NOBLE PURSUITS

Chautona D Havig

Copyright 2008 ©

ISBN 978-0-557-03787-2

I've read thousands of 'dedications' and 'thanks' at the beginning of books over the years and I've always wondered how the authors choose whom to thank or to whom to dedicate. Well, I still don't know. I could be filial and mention my parents, but I'm fairly certain they wouldn't care for this book. I'd thank my husband for being my inspiration for Nolan but then I'd have to admit that Nolan doesn't hold a candle to my husband and that kills the whole 'inspiration' angle. Some have asked me if Nolan was named after my son Nolan and I can't say he was. I just needed the meaning and used it anyway. I'd say that I hope my Nolan will be as wonderful as the character but really, I think he's far superior so that won't work.

There are friends who walked me through every agonizing step and who can give you every single solitary error I've eradicated and have a list alphabetized and numerically ordered of the remaining ones but they've been kind enough to decide that publication is more important than perfection. Thanks guys- you know who you are.

However, my dear friend Teresa needs credit for the "Last Supper" concept. I stole it, without permission, and hereby give her credit in hopes that she won't sue me and hate me for life. Love you gal! In addition, I need to thank my friend Glenda for letting me 'borrow' her husband's name. Without permission. Again. (Is there a trend here?)

To meet other members of the *Rockland Chronicles* cast, visit

www.fairburytales.com

and for more information about Chautona and her books visit

www.chautona.com

Chapter One

July

"As you can see, in this contract, Noble Solutions is only responsible for any trouble with upgrades or changes made by myself. Integrating any of your company's adjustments with my software will be billed to your account. Is that agreeable?"

"No."

Amid the muted sounds of a fine restaurant, Nolan Burke attempted to explain the terms of his standard contract to a potential client. Nolan's frustration mounted as the woman ignored his explanations in favor of overt flirtation. While he spoke of contract renewal dates, she suggested a dinner date and chose not to acknowledge that he declined the offer.

"No? What part of the contract do you have a problem with Miss Walker?"

"My name is Michelle; I loathe Miss. It's archaic and patriarchal." Nolan cringed as Michelle Walker crowded into his personal space once more. She'd been excessively warm and friendly from the moment they introduced themselves in the restaurant lobby. As he averted his eyes from a fine view of more cleavage than any man should be subjected to in public, he adjusted his pen and prayed for patience. Instead of the instant escape he hoped to receive, an opportunity to practice patience surfaced. "Michelle will do, Nolan. I'm not a very formal person."

Michelle gave another slow smile and a sultry wink. Groaning inwardly, Nolan ignored the overture and tried steering the conversation back to the subject of their meeting. "Well then Ms. Walker-"

"Michelle." The woman's tone was determined, almost fierce.

Nolan signaled for the check and snapped the file folder shut with finality. "Miss Walker. I don't think that my company can offer you what you are looking for."

Rising to exit as quickly as possible, he continued. "May I suggest Lynn Graves over at *Computing Concepts*? I thank you for your time and will of course, cover the check."

Before Michelle could respond, Nolan signed for their lunches and with a formal nod, wove his way through the diners. Left alone at the table, the young businesswoman fluctuated between admiration, fascination, and irritation at his apparent immunity to her. Men did *not* resist Michelle Walker. Period.

She scrutinized Nolan as he walked away. The cut of his suit, style of his hair, and the perfect shine of his shoes practically screamed success. He gazed briefly at a little girl wearing a paper crown and blowing out candles on an elaborate birthday cake. Nolan Burke hadn't smiled at her like that. In fact, after their initial handshake, he hadn't smiled at all. Michelle wondered what kind of woman *could* spark his interest and couldn't conceive as to how she had failed.

Michelle Walker was fully conscious of her attractiveness and allure. The hours and expense required as well as her hard work in sculpting the perfect physique was evident with every move. Of course, she rewarded herself by shopping for impeccable clothing designed to accentuate her hard-earned body. Michelle's recreation hours were all about keeping her fingers carefully manicured, and her cosmetics applied with precision. Her stylist made his car payment on time, every month, thanks to Michelle's highly pampered hair follicles. She had been on the top of her flirtatious game. The fact that he'd resisted her allure nearly convinced Michelle that he was training for a monastery.

Michelle hadn't considered Nolan's company for the computer system she needed to integrate her office until she heard about its exceptionally handsome owner. Her administrative assistant, Janice, assured her that the owner of Noble Solutions was 'really hot'. After a recommendation like that, the decision was easy. Didn't she deserve to enjoy her success? Michelle ruefully admitted to herself that Janice had been right. Nolan Burke, despite his other deficiencies, was definitely hot!

"What a self-righteous chauvinist! He probably wants a domestic little trophy wife in a yellow house with a picket fence, two point three kids, and Sunday school for all. Man, has anyone ever told him that this is the twenty-first century? Queen Victoria has been dead for several generations now-" Michelle Walker continued her mental tirade as she watched Nolan step out of the restaurant, hail a cab for an elderly woman, jump into his waiting SUV, and pull away from the curb.

"Bet he was a boy scout too." She muttered with annoyance under her breath.

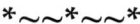

"What is wrong with me? Why is every woman I meet like a female masher?" Nolan Burke put his Escalade in gear and turned up the air conditioning to cool the stifling summer heat as he eased into the lunch traffic. As he drove toward home, Nolan reflected on his disastrous lunch meeting.

The successful computer consultant drummed his fingers on the steering wheel, apparently lost in thought. Stopping at a red light, he noticed a striking Asian woman smiling up at him from a convertible. As the light changed, and with an audible groan, Nolan rapidly accelerated and robotically drove home, once again, mentally absent from the world around him. At the next light, he scribbled a note to have his windows tinted.

Nolan had no family. Born late in his parent's lives after years of childlessness, he was their pride and joy. His mother poured her heart into rearing her only child and under her careful nurturing Nolan flourished. Mrs. Burke had called him her "little man" and his personality, even from childhood, showed it. Handsome, intelligent, and successful, his parents had passed away with the knowledge and comfort of their son's strong faith and unwavering standards.

Nolan was honest with himself. Home and family were important to him; he knew what he wanted in his life and prayed daily that his desires were within God's will. If a wife and children were not in his future, Nolan often prayed that God would remove his deep desire for a family.

He knew, without a doubt, that what he did not want was the kind of woman that impressed many of his friends and acquaintances. Nolan's idea of an attractive woman went far beyond the superficial. Even the intelligent women in his social circles seemed to care more about a lifestyle than sharing a life. While he knew that his ideal might not exist, Nolan had no doubt that God would have someone perfect for him if marriage was part of the Lord's plan for his life. He had no interest in the forward women who'd been throwing themselves at him lately.

Nolan dialed his best friend's home number. Sounds of squealing children in the background made it difficult for Mike's wife Traci, to hear him. "Is Mike around? Does he have a few minutes?"

Nolan filled Mike in on his botched meeting. "Mike? Is it just me? Am I just dreaming or is there a chance that somewhere out there is a woman who doesn't find it necessary to throw herself at men?"

Mike roared with laughter. "Well, when you look like you and have your bank account-"

"Man, I'm serious! This is getting pathetic!"

Toning down his voice, Nolan's friend tried again. "Your problem Nolan is that you've always compared every woman you meet to your mom. Women like your mother are extremely rare these days."

"Mike, I just would like to meet a Christian woman who isn't out there flaunting her self like a baptized prostitute or trying to prove that anything a man can do she can do better. There have to be some women left that are secure enough in their femininity that they don't feel a need to compete with men too."

Nolan wished his friend a pleasant evening and tossed the handset on the couch beside him. Booting up his laptop, the frustrated man opened *the* file and scanned his dream wife 'order form'. One evening after a particularly draining charity dinner Nolan had left early, gone home, and created a 'wish list' for the wife he prayed the Lord was saving for him. The list had a few additions now and then, usually as the result of an unpleasant encounter somewhere.

Christian
Feminine- loves being a woman
Strong
Modest

Sense of humor
Intelligent
Low-maintenance

After reviewing his list, he added number eight.
Loves children

Nolan sighed and closed the laptop. At thirty-seven, he was not exactly old but he was very alone. Apart from his best friend from childhood, he had no family and though the fellowship of Christians was always encouraging, lately it wasn't enough. Should he move? The women he knew from his church weren't right for him; the fact that they made their interest in him perfectly clear sent up red flags. Where was maidenly modesty anyway? If he left Rockland, where would he go? Did strong *and* feminine ladies even exist anymore? Maybe he should move to the South. Southern Belles might be a good idea. Ideas and questions whizzed through his mind at lighting fast speed. Lost in thought, Nolan grumbled unconsciously, "'A virtuous woman, who can find?' is right!"

Chapter Two

August

Nolan wove his way through the ballroom looking for David Corbin. Friends beckoned him to join them but he smiled and kept weaving. A waiter handed him a glass of zinfandel while he stood waiting for David to finish talking to the emcee.

"Hey Burke! Did you try the Rangoons? They're great."

"I'd rather not spend the night at the ER, but thanks."

The emcee disappeared into the crowd and Nolan and David made their way to a table. Before either man could say a word, a woman slipped into the empty chair next to Nolan. With all of her attention fixed on Nolan, she missed the amused expression in David's face.

"Nolan Burke, I'm mad at you!" she asserted playfully, one hand resting lightly on his arm. "You said you'd call and it's been two months already."

His face seemed to sigh though laughter rang out hollowly. "Now that's not how I remember it, Tara. I distinctly remember you telling me I would call and me assuring you that I would not."

"Well, of course you couldn't mean that. Don't you think it's time you took me to dinner?"

Nolan dreaded these scenes. As hard as he worked to avoid openly rejecting friends and acquaintances, sometimes it was impossible to avoid. "I don't think that'd work for either of us but you're good for my ego Tara."

Relieved to see Mike and Traci meandering toward their table, David came to his friend's rescue. "Tara, I don't mean to be rude but the Finches are coming this way and this is their table. Maybe we'll get a chance to talk more after dinner."

Tara stood, half-glared at David, and smiled once more at Nolan. "I still think dinner is a great idea. I'll call you."

She slipped from her chair and sashayed across the room before Nolan could respond. Mike and Traci saw the scene on their way to the table and arrived with barely suppressed mirth in their voices. "She never gives up, does she?" remarked Traci wryly. "I've never understood why she can't see that you're just not interested."

"Nolan gets that wherever he goes. Who can resist charm, looks, and bucks? He's a triple crown winner!"

"Thanks Dave. That's how I always wanted to be perceived." A glance at Mike sent Nolan's head wagging. "If I hear a single word about just horsing around…"

A waiter with their meals interrupted the conversation before jokes followed. "I have three fish and a chicken?"

Nolan raised a finger. "Chicken here."

"Are you the allergy to shellfish?" The waiter pulled a note from his pocket.

"Yes. Is there a problem?"

"Here is a note from the chef." Without another word, the waiter hurried off to the kitchen.

A glance at the note made Nolan smile. "I'd like to speak to the chef. Please don't let me forget after dinner."

"What was it?" Traci asked curiously.

"Nothing major. He just heard that there was a shellfish allergy here and he wanted to assure me that the crab rangoons and shrimp dishes were assembled off site and cooked in a separate kitchen once they got here."

"That's service. I'm impressed," remarked Mike as he took a bite of his salmon. "This is good."

Nolan swallowed his bite of chicken Kiev. "Frank is one of the best. He apprenticed under Claude over at *Mon Deux*. At a wedding reception, of the sous got careless with prep and a guest had an anaphylactic reaction. It stuck in Frank's mind and he's been conscientious about it ever since. He likes to assure his patrons that it is safe to eat."

Before anyone could respond, Nolan felt a tap on his shoulder and looked up. "Yvette, how are you?"

"Better now that I see you here. Going to ask me to dance later?"

With a fork loaded with chicken, Nolan shrugged. "Depends on if you're around when I get around to the dance floor. See you later perhaps." With that, Nolan took his bite and smiled a goodbye. Yvette, accustomed to Nolan's deflections, gave him a wink and waved to the rest of the table as she moved toward the ladies lounge. Traci stood to follow.

"I have to hear this. I've been watching and there's an eligible female convention going on in the powder room. I'll see who else is on the prowl and be back before you're done with your chicken."

The three men watched amazed as Traci disappeared into a crowd of females near the door Yvette had disappeared behind only moments before. Traci had an ulterior motive. She knew what Nolan wanted in a woman and realized this was the perfect opportunity to do a little reconnoitering.

The conversation inside the lounge revolved around the latest scandal, the mayoral election, and Nolan Burke. Sequestered in a stall, Traci had the perfect listening post.

"Tara, will you never give up? He is *so* not interested." Claws emerged from the brunette crowd.

"I'll give up when I see him with a wife on one arm."

A collective titter rippled over the room. Amita Patel queried over the din, "Has anyone here actually gone out with Nolan?"

The room hushed. No one spoke. Traci heard Tara's smug retort seconds later. "Well, then I'd say no one has room to talk. Y'all want to act superior and all but it's not like I'm the only one he hasn't fallen for- yet."

"Well he goes to my church," a voice in the corner said. "He doesn't even attend the singles activities."

"He took that chick from Chicago to the symphony last year. The one in the red dress?"

"That cow? She was ridiculously homely."

Traci listened to the chatter amazed at what she heard. She'd always thought Nolan was a bit overly dramatic about his frustration with the women in their circles but tonight she saw a glimpse of the reality of his life. Another voice pierced her musings.

"I'm convinced he's either gay or a modern eunuch."

She'd had enough. Traci left the stall, barely remembering that she was supposed to be using it as intended and flushing as she left. She pushed through the throng around the mirrors and claimed an empty sink. As she reached for a towel from the room attendant, she turned to the group.

"Nolan Burke is not gay, he's not a eunuch, and he's most certainly interested in finding the right woman. Did it occur to you that he's looking for something different? Someone different?"

The women looked thoughtful as Traci wove her way through the room to the door but at the sound of the band, the atmosphere changed back to the primping she'd found when she entered. "So much for making a difference," she muttered to herself.

At their table, Nolan looked resigned. "Too early to leave, rude not to offer, I guess I'll get it over with."

As he passed her chair, Traci caught his arm. "I heard them in the bathroom and well, I get it now. Avoid Tara if you can. She has on her war paint."

For the next fifty minutes, Nolan danced and evaded. Mike and Traci occasionally crossed his path and each time, Nolan danced with a new woman. He waltzed with each partner around the floor, mentally cursing the genius who decided to make the evening a 'tribute to Strauss.' As he whirled, Nolan tried to ignore the barrage of pushy females shamelessly angling for an invitation to dance.

Finally, Mike leaned in and said, "Gives new meaning to dodge 'ball' doesn't it?"

~~~~*

Sunday morning, Nolan prayed all through the worship service. The sermon escaped his notice, he didn't sing, and he almost missed the communion trays as they passed by him. His heart was laden with the feeling that there was something terribly wrong with him. He'd been curt with several women and hardly cordial to others.

Pastor Zimmerman found Nolan waiting in his study an hour after the congregants disbursed. "Um Burke, you look awful."

"Sums up how I feel if you want the truth."

Tim Zimmerman sat in his chair behind an immense desk and propped his feet on the top. "Tell me about it."

"Do you mind? Will Mrs.-"

"We don't eat lunch together. Sundays are our free days. Talk."

"I've got female troubles."

"PMS or PPD?"

Nolan laughed. "Thankfully PPD isn't an issue but I appear to be trigger for PMS anyway."

"PMS? I really don't think you're responsible for the hormonal rages of biologically timed-out women."

"I'm speaking of the lesser known but just as dangerous, Pre-Marital Syndrome."

Chuckling, Tim reached into his drawer and pulled out an insulated lunch bag. "Here, have a sandwich. I have a feeling we're going to get hungry. There are water bottles in that fridge next to you. Pass me one, will you?"

For the next hour, Nolan described the constant influx of eligible females that flocked to his side. He was embarrassed at how conceited he sounded but desperation called for strict honesty about both the situation and his dismay over it. "Am I doing something to encourage this? Is there something I should do to prevent it? I don't want to attract this kind of attention-"

"You can't prevent it all, Nolan. Women, many of them anyway, find money and power very attractive. You could look like Quasimodo in the looks department and still attract attention. Unfortunately you don't even have the Quasimodo thing going for you."

"So do I just disappear into the wilds of Colorado and hope some cattle rancher's daughter likes me?"

Tim stifled a laugh and said, "Nolan, rancher's daughters, coal miner's daughters, and welfare-dependent single moms. You know there will always be women who will throw themselves at you.

"You know, maybe a change of scenery would do you good. Go somewhere where you aren't well known or recognized. At least you'd have a little time before your reputation and financial information became household gossip."

"I thought about moving but I just assumed it'd be the same thing anywhere I went."

Tim sat thoughtfully considering Nolan's concerns. "I really thing moving might be the best thing but where you move counts. Don't stereotype women by locale. Find a place with a high percentage of single women and get to know them. Visit the churches in the cities and towns around the loop. Check out Hillsdale, Marshfield, New Cheltenham, Westbury, and even

Fairbury. I always thought Alexa Hartfield would be a good match for you."

"I know her brother…"

"Talk to him," Tim insisted.

"Call him and say, 'Hey, you've got a sister and I'm looking for someone so how about fixing us up?' That's insane."

Tim leaned forward on his forearms and rubbed his knuckles with his thumb. "Nolan, tell your friend your problem. Tell him the kind of woman you're looking for and tell him you're looking at the towns on the loop and you want any information he has about Fairbury. If he thinks you're good for his sister, I'll bet he says so.

"Tim, he tried to fix me up with her in the past but there are a few problems. I want a family. She doesn't."

"Well, that is one problem but it doesn't negate his knowledge of Fairbury. Call him. I think the church needs to start helping one another in this area." Tim's eyes earnestly urged Nolan to step out of his comfort zone and take the first step toward his future.

"I'll do it, Tim, thanks."

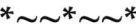

"Wes, good to see you man. Where've-" Nolan paused to acknowledge a couple passing their table. "-you been lately?"

"Just got back from Afghanistan."

"You know, I've never asked. How does your family feel about those trips to Afghanistan and Iraq?"

Wes grinned. "My parents don't ask. Alexa gets concerned but I tend to be vague with her. This time I said, 'I'm off to one of those 'istans'' and I hope she assumes that its one of those lesser-known ones."

"A little deceitful but understandable."

Wes signaled for another Coke and leaned back in his chair. "So, what is up with you? Found that dream woman yet?"

"No, that's one of the things I want to talk to you about."

"I still think you and Alexa would hit it off nicely," Wes asserted.

"When we talked at her house last January, we both knew that it wouldn't work. It's too bad though, she was one of the nicest most real women I've ever met."

"And I'm sure it didn't help that she didn't throw herself at you."

After a few moments of concentrated eating, the conversation picked up as though it'd never paused. "Well, if I didn't know you want children so badly, I might be a bit insulted on her behalf, but as Alexa's only brother, I can say that your life is safe from death at my hands for not being interested. For now."

"So what about the rest of Fairbury. You've been around a lot lately, is it worth checking out?" Nolan felt like a desperate teenager looking for a date to the prom.

"Lots of singles in Fairbury if that's what you mean. They have movie night once or twice a month there. People come from Brunswick, Marshfield, New Cheltenham- even Rockland. I don't know who fits with Fairbury and who is an outsider half the time but it's a healthy mix."

"I'm considering a move."

The statement hung between them as though daring either to touch it. Finally, Wes sighed and shoved his plate away from him. "Nolan, I know you've always wanted to have a family of your own. I know that you miss your parents and want what they had and until recently, I didn't really get it but-," Wes continued in spite of Nolan's raised eyebrows and alert expression. "I want to ask one question before you make life altering decisions."

"Shoot."

Wes tossed him a 'you asked for it' glance and said, "Is this move a consideration because you want a wife or because you want the women you don't want to leave you alone?"

Chapter Three

Labor Day

London and Mickey tore through the living room squealing and squirting water pistols at one another.

"Take it outside!" Traci ordered in a stage whisper. "The baby is trying to take his nap."

London turned her gun on her mother and squeezed the trigger. A stream of water splashed across the photographs Nolan had spread out on the coffee table. Mike jumped and raced for a towel and Traci wailed trying to save the pictures as she scolded her daughter.

"It's ok Traci. I can print more. Don't worry about it." He beckoned to London who raced for her 'Uncle Nolan' and buried her face in his chest.

"I'm sorry Uncle Nolan! I didn't mean to-"

"I know you didn't sweetie-"

Traci interrupted angrily. "London Finch! You march yourself up to your room right now young lady. You know better than that..."

The irate mother's voice followed her daughter out of the room, up the stairs, and to the opposite corner of the house. A door slammed and then the cry of a disoriented toddler followed.

"Oh great, there's Parker," Mike groaned and disappeared up the stairs after his wife and daughter.

Mickey gave Nolan a smug look. "Little kids are always messing things up."

"It seems like I remember something about a can of acetone and a not-so-shiny paint job last week. I think mistakes are ageless Mickey."

Indignant, Mickey protested hotly, "I thought it was the wax. It was a surprise for Daddy's birthday." Embarrassed, the child raced from the room into the back yard.

"A fifteen hundred dollar surprise. Happy Birthday to Mike from Mickey," Nolan muttered.

Mike and Traci hobbled downstairs, Parker on Mike's arm and a sobbing London holding Traci's hand. London dragged her feet to Nolan's side and said, "I's sorry Uncle Nolan." Before Nolan could respond, the child thrust her hand in her pocket, pulled out a handful of change and dollar bills, and dropped it in his lap. "I have to pay for it."

Nolan began to protest but one glance at Traci's face silenced him. Something in her eye told him he'd be better to take the money. "Thank you London. That's very responsible. I'm proud of you."

While London skipped off to continue the water fight outside, Nolan gathered his ruined photos and threw them in the garbage. Traci picked up a package and pulled the prints from inside of it. "These are fine-" She stopped abruptly. "Why are there pictures of houses? You do trees, animals, insects, flowers- you know, natureish stuff. Why the suburban sprawl?"

"That's the other reason I wanted to talk to you and Mike..."

Mike accepted the pictures from his wife and flipped through them quickly. "You're investing in rentals?"

"I'm thinking of moving."

"Out of state?" Traci's dismay was heartening.

He shook his head. "No, one of the cities around the loop. I've considered Brunswick, Marshfield, and Hillsdale. They are all close enough for a commute into Rockland. Marshfield is the largest but it's packed with planned communities. I don't want a covenant or association to dictate if my vehicle is too large to park in my driveway."

Mike and Traci Finch looked over the information Nolan spread before them. "Have you attended any of the churches?"

Nolan shook his head. "I've spoken to several pastors and ministers and found that Brunswick has a few doctrinally solid churches both denominationally and non-denominationally. It'll be hard to choose there I think. I'd hate to choose a church based upon the percentage of single females-"

"Why not?"

Nolan looked askance at Traci. "Choose a church because of the number of single women? Are you crazy?"

"Once you've determined doctrinal agreement, why not? Why do we play these games as if it is somehow more spiritual to pretend we don't know how many eligible females are present? If 'he who finds a wife, finds a good thing,' then why isn't it a good thing to go where the highest potential for finding a wife *is*?"

Mike looked at Nolan and back at his wife. "Traci, I think you are onto something. I wonder if that is what is wrong with modern dating. It is taboo to admit that you are looking for someone to *marry*."

"Exactly." Traci nodded sagely. "We are in the market for a spouse but we're not even supposed to say we are window shopping; we're just supposed to be passing by and the right one drops in our lap. The fact that we set up the meeting, paid someone to push them into our lap, and made sure we were perfectly situated to impress at that particular moment is just a deliberate accident of pure happenstance."

Mike shoved his open laptop across the coffee table and pointed to the results of a Google search. "Brunswick. The per capita of single females in Brunswick is eleven percent higher than Marshfield or Hillsdale."

"Brunswick it is," replied Nolan wryly.

Chapter Four

Mid-September

"… And what are the prices on the pears this year?" Grace Buscher mentally tallied her large order. Suffering a short-term financial famine, she mentally kicked herself for taking a weekend trip to Mackinac the previous month. The money spent on that trip would have covered her groceries for months.

Each year she struggled with the idea of taking a vacation. In prior years, her father had been the one to insist that they go. "Vacations are medicine for the heart, soul, and body. It's preventative maintenance that you can't afford to ignore any more than oil in a car or a tune-up."

Grace stopped her reminiscing, confirmed her order with the orchard, and hung up the phone. The Buscher family bought their fruit from Stead's Orchards every fall. In addition, the orchard gave Grace many boxes of seconds that they couldn't sell at their trips to Farmer's Markets in nearby Rockland and Fairbury. Canning the fruit would take the next two weeks and though it was hard work, Grace loved it and had customers who paid well for freshly canned fruit. Few things, in her opinion, produced a greater feeling of accomplishment than seeing glistening fruit lining her pantry and mudroom shelves.

Grace opened the front door and sniffed the brisk afternoon air as autumn rushed at her in the breeze. In a matter of weeks, she'd wear her sweaters and her favorite corduroy skirt. Geese flew overhead as she looked up at the sprawling oak tree in her front yard. The leaves were already turning colors. Before long, the streets would be a riot of color with leaves crunching under the tires of her neighbors as they drove home after a long day at work.

The living room clock chimed the hour. Humming Glen Miller's *In the Mood*, Grace cleared her budgeting from the table and headed for the kitchen. Cade was coming soon, and on Fridays he tended to have extra homework. She pulled lasagna from the fridge and set it in her pre-heated oven. Cade's mother, Mrs. Crenshaw, paid Grace extra every other Friday for two-third of a pan of her excellent lasagna.

As she returned to the front of the house, she saw Cade and waved through the window. The careless boy dashed between two cars waving a handful of papers jubilantly before she could call out a warning. A metallic midnight blue SUV hit Cade before the driver could brake. His papers fluttered across the street much like the leaves of the sprawling oaks. Grace rushed from the house and raced across the street almost before the driver hit the child, arriving just after the vehicle stopped. Cade moaned as Grace felt his limbs and head.

The driver hurried from his vehicle, calling for help on a cell phone. "Is he ok?"

Grace listened as he explained what happened and received instructions from the dispatcher. At each of his questions, she shook her head or nodded in response. When they heard sirens in the distance, the 9-1-1 dispatcher disconnected the call and Grace asked permission to use his phone.

"I need to call his mother. She's usually not here until after six on Fridays and he could have internal injuries. It looks like your bumper might have hit his belly. It's the perfect height."

The driver sighed and kneaded the back of his neck with his fingers. "I don't know where he came from. I didn't even brake."

Briefly, Grace focused her attention on the driver. The man was visibly upset. Her voice gentle and firm, she reassured him. "It wasn't your fault. Cade had something to tell me and didn't look. I've told him a thousand times to look first and he was careless.

"I'm Grace by the way, Grace Buscher."

"Nolan Burke. I'm moving in this weekend, I just- Do you really think he's going to be ok?"

Grace nodded and dialed the boy's mother. Staring confused at the phone in her hand, she mumbled, "It's not ringing."

Nolan looked at the screen and smiled. He reached over, pushed the send button, and nodded at her before kneeling beside the whimpering boy. "Hey buddy, the ambulance is here to help you. I'm very sorry that I hit you."

The boy's voice was soft but steady. "It's my fault. Miss Grace is right, I didn't look."

The paramedics edged Nolan from their space as they examined the child. An officer pulled him aside and questioned him, while Grace tried to relay messages from the paramedics to his frantic mother.

"Cade honey? Your mother is going to meet us at the hospital. They're taking you there just to make sure nothing is wrong inside. Ok?" Grace smiled at the young boy as he grinned and nodded.

She ran inside the house and grabbed her purse and medical authority note. Dashing back out the door, Grace barely remembered to lock it. She climbed into the back of the ambulance with a wave and a reassuring smile to Nolan as they drove toward the hospital.

Once the officer finished with his report, Nolan realized that Grace might not have a ride home and asked directions to the hospital. Though he hardly expected her to accept it, considering he was a perfect stranger, he felt obliged to make the offer. If nothing else, it was a good excuse to find out if Cade was truly fine.

~~~~*

"Miss Buscher? Is Cade's mother here yet?" Nolan saw the strain in Grace's eyes and it bothered him. He thought it probable that she felt responsible however impossible it was for her to prevent the accident.

Grace jumped at his voice. "I didn't know you were here!"

"I was concerned that you might not have a ride home. I know you don't know me, but I had to offer. I can provide references, if that helps. I had to bring them for the realtor." Nolan's eyes twinkled as he joked.

A shrill woman's voice interrupted them before Grace could reply. "Grace, where is he? Is he going to be ok? What am I going to do with that boy?"

Turning from Nolan, Grace spoke quietly and calmly to Mrs. Crenshaw. Cade's mother listened intently and watched her son as he waited for an ultrasound. Grace introduced the worried mother to the doctor, told her the investigating officer's name, and then left her alone with her son.

Nolan watched the calm, capable manner that radiated from her. Grace was unruffled, her name perfectly suited to her. As she signed release of responsibility forms, Nolan observed her more carefully and wondered how someone would describe Grace. It seemed that her personality overshadowed her physical appearance. Instead of observing her eye color, he noted that they were clear and kind. He did not notice her height as much as he did her poise. As he considered the impression she left upon him and the hospital personnel, 'casually regal' came to mind as the optimal description for Grace. She conducted herself like a princess, yet without pretence or self-awareness.

Grace turned back to Nolan as she finished and noticed his scrutiny. A more self-conscious person would have been bothered, but Grace found it amusing. She knew that in the minds of many men, there was not much to look at, though that fact never seemed to bother her. In her opinion, life was too short to be concerned with the conjectures of people based upon superficial things like how she styled her hair or what size dress she wore.

"May I borrow your phone? We'll have to step outside but I know from experience that the pay phones here are coin eaters."

"Accident prone?"

Grace laughed. "No. I just spend time reading to a few older patients once in a while and my Aunt Fran has been here a few times."

Outside, she dialed the number and then searched for the elusive send button. Knowing how irritated some women became at the slightest offer of help, Nolan refrained from doing it for her. Grace eyed him in mock annoyance. "You're enjoying this aren't you?"

Nolan raised his eyebrows and cocked his head questioningly. Exasperated, Grace pointed to the phone. "You know where that stupid button is and won't show me."

Nolan laughed, and this time showed her where he punched the button. Grace responded mockingly. "Send? You have to hit a button that says 'send'? Why not 'go' or even 'call'? Doesn't that make more sense?

"Mel? Is Craig around?" Grace smiled at Nolan and nodded into the phone. Nolan found it comical how often people made gestures while speaking on the phone, as if the person on the other end could actually see what they were gesticulating with their hands and faces.

"Hey, Craig. I'm at the hospital. Cade was hit by a car- ran right out between two cars and splat. Thankfully, the guy wasn't one of those crazies who tear around that corner."

Grace nodded again and Nolan stifled a snicker. She looked at him sharply but continued her conversation. "Listen, Mr. Burke, the driver? He's offered to drive me home; I think he's renting out the house across the street where Mabel Gantry lived. What would you like me to do? Uh huh- don't start Craig. That's not funny. Ok, I'll do that. Call you when I'm home and settled. Love you too. Tell Mel to give you a scoop or two of ice cream to cool you off. Uh huh-bye."

Snapping the phone shut, Grace handed it back to Nolan. "Thank you for the offer but my brother would be more comfortable with me taking a cab. He's calling one for me now. I hope you understand." Grace's smile was genuine and slightly apologetic.

"Not at all. I wouldn't want my sister, if I had one, to ride home with a relative stranger." Nolan paused.

Grace and Nolan chatted for a few minutes until a cab turned into the parking lot. As she signaled her position, she smiled at Nolan. "Feel free to stop by if you need help with anything. I'll be gone for a while tomorrow morning, but then I'm pretty much chained to the house for the next week or two."

Nolan opened the door for Grace as the cab drove under the portico. "I'll remember that. Have a good evening."

Nolan sprinted across the parking lot and tried to follow the cab, but it was already out of view. Retracing the streets he had driven en-route to the hospital, Nolan realized that he was likely taking a shorter route back to Grace's street. He found himself on residential streets and outer main roads. Traveling well within the speed limit, he turned into his new driveway just as the taxi rounded the corner.

As he stepped outside his vehicle, Nolan smelled the distinct odor of something burning. "Some poor guy is having a charred meal tonight," the bemused man said under his breath. A wistful pang followed. Charred food might even be enjoyable providing you had someone special to laugh with as you tried to eat. If you couldn't choke it down, experience had taught him that take-out food could right many culinary wrongs.

Nolan mentally calculated the cab fare and stood ready to pay the driver, as Grace's cab turned into her driveway. As he opened the door for her, Nolan leaned through the passenger window and paid the middle-aged man behind the wheel. He dismissed Grace's protest, waved, and sauntered to his new home. As he started to unlock the door, a wail from Grace's direction stopped him. Rushing back, he found smoke billowing from the doorway and Grace laughing as she choked her way through the house to the offending oven.

"Oh boy, I forgot about the lasagna. Mrs. Crenshaw will be disappointed. Well, I guess she has other things on her mind doesn't she? Oh, Grace Buscher, you have to learn to think before you rush into things. You could have burned the house down!"

Amused to hear her talking to no one, Nolan realized that she wasn't aware of his presence and turned back toward home. He flicked open his cell phone and placed two quick calls. Thoughtfully, he ordered a split pizza for his neighbor, pepperoni on one of the halves and everything but anchovies on the other. For himself, he ordered Chinese. Nolan had not realized how hungry he was until he began placing his order. He added rice, egg rolls, and soup to his order, and asked twice for utensils.

While he wandered through the house making notes on his PDA, Nolan realized that the house was still larger than he truly needed. He briefly considered trying to find a smaller home but the sounds of children playing ball down the street and the memory of his new neighbor checked him. Too large or not, this house was considerably smaller than the home he'd just sold and the neighborhood was perfect.

By the time the doorbell rang, Nolan's stomach growled audibly. He groaned as a perky teenaged girl handed him the pizza he'd ordered for Grace. It wasn't hard to assume that his Chinese was probably en route to Grace's house. As he debated what to do with the pizza, a white mini van, marked *Wong's Wok*, stopped across the street. He tried to intercept the driver and swap boxes but the

Asian man hurried past. The little man obviously thought that Nolan was trying to steal the food and scolded him angrily.

Standing behind the irate Asian holding the pizza box, Nolan looked sheepish as the little man shooed her back into the house. Irritated by Grace's lack of cooperation in protecting herself from the evil pizza swapper behind him, the deliveryman drove away indignantly. "You got my Chinese. I sent you a pizza. They didn't have lasagna, and pizza was the closest they could offer."

"Uh huh, bub! I don't give up Chinese easily." Grace sniffed the box. "Kung Pao and egg rolls at the least. My favorite."

Nolan laughed and started to say goodnight. Before he could realize her intention, Grace snatched the pizza box and disappeared inside and minutes later, she re-emerged carrying a tray holding the pizza and two heaping plates of Chinese food. She placed the food on a wicker table and motioned for Nolan to sit in the nearest chair. "Would you like something to drink? Water? Soda? What can I get for you?"

Nolan hesitated and then asked for soda. "Water makes the spices stronger and my mouth burn longer!"

Minutes later, she sat drinks before their plates and the multi-cultural dinner commenced. They ate in comfortable silence at first. Eventually, Grace asked where Nolan was from, and he in turn, questioned her about the neighborhood, different churches, and the length of Grace's residence in her house. That question got him more than he bargained for.

"I was born here."

"Born here as in this town, your parents lived in this house at the time; you were born in this house? Which?"

Grace shook her head. "No. Here. On these steps. They couldn't move my mother, she screamed in pain if they jostled her the slightest bit, so three ladies held quilts up for privacy while I was born right on this porch. My brother drove everyone nuts by sneaking over the back fence to come find mom and see me."

"I guess you could say that you have roots in this house then couldn't you?" Nolan tried to imagine a woman giving birth in such a public way, but didn't quite succeed.

"Mom used to joke that when she decided to try for a natural birth, she went all the way." Grace's laughter was infectious.

Grace's neighbor, Verily Wirth walked to his mailbox to make sure that the mail carrier hadn't decided to make a late night delivery. He watched in delight as Grace sat on her porch with a handsome man laughing and having a delightful time. For the past five years, the lonely widower occupied his time by inventing exciting romances for his young neighbor across the street and reliving the wonderful years that he'd spent with his wife.

When she was finished, Grace gathered the plates onto her tray. Nolan offered to help clean up from the meal but Grace demurred. "Thank you for offering, but I'll get it. I should go in, Mr. Verily is likely ready to call my brother and give him a play by play of our meal. Have a nice evening and thank you for providing dinner- I was hungry.

"If you need help moving, finding your way around town, or just need a cup of sugar, please don't hesitate to ask." She turned, dragged the screen door open with her foot and without looking back said, "Oh, and if you hear rattling late at night, it's Joe Alden's dogs from across the fields getting into the old metal trash cans in the alley behind your fence. I'd appreciate it if you'd get rid of those."

She heard him chuckle as he wandered back to his dark, empty house. Minutes later, she saw Nolan's headlights flash across her living room wall as he made a u-turn and drove out of the neighborhood. "Well, at least he has a sense of humor. That's a good thing, isn't it Grace?"

Her hearty laughter rang out a short time later as she heard the faint rattling of metal trashcans. "I think he's is taking them away tonight! Wait 'till Craig hears about that."

Grace sobbed into her pillow. She didn't know how she was going to get through the night. After three showers, Grace felt no more relaxed than she had when she saw Cade's little body fly through the air. At the thought of the thud that must have followed, a fresh wave of tears threatened to overtake her. Pulling her Bible back to her, Grace re-read the words that had always comforted her at times like this.

"Then your light will break out like the dawn,
And your recovery will speedily spring forth;
And your righteousness will go before you;
The glory of the LORD will be your rear guard.
And if you give yourself to the hungry
And satisfy the desire of the afflicted,
Then your light will rise in darkness
And your gloom will become like midday.   Isaiah 58:8-10

As Grace lay on her bed praying, tears still streaming from her eyes, the phone rang. Instinctively, Grace knew it would be her brother. "Craig?"

"I knew you'd be struggling. I'm so sorry honey. Do you want to pray for a while?" Craig's voice was filled with love and concern.

Grace hesitated. "What about Mel? Doesn't she need her sleep?"

Craig assured her that his wife slept peacefully while he paced the floor of their living room in concern for his little sister. "Grace, let's pray. You need to take this to the Lord."

An hour later, Grace slept. The Lord's peace had stolen over her as her brother prayed for the 'peace that passes understanding' to fill her heart and mind. As Grace slept, Craig continued to pray until his alarm clock woke his wife and started his day.

Chapter Five

Grace awoke, dressed, and rode with Craig and Melanie to the orchard early Saturday morning. Several boxes of seconds needed immediate processing but the free fruit was something she'd never refuse. Nolan's moving truck sat parked half way into his garage when they returned.

Grace sang old songs while she and Craig lugged her fruit into the house. She chose to keep her mind off the monstrous task ahead of her by singing of Kalamazoo and Chattanooga with Glenn Miller playing in her head. Grace had been on a big band streak lately to the bemusement and relief of her family. The Cindi Lauper kick a few months back had been especially annoying.

Nolan noticed his busy neighbor in between loads of his own and started toward her house to help. Torn between the instinct to help Grace with her burden, and not wanting to create an uncomfortable situation, Nolan paused in his work. In his experience, women generally took offers of help as a sign of his interest in them and occasionally even resented the implication that they needed a man's help. Nolan was still working on how to get around that one. He finally overrode his cautions as he saw her make a third trip to the back of the mini-van.

Before he could cross the lawn, he noticed a man and very pregnant woman helping her. Nolan winced as the woman waddled to the back of the van and reached for a box of what appeared to be fruit. Before she could heft the heavy carton, the man with her took the box away and shooed her into the house ahead of him. Grace chuckled and started singing about a naughty woman on a street somewhere. Nolan returned to his moving with a light heart. If his neighbor turned out to be the friend that he thought she would, he'd find out about that song later.

~~~~*

"Craig, you are too funny!" Grace and Melanie giggled at Craig's serious over reaction to her impromptu dinner with her new neighbor.

Grace led her exhausted sister-in-law down the hallway to her spare room as they mocked her brother's over protectiveness. "You rest. I have to have words with your husband. Wake up in an hour and I'll put you to work peeling."

"I told him that he was being ridiculous. Don't be surprised if he goes across the street and checks out the masher." Melanie winked, turned on her side, and was asleep before Grace could get back to the kitchen.

"*Craig*! Those are for canning, not for your perpetually empty belly!" Grace smiled as she poked at her brother's stomach and started a sink full of water and fruit soap.

"Tell me again why you sat on your porch and had dinner with a complete *stranger*?" Craig's tone was heavy with concern. "That's not *like* you Grace!"

"I told you. He hit my boy. My food was in the oven. He drove to the hospital to check on Cade. He realized I didn't have a car. He offered me a ride knowing I wouldn't accept his offer. I only called you so that it wouldn't seem like I was ungracious..." Grace continued giving Craig a play-by-play of the evening's events. Again.

Craig listened closely but still seemed skeptical. "I am just amazed that you sat out there and ate dinner with him. Since when do you have dinner with strange men?"

"Since the children that I am responsible for dash out in front of moving vehicles and subsequently cause me to ruin my dinner. Well, I only eat with the ones that also replace said ruined dinner." She paused and forced him to meet her eyes. "Craig, I didn't let him in the house. I had the porch light on and Mr. Verily was watching every move we made. He checked his mail at almost nine pm." Grace winked and started scrubbing a box of apples. Her humor was wasted. Craig was already on a mission.

"I'm going to go help him, got any sodas?" Craig wasn't the subtlest of men but Grace knew that he loved her and took his role as her brother very seriously.

"There are some on the top shelf. Drink those. Leave the ones on the second shelf alone."

Craig looked at her strangely. "Why?"

"Because *Squirt* fits you and I'm afraid of the subliminal messages you might get if you take a *Mug*."

~~~~*

"Need a hand with that?"

Nolan, deliberating as to the best way to get his couch through the doorway, looked up. He seemed happy for the diversion. "Thank you, I'd be grateful for any help I can get. I'm Nolan Burke."

"Craig Buscher. Grace is my sister."

"Did she tell you what I did last night?" Traces of pain laced Nolan's voice

"Grace told me what Cade Crenshaw did- foolish boy. He knows better. Maybe now he'll obey when he's given rules to follow." Craig's concerned tone softened the apparent harshness of his words.

"I called the hospital this morning; they said he was released late last night. Everything came back normal. He got away with just losing a chunk of the back of his head. I'll bet his jacket is a goner though."

Craig nodded. "Grace is hoping to buy a Cubs jacket he's been wanting as kind of a 'hope you've learned your lesson' gift."

"Cubs? He likes the Cubs? Doesn't he know that they are practically the worst team in baseball?"

"He knows it. Says he likes the uniforms. Maybe he thinks the "C" stands for Cade or something. Kids. Go figure."

The men grunted through their chuckles as they maneuvered the couch into Nolan's new living room. Craig started to push it against a long wall but Nolan stopped him. "I'm thinking about setting it here. This will create a separation from the breakfast bar over there."

Craig nodded and they hefted the couch once more to shift it into the new position. "Do you have time to help me with my mattress?"

Craig answered Nolan's question with a silent nod. Those who knew Craig well would know that he had something to say. Craig tended to become very quiet just before 'speaking his piece'. Nolan sensed that his visitor was there for more than a neighborly visit and puttered around the room opening boxes and setting out personal items.

A framed photograph caught Craig's eye as Nolan held it against the wall here and there looking for the right place to hang it. He recognized the view from nearby Lake Vienna. "That's a great picture. Did you take it?"

"Mm-hmm. I climbed the rocks behind the lake and snapped it at sunset.

"You're good." Before Nolan could reply, Craig continued. "Nolan? Got a question for you." Craig's voice was serious.

"Friendly." Nolan countered in a firm but pleasant tone.

"You sure?" Craig surveyed the man in front of him. Nolan was tall, he was extremely handsome, and it was obvious that he was also successful. Craig didn't want a womanizer to trifle with his sister's affections.

"Do you doubt it?" Nolan returned his new friend's gaze. He wasn't quite sure how he knew that Craig would be a friend, but he had no doubt.

Craig's gaze didn't waver. "I have to be sure. She's my sister. I am almost all the family that she has."

"Craig, what would you have done in my situation? Would you have driven away without checking on the child or ensuring the woman had a ride home?" Nolan's respect of Grace's brother rose by the moment.

Craig looked at Nolan. His eyes were honest, and he was not offended by Craig's interrogation. "You're right. Grace is right. I overreacted. Thanks for understanding. Let's go get that mattress."

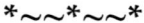

Grace watched from her window as the two men laughed and carried in Nolan's things. He had a credenza that Grace would have paid a fortune for, if she had a fortune to spend. Grace sighed. Making ends meet was hard enough without dreaming of furniture that she couldn't afford.

Grace carefully measured the cinnamon and the trace bits of nutmeg and ginger she used in her applesauce. With everything ready, she set up her pans. Jugs of apple juice stood ready to add liquid if necessary. She arranged a chair with a Dutch oven on the seat, and set up her apple-peeling gadget. She was on her second box of apples before Craig returned.

"I found you some more hands Grace. Where do we start?" Craig stood at the sink scrubbing his hands in preparation for a morning of fruit peeling.

"Why don't you scrub? Do you mind? The water is really drying out my hands for some reason."

Turning to Nolan, Grace smiled her welcome. "We're happy for the company and you're welcome to just sit there and amuse us." Grace chuckled and went back to turning her apple crank.

"I can turn that. Why don't you do something that you don't trust me on? Peeling fruit would not be a good one. The last time I peeled a potato- well, let's just say that I've seen larger plums than that potato after I was done with it."

Grace laughed. "This little jobbie does the peeling for me and doesn't take off more than I want it to."

She showed Nolan how to pull the peel away from the fruit and dump it into her compost bucket. As they worked together, the fruity trio joked, laughed, and the rest of the morning flew past. Before long, the spicy aroma of Grace's applesauce drifted down the hallway and woke Melanie from her extended nap. They all jumped when Melanie's voice called from down the hall asking what they were having for lunch.

"And you joke about my bottomless pit." Craig smiled at his wife as she waddled into the room. He turned to Nolan.

"This is Melanie, my wife, and recently she's become the meal monitor." Nolan's chuckle grew deeper as Melanie bopped her husband's head on her way to the saucepans.

"I am so exhausted. Did I mention that I'm tired? I want to sleep some more. But, this baby thinks it's lunch time, and looking at that clock, I must agree with him." Melanie stood over the stove smelling the delicious aromas and kneading her back with her fists as she tried to work out the kinks of her unbalanced body.

"Sandwiches anyone?" queried Grace as she mentally calculated the amount of leftover roast in her freezer.

"Ok, but if you provide lunch, we're taking you out for our *Last Supper*. That ok with you Mel?"

Craig looked at his wife's expression before continuing. "You're welcome to come too Nolan. We'd love to have you."

"Last Supper?" Nolan and Grace both waited, confused, for an explanation.

Melanie smiled. "It occurred to us last night that this baby might arrive any time now, I was due yesterday, so we should go out, one last time as a couple, without 'visible' children."

Grace shook her head as Melanie finished her explanation. "That's a great idea and I wish I could join you but I just can't. I'll be up until almost midnight as it is finishing these apples. Tomorrow, after church, I have the peaches to do. They'll peak by then. I can't go anywhere until I've canned all of this. I can't afford to lose the fruit or the money *from* the fruit."

Nolan saw through Grace's words. She wanted her brother to have his 'last supper' alone with his wife and the truth made a beautiful excuse. The fruit would wait. He knew enough about fruit to know that a couple of hours wouldn't make a difference but she used it as a semi-legitimate excuse.

Grace's hospitality was casual but thorough. She made sandwiches, cut up peaches, and shook up a box of instant pudding. She served mint tea and the chocolate pudding in her living room after they finished their sandwiches.

Craig, noting Melanie's continued exhaustion, finally insisted that they leave. "I want you perky enough to enjoy our dinner."

Melanie smiled at her husband before turning back to Grace. "Honey, are you sure you don't want to come with us? This can wait can't it? I mean, the apples should still be good on Monday."

"No way. I am going to finish my apples and then I'll study for the lesson tomorrow. That class is getting harder every week." Grace grimaced as she thought of the work ahead of her.

"You guys have fun, eat some dinner, and if that baby of yours doesn't arrive soon I'm going to bring over a few gallons of castor oil. Or is it cod fish oil? One of those is supposed to work isn't it?"

"I am *not* taking castor oil, cod fish oil, or even *baby* oil! The baby will get here when he is good and ready. Meanwhile I need a nap." Melanie looked like a twelve year old with a basketball under her shirt. Rubbing her eyes, she yawned as she waddled slowly out the door.

Grace waved her brother and his wife goodbye and then went back to work filling jars of applesauce. She chatted with Nolan for a little while before he decided to return to unpacking and unloading. As he opened the front door, Grace called him back.

"I'll bring over a bit of my dinner if you like. There's no reason for you to try to cook *and* move.

Sensing Nolan's hesitation she added, "I have soup all made and ready to heat up so it's no trouble."

"Thank you Grace. I'd appreciate that." He didn't know what else to say. Nolan considered her offer, as he walked to his house, and decided that Grace was probably more generous at heart than her pocketbook would allow.

He was right. While Grace enjoyed her life as a homemaker, she found making ends meet a deterrent to her natural giving and hospitality. Though she earned very little, Grace was determined to avoid the career world. She knew instinctively that it wouldn't make her happy. She held a degree in Physics, but she had no intention or desire to use it. She'd been interested in learning, had a scholarship to Rockland University, so she'd taken advantage of that opportunity but her heart was in serving people through domestic arts.

As a young teen and into her early twenties, she focused on perfecting those things that make a home special. Somehow, even after the death of her father, she had been able to support herself by caring for children, cooking for friends, and occasionally sewing for those who wanted something more original than department store clothing. She used skills that most of her contemporaries disdained to live a rich life and provide or her physical and financial needs.

Once each year, Grace accepted a wedding to sew for and cater. She'd considered making it a larger production and growing a full business doing wedding consulting and providing services needed but she knew she'd learn to hate it. Grace had a mission for her life and until God sent her something else to do, she planned to stay focused on that mission.

As Grace closed up her house that evening, the lights across the street made her smile. She'd been sad to see Mabel Gantry move to Milwaukee to live closer to her grandchildren but the prospect of a new friend and neighbor was encouraging. "You're good to me Lord. I can't complain. Now, do you think you could help me get these millennial positions straight in my head? I'm failing miserably right now."

Chapter Six

"Good Morning Miss Grace!" Amber Christiansen's elfin face beamed up at her.

Sitting quickly, Grace leaned over the pew. With her arms resting on the back, she grinned at the darling little girl. "Morning sunshine! How are you this morning?"

"Mrs. Buscher wasn't here this morning so we didn't have class. I get to sit with mommy instead!" The little girl snuggled closer to her mother.

Marci Christiansen's love shone in every thing she did with and for her child. Though she spent much 'quality' time with her daughter, it was never enough for Amber. It seemed to Grace that the precocious child wanted her mother's time more than the experiences that the overworked lawyer lavished on Amber seemingly in every spare moment.

"Well, I think that Melanie is just feeling extra tired these days. I'm sure she'll miss you.

"Marci, do you still have to go to Chicago in the morning?" Grace looked back for her friend Paige as she waited for Marci to answer. Paige was MIA.

"They rescheduled the meeting and I have to be there by seven tomorrow morning. I had to rearrange my flights and now I'm leaving immediately after church. There aren't any flights to get me there in time unless I leave today so, off I go!"

The smile on her face did little to hide the pain in Marci's eyes. Grace wondered how often her friend's work forced her to cut her weekends short due to the following week's workload. Looking into Marci's weary eyes, she realized that it must happen more than she'd previously thought.

Life as a single woman was sometimes lonely, but Grace knew that she avoided much pain and heartache as well. Her relationship with the Lord was both genuine and intimate. It would take an extremely special man to tempt her to give up some of that closeness. In her prayers concerning a husband and children, Grace prayed for a complete peaceful understanding that the Lord was behind any relationship she might enter. Voluntarily sharing her innermost person with the Lord had taken years to accomplish. If it was that difficult with One who knew all anyway, she didn't plan to jump into another relationship lightly.

The Apostle Paul's cautions were serious. A single person did have a different relationship with the Lord than a married person did. Grace didn't consider one better than the other, she believed that the Lord intended for most people to marry, have children, and shine as beacons in a world of pain, darkness and sin. Until that day, or in case she was one of the exceptions, Grace's father taught her to rely solely on the Lord for her strength, identity, and even the emotional support that women need so desperately at times.

Amber's voice interrupted her reverie. "Look! There's Miss Paige. Isn't she beautiful?" Everyone seated nearby heard the delighted exclamation and all silently agreed. Paige Matthews was most certainly a remarkably beautiful woman.

Grace nodded. She's the most beautiful person that I know, both inside *and* outside, and that is a rare combination."

"Yep! Mommy says it's a lie to be beautiful on the outside and ugly inside. We need to be beautiful inside and then we're always beautiful!" Amber nodded solemnly and reached for Paige.

Before Grace could welcome her friend, she noticed Chuck Majors charging toward them. Visions of bovine marauders in specialty gift stores came to mind as he plowed past several children and narrowly missed toppling the fichus tree that stood by the side doors. "Storm brewing on the starboard bow."

Everyone around her understood Grace's mutterings and prepared themselves accordingly. Amber, with a child's fresh honesty, stared stonily at the approaching man. She was used to being the center of attention and Chuck Majors tended to be too full of himself to notice a little girl starving for male attention.

Paige sat down and began thumbing through her class folder to find her notes. Marci helped Amber settle down with a coloring book and some crayons. Grace sighed and squared her shoulders.

This was going to be an interesting moment. Chuck had been after Paige for months.

"Paige! Where were you Friday night? I arrived right at eight and you weren't home! I waited for thirty minutes! I mean, I knew something important had to have come up and all. You don't have my number do you?"

Chuck continued his monologue until the teacher started their class on eschatological views. Grace could feel Paige sag in relief as she settled into the corner of the pew. Chuck, irritated that Grace sat between him and his current object of interest, finally settled himself in the next pew behind them. It was annoying, but Grace couldn't blame him; Paige was too beautiful not to want to have in your line of view.

Moments later, she choked into her sleeve as she saw the minister's oldest son usher Nolan Burke to Chuck's pew and asked Chuck to shift down a bit so that they could sit there. Paige was completely out of view and now, Chuck's fine view was reduced to the side of Grace's neck.

Whispering to Paige she chuckled and said, "I bet he *loves* the look of that mole back there!"

Nolan over heard the comment and wondered. "What mole was Grace talking about and who was 'he'? Was it him, the minister's son Jason, or the macho guy that they'd displaced?

When Paige turned to pass back the handouts for the morning's lesson, Nolan couldn't help but notice the quiet, graceful way that she had about her. To his natural delight, she was also refreshingly beautiful. Most women of his acquaintance with her features were models, or the daughters of wealthy businessmen and brazen, forward, self-absorbed, or some combination of the three. As frustratingly irritating as his experiences with attractive women were, he certainly appreciated a lovely face that didn't flirt when given half a chance.

Nolan liked *The Assembly*. The class was stimulating and informative. He now understood a wide variety of eschatological views as well as when and how they became popular. The sermon and time of communion were refreshingly real- completely without pretense. As the congregation welcomed him, he appreciated their warmth yet noted the careful way they attempted not to smother.

The church obviously was truly a piece of the family of God and not just a social club for 'good people.'

"Hey guys. Let's go to Kirkland's Buffet for lunch! I'm starved." The group at large so quickly declined Chuck's invitation that Nolan decided to follow suit.

He raised an eyebrow at Grace when Chuck continued after four flat refusals, "Great, I'll see you all there in ten. Paige, your lunch is on me- desert and everything."

Nolan waited until Chuck was out of earshot and asked, "Did I miss something, or did all of us decline?"

Grace's laugh was infectious. "Chuck never hears what we *really* say; he just hears what he thinks we should say. It will take him about thirty minutes to decide that *all* of us had an emergency and couldn't show."

He indulged in an amused chuckle as he turned to introduce himself to Paige. Well aware of the attention Nolan directed toward her, Paige skittered away before he had a chance. Turning to Grace with a bewildered look, Nolan asked if he'd been offensive.

"Not in the least. Paige is just very shy. It'll take her a few weeks to feel comfortable around you. It's nothing personal." Grace smiled as she watched her friend slide into her little sports car and drive toward home.

She turned to say something else to Nolan but at the sight of Marci and Amber, she hurried over gesturing for Nolan to follow. "Hey you two, I had an idea. What do you think about Amber coming home to stay with me tonight? We can make applesauce together, roast marshmallows over the stove, and watch an old movie. Would that work?"

Grace looked eagerly from Marci to Amber hoping they would accept. Seeing them eyeing the man with her, Grace motioned Nolan closer. "Oh, Marci, I am sorry, this is Nolan Burke; he's my new neighbor. I was happy to see him here today! Wish Craig was here to see it."

At Marci's pointed look, Nolan choked back a snort. "Her brother was concerned at my intentions in regards to Grace. I assured him I intended to live in the house and be a good neighbor to his sister."

Marci looked at her watch and shrieked. "Arrrghhhh I have to be at the airport in an hour! Are you sure that you want to take her Grace? I have the sitter all lined up..."

"I'd be thrilled, honestly."

"Go get your stuff Amber and put it in the bus. Jason looks like he's getting ready to go." Amber squealed in delight and skipped off to her car. Marci unlocked their mini van with a remote lock while she thanked Grace again.

Nolan waved at the two ladies and began walking to his car. Seeing Amber wrestling a suitcase, Nolan took pity on the little girl. "Can I help you with that Miss Amber?"

Amber giggled. "No one calls me Miss. That's what I have to call the ladies who are my friends. Mommy says it is called common courtesy."

"That's true. But, it's always courteous for gentlemen to call any lady 'miss', even if she's a little lady. So, if it's okay with you, I'll call you Miss Amber."

Amber's fairly sparkled as Nolan talked with her and transferred her little suitcase to the church's van. Grace glanced at Marci as they watched the proceedings and saw the pain creep back into her eyes.

"It still hurts, doesn't it?" Grace rarely beat about bushes.

"She's so precious- and Roger never saw it. All he could see was bills, sleepless nights, potty training, toys on the carpet, and that I wasn't as 'polished' as I was before she came along." Marci fought tears.

"Care to hear what I think, Marci?" Grace was blunt, but she wasn't tactless. She knew when to speak out and when to ask first.

"I'm better off without him?"

"Amber is better off not seeing him reject her day in and day out. It happened once, not repeatedly."

Marci knew that Grace was right. Marci's own father had been emotionally, and sometimes physically, detached, as she'd grown up. Marci didn't want that for her little girl. Perhaps the clean break would turn out to be a better thing.

With tearful and silly goodbyes, Marci drove toward the airport while Grace and Amber rode home. They debated fish sticks over grilled cheese and salad over celery sticks. Grace was at peace. She may not have children but she was able to be a substitute mommy now and again and that was a beautiful thing.

~~~~*

"Amber! That's my brother on the machine. Mrs. Buscher is having her baby! They're at the hospital right now. Let's pray that everything goes smoothly, and that babykins shows up soon, shall we?" Grace danced about thinking of the new baby.

They prayed, ate, and began marathon applesauce making. After a time, Grace noticed that Amber seemed to be losing interest. "Amber honey, why don't you go play out front with the soccer ball? I'll be done here soon and then we can play a game."

Amber ran to the toy closet and pulled the ball from a box of 'outside' toys. Soccer was the little girl's passion. Between playing on two different teams and watching every televised event that she could find, Amber seemed unable to tire of the sport. Marci joked that it was a beautiful way to kick out her frustrations and though it was a tricky juggle of her work schedule, she supported Amber's dedication to it.

"Grace, you need to go to more of her games. Marci probably misses a few and it would mean a lot to Amber if you went. Now find out when her next three games are and get them on your calendar." Grace's mutterings to herself tended to serve as a mental reminder of what needed doing, and though she received a few raised eyebrows at the grocery store and the dentist's office, she never seemed to mind.

Grace giggled as she observed Amber attempting to con Nolan into a game. The enchanting little girl sweet-talked him from his car and moments later, they were chasing the checkered ball across the yard with gusto. From her window, Grace saw Nolan straining from his exertions but he, with an excellent display of sportsmanship, continued to play despite his obvious desire to quit. His slippery dress shoes didn't make the job any easier.

Amber was incapable of exhaustion, or so it always seemed. She ran Nolan ragged. Amber wouldn't coax the poor man into a 'pick up' game again anytime soon! Never knowing the meaning of the word quit, Amber went in for the kill and scored a goal, right between Nolan's ankles.

When Grace saw Nolan collapse on the lawn, breathing heavily and wiping sweat from his forehead, she went into action. She made lemonade and placed it on a tray with three glasses. Opening the pantry for some napkins, Grace jumped, screamed, and then went on a rampage. Nolan and Amber, concerned that a rabid dog or something equally horrifying was mauling Grace, rushed into the kitchen. Initially, it wasn't apparent to them what the problem was, but Grace was literally throwing items out of the pantry searching for something. At the sight of Nolan's shoes, Grace grated between clenched teeth, "Get me that broom that's hanging beside the fridge will you?"

"Is everything alright?" Nolan's voice was tentative. Amber slowly backed into the living room while tugging on his sleeve.

"Mr. Burke." Amber tugged at his sleeve. Let's go back outside."

Nolan whispered back in typical, over loud, male style, "What is it?"

"*Mice*. That's what it is. *Mice*! Who do they think they are?" Grace's tone was angry, appalled, and terrified all at once.

Nolan watched in awestruck fascination as Grace tore apart the pantry searching for the mouse and his home. She was a whirlwind; being a good fifty pounds overweight hid her energy. This woman had strength, energy and passion, and all over a mouse in her pantry. Nolan had never witnessed anything like it.

Finally, the mouse scurried past her toe and darted across the floor. The broom came down with a sharp 'whap' near Nolan's foot, before the mouse darted behind the refrigerator. "Ha! Gotcha now you nasty little beast!"

Grace was on her feet and dragging the fridge away from the wall before Nolan could offer to help. She narrowly missed tripping over a can of pumpkin before bringing the broom down hard on top of the mouse. The critter had foolishly decided that it was time to make a run for it but that was precisely what Grace had anticipated. With a final squeak, the mouse lay still at her feet.

Nolan didn't know what to do next. Should he offer to help the woman? He didn't know. Some women would love the help but others would resent it. Before he could offer, Grace shuddered. "Can you please get that thing out of here?" she ground out between firmly clenched teeth.

Nolan snapped his head up and eyed Grace. She looked exhausted and emotionally 'done in'. "I'd be happy to. Why don't you go sit down?"

Grace stepped over the offending rodent with a goofy little side step dance, and collapsed into her favorite chair in the living room. She was exhausted from her ordeal and listened as the Nolan and Amber worked on cleaning up the kitchen. Amber told stories about Grace's encounters with mice but Grace was too tired and emotionally spent to defend herself.

"They come from the fields across the road there... she hates them Mr. Burke. She goes from being calm and cool to totally freaking out! I mean I saw her jump on one once. After she squished him, she barfed in the sink. It was so gross."

"I see. Well, it looks like she got this one. He won't be bothering her any more... or do mice have more than one 'life' like cats? Let's wash off the shelves and put this stuff back for her. Ok?"

A short while later, Grace opened her eyes and saw a glass of cool lemonade with two sweet hazel eyes peering over the top of it. "Miss Gracie? Want some lemonade? The kitchen's all clean and pretty so you can relax and enjoy it. Mr. Burke and me will go play outside and let you rest if you want..."

Grace tried hard not to laugh. The little girl seemed to have spent one too many days the Buscher home. She obviously knew how irritated Grace became over mice. Grace had exceptional control over her fear of mice. That is, until she saw one. Generally, at that point, her fear manifested itself as fury and the results were predictably comical.

"Go outside and play honey, I'll get to work on the kitchen. I have a few things that I need to do now. Thank you for picking everything back up."

"We washed the shelves too. Just in case... it... was on them." Amber's eyes looked too wise for her years.

Grace sent Amber back outside with Nolan before attacking her kitchen with a vengeance. Experience told her that where one mouse was, more were likely to follow. Armed with several boxes of zip-lock bags, Grace began to secure her domain. All of her silverware was rinsed in bleach water, dried, and bagged. Her tea, crackers, and other 'open' containers were bagged. She bagged the butter crock, sugar bowl, and salt and peppershakers. There wasn't an empty plastic storage container in her entire kitchen by the time she was finished.

Nolan looked up in surprise when he heard the back door slam shut. Grace carried her broom in one hand and a bottle of disinfectant cleanser in another. Fascinated, he stared as she poured half the bottle of cleanser over the bristles and then 'swept' it into them by fiercely sweeping the broom back and forth on the driveway, apparently trying to rub the solution into the broom. Finally, she rinsed the broom with the hose.

"Getting out the gore?" Grace heard Nolan's taunt from across the lawn but continued in her cleansing rite.

"Awwwwww come on Grace, the poor broom is clean already! Give the thing a chance!" Nolan's wheedling voice seemed to make no impact on Grace.

When Nolan reached her side, he saw that things were much worse than he had realized. Grace wasn't just angry over the mice; she was terrified. Her knuckles gripped the broom like a pair of vice grips. He eased the broom from her hands and drew Grace back into the house. Grabbing an afghan from the back of the couch, Nolan led her to the recliner, tucked the blanket around her, sat on the floor beside the chair, and prayed.

"Lord, we ask that you comfort Grace right now. Please help her to have the strength to release her fears and frustrations to you. We ask for a restful nap, and a pleasant and vermin free day tomorrow. In the name of Jesus, Amen."

Grace mumbled something about finding the money for an exterminator and then something about protecting her fruit before falling into an exhausted sleep. Nolan stood and watched her for a moment. Did she expect an exterminator to be open on a *Sunday*? As he headed into the kitchen to consider how to protect the fruit he realized that Grace had been talking to herself again. A bemused smile crept into his features as he went outside to rejoin Amber.

"Does Grace often talk to herself?"

Amber snickered as she practiced dribbling across the yard. "She carries on entire conversations by herself... she even repeats the conversation with different answers and stuff. It's like she practices what she could have to say or something."

Amber gave an impish little smile before adding, "And she is funny sometimes too! I heard her talking once; she was really letting some company have it for not sending the right stuff and then charging her for it and the right stuff too. When I went in, she was making her bed... and there was no phone anywhere!"

Nolan chuckled at the mental picture but quickly sobered. "I don't want to sound like I am reprimanding you, but... well; some people might call it gossip to tell a story like that. I shouldn't have asked. Forgive me?"

Amber looked at him curiously before nodding cautiously. "Do you really think Miss Grace would mind? She is always making fun of herself for her 'inside conversations'. I didn't know it was wrong to talk about it."

"Well, technically it might not be wrong to have told me that story, but my asking was tempting you to gossip... and in the very strictest sense, talking about Grace, with her not here, could be considered gossip." Nolan paused to try to clarify his thoughts. How do you explain gossip to a child who wouldn't consider maligning her friend?

"So just in case someone thinks you are being mean you shouldn't talk about them unless they are there?" Amber seemed fascinated by the direction that the conversation had taken.

"That's right." Nolan's relief was evident.

"But how would they know you talked about them if they aren't there?" Amber's eyes began to look suspicious.

"That is the point Amber. If who you spoke to mentions the conversation, then the person, if they felt gossiped about, might not feel comfortable talking to you anymore. See?"

Amber looked as if she had another question but before she could ask, remembered something. "*Wait!* We forgot all about Mr. and Mrs. Buscher! They are having their baby right now. It might be here. Miss Grace wanted to go see them when the baby came. Should we go see for her?"

Nolan laughed at the little girl's obvious delight in her scheme. "Well, there are two problems with that. First, I can't take you anywhere without Grace's permission, and secondly... well... I think that her brother will call her as soon as that baby arrives. What we can do though, is go inside and make dinner for her and for her to

take to them in the hospital. I don't know if they let dads eat too...
and if they do, I doubt if Craig would enjoy the food."

"Hospital food is yucky!" Amber's face was comical. It seemed
as though she was no stranger to the bland fare of institutional food.

Inside, Nolan stood before the sparse refrigerator, hands in
pocket and tried to figure out what could be made with the scanty
contents. There was leftover chicken soup, and sandwich fixings, but
not enough to take to the hospital. The freezer showed more promise
but it was empty as well and there was no time for defrosting.

"Looks like we'll have to be creative Amber. You see if you can
find a clean box and a towel to put hot food into, and I'll go see what
I have at home to contribute to dinner."

~~~~*

Grace heard ringing and wondered sleepily what it was. She
struggled to wake up and climb out of her chair. Nolan brought her
the phone before she could become fully coherent. "H'llo?"

Grace listened a moment and looked around the room with
fuzzy eyes. "Amber? Your mom's on the phone. Do you want to
talk to her?"

As Amber prattled on about her soccer game, the mouse and
their current preparations for dinner for Craig and Melanie and the
upcoming birth, Grace rubbed the sleep from her eyes, and stretched.
Dinner smelled wonderful and the smell caused a rumble in her
stomach. "Hungry Grace?"

Grace smiled at him. "What are you cooking... that smells
great!"

"Lemon Pepper chicken. Just chicken, rice, snow peas and a
brothy sauce over it. Have a seat; it's almost done. We were thinking
about taking some to the hospital for Craig."

Grace sat at her table and enjoyed the aroma of the plate of food
that Nolan placed before her. Nolan glanced at Amber who was
cheerfully chatting at her mother and suggested they pray without
her. "She's busy with her mom. We'll pray for her."

As they raised their heads to begin eating, Amber bounced over
to Grace. "Mommy wants to know if you need anything from
Chicago."

Grace started to shake her head but remembered Cade's accident and took the phone. "Marci... do you know if there is some kind of discount sports store there where you could find an affordable Cub's jacket?"

For the next few minutes, the two women bantered back and forth on the exact description of the jacket, and if Marci would let Grace repay her for the jacket. Finally, Marci put her foot down. "Grace. What I'll have to pay for this is half what it would cost me to have left Amber with a sitter, and she's having a blast. You're still giving me a gift of taking care of my daughter; let me pay for the jacket. You've more than earned it already. I'll pick up Amber tomorrow night sometime after seven."

Before Grace could argue, Marci hung up. Her face was masked with frustration. "I'll figure this out. She won't get away with it that easily."

"Trouble in paradise?" Nolan found Grace's discomfiture to be comical.

"She doesn't want to let me pay for Cade's new jacket. How can I give some a gift that someone else paid for?"

Thinking for a moment, her new neighbor shook his head. "I'd say that you would be paying for it. I don't know much about childcare expenses but I can imagine that overnight care and taking a child to and from school would be expensive. Much more expensive than a jacket."

"That jacket is almost a hundred dollars. I can't really afford it but his jacket is ruined and I don't want him to feel like he is 'in trouble' with me. I thought it might be nice."

Amber piped up, her voice thick with disgust. "He deserved to lose his jacket. He was foolish."

"Amber!" Grace was at a loss. The two children that she loved most had an extreme disdain for each other.

"Well he did. It's stupid to walk between cars like that. I know that and I am almost a whole year younger than he is." Amber crossed her arms defiantly across her chest.

"Amber. I think you should go hang up your school clothes and cool off. You're out of line." Grace was calm and matter of fact. Many children would have taken her lack of visible anger as an indicator that they didn't need to obey, but Amber was well aware that Grace meant business.

"Yes Miss Grace. I'm sorry." Amber left the room and shuffled down the hallway.

Nolan watched the byplay curiously. "Wow. I've seen moms and kids at stores, churches, and restaurants... I've never seen a kid so quickly subdued. What'd you do?"

"She knows I mean business." Grace savored another bite as she considered the jacket situation once more. Maybe Marci and Nolan were right. She was doing what she was generally being paid for and the price of the jacket would likely be much cheaper in one of those discount stores that Marci always shopped at.

"So most parents don't mean business?"

Grace thought about that. "I don't know about that... I just think that a lot of parents spend more time negotiating good behavior rather than requiring it."

"What would you have done if she hadn't complied?" Nolan was taking swift mental notes. His friend Mike had three somewhat unruly children that he and his wife worked hard to raise but felt like they were failing at every turn. Perhaps Grace had insight that might help his friends.

"Well, I probably would have told her that dinner would now be served in her room only and to go immediately."

"And if she refused?" Nolan had seen similar scenes in Mike's house numerous times.

"Well, with my own child, I would have more leeway. I don't keep children if the parents don't agree to pick up the child immediately if they refuse to obey." Grace sounded sad even to think of such a thing actually happening.

Nolan thought of something. "How would Marci be able to get Amber immediately? I mean, she's hundreds of miles away."

"Marci would get on the next flight, even if it meant missing her meeting and Amber knows it. I know I wouldn't want to go home with a mom who had to fly home from a business meeting that puts food on the table. It's a deterrent. And they know I'd do it without thinking twice."

Nolan thought about the idea as he stirred his food together and took another bite. Swallowing quickly he asked, "So, what you are saying is that you have to make them want to obey you?"

"Not quite, but that is a good goal as well. You just have to make any undesired behavior counter productive. If they do something that you don't like, make them want to never do it again."

Before the conversation could continue, the phone rang again. Grace jumped up and answered it excitedly. "Craig? *Mel!* Are you ok? Is everything ok? Is the baby there? What is her name? His name-"

Nolan laughed as Grace became immediately silent. Her head bobbed and shook as she gave silent squeals and jumped around. "Amber... come in here... the baby is here!"

Absentmindedly, Grace hung up the phone and grabbed her jacket. She grabbed Amber's hands and danced about the room in excitement. "Come on guys... we have a baby to see! Visiting hours are over in an hour. Craig is coming right now to get us. Would you like to come, Nolan?"

Nolan considered going but the idea of being that close to a little baby was too much for him. "I'll stay here and clean up my mess. I'll lock the door on my way out. Give my best to Craig and Melanie."

Grace headed out the door only to pop back in quickly. "Can you call Mrs. Crenshaw and tell her to tell Cade to help Amber get the right bus after school tomorrow? Her number is on that sheet by the phone in there."

Nolan nodded and waved her off. Picking up the phone, he made the call for Grace and relayed her message, as well as the good news about the baby. Her kitchen was cleaned and Amber's plate of food covered and set into the fridge. Looking around the kitchen, he saw nothing out of place. As he snapped off the light, he prayed that no unwelcome visitors would invade while Grace was absent.

On his way out the door, he saw a photo album and his curiosity got the better of him. Sitting on the floor, Nolan thumbed through the pages. The album was arranged in chronological order and Nolan watched as Grace and Craig were born, grew, and changed. Grace was an adorable little girl and Craig appeared to have been a local football hero.

Nolan snapped the book shut sharply. Thoroughly ashamed of his invasion of Grace's privacy, Nolan turned off the lights and shut the door. Testing to assure that the door was locked, Nolan stepped out into the night and walked home praying. "A baby Lord. A baby girl. Keep the family safe, happy and in Your care always."

Chapter Seven

"Is this your classroom?" Grace looked through the little window in the door.

"Yes, that is Mr. Minchin. He says that he is a great decadent of Miss Minchin in *A Little Princess*. I think he's joking 'cause that's just a story."

Grace managed to stifle a chuckle over Amber's malapropism. "Ahh. A descendent of the right, dishonorable Miss Minchin huh? Is he nicer than she was?"

Amber nodded, and waving cheerfully, skipped into her classroom. Grace grinned as the teacher sent Amber back to the door to walk in properly. Turning leave the school, Grace sighed to herself. "Some things never change."

Grace eagerly rode to the hospital on the 'dial-a-ride' bus to practice her new role as a doting aunt. She found Melanie taking a shower and getting dressed while Craig sat in the chair and held his sleeping daughter. "How is Mel feeling?"

"The doctor says it's been over twelve hours, the pediatrician has agreed to release her, and everything looks good so we'll be going home in about an hour."

Grace took her niece from Craig and cooed over her. "They made me scrub up before coming in so I'm all clean sweetie. You're one blessed little girl. My big brother is your daddy and he picked out the sweetest mommy in the world for you.

"Let's ask your Daddy what they've decided to name you." Grace looked pointedly at her brother. She knew that they had considered many forms of Anna and Grace and had tentatively settled on Hannah as a compromise.

Craig shrugged his shoulders in mock annoyance. "We haven't come to an agreement yet. We're still deciding."

"What are the options today?" Grace traced the baby's features with her fingers as she listened to the great debate begin again in earnest.

"I want Hannah Grace but Craig says that's like naming someone Grace Grace since Hannah means grace." Melanie, walking in with a towel wrapped head, sounded ready to cry. Grace rocked the baby with slight exaggeration to hint to her brother that the new mother might need a little more understanding.

"What do you want Craig?" Though hesitant to ask, Grace was curious.

"Anna Grace. After mom. I'd like to name her after both mothers but I don't like Adeline or Lynn with Grace or Anna."

"Doesn't Anna mean grace too?" Grace winked at her sister in law.

Names were tossed about the room until the doctor came to sign the discharge papers. Melanie began to act a little panicked at the idea of leaving the hospital without a name for her child. With an air of resignation, Melanie took the baby from Grace and sat in a chair next to her husband. "Name her anything Craig. I just want the birth certificate filled out before I walk out that door."

Grace stepped outside the room and pulled the door shut behind her. A nurse came with more papers to be signed, but Grace waved her off. "They need a moment to discuss something; I'll let you know when they are ready."

Ten minutes later, the door opened with a grand flourish. "Grace… May I formally introduce you to your first niece, Graceanna Lynn Buscher. Emphasis on 'ahnnah' in -anna."

Grace took her niece from the little one's proud papa. While Melanie signed papers, Craig gathered Melanie's and the baby's things and headed to their car. Walking down the hall, Craig listened to his sister crooning over his little daughter and was happy with his lot. God had given him a beautiful wife, a loving sister, and now the world's sweetest baby. With a heart full of gratefulness, he thanked the Lord for His blessings and prayed for wisdom in the coming months and years. To a Buscher, family is a sacred trust and Craig was feeling a new weight of responsibility in that trust.

Warm cookies cooled on a rack next to the oven as Cade and Amber burst into the house that afternoon. Grace welcomed the children and listened to the tales of their days and competed for her attention. Several squabbles were quickly settled by Grace in her no nonsense manner. Once full of cookies, the two children worked on their homework and Grace prepared supper for herself and Amber.

"Oh, Amber... they named the baby today. Cade, would you like to see a picture of her?"

Cade looked at the baby's red wrinkled face and laughed. "She looks like a chicken with no feathers."

"She does *not!*" Amber was indignant.

"Enough you two. You are both being deliberately unpleasant and I've had enough already. When you're ready to behave, I'll tell you the baby's name."

Grace continued her food preparations and told the children to finish their homework. Several minutes later Cade came over and apologized. "I'm sorry. She just bugs me and I let her. I should be better 'cause I'm older."

"You owe her an apology too. You've been picking on her since you walked in the door, and I imagine all the way here." Grace gave him a pointed look.

Cade obviously hadn't counted on women's intuition to get him into trouble. He turned to Amber and hesitated a moment before squaring his shoulders and offering his apology. "I am sorry. I'll be nicer."

Amber's little chin shot up as if to reject his apology but a glance at Grace stopped her short. "Me too. I tried to bug you. That was rude."

After Cade went home with his mother, Grace and Amber ate dinner, cleaned up, and then began packing Amber's things in readiness for her mother's arrival. "Amber? Why do you and Cade have such a hard time with each other?"

"I don't know. I try to be nice to him... I do! But..."

Grace looked concerned. "What is it Amber? I need to know."

Amber shrugged. "He's just a boy and boys are mean to girls. I don't like it so I pick back. I'm sorry"

Grace knew that there was more to the problem than Amber was sharing, but her little friend seemed bothered by the conversation. As Grace watched her carefully fill her little suitcase,

Amber pretended to be very busy with her task and avoided looking into Grace's eyes. Her silence was extremely surprising to Grace. Amber was known for being exuberantly talkative.

Grace answered her phone cheerfully. "Good Evening!"

"Feel up to a game of checkers?"

"Sure! Your porch or mine? We have to enjoy it while we can. The weather is going to send us inside soon." Grace began searching for her cardigan and knit cap.

"Oh, let's give Mr. Wirth a show. He has a better view from your porch. I'll bring some nuts and a thermos of hot chocolate. Mom's recipe." Nolan grabbed his snacks as he hung up the phone and started across the street.

Grace had warm blankets, gloves, and two cups arranged on the porch when Nolan arrived. While Nolan set up the playing board, Grace settled into one of two beanbag chairs that she dragged out onto the steps for a more comfortable game. When everything was arranged, Nolan took one black and one red checker and shuffled them in his hands. Holding out his fists, Grace chose.

"Red. You go first." Grace turned the board so that the red checkers were on her side and began to plan her strategy.

For the next twenty minutes, moves were carefully plotted and executed. Grace made strategic moves to indicate that she 'missed' a good opportunity and tried to set up a surprise attack. Nolan countered and stopped her cold. Finally, after whittling each other down to one king, the match was tied. To win, one or the other would have to deliberately put themselves in harm's way and neither would concede.

"Good game. What do you think? One more or is it too cold?" Nolan watched, concerned that his opponent was too chilled for another game.

"We can't quit without a winner! I want to either know I failed or make you taste defeat. Ties are unacceptable!" Grace's lighthearted tone gentled the fierce competitiveness of her words.

The next game was fierce and swift. Some moves were made with much thought and deliberation, while the next might be executed without hesitation. In the end, Nolan was victorious. "Rematch tomorrow night?"

Grace's smile was the only answer necessary, yet she assured him that she would be on her toes and there would be no chance of him beating her again. "I have to lose now and then so that winning is 'worth' it. Does that sound believable?"

"That sounds like an excuse Miss Buscher... and I don't accept excuses!"

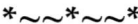

Grace greeted her friends as she neared the retirement home. Couples walking to the center of town, elderly gentlemen shuffling to the park to feed the birds, and silver-haired ladies out for a bit of fresh air and gossip, waved and called out greetings as she passed. She never wondered if Aunt Fran would be inside. Aunt Fran never left. Her father's sister's hobby was languishing in misery in Brunswick's finest, and only, retirement home.

Tara Boyer shook her head and made a slicing motion across her neck as Grace entered. She squared her shoulders, held up a stack of photos of the baby, and made praying hands motions as she slipped past the reception area and headed toward Fran Bucher's apartment. Obviously, this wasn't a good day to visit Aunt Fran. She knew that no matter what choice she made, her aunt would be difficult. Come too soon, stayed away too long- it didn't matter what anyone did, Aunt Fran just liked to complain.

"Oh it's you. Weren't you just here last week?" Fran whined as Grace entered.

"I love your new color. I wasn't sure when you showed me the paint chip but it's a lovely green."

"You just never have had an eye for color. What are you doing here?"

Grace settled herself next to Fran and pulled out the stack of photos. Before she could share them, Fran scooted to the side. "You really need to lose some of those pounds Grace, I feel like I'm on a teeter-totter."

"Well, take a look at little Graceanna. She was born on Sunday."

"She's been here for nearly a week and I'm just seeing pictures? I tell you, you and Craig don't have the basics of courtesy anymore."

This was normal. One minute she was attacked for coming too often and in nearly the next breath, she heard the whine of being forgotten and unwanted. Nothing Grace could do or say would make a difference, so she smiled and pointed out the natural dimples in Graceanna's cheeks and chin, and the wide-eyed look they'd already captured from her.

"Have you gotten a job yet?"

"I already have work to do Aunt Fran. I don't need a job. How do you like the new exercise room?" Her deflections always failed but she never failed to try them.

"Listen Grace, you need to quit playing house and take charge of your life. You have a degree for G-"

"I don't want to hear it. I know what I can do. I can do what everyone else does. I want to do what I want to do and I will for as long as I can afford to do it."

"You're living like a pauper."

Her laughter made the attendants in the hall smile. Fran was always in a better mood after Grace left. "Aunt Fran, I *am* a pauper."

"Well quit acting like it! You are being ridiculous. You could have everything-"

Grace stood setting the pictures on the coffee table. "I have everything I want. I need to go. I think I'm upsetting you."

She leaned in, kissed her aunt's cheek, smiled into her eyes, and said genuinely. "I love you Aunt Fran."

As the door shut behind her, Fran Buscher crossed her arms and legs and leaned back into the comfortable couch cushions with a self-satisfied smile on her face. "You have everything but a man and with all that flab and stuck at home, you'll never find one of those either."

Chapter Eight

Grace awoke with renewed vigor. The last week had been physically exhausting but Grace attributed it to the many quarts of fruit that she'd canned. Her friends paid handsomely for the jelly and fruit that Grace worked so hard to process. The proceeds would feed her through December and then some. Grace often wondered if her customers didn't pay more for her cooking than it was worth, but she was always assured that hand canned fruit and jelly was nearly impossible to buy and very expensive if you were so fortunate as to find a source.

"Well Missy, you have a full plate today. Mel and the baby are coming to spend the night while Craig is in Rockland for that silly conference and you need to get their room ready, get dinner started, and then pull out those catalogs to plan Gracie-anna's spring wardrobe."

Grace continued with her running dialog as she brushed her hair, made the bed, dressed, and moved from room to room readying the home for the day.

Craig often insisted that Martha Stewart could take lessons from her. Grace always blushed as he talked but appreciated that her brother valued her contribution to the family. His most memorable assertion was, "Martha may love doing everything at home and being involved in the home, but Grace makes an art of it without a large expense account."

"Mom taught me well didn't she Lord? I miss her. I miss dad too. Life can be hard and lonely at times but I love the work that You've given me to do and I thank you." Grace's prayer continued while she began mixing a triple batch of muffins.

As she looked across the street, the loneliness of Nolan's house prompted a new line of ramblings. "Nolan is home today Grace.

He'd probably appreciate some hot muffins. If you hurry, you can fix him a basket and get back before Melanie arrives."

Grace enjoyed the easy friendship that had grown between herself and her new neighbor. Nolan appreciated the candor and ease of their discussions as well as the lack of flirtation. Grace simply appreciated not being perceived as less than a 'real' person for not having a traditional career. They discussed politics, the Word, and music over endless games of checkers on his porch or hers. As the evenings grew cooler, they held fewer matches outdoors, but with Melanie coming to stay for a few days, they had been looking forward to a three-way championship.

~~~~*

"Howdy neighbor! I made muffins for Melanie and thought you might like to have a few while they are hot."

Nolan smiled at the sight of the basket in Grace's hand. This wasn't the first time that Grace had shared her larder with him. Her generous nature was evident at every turn, but Nolan was quite aware of her lack of financial resources. Eventually he would devise a way to contribute to her housekeeping without it being obvious or insulting.

"Morning Grace! Thank you, I haven't had breakfast yet. You know, I was thinking about inviting myself to dinner tonight if you didn't mind."

Grace controlled her expression with some difficulty. Her hospitable nature made it impossible to refuse him, and though her carefully planned budget wouldn't easily stretch to cover the cost increase, she'd find a way. "We'd love to have you. Anytime you want to come on over, feel free. Mel and Graci-anna will be here through Friday evening."

Nolan stopped Grace as she turned to leave. Tugging on her sleeve, he said, "Well, I can't invite myself to dinner without bringing something. I have these steaks in the freezer. Do you like steak?"

"Thank you! We'd love to have them! I-"

Grace stopped mid-sentence as she noticed Melanie getting out of her van. Grace called a greeting to her sister-in-law, and with a quick wave at Nolan, jogged across the street. "Come when you can Nolan!"

Nolan watched as Grace helped Melanie bring in her things, cooing to and casually holding the infant all the while. He felt a twinge of awe. Though he loved children, babies made Nolan nervous. His fear of infants was so acute; he'd managed to avoid ever holding one. However, Nolan also knew that tonight he might find himself unable to refuse. "Aaarrrgggh. What was I *not* thinking, inviting myself to dinner?"

~~~~*

"Mel, what about this one?" Grace lingered over yet another picture of a delicately smocked dress and sighed at its beauty.

"Grace, you don't know how to smock. How do you expect to learn how and make that before spring?" Melanie laughed at Grace as she nursed her two-week-old daughter.

"I just *have* to learn how to do this. These are too precious! I think I could do quite well if I made these for that upscale boutique we saw in Rockland last summer. You know that one where we loved everything but the price tags?"

Melanie was thoughtful. "Ok, let's make a deal. You can make the dress if I buy the materials for 3 of them and the supplies to get you started."

Grace shook her head. "That's no gift! I was supposed to get to give Graci-anna her first Easter dress and if you pay for it all, what kind of gift is that?"

"Grace." Melanie's tone was firm but gentle.

"What? It's like me buying you a birthday gift but you insist on paying me for everything but the shipping?" Grace's hands were on her hips, and her eyes were flashing. When it came to her financial 'worth', Grace tended to become somewhat unreasonable.

"Grace, listen to me. The hours that you will spend making this dress will be more than an incredible gift. You can even make more smocked dresses if you let me do this but as hard as it is for me to say…"

Melanie paused. It was almost an unwritten rule in the Buscher family not to mention Grace's minimal income. She finally took a deep breath and continued. "Grace, you can't afford the classes, books, or supplies to learn this and you know it. I have stood behind your desire to 'make it' on your own. I understand it, and I will back you up all the way, but you can't afford to spend your hard earned money on things for my baby."

Grace looked at her feet a moment or two before starting to protest. "Melanie, I don't think it's..."

"Grace." Melanie's tone grew stern. "Grace, this is your pride talking. I know you love to give. I understand that, I do. But Grace, we both know that desire doesn't produce cash, and for you to insist will hurt you in the long run and what kind of gift is that for us? Can we appreciate and love something that you've given that costs you more than you can afford?"

Tears stood in Grace's eyes. Melanie was right as usual. The gentle woman very seldom stood against anything that Grace or Craig wanted, but when she did, they wisely listened.

"Ok, let's find out where to buy the stuff. Who do we know that smocks?" Grace was eager to get started and get her mind off her financial difficulties.

"I don't know... Paige seems to be here. We can ask her, but somehow I don't think she'll know."

Before Grace could get up to open the door, Paige knocked gently and entered. "Sorry for just coming in but I didn't want to wake the baby if she was sleeping."

"What brings you by at this time of day?" Melanie transferred her little daughter to the arms of her aunt before adjusting her clothing and turning her attention to Paige.

"Well, I drove by your house on my way over and the kitchen floor is all over your driveway and the wind is picking some pieces up and tossing them in the street and the neighbor's yards. I thought you might want to call the installer and have him take care of it before something gets damaged."

Melanie made a beeline for the phone. "Why didn't you just call? I feel badly that you came all this way."

"Well, it was an excuse to see you and the baby- and Grace of course!"

"I knew that I should insist on staying home while they did the work. Craig kept going on and on about how I needed my rest, and without someone to help if the baby wouldn't sleep at night..."

Melanie turned her attention to the contractor who finally answered the phone. Paige and Grace quickly began pouring over the different catalogs and magazines. If the two women had been allowed free reign, they could have easily outfitted ten children with their 'favorites' alone.

Before long, Paige told her friends about seeing Nolan at a business lunch that day. "The woman was beautiful and obviously quite interested in him but he was all business."

Paige went on to describe the woman's constant flirtation. The three women laughed hysterically when Paige told about Nolan's smooth handling of the woman's insistence that he 'be a man and drink a *man's* drink'. Paige assumed a sultry tone as she imitated the woman's command.

"So then he turned to the waiter and said, 'Just bring me a universal solvent on the rocks please.'"

"He didn't! What did the waiter do?" Melanie was laughing so hard the tears ran from her eyes.

"That was the funny thing, the waiter obviously knew what he was talking about, but the woman was absolutely clueless. She sat there looking smug until the waiter showed up with a glass of ice water."

Grace giggled. "So what did she do then? I mean, could she tell it was water and not just one of those clear drinks like Vodka or something?"

Paige nodded. "It was obvious. The waiter brought it in a regular water glass and everything. The chick stared daggers at him. He sipped the water, signed the check, closed up whatever he had been showing her, and left."

Grace was stunned. "I know about that account. It would have been a huge one. I wonder if there was more to it than the drink thing or if he is that opposed to alcohol?"

Paige shook her head. "I think he just didn't like her trying to 'pick him up'. She was awful. I know I am backward and not very 'outgoing' but this gal was the worst I've ever seen. She put her hand on his leg at one point!"

"No way." Melanie shook her head sadly as she considered what today's men had to go through. For years, she had been upset with the rude and crass way that men tended to treat women but lately she'd seen that things were now on the other foot. Women were just as bad as the men were- often worse.

Grace couldn't contain herself. "How did he get out of that one?"

"He stood and moved to the chair across from her as though she needed more space. Uh oh, speak of the devil- the lady-killer himself. I'd better go." Paige stood briskly and gathered her purse.

"He doesn't bite, you know." Grace shook her head and tried to stop Paige from leaving. Several times, she had wondered if Nolan was becoming interested in her friend and wanted to see them together in hopes of confirming her suspicions. Grace thought that Nolan and Paige would make a beautiful couple- and she was right.

"I know he doesn't but I don't know him and..." Paige turned and dashed for the back door. "I'll call you tomorrow.

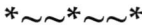

Nolan stood at his kitchen sink seasoning the steaks when he saw Paige Matthews drive up to Grace's house. "Ahh... now what perfect timing. Perhaps I can finally have a regular conversation with you Miss Matthews. I think I'll go to Grace's in just a little while. She did say anytime was fine!"

He whistled as he covered the steaks carefully and washed his hands. Chuckling at talking to someone who wasn't there, Nolan changed clothes, answered a couple of emails, and then sauntered across to Grace's house.

From his first meeting with Paige, Nolan had been intrigued. Paige was beautiful. There was no way getting around the fact that the woman was completely stunning, but she was also feminine and her shyness was a welcome relief from the over-aggressiveness he dealt with daily. He wanted to know more about her as a person but thus far knew only the little that Grace shared with him.

As Nolan knocked on Grace's door, he saw Paige climb into her car. Waving cheerfully, the young woman put her car in gear, and sped away before Grace had the chance to open the door. "Paige saw you coming and was out of here before we could invite her to stay! Either you intimidate her more than most people do or she knows something about you that we might need to know!"

Grace took the platter of steaks to the kitchen and carefully arranged them under the broiler. A salad was in the making, and Melanie was resting as her baby drifted to sleep. "Is she really that shy or have I done something? I'd like to get to know her but she isn't being very encouraging."

"She's shy, and I think you are doing the right thing by letting her warm up slowly. Guys like Chuck- well they think because she's beautiful, that she should love the attention. If they are good looking, they tend to scare her and... well..." Grace blushed as she searched for a way out of hole she'd dug for herself.

Nolan considered pretending that he didn't notice her fumbling, but opted to drum his fingers on the table instead. Grace grew more embarrassed and finally blurted out, "Well, it's not like you don't *know* how handsome you are, so why should I pretend that I don't either?"

"Thank you Grace. What a lovely compliment. Brilliantly executed as well." Grace only grew more flustered at the amusement behind his eyes.

Suggesting that Nolan set the table, Grace turned back to her dinner preparations. She heard Melanie's chuckles floating from the recliner and snapped, "You knock it off Mel, or no dinner for you."

"You going to starve your niece? If I don't eat, she don't eat!"

Nolan chuckled at Grace's groan and pulled out the plates and silverware. He mulled over Grace's response to her admission of her finding him handsome. Most of the women of his acquaintance would have used that moment to flirt with him. Grace was too forthright for behavior like that. She was honest, and truthful, but she didn't want to talk about him in such a familiar manner. Nolan found it refreshing... very refreshing.

His musings were interrupted when Melanie handed him Graceanna. "I need to excuse myself. Will you please hold her for a minute?"

Without waiting for a response, Melanie walked awkwardly down the hallway as if her legs needed re-circulation. Nolan's expression was priceless. He held the baby in the gingerly-extended manner of most men. Grace took one look at him and quipped, "You know, most men hold a football more tenderly. Pull her inward toward your chest. She needs to feel secure."

He shifted his little bundle until the baby was tucked into the crook of his arm. Grace smiled to herself as she watched the big man grow goofy with delight at the baby's soft sighs and gurgles in her sleep. His eyes didn't leave the infant's face until Melanie returned to claim her baby.

"I think she is ready for a nap now." Melanie's voice was choking back laughter.

"You did that on purpose! She didn't need to be held!" Nolan's voice startled the infant, which reminded him to moderate his tones. "You may live to regret that trick Melanie!"

"Yeah… maybe. But you won't regret it I'll wager."

Grace interrupted before he could reply, "Nolan, what would you like to drink with your dinner?" A mischievous twinkle in Grace's eye kept Melanie from taking the baby from the room.

"Well, what do you have to offer?" Nolan's eyes were back on the sleeping infant and were oblivious to the plot thickening around him.

"Well, I have soda, tea, coffee, lemonade, milk… or the house specialty." Grace waited for his response and held her breath. Everything hinged on if he would ask.

"I feel daring. I think I'll take the house specialty." Nolan's nonchalance was a relief to Grace who consciously let out her breath slowly.

"Ok, one *Universal Solvent on the Rocks* coming up!"

Nolan's jaw began working as the familiar phrase bounced through his mind. The women stifled their titters as they watched him consider how they knew of the incident. Understanding dawned swiftly. "Wait a minute. Paige! The gorgeous woman seated behind my client- that was Paige Matthews wasn't it?"

Grace nodded and dodged the cherry tomato that Nolan picked out of the salad bowl and tossed at her. Graceanna whimpered in her basket and Melanie took up the fight. "Now look what you've done. Gracie is upset that you called another woman beautiful."

Nolan, misunderstanding which 'Gracie' Melanie spoke of, turned sharply to look at Grace and was momentarily confused. Grace looked amused rather than embarrassed. 'I don't-"

Melanie interrupted him before he could say something to embarrass both Grace and himself. "You've stolen her heart. My daughter is in love at the ripe old age of two weeks."

Grace giggled. "Well, she's over nine days old… she can't be the *Naughty Lady of Shady Lane* anymore."

Narrowly escaping an embarrassing position, Nolan asked about the song. "I heard you singing that when I moved in. What's up with you and the risqué songs?"

Melanie laughed and launched into a rendition of the misleading song. Grace quickly joined her in theatric harmony. Singing 'of trying to pin things on 'her' that won't hold water, and never refusing liquid refreshment, the two ladies ended with an exaggerated flourish.

Melanie sighed. "I've loved that song ever since I was a little girl. When I found out that Craig lived on Shady Lane, I knew he was the one for me."

Nolan enjoyed observing the camaraderie between the two women. He had heard horror stories about 'in-laws', but these two women appeared to truly love and respect each other. Melanie didn't seem to mind that her husband had another woman to 'protect' while Grace shared the big brother she had adored since childhood with tact and, well, grace.

They ate the meal amid laughter and much teasing. Grace held her own and at times, Melanie appeared to be her twin. Nolan wasn't the first to wonder how much of his sister's personality that Craig had looked for in a wife.

After dinner, Melanie spontaneously decided to make a Hungarian Coffee Cake. "It'll be great! You guys go play some checkers in the living room and I'll join you as soon as I am done with the dough."

"Mel! Those things take around three hours with all the risings and bakings and dipping... are you sure?" Grace loved the pull-apart cake that tasted better than any cinnamon roll ever created, but knew it wouldn't be ready to eat until nearly ten o'clock.

Melanie shooed the would-be checker players out of the kitchen. Based upon her observations, Melanie concluded that Grace was feeling awkward after her comments on Nolan's appearance. She hoped by encouraging them to begin a game of checkers, Grace and Nolan would ease back into the comfortable friendship that had grown so easily between them.

Three hours later, they all munched on the cinnamony goodness of Hungarian coffee cake. Nolan and Grace took swipes of the icing drizzle that pooled at the bottom of the pan while Melanie tried to both nurse baby Gracie and lick her sticky fingers. Feeling the exhaustion of an early morning, and now a very late evening, Nolan walked slowly home. As he entered his empty house, he began praying.

"Lord, that is one incredible family. Please help me to build a family that is as close and loving as they are... and Lord... that baby. I want to put my order in now for a half a dozen just like her."

Chapter Nine

October

"You know what Mel? This is just like cross-stitch. It's not hard at all. Now, threading all of those needles... *That* was hard." Grace counted the pleats in the fabric of a plain white dress and gave Melanie a play-by-play about her progress.

"Hey, whatever you are doing... just get good at it. I mentioned the dress you're making to one of the ladies in my Bible Study, Leigh Ryder, and she wants one for Emme's shower."

"These won't be cheap though. The time investment will probably be at least four hours just for the smocking portion. Well, once I know what I am doing. This one will probably take me a month." Despite her words, Grace was excited. Her reputation was going to ensure that she would sell as many of the hand-smocked dresses as she could produce.

"Oh Grace, I was thinking. Did you get the impression that Nolan might be interested in getting to know Paige better? I was thinking about trying to set them up."

Melanie did not like where she was taking the conversation but she did know that her husband was not happy to hear that Grace found her new neighbor attractive. Craig had jumped at the news that Nolan could be interested in Grace's best friend. His final words were, "Well, I don't want Grace getting her heart broken. As much as I like Nolan, he's too good looking for my sanity."

Grace looked up from her sewing with a little smile. "Wasn't that funny? Do you think I can talk her into riding with him for the progressive dinner next week?"

"Well, I had the same thought but... Well, what if we're wrong and he wouldn't want to?"

Grace reached over and picked up her phone. As she waited for the answering machine to pick up, she snatched an afghan off the back of the couch and pulled it over her head like a shawl and began singing *Matchmaker* from *Fiddler on the Roof*.

Moments later, she did a goofy little dance around the room and sang an impromptu little ditty about turning a page for Paige. "Now, to work on Paige. That won't be as easy. Hmmm... I wonder... We could just tell her that she can choose between Chuck and Nolan. Do you think that she'd fall for it?"

"And she wouldn't say, "Ummmmmm, how about 'neither'?" Melanie looked skeptical.

Grace got the devious look in her eyes that always created nervous knots in Melanie's stomach during a fierce game of hearts. "We just have to make her choose immediately- then she's committed! She'll try to back out but if I make it scary enough, she'll snatch Nolan before I finish offering Chuck."

Within the half hour, Grace's two friends had plans to share a car for the progressive dinner. Grace was excited. She hadn't played matchmaker since she met a pretty little southern blonde at the little Bible bookstore in town the year before her father died. She'd forgotten how fun it was.

~~~~*

Craig double knocked on the back door before entering. "Hey... there are my women! The three most beautiful women in the world are in this kitchen and they are all mine!"

Grace snapped her brother with a wet towel as he made a beeline for his wife and daughter. "How was the convention? Worth not commuting home to?"

"I think these late night conventions are a waste of time. None of us could think clearly after dinner, and the late 'lectures' were on stupid things like, 'How to wine and dine your client'."

Melanie hugged her husband before getting up and gathering her things. "I don't want to rush out of here Grace but I'm anxious to see how my kitchen looks- and see if they cleaned up their mess."

"You go home to your new kitchen. I know I'd be eager to see it in your place." Grace quickly gathered the baby's diaper bag and car seat as she rambled about the projects that the two women had started.

Grace felt a slight sense of loss as she walked through the empty house an hour later. She picked up a tiny sock that had worked its way into the couch cushions and gave a tight little smile. The scent of the baby's bath cleansers and lotions lingered in the bathroom and the impression of Graceanna's little body was still evident in the beanbag chair. Melanie had propped her little daughter in the chair to observe as she and Grace cut out the little one's spring wardrobe.

"Grace, get out of this house and work on the yard or something. Go rake up those leaves; pull out the dead flowers, anything but this!" Just talking to herself again felt good. Days of fighting the tendency had been extremely difficult.

Nolan watched as she raked the yard's leaves into one enormous pile. He wondered if she planned to create a bonfire or if she was just a hyper-perfectionist. His laughter rang through his half-empty house as he saw Grace run and dive into the pile. Grace tended to be a little circumspect in her behavior but her eyes always held a glint of mischief that made him curious. This was a side of her that he hadn't seen. As she ran for a second dive, Nolan decided to join her.

"Hey, save some for me!" Nolan's voice rang out across the street.

Grace grinned and began raking the pile back into the mini haystack that she'd been able to jump on. "Isn't it fun? I can't stand just leaving a perfectly good pile of leaves sitting there all lonely."

They jumped and rolled for a few moments before Grace began transferring the pile of leaves into her wheel barrow and moving them to an enormous compost pile at the back of the house. As Nolan helped, he began questioning Grace about the progressive dinner the following night. "So, how did you pull that off? When you asked me about it I thought that there would be no way that you could talk her into going with me. Spill it."

Grace grinned wickedly. "Well, you have to promise to tell me everything about the 'date'. I won't always pry but I just *have* to hear this one!"

Nolan was thoughtful. "I think I can promise to tell you everything that Paige agrees to."

"Deal. It was simple. I described a horror date with Chuck Majors and said either that or she could ride with you. She was so relieved to get away from Chuck that she agreed to go with you. Then, when she tried to get out of it, I told her that Melanie had already walked across the street to give you the good news."

Nolan laughed at the mental picture that Grace drew before growing thoughtful. He rubbed the back of his neck and finally came to a decision. "Grace, can I have her number? I think I should call and offer her an out. I don't want her to feel trapped or she'll never relax enough to really get to know me."

"You're definitely interested in her, aren't you?" Grace grinned at Nolan's discomfiture.

"Grace, I've never met anyone like her. She's intelligent, or appears to be, she's feminine, and she has a modesty about her that I rarely see. It's hugely refreshing."

Grace snickered. "And it doesn't hurt that she's gorgeous too."

"How is it that she seems oblivious to that? Men must surround her like sharks."

They sat in the last of the grand leaf pile and talked. With his knees drawn up to his chest, Nolan listened intently as Grace told the story of Paige's awkward Jr. High and High School years. The teasing and torment that the girl endured had carried over to her adult years. "She still sees herself as the gawky, awkward girl that the guys tormented. To this day, if a man shows her any attention, she assumes that it is to dump her in an emotionally stripped heap later."

"Ouch. That would be traumatic enough to make one overly cautious. Children can be cruel. My father had a business partner that home schooled his children, before it was popular, for that very reason. He spent hours in court fighting for the right to do it, but his daughter had an enormous port wine stain that made her an oddity and he decided that adults were cruel enough. He wasn't going to subject her to children too."

Grace nodded with understanding. Her school years hadn't been unpleasant but she'd witnessed worse than Paige's torment over the years. "I think that, should the Lord bless me with children, that I'd like to home school them. I love children and five year olds are so much *fun*! Why should I give them up just as they get to be so quirky and intellectually spongy?"

Nolan was thoughtful. He had always dreamed of children but had never considered their education. Schooling was a given, but specifics were still fuzzy in his mind. The picture of a faceless wife quizzing a little girl in pigtails on addition facts before a romp in the fall leaves enchanted him. In a rare moment of spontaneity, Nolan made a decision.

"I think you've got something there. I hadn't considered home schooling, but now that I think of it, I don't want to miss the relationship that could develop within family dynamics like that. Imagine being there to watch your child's fascination as they learn to read, or hear the Declaration of Independence *and* understand it."

Grace nodded but was silent. She didn't like to dwell on future dreams too often. Brushing aside the longing for a family to fill her home, she began offering pointers on how to keep Paige from backing out of the driving arrangements for the following evening.

Verily watched them from his living room window and found the picture on Grace's lawn to be an especially lovely one. Nolan listened earnestly as Grace chatted animatedly. Grace sat with her legs tucked behind her and leaning on one arm with the autumn breezes occasionally flicking her hair into her face. Verily sighed remembering days past as Nolan pulled a leaf from Grace's hair. Had he known that Grace was planning a date between her new neighbor and her best friend, Verily's disappointment would have been keen.

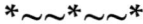

Nolan nervously rubbed the back of his neck as he spoke into the phone. "Hello Miss Matthews. This is Nolan Burke. Grace tells me that she has hoodwinked you into riding with me for the dinner tomorrow evening... Drat it Nolan, that won't work! She'll run for sure. Keep it mellow. Grace insisted on mellow. Try it again..."

After several more tries, Nolan had his conversation rehearsed. It was perfect. Flawless. There was no way that she would back out. He hoped. "Hello?"

Paige's voice became uncertain the moment she heard Nolan's deep voice on the line. His carefully rehearsed speech dissolved into a pool of sludge and he stammered something about the weather being fine and then asked how she liked her health.

Paige chuckled. Hearing his awkward tone gave her courage to speak up. "Nolan Burke. Are you trying to get out of Grace's impossible matchmaking scheme?"

"No! Um... actually I am trying to give you an out that you won't take." Nolan mentally kicked himself. How pathetic could he get?

He interrupted Paige before she could turn him down flat. "Paige, I wanted to ask you and didn't know how you'd take it. I guess that I played the coward. If I didn't know that you'd say yes, I wasn't willing to risk it. Forgive me?"

Without waiting for an answer, Nolan continued with his request before he lost his nerve. "I would really love to take you. I've wanted to get to know you better and this is a perfect opportunity but I knew if you just went with me because you were tricked into it, we'd both be miserable."

Paige stammered something about answering the door and fled the phone. Nolan took a moment to re-gather his dignity and prayed for the proper words. "Dumb jerk, Nolan, you should have prayed *before* you called her."

Paige heard him and chuckled. "Well, to be honest..." Paige's words were a little more relaxed.

"To be honest, I would have loved to get out of it. I don't' do well with people I don't know but... we are supposed to ride in pairs or quartets so if you really don't mind..."

Nolan pumped his fist in the air. "Paige, I'll be looking forward to tomorrow night. I appreciate you being willing to give it a chance. Then again, I hear the alternative wasn't to your liking either..."

"Oh! Oh my! Um... Nolan? Can you pick me up early? Or, maybe I'll drive over to Grace's." Nolan could almost see her chewing on her lip.

"Mr. Majors thinks he's driving you?"

"After four no's you'd think he'd leave me alone. Why are men so determined to make a woman's life miserable?"

Nolan was silent for a moment. Paige became concerned that she had offended him but before she could apologize, he answered. "Paige, not all men are like Chuck. Honestly, most aren't. And, if you don't mind my being quite blunt, with a woman as beautiful as you are, men are apt to become somewhat goofy."

Paige was stunned. She'd been told of her attractiveness in the past, but had always assumed that the men were mocking her. "Well... I ... I ... I guess I'll see you tomorrow night then. At Grace's. Bye."

Turning from the phone, Paige walked with determination to the bathroom mirror. She habitually avoided the mirror at all costs. Quick brushes to the hair or occasional cosmetics to cover a pimple, kept the need to a bare minimum. This time, Paige studied the reflection systematically. Trying to look through the eyes of a stranger, she picked apart each of her features.

Beginning with her hair, Paige scrutinized her eyes, nose, skin, teeth, and even the shape of her face. When finished, she found her favorite catalogs and flipped through them page by page. Eventually she found three or four women that she considered beautiful. Holding the catalog next to her face, she compared herself to them in the mirror. With the exception of hair color, Paige could have been each of the women's sisters. Paige had chosen red heads, brunettes, or platinum blonds. Not one of the pictures showed a honey blond woman.

Thoughtfully, Paige closed the catalog and put it away. She wondered how she had gone from such an awkward, pimple faced, buck toothed girl, to looking nice enough that a man like Nolan Burke had called her beautiful. The idea seemed preposterous. The most eligible man at church considered Paige Matthews, the class freak at Brunswick High, attractive.

~~~~*

Melanie opened Grace's door with a flourish. "Mr. Burke. How good to see you. Would you be interested in entering this fine abode?"

Grace tittered as she walked past her goofy sister-in-law. "We told her to stay out of the buttermilk but you know how some people are..."

Nolan's laugh died in his throat when he saw Grace. She wore a royal purple dress that reflected into her eyes and gave her color that he'd never noticed before. "Grace, that dress looks wonderful on you. You look very nice."

Grace looked somewhat confused. Before she could respond Nolan hastily added, "You too Melanie... motherhood certainly agrees with you."

Craig lay relaxed in the recliner with a sleeping Graceanna. Alarm shadowed his face upon hearing Nolan compliment Grace. It was obvious that his remark to Mel had been an afterthought. Melanie shook her head at the storm brewing in Craig's eyes but was deliberately ignored.

Paige's knock broke the awkward tension that had descended upon the group. Grace welcomed Paige and began bundling Graceanna into her car seat. Melanie took her child, car seat and all, from Grace and led the other two women to the waiting vehicles. At the door, she turned back to Craig and in a tone that pleaded for peace, said, "Honey, will you get the diaper bag?"

Melanie knew that Craig would say something and she also knew that if he couldn't get Nolan alone, he might lose all discretion and blurt out a biting comment or accusation in the middle of the dinner. Despite her dislike of confrontation, Melanie prayed that her husband's over protectiveness toward his sister could be swiftly and painlessly resolved. This was effectively Paige Matthew's first chance at a good date and Melanie did *not* want that ruined.

With a stern face, Craig picked up the requested diaper bag and turned to Nolan. "I thought we were becoming good friends Burke."

Nolan's face went blank. He hadn't recovered yet from discovering that Grace was a woman. In a moment of detachment, it occurred to him that this was a perfect example of the difference between head knowledge and heart knowledge. Shaking his head slightly to clear his thoughts, he turned back to Craig. "Pardon me? Did I miss something?"

Nolan's hesitant laugh irritated Craig further. "Well, you've known me approximately as long as you have Grace and haven't once told me that you liked my shirt or my tie."

Still in the dark, Nolan shrugged. "Uh... Craig? You feeling ok?" Craig's stony silence prompted him to try another approach. "Honestly Craig, the next time you wear purple, I promise, I'll notice!"

Finally, exasperated with Craig's refusal to be drawn out, Nolan quipped, "Well, if your face counts... then I'll comment now. Your face so purple that it could get lost in Grace's dress!

Craig fumed. "This is my *sister* that you are talking about Burke! It's apparent that you've discovered that she isn't just 'one of the guys'."

"Well, you're right there. I hadn't thought of Grace as anything but a great person to know once I got over my wariness of her."

"Wariness of *Grace*?" Craig's face was comically offended.

"Craig. I have not had a female who happened to be a friend since elementary school. Girls just don't make good friends. But when I met Grace, she was just a person who I clicked with. You know? I never thought of her as male, female, or otherwise."

Craig's doubtful "uh huh" showed that he was unconvinced. "So you are saying she's androgynous."

"No! That's exactly why it's so weird. She's ultra feminine and womanly but she doesn't slap you in the face with it."

Melanie stuck her head in the doorway. "Guys, Paige is looking ready to bolt. Are you done marking territory? Can we go?"

Classical music played in the background as Paige and Nolan left the house where they'd enjoyed soup and salad, and were now driving to the Hocking's for the main course. Their first moments had been awkward. Nolan worked hard at not pushing his guest to open up, while Paige struggled to overcome her intense shyness. The combination was socially horrific. The painful pauses slowly grew into comfortable, companionable silences and the subsequent conversation was 'real', not stilted and forced. Nolan would have been having a very good time had he been able to get the conversation with Craig out of his mind.

Paige looked at the thoughtful man beside her and decided that it was time to step outside herself and help her friend. It had occurred to her that Grace and Nolan had much in common and would make a fun pair. Grace had always been there for Paige through all of the awkward, uncomfortable years and the subsequent lonely ones and for once, Paige thought she had a way to repay her.

"Doesn't Grace look wonderful in her new dress? I love that particular shade of violet on her. It's her best color."

Nolan started visibly. The last thing he expected Paige to mention was Grace's attire and after the dressing down he'd received for noticing it, Nolan wasn't sure it was a topic he wanted to pursue. "I did notice the dress. It is lovely, as is yours. Sapphire blue is one of my favorite colors. The three of you looked like stones from a jewelry store. You know- the blue, green, and purple." Nolan felt like a fool. *Gems from a jewelry store? How stupid can I get?* " he thought to himself.

Paige eagerly pounced on Nolan's 'obvious' willingness to discuss Grace. "I don't know how she does everything that she does. That dress would take me ages to finish but Grace just seems to whip them out between any one of her other several dozen projects that she always juggles."

"Grace made that dress?" Nolan mentally kicked himself. "I mean, did you mean to say that you sew as well or are you saying that you don't care for sewing?"

"I can sew. I took Home Ec. from the same teacher that Grace did but she was already an accomplished seamstress. Her mother taught her the summer that we were ten. After I ruined my third skirt, Mrs. Buscher suggested that I try again the next summer."

"Do you enjoy it? Sewing that is?" Nolan didn't know much about sewing but it sounded like something that a creative person would enjoy.

"I am adequate. If a niece needs a costume for a play or something, I'll do in a pinch. Grace though, she sews costumes for half of the plays in this town! It's good money for her though."

"How does she manage to keep financially afloat? It's glaringly obvious that she doesn't live on much."

"She is a financial genius. I don't know how else to put it. She lives on two hundred a month from the life insurance, plus whatever she earns. The house is paid for but there are taxes and things."

Nolan was thoughtful. "So… utilities, taxes, food, clothes, gas and her own insurance. She must have to come up with thousands of dollars a month!"

"Not really. She's a financial genius like I said. She can eat on about thirty dollars a week without scrimping on quality and half the time feeding someone else a few times a week. She shuts off the house in winter and lives in the three front rooms. Then, at night, reverses it and only turns on the heat to her room. She is just extremely frugal."

"Must be hard. I've noticed that she's very giving."

Paige sighed. "That's her downfall. Anytime her finances get extra tight, it's because she's spent more for a gift or to help someone by spending more than she could afford. We've all tried to 'help' her from time to time, but she can spot it a mile away."

"Can't Craig help? Does she not have any job skills or what?" Nolan was becoming irritated at the idea of someone having to live so frugally.

"She has a degree in physics. She even went through grad school but that's not what she wanted to do."

"And Craig and Melanie didn't want her to live with them?" Something about the scenario felt strange to Nolan and though he knew it wasn't his business, he was curious.

"Oh Craig lived there until Melanie got pregnant. Then Grace shooed them out. She said something about mama birds needing their own nests to build."

A chuckle erupted unbidden. "That sounds like Grace alright. And it's too much for Craig to contribute huh?"

"No. If she needed help… really needed it, he'd insist on her accepting it. She just really wants to try her 'experiment'." Paige looked thoughtfully at the Hocking home.

"What is her experiment?" Nolan started kicking himself again. When would he learn to control the subject better? This was a time for him to get to know Paige, not to learn Grace's personal history.

"When her father got sick a couple of years ago, he talked to Grace. He expected to live to see Grace married and taken care of, but you know how unpredictable life is. He told her that she would have to support herself, or live with Craig until she married. She thought about it for a few weeks, and decided against using her degree to support herself and decided to live her dream. So right now, she's still experimenting. She gave herself five years to make a success out of housekeeping for herself for a living and she's making it. Her mother would be proud.

Paige paused. A lump formed in her throat as she tried to explain the story. "Mrs. Buscher died when Grace was sixteen. Car accident. What they didn't plan for, was Grace not finding the right man."

"Ouch. That would be difficult..."

"But, Grace is a beautiful person. Everyone speaks very highly of her but rarely thinks of her as more than the nice girl at church. I don't think she's been on a date since ..."

Nolan was dying to hear what Paige started to say but the woman turned quickly to him. "Guess we'd better get out. They're waiting for us to go in and the baby shouldn't be outside in this wind."

"Quite chatty aren't they?"

Craig was encouraged to hear the delight in Grace's voice at the apparent ease with which Paige and Nolan conversed. "They're a nice looking couple too."

He was right about that. Paige was tall, willowy, and very fair. Her Scandinavian heritage was evident from her blond hair and blue eyes, to her broad shoulders and height. Nolan was just as tall and broad shouldered, but his hair and eyes were dark. No Hollywood movie could have produced a more attractive couple.

Grace's excitement at the possibility of a relationship developing between her two closest friends was evident. "I just hope that Paige will give it a fair chance. My newest and oldest friends. How neat is that?"

Chapter Ten

A radio droned the latest news as Grace carefully put her house in order. The days were staying too cold to keep the house open any longer and Grace was readying it all for winter. She had windows blocked off with quilted fabric to keep the cold out, and weather stripping was screwed to the bottoms of the doors. It made opening the doors harder but it did keep out drafts.

"...has attacked women in three different neighborhoods already. The police are asking women at home alone in the mid morning to early afternoon time frame to keep all doors locked and to call 9-1-1 immediately if they see any suspicious activity. In other news..."

Grace immediately prayed for the women who had already been attacked. "Lord, you know, you'd think that the safest place to be in the world would be your own home. This kind of thing just reminds a person that the only safe place *anywhere* is in the palm of Your hand..."

She continued praying and chatting with herself as she finished her winter preparations. Craig planned to go wood cutting the coming weekend. She'd have to get the woodstove readied and clear the furniture off the porch to make way for her woodpile. The day promised to be a very busy one.

Seeing Nolan drive up from his lunch appointment, Grace dashed out the front door. "*Stop*, you!"

The startled man whirled around in confusion. "What'd I do?"

Laughing, Grace shook her finger at him. "You *didn't* tell me about your 'sorta-date' the other night."

Nolan had strategically avoided this conversation. Paige had been more than willing to grant full permission for Nolan to discuss each and every word that had been exchanged. Nolan was beginning to think that she delighted in the prospect that Grace might actually extract the evening's conversations from him.

Considering that almost the entire evening had been spent in discussion of Grace, Nolan was at a loss as to how to handle the situation.

"Well, really, there isn't much to tell. I had a wonderful time. Paige is very easy to talk to once she opens up."

"Uh huh. Did she say that she didn't want you telling me?" Grace knew that it was unlikely but people became skittish about personal relationships.

"No, she actually said that I..."

"Come on; don't leave me in the cold. I can get it from her too you know." Grace's impatience was becoming comical.

He realized that Grace was really looking forward to a serious relationship brewing between her friend and himself. Wondering at her obvious lack of interest in him as a man, Nolan felt a bit of a blow to his ego. He wasn't used to women being immune to him. Months before, Nolan would have assumed that he would love knowing there was at least one woman out there not trying to attract him.

Realizing that Paige would delight in telling Grace about their evening, Nolan decided to come as 'clean' as he could without thoroughly embarrassing himself. "Well, she actually opened up a lot. She told me about her growing up as your friend, about your mother trying to teach her to sew- ummm..."

"You talked about sewing and my mom? Her awful years of junior high?" She mulled the idea that this might be a very good thing. Paige had obviously been very open and forthcoming with Nolan. She didn't open up to people she knew well, that easily.

"Yes. She talked a lot about you. It is obvious that you've been friends for years. She even told me a bit about your upbringing, about Craig and Melanie living with you for a while. She really respects you, you know."

Grace nodded. "You planning to ask her out to dinner or something soon?"

Verily Wirth, watching from his living room window, heard Nolan's deep rumbling laugh and it warmed the widower's heart. The older man made plans to ask Grace to make him one of her pot pies so that he could find out more about Grace's new beau.

"Grace, you don't give up do you? Actually, I was going to see how she felt about e-mails. I thought it would be less uncomfortable for her. If we saw each other at church and occasionally at your house, while we emailed each other..."

"That would work wonderfully!" Grace was beaming. She was going to get to be in the middle of another budding romance. What more could she ask for?

~~~~*

The next morning Grace decided to walk to her Bible Study. The air was crisp but with a sweater and a brisk walk, she'd stay warm enough. Stepping outside, she found her legs were cooler under her denim skirt than she'd expected. She hurried back indoors to put on a pair micro fiber tights to keep them warm.

This short delay gave Nolan time to return from an appointment, go inside, and fill a glass of water. He watched as Grace left her house and strolled down the street with a little wave to the tall, lanky elderly man who lived next door to him. Smiling, he turned on the radio for the mid morning news and went through his messages on his answering machine. The third one made his stomach churn. "Hello handsome. It's Michelle Walker here. Look, I'd like to have another meeting. Your gal at Computing Concepts is completely incompetent and I really would like to get this system in the works. Call me."

Before he could respond, the latest news bulletin on the radio caught his attention. "-on the look out for a male, Caucasian, average height, red hair, mustache and approximately 180 lbs. Today's victim makes the fifth in a rash of attacks in the town of Brunswick which lies to the south of Rockland. Today's attack in Brunswick, combined with an attack yesterday afternoon in Ferndale that may be related, has sparked a county wide manhunt..."

Nolan grew concerned as he listened to the announcer talk about the neighborhoods and women that the man chose. All were women, home alone in deserted neighborhoods between ten in the morning and two in the afternoon. His alarm grew as Nolan considered the situation.

"That could have been *Grace*! And she's out there walking in the open almost begging to be attacked."

Debating his options, Nolan picked up the phone and called Craig at his insurance office. "Craig? Hey, it's Nolan. Have you been listening to the news?"

Nolan listened intently. "The dog is a great idea but... well; Grace just took off on foot somewhere. She had that flowery bag with her. Any idea where she went?"

Holding the phone away from his ear, Nolan shook his head in wonder at the fierceness of Craig's protective side. "Craig. Down boy. Maybe Melanie knows where she went and could give her a ride home?"

He hung up the phone reluctantly. Grace wouldn't be very happy when she heard the trouble Nolan had gotten her into. After debating whether or not he should go in search of her, Nolan finally turned back to his messages and turned the problem of Grace over to the Lord.

~~~~*

"Craig... I do not want a dog!" Grace's voice was firm but her brother on the other line was not budging.

"Craig... I..." Quickly, she realized that, like it or not, she'd have to get a dog. If she resisted for too long, Craig would go to the pound and get one himself. It would likely a huge Rottweiler that ate too much, and took up way too much room. It was also a little known fact that Grace did not like large dogs. While not terrified of them, she found them intimidating and unpleasant memories ensured that she'd shy away from them whenever possible.

"Fine. I'll go right now. I'll get the one that barks the most I promise. Right... fine. Thanks for nothing bro. Tell that wife of yours to slap you when her hands are free."

Grumbling all the way down her walkway as she headed to the bus stop, Grace was ready for battle when Nolan waved from his window. She crooked her finger menacingly. He gave an exaggerated shrug and jogged outside.

"Yes?" His tone was far too innocent.

"You are taking me to the pound. Thanks to you, my brother has demanded a dog. I think you can pay for him too. I want the dog, the bowl, the leash, a two-week supply of food and his first Vet bill as recompense for getting me into trouble. Got all of that?" Grace's smile belied the fierceness of her words.

Nolan jogged back inside to retrieve his checkbook and they drove to the pound. The howls of lonely dogs were audible a block away and Grace's face showed her irritation. "I hate places like this. I want to take them all home and it seems so unfair just to take one. I can't believe you got me into this."

Nolan tried to defend himself but immediately gave up and resigned himself to being the 'bad guy' for the afternoon. It was enough work to follow her through the facility and drag her away from homeless kittens, rabbits, and birds to the dog cages. There the struggle began in earnest.

With tears in her eyes and a heavy heart, Grace went from cage to cage greeting the 'inmates'. Nolan noticed that the smaller dogs received more attention than the larger ones and a large mastiff barely received a hello. A shelter volunteer recognized Grace and led her to the back. Snuggled up on a blanket arranged in the middle of a rabbit cage, lay a ball of fluff. Grace lost her heart immediately.

"They found him in a dumpster. He was barely old enough to be weaned. We don't know if he got in a bag of trash, fell asleep and the owners threw him out or if it was deliberate. He's a frisky little guy but he needs more care during the next two weeks than we can afford to spare."

"What kind of dog is he?" Grace was already trying to name the yapping little fellow.

"Pomeranian. He could be a purebred. A vet could tell you most likely." The volunteer looked hopeful, too hopeful to Nolan's eye.

"Grace… he looks like a rat on steroids. This is supposed to be a watchdog. How do you expect him scare away an intruder?"

Grace's look squelched any other objections. "Look Nolan, all I promised was to get the dog that barked the most. This guy here fills the bill. Now, I suggest you get out your checkbook and pay for your mistake."

Nolan laughed as he took the dog's identification card to the front desk to pay all fees associated with the little bundle. He joked with the ladies behind the counter about getting a discount according to size but they were merciless. One of them smugly remarked. "I heard that you are in the doghouse and that's why you are paying for him. I don't think your girlfriend would appreciate us making it easy on you."

Nolan quickly decided not to correct the woman's assessment of his relationship with Grace. What purpose would it serve but to make him sound like a heel? He smiled and said, "I got her in trouble with her brother and the dog is my penance. I'm afraid of what she'll name him. Can't you just see him being named Killer or Cujo or something equally ludicrous?"

"His name is Rolex you traitor."

"Rolex? What kind of name is that?"

Grace's grin was wicked. "He's a watch dog isn't he?"

"And he's costing as much as one too..." Nolan muttered under his breath.

Grace's expression was smug. She left him to fill out the paperwork and get recommendations for food and a Vet while she went to the car with her little bundle of fur. Rolex was sleeping peacefully on her lap seconds later, which gave Grace a moment to pray for patience with her friend and brother before that friend returned to the car. A peace settled over her as she prayed. She knew how to make it right.

Nolan joked and teased about the fierce puppy all the way home. While Grace found an old blanket for her sleeping pooch, He headed to the pet store. Grace started her dinner as she waited for the coming supplies and continued her running conversation with the Lord.

"Knock, knock. Got your stuff Grace. Need anything else? I have a business appointment in thirty minutes and I smell pound on me." Nolan checked his watch and seeing the timepiece made him smile.

"Thanks Nolan. Oh, and make sure you give the receipts to Craig next time you see him. He owes you for your expenses."

"What? Thought I was paying the price for this one?" Nolan was starting to see Grace's plan and was feeling cheated. He liked being able do something for her, especially since he'd been the one to prompt the order for the dog in the first place.

"Nope. I just had to make you sweat it a little. Give those receipts to Craig- better yet, give them to me. I'll give them to him." Grace went inside with a smug look of satisfaction on her face.

Knowing he was going to be late for his meeting, Nolan pulled the receipts from his pocket, followed Grace inside, and handed them to her before darting across the street to clean up for his meeting. Moments later, his SUV pulled swiftly out of the driveway.

As he passed the two cars that Cade had darted between only weeks before, Nolan slowed down. The mere sight of the cars reminded Nolan that no meeting was worth risking the life of a child. Grace saw the slowing of the vehicle and smiled. Moments later when she saw an expensive velvet dog bed in the bag of supplies, Grace smiled again. Guilt certainly had its advantages.

~~~~*

"You call *that* a dog? It looks like an overgrown hamster!" Craig's voice was incredulous.

"Rat."

"Do what?"

"Nolan calls him a rat on steroids." Melanie stifled a guffaw at Grace's exaggerated wink.

"He's right about that. Grace, I said a watchdog. This is not a watch dog!" Craig was becoming genuinely angry.

"Sure it is! It barks a lot, when he's awake anyway, and his name is Rolex. Can't be a better watchdog than a Rolex. You know me. I've gotta have the best; especially on your dime. Here are the receipts. Nolan will expect reimbursement for his expenses by the end of the week." Grace and Melanie collapsed in helpless laughter at the look of disbelief on Craig's face.

It took little time for Craig to concede defeat. He couldn't help it. The rat was adorable, and the women in his life loved him. What the dog wouldn't do in deterring an intruder, he would make up for in companionship. Moreover, he wasn't exactly surprised that Grace had chosen a small dog. She hadn't hidden her fear of large canines as well as she thought she did.

"Just keep the doors locked and take the bus or call Mel when you have to go somewhere ok?" Craig's concerned tone caused Grace a moment of guilt.

Cade had been working diligently on his homework during Grace's introduction of her new pet to her brother's family. He and Rolex had become that fast friends upon Cade's arrival from school.

Rolex whimpered at Cade's ankles as the boy worked hard to finish his work. He was eager to play again with the little dog but knew his mother was due to arrive momentarily. With great disappointment, Cade put his books in his backpack and after patting Rolex's head, ran to his mother's waiting car.

Grace watched the boy talking animatedly to his mother as they drove away before turning to her brother and his bemused wife. "Anyone feel like taking me to dinner? I am famished and I sorta spent my late morning and early afternoon having a baby." As an after thought she added, "Oh and you can tell Aunt Fran about Rolex. I am not going there."

Chapter Eleven

November

Exhausted, Grace lounged on her couch and worked diligently on a smocked dress. Every stitch seemed to take an amazing amount of effort but Grace continued to plod along, determined to be productive even as she rested. Across the street, an expensive looking sports car roared up to Nolan's house and screeched to a stop. While Grace tried to determine if the hood ornament was a Jaguar or not, the driver exited looking like a model from an Eddie Bauer catalog. His dark skin looked amazing against the cranberry sweater he wore.

"Either he's the casual riche or he's trying to look the part of a bumpkin on a millionaire's salary," she muttered amusedly to herself.

Nolan hurried from his house and greeted his guest. "Hey David, glad you made it! Did you find me ok?"

David Corbin slapped his college buddy on the back and immediately started teasing. "Well, actually it was easy enough to find but I was sure I was in the wrong place man! What, are you slumming it?"

Unaware that snatches of their conversation could be heard through the slight crack in Grace's window, Nolan laughed good-naturedly. "Well, you know me... always have to try something new."

From many of Nolan's acquaintances, the question would not only have been serious, but a deliberate cut. While none of them would admit to being snobbish, the fact is, most of the people Nolan knew well were extremely well to do and lived in a style unseen in Brunswick. They simply would not have understood Nolan's desire to blend into the woodwork of life in his new town.

Nolan saw Grace at the window and waved. "That's my neighbor, Grace. She's great. I'll have to take you over later and meet her. With any luck, she's been baking."

"Housewife?"

"Homemaker anyway. She's not married." Without realizing that he appeared to be deliberately changing the subject, Nolan led David into his house and gave him the quick but grand tour. "In here is my formal living room which I use for an office. I started off down the hall but I like being nearer the front where I can watch the kids playing and keep an eye on Grace. We've had a rash of attacks-"

"Yeah, I heard about those. I've never been here before and as I drove in and saw how much smaller it is than I realized, I wondered if everyone knows how new you are. Could you be a suspect?"

Nolan's laughter echoed through the rooms. "Not on your life. I'm too tall for one thing and I've been with people during attacks so even if people did figure out I was new, they wouldn't think it was me. The town has nearly thirty-thousand people Dave- It's not like we're Backwater Village, population one hundred twenty-two... until Ina Mae has her baby anyway."

The men laughed and Nolan poured coffee for Dave as they continued through the kitchen. "Black right?"

"Well I don't mind but it's not politically correct these days..."

"The coffee man," Nolan growled as he shoved the cup into his friend's hand.

"Well if you insist. So you make your own coffee? Do you cook too?"

"It's a different world here. I wanted to blend in so I rented something small- except that it's really bigger than I need-"

"Sounds cramped to me. So tell me Nolan, why are you here? Be honest with me because you've got friends in Rockland who are concerned about you."

Nolan relaxed in his favorite chair and propped his feet on the ottoman. "How many of these friends wear spiked heels?"

"Touché."

"So, what is up at the church? Did they agree to help the homeless mission down on Washington?"

The men drove for snacks and talked about things back in Rockland. Once parked in front of Nolan's enormous television set, the conversation lulled to short sound bytes during muted commercials as they watched the Rockland Warriors fight for their place in the upcoming championship. Nolan needed this day more than he'd realized. Just the presence of someone who knew him, knew his likes and dislikes, and accepted him, was a huge relief. For the first time in weeks, Nolan didn't have to explain himself. He could just be.

"So what's with the suburban life, Burke? This place isn't much bigger than your old guest house."

"Well, for one thing, Brunswick is a solid middle to lower middle class town. There are some nicer homes on the outskirts but nothing like what we're accustomed to. I just rented-"

"Well at least you're renting but man this place has to be twenty years old! Why not rent something newer? A townhouse maybe?"

"The house is over thirty years old. Built in the early seventies I think." Nolan wondered, as he did it, why he answered such an irrelevant question. "I rented it because it was in an established neighborhood with children and a nice view over my back fence. Just fields of nothing right now. Come spring there will be alfalfa or something out there."

"That still doesn't make sense. If you wanted out of the city, why not try Fairbury or New Cheltenham, or even Marshfield. All of those places had nice homes, cultural centers, and good restaurants. This is soccer mom central."

"Because the church here had the highest number of unattached females."

The answer hung over the room. Finally, David said, "Well if that isn't forthright, nothing is. So you were on a woman hunt and none of your friends in Rockland were good enough?"

A slight edge to David's voice unnerved Nolan. He wasn't used to his friends not understanding. "Dave, can you see me with Sheila or Jennifer? Do you think I'd be satisfied with a life of nannies and trips to the tropics?"

"Did it ever occur to you that the women you know might also want something different but not know how to go about it?"

Nolan's mouth opened to answer but nothing came. He sat there, slack-jawed throughout the rest of the commercials before taking a drink of his root beer and returning his concentration to the game. At the next break, he turned to Dave and admitted, "I didn't. I never thought of that. I guess I assumed that they would have shown some kind of desire somewhere for something different. All I saw was the perfect manicures, the perfect wardrobes, and the stilted conversations about whatever was the 'in' thing of the week. Why wouldn't someone ever mention a desire for change?"

"Because like you, they weren't willing to put themselves on the line."

"What do you mean? What do you think I'm doing?"

At the next commercial break, the conversation continued as though without a pause. "You're running away. You're pretending to be someone you aren't in order to find what you're looking for."

"Are you saying you think I'm a fraud here?"

"I'm saying," David replied carefully, "I'm saying that you appear to be just another guy here but you're not. You're a very wealthy man who is accustomed to a much more lavish lifestyle than you can find here."

A whole quarter passed without another word. Near the final two minutes, commercials drove them nuts as the score hung at thirty-four Warriors, thirty-five Cardinals. "After this is over, I want to take you over and introduce you to Grace. Maybe you'll understand why I haven't flaunted my-"

"I'm not talking about flaunting. I'm talking about hiding. You seem to be hiding under a façade of suburban middle class when we both know even your parents had a hard time remembering those days."

"Look who's talking! Mr. Son of a real estate developer!"

"But I don't pretend."

The game exploded on the screen effectively silencing both men for several minutes until they finally threw popcorn at the screen in disgust as their team lost. Dave branched into a new topic. "So, in this paradise of available females, have you met anyone?"

"Paige Matthews. She's intelligent, modest, and incredibly gorgeous. I'm just getting to know her but it's nice to have to do the pursuing for once."

"Oh so this is really about your desire for the hunt."

Laughing, Nolan shook his head. "The hunt is an enjoyable novelty- it's not as easy as you'd think- not with Paige anyway. But, what I really like is that I'm not on the defensive. I don't feel like a car on the showroom floor. Everyone's looking, wanting to take it for a test drive, and I'm terrified to find out who finally buys me."

The look on David's face was priceless. "Come on, Dave; let's go drown our sorrows at Grace's house."

Ignoring the unfinished discussion, both men ambled across the street and their stomachs rumbled at the scent of stew and pumpkin pie as they climbed the steps of her porch. Grace's call of, "come in" sounded closer than Nolan expected and he was surprised to find her sitting on the couch stitching something. He introduced his friend and insisted she stay seated as he did.

"Oh stay there. I rarely see you sitting you know. It's a nice change."

"I'm just so tired and cold today. I hope I'm not coming down with anything. I'd hate to get you or David sick."

She turned to David and without giving Nolan a chance to respond, insisted he take a seat. "So what brings you to Brunswick today?"

"We watched the Warriors vs. Cardinals game."

"Warriors lost."

Before David could comment, Nolan asked, "You watched it?"

"No. I could tell by the tone of your voices that you weren't happy. Are you guys hungry? Stew is done and there is pumpkin pie in the oven."

She moved to get up but Nolan threatened to sit on her if she tried it again. "I'll take care of it. Should I check that pie? Knife in the middle, right?"

"Right. You remembered."

David watched in shock as Nolan tested the pie and sent it back into the oven declaring it 'not quite done.' He brought a tray and three bowls into the living room and ladled the stew from a cast iron Dutch oven on the wood burning stove. The scene was so utterly foreign to David on so many levels, that he was dumbstruck. Nolan hurried back into the kitchen for spoons, napkins, and glasses of water for everyone. The sound of the oven timer sent him racing back to the kitchen to check on the pie.

"Are you staying over, David?"

"No, I was going to try to talk Nolan into a movie and dinner and then I planned to head back to Rockland. I'm supposed to fill in for a friend at church tomorrow."

Nolan overheard and commented, "I think Nick does that because you get those kids hungry for more. You really should take over the thing."

Grace ignored the tangent and returned to the topic. "Are you set on that? I mean the whole dinner thing because my stew is pretty filing and if you eat pie-"

"How about a triple checker round?" Nolan interjected.

"I'm lousy with checkers but I'm game." The game itself sounded dull and monotonous but watching Nolan in this new environment was far from uninteresting.

Nolan and Grace grinned simultaneously as Nolan pulled the checkerboard out from the lower shelf of the coffee table. "Set 'em up!"

~~~~*

Nolan stood next to David's window rubbing his arms. "Thanks for coming man. I've missed you."

"This is your new life then huh? Pie and stew and checkers on a Saturday night?"

"Be honest Dave, did you have fun?"

He nodded as he rolled up the window, whipped his car around, and drove down the street. "I had fun man," Dave said to himself, "But mostly watching you. I had no idea that the domestic scene fit you so perfectly."

Chapter Twelve

For the next two weeks, Grace taught a puppy to 'go' on newspaper, sleep in his bed, and not cry at night. She mastered smocking and worked hard to be ready for an upcoming craft show. Her life was a whirlwind of activity and though she enjoyed keeping busy, she began to look forward to the quieter days of winter after Christmas.

Exhaustion kept her from the retirement home until even Craig finally said something to her about it. The next morning, Grace left the housework and met the early bus. It was time for a visit with Aunt Fran.

"So I have to hear about your new pet from your brother. You caved, Gracie."

Grace's expression was priceless. "I got him though. I knew he'd pester me until I went crazy so I agreed to the dog and then chose one on my terms."

"Craig wanted a shepherd. He's always loved them. What'd you get?"

"A Pomeranian puppy. Seven weeks old."

Even Fran Buscher had to laugh at the mental image of a dog like that as her solution to her supposed need for protection. "I bet he wasn't happy. He said he wanted a watch dog."

"His name is Rolex. That's a watch; he's a dog… perfect."

"I always knew you had more spunk than you seemed. So, what about your new neighbor?"

Grace spent the next half-hour talking about Nolan and how thoroughly he'd integrated himself into their lives. "It's like we've known him forever. He's very good to Verily and my kids."

"You shouldn't talk about those brats you watch as 'your kids'. People are going to get the wrong idea and think you actually had the backbone to stand up to the Puritanical ideals my brother brought you up with, and enjoyed a little old-fashioned carnality."

"Aunt Fran, that was just crass," Grace protested. "I don't appreciate you speaking like that about my dad."

Ignoring her objections, Fran took the conversation in a new direction. "What about this Nolan? Any chance at a-"

"Don't even dream it Aunt Fran. He's attracted to Paige Matthews-"

"That homely thing? Even you were more attractive than that girl," she began

Ignoring the sting of 'even you', Grace interrupted to defend her friend. "Paige is now one of the most gorgeous girls in the greater Rockland Metro area. You've seen her. The one who picks me up sometimes. Blond hair, tall, very fashionable-"

"If that's the girl you ran around with in junior high, then find her makeover place and get them to work on you girl, they did great."

"I love you too Aunt Fran."

While Grace created ornaments and household decorations for the coming Christmas Craft shows, Nolan began corresponding with Paige via email. Initially, he sent a simple email to her address in the church directory, with a short note suggesting they get to know one another via email. When he received an unexpected but pleasant and warm response, Nolan hoped that he would find in Paige, the woman that he'd been seeking for so long. Thus far, the experiment was a monstrous failure. All of their conversations seemed concentrated upon Grace.

It was soon apparent to Nolan, that Paige was not the kind of woman that he hoped to find. She looked feminine, and acted feminine, but illogically, she appeared to resent her femininity. Nolan was looking for a strong woman, but Paige paradoxically exuded an air that reminded him of a damsel in distress. The more that he realized how wrong she was for him, the more she seemed to be pushing him toward Grace. Surprisingly, Nolan seemed to welcome the switch.

Sitting in his home office, Nolan was working hard on a new project. His email icon popped up at the bottom of his screen and he clicked it open. "That was fast! I just emailed you an hour ago."

He opened Paige's latest email. She was asking for an escort to the church's Thanksgiving supper two weeks from Wednesday. "Chuck Majors has informed me that since we seem to 'miss' each other so often that he'll just meet me there. If you feel up to rescuing me this once, I'd appreciate it. I'd suggest that you take Grace too but she's on the cooking crew. She wont' be dining with the rest of us. Please let me know. I appreciate this email correspondence. I would never have had the courage to ask you in person."

Nolan fired back a quick 'absolutely, and thank you for the offer' missive into the great wide web, and pondered his correspondence with Paige. He scrolled through several of the latest emails and then began laughing. The tears rolled down his eyes, and his belly hurt from his guffaws. "Those two women are going to drive themselves crazy!"

He felt foolish. It was obvious and yet he'd missed it. The two women were both working hard to play matchmaker between Nolan and their friend. Paige extolled Grace's virtues from her opening sentences to her closing ones. She was discreet but Nolan should have been able to guess from that first conversation during the progressive dinner.

Grace was her charming self. Never one to beat around the bush, she gave him tips, hints, suggestions and generally conspired with him to make the relationship work. Nolan thought about that. He wasn't a romantic in the original sense. He knew that life could be hard, and that problems generally required work more than simple hope. On the other hand, did he really want to begin a relationship that would require so much work from the start?

He thought about the past weeks. From the first few moments of his acquaintance with Grace, there was an ease and a friendliness that he had rarely found with anyone but his parents. When she didn't blame him for Cade's accident, he'd been relieved. When she placed the responsibility on herself and the boy, it impressed him. People were all too willing to shift blame, but not Grace.

He'd thought of her as 'just another guy' from the first. How could he have done that? She was the epitome of womanliness.

What made him blind to that? Nolan's musings took him to places that were uncomfortable for him.

"*Am I that shallow?*" Nolan's questions to himself hurt. Surrounded, as he was, by attractive and beautiful women, he'd always imagined himself with a more modest version of the stunning women of his acquaintance. However, he had not given much thought to appearance on his 'Order Form' for a wife. Pulling up the document on his laptop, he did much soul searching.

Christian
Feminine- loves being a woman
Strong
Modest
Sense of humor
Intelligent
Low-maintenance
Loves children

Reviewing the list, he added,

A best friend
An attractive personality

Nolan thought about Grace as he looked at his list. It seemed as though someone wrote a want ad with Grace in mind. "*Attractive personality... what does that really mean? Am I saying that 'looks' don't matter? Or, am I really saying that Grace's looks don't matter? What does she look like anyway?*"

He thought seriously for some time, and then felt foolish. Men were stereotyped as being annoyingly visual and often for good reason. Modesty was an important virtue to him because of it. Indecently clad women were always a stumbling block and he had turned down many accounts that were sought by women wearing too little for him to keep decent thoughts in his head.

He puzzled over Grace's features for a time. While fairly certain that Grace wore her hair chin length, he wasn't sure of its color. He finally decided on honey blonde before realizing that he was thinking of Paige. He thought her eyes looked purple the evening she wore her purple dress, but later realized that it must have been a chameleon effect. Regardless of their color, Nolan knew that Grace had the kindest eyes he'd ever seen.

Grace was somewhat plump... actually, she reminded him of his mother. Martha Burke had called herself, "softly contoured". While Grace didn't strike him as obese, he couldn't have guessed her weight. When Nolan realized that he had no clue as to Grace's height, he laughed.

"Lord, I've always prayed that I wouldn't marry superficially. That the woman I married would be so perfect to me that I didn't even notice if she was outwardly attractive. If Grace is your answer to that prayer... the joke is on me because I certainly didn't notice either way."

His thoughts came swarming around him like a heavy blanket. He'd just discovered that Paige wasn't the right woman for him and already he was looking at Grace in a different way. Thoroughly disgusted with himself, Nolan stood to retrieve the paper. "Nolan. Down boy! Your biological clock isn't ticking and neither is Grace's."

Had he not been working so hard to focus on his friendship with Grace, Nolan would have found himself quite amusing. Even in verbal chastisement, Nolan's mental shift to Grace was apparent. New ideas had opened to him and he was finding it hard to let them go.

~~~~*

Tuesday before Thanksgiving, Grace knocked on Nolan's door with vigor. Upon hearing the upcoming dinner plans, she realized that Nolan might like to see a swatch of the fabric left over from making Paige's dress. With the swatch in hand, Nolan would be sure to get the perfect corsage.

"Nolan!"

Nolan answered the door with trepidation. Should he treat Grace differently? For the past few weeks, he had slowly become aware of the fact that one of his best friends happened to be a woman. Her smile relaxed him and until she bubbled over about him escorting Paige to the up coming dinner. "Yes, she asked me to do that the other day. Wasn't that improvement for her? I really think she is on the way out of her shell."

Grace cocked her head in the charming way that she'd developed in the last few weeks. Having the puppy had given her new mannerisms that were comically endearing to her friends and family. "Ok, what's wrong?"

Nolan had a feeling that he'd never be able to hide anything from Grace. She was very intuitive. "Grace, I've been thinking and praying today and, well, Paige is not what I am looking for in my life. She's very attractive on many levels and I do enjoy her company in somewhat limited doses, but after this dinner I won't be escorting her anywhere."

Until he articulated his thoughts to Grace, he hadn't realized how fully convinced that Paige not what he was dreaming of in a wife. Grace looked at him with hands on her hips and laughed. "You really aren't interested are you?"

"You have no idea..." He quickly caught himself. Sheepishly, he shook his head and turned his attention to the fabric in Grace's hand.

"What is this for?"

"Well, this is what Paige will be wearing."

Unable to resist an opening like that, Nolan teased her in hopes of relieving some of the tension that was beginning to build. "I think she'll be a little cold... don't you think we should buy her a sweater or something?"

Verily heard Grace's laughter from his house and watched in delight as Grace flicked him on either cheek with her piece of rosy fabric in the manner of old British gentlemen as they challenged one another.

"You're terrible. I just thought you'd like to see the color so you could match a corsage- it's customary to have one for her. I was going to suggest roses but if you're going to distance yourself, maybe carnations would be good."

"No Grace. I'll find the prettiest ones I can that will match. There isn't any reason for her not to receive the best. I doubt that she's received many flowers that she felt free to accept."

"She hasn't but..."

Nolan cut her off quickly. "Grace, Paige will be relieved to know that I don't intend to continue to pursue a relationship with her. Not because she's afraid of me, or doesn't trust me, but because she is no more interested in me than I am in her."

A wicked grin crossed Grace's face. "Can I interest you in a lovely lawyer with an enchanting child? Marci…"

"Grace… I'm just realizing what I am really looking for and I'd kind of like to see where the Lord takes that right now."

Misunderstanding the look in Grace's eyes as disappointment, Nolan added, "Let's make a deal. In four months, if I haven't found Miss Right, you can set me up with any woman who is a Christian and doesn't ask me out first. I can't stand that."

"Well, I was sort of joking but now that I think about it… I'll keep her in mind when God doesn't drop a gorgeous woman in your lap before our three months, twenty nine days, twenty three hours, fifty-seven minute contract is over."

Nolan's deep rumbling laugh made Grace smile. She started back down his steps but paused as she heard him say, "The kind of woman I am looking for might not be obviously gorgeous to the casual glance, but she'll be the most beautiful woman in the world to me."

"I'll keep that in mind. There has to be somebody… but I'll bide my time. I agree; if there is one thing I can't stand, it's a pushy woman…" Grace's words trailed off in thought.

He listened to her chuckle as she crossed the street and retreated into the warmth of her house. Nolan stood in his open doorway, letting the stiff autumn breezes push their way into his warm office area and didn't notice. The sharp jangling of the reproduction telephone that hung in his kitchen snapped him from his reverie. Without waiting for his answering machine to pick up, Nolan answered.

"Noble Solutions, this is Nolan Burke speaking, how may I help you."

Nolan sank into his couch in frustration. This was the third call that he'd received this week. All of them were recommendations on his 'excellent service and integrity' by Michelle Walker. "I think I should have moved to another city… not just the suburbs."

"Pardon me ma'am… thinking out-loud. I can meet you for breakfast on the 29th or lunch on the 30th at the earliest…

"I see. Breakfast it is. I'll leave my name at the hostess desk so they know where to seat you. Thank you."

As he disconnected from the call, it occurred to him that he should order a corsage immediately. The dinner had unintentionally become an 'event' among the church's singles. If he waited too long, he might find it necessary to drive to the city for what he wanted. He swiftly exited the house, backed out of his driveway, and drove to town.

"Do you have something that would look nice with this fabric?"

Nolan was ready to give up and get plain white roses when he saw an exquisite orchid nestled in a flower arrangement. "That... that is what I want. Can you make me a corsage out of that?"

The woman tried to explain that it would cost him more for the corsage than for the entire arrangement but Nolan insisted. "Take the other flowers and stick them in that plant over there. The one inside that picnic basket- and I'll give you a card for it. Can they be delivered before closing tomorrow?"

The assistant assured him that it would be delivered before four and wrote up his order as he signed a card for Grace's plant.

"Thank you for all of your hard work and effort extended to make this a special night for all of us, Nolan. P.S. This scripture reminded me of you as I read it this morning. Proverbs..."

Nolan frantically racked his brain for the proper reference but couldn't remember which one it was. He dashed out to his vehicle. After checking the place in his Bible and finding the chapter and verse in Ecclesiastes that says,

"Moreover when God gives wealth and possessions, and enables him to enjoy them, to accept his lot, and be happy in his work, this is a gift from God."

Nolan dashed back indoors, added 5:19 to the bottom of the card, paid for his order, and drove home happy with his purchases and feeling like all was well with the world.

~~~~*

The following afternoon, Cade and Grace played catch in her front yard and it was obvious that Grace was thoroughly enjoying herself. They both waved at Nolan between tosses, while Cade proudly wore his new Cubs jacket and threw awkwardly. As Nolan watched from his window, he could see that Cade was trying but having a very difficult time throwing straight.

Grace patiently tried again to show him how to hit the 'target' and Cade kept trying. All too soon, or so Nolan thought, they went inside for cocoa. "Miss Buscher?"

Grace looked up from her steaming mug of marshmallow-laden chocolate. "Got a problem Cade?"

"How come my mom is always working? How come she can't be home when I get home? I mean...I like coming here! I just wondered why you can be home when you don't have kids, and mom has two kids she could be home with?"

"I think your mother would say that she works so that you all have enough to eat, a home to live in and clothes, schooling... the things that are important to mothers to provide for their children." Grace hoped she was right.

"But what is Dad for then? I mean... Dad makes a lot of money. Why can't he buy that stuff so mom can be home like you are?"

Grace's concern grew. It seemed as though Cade was bothered by something and had determined that if his mother were home in the afternoons, then the problem would go away. "Cade, I don't know your parent's financial position. People often have bills that they can't pay with just one income."

"But you live on next to nothing. Mom said that you are the only person that she knows that can squeeze blood from a turnip."

Grace's laugh muffled the knock on her front door. She started to explain why she chose to live the way that she did but a second knock brought her to the door. When she saw the plant laden picnic basket in the deliveryman's hand, her delight was evident, even from Nolan's vantage point across the street.

As she read the card, she instructed Cade to get a Bible. "Proverbs... 5:19 is what we are looking for... it's after Psalms right in the middle there... good job." Grace hardly paid attention as she fussed with the flowers. The plant was beautiful but looked especially lovely with fresh flowers were carefully added here and there. The effect was stunning.

Cade began reading eagerly. "As a loving h-ind and a graceful doe, let her... let her..."

"Is it a hard word Cade? Need help?" Grace was hardly listening as she continued to fuss with the fragrant flowers.

"No... um... let her br- breasts satisfy you always a-..."

Grace stopped him quickly as she snatched the Bible from him. "Wha- Um... Cade, I ..."

Cade was blushing furiously, though Grace was an even deeper shade of crimson. Mentally she railed against Nolan as she struggled to cover the faux pas. "Um Cade, well... I think that this card is meant for someone else. It's probably a mistake.

"Let's go back to our other discussion." Grace seethed through the entire conversation. She knew that her boy wasn't getting the answers that he needed but her anger was difficult to overcome.

A very relieved Grace sent Cade to his car the moment his mother knocked on the door. Mrs. Crenshaw laughed at the entire situation but became sober as she heard of Cade's desire to have his mother home. "I think there is more to it than it sounds. He's really fixated on it right now. I thought you should know."

Grace curled up with her Bible and began praying. She was angry... no, she was furious. What kind of sick joke did Nolan think he was playing? "As a lovely hind..." Her face burned as she remembered explaining to Cade that this was a large deer like animal, not someone's backside.

Her anger got the better of her and she stalked out the door. She was so focused on the object of her wrath that she didn't notice Melanie and the baby entering the back door. As Grace pounded on Nolan's door, Melanie saw the flowers and innocently read the card. She stared at the reference in disbelief.

"Come on Craig... pick up!" Melanie prayed that Craig remembered to turn on his cell phone.

"Craig. You'd better come to Grace's. I stopped by to talk her into dinner at our house and ... it appears she has received flowers... well a plant really, from Nolan....

"Craig... it's not that simple. There was a Bible reference on the card and-" Craig's uncharacteristic defense of Nolan irritated and saddened her. This was going to get ugly. "*Craig*, it's Proverbs 5:19!"

Craig's heart grew cold as the rest of him grew angry. Any other verse in Proverbs might have meant nothing to him but Proverbs 5:19 was a verse that he often quoted to his wife during intimate moments. "I'm just a couple of blocks away, I'll be right there. Where is Grace?"

Hearing that Grace was already in animated conversation with Nolan wasn't comforting. "She'll murder him."

Melanie's relief that Craig felt some concern for Nolan's welfare was short lived. "No Melanie, I just want some left for me to kill."

~~~~*

Murder wasn't on Grace's heart. She was too humiliated and hurt. Nolan had seemed so genuine and gentlemanly. She was shocked at his crassness but more than anything, she was hurt at the loss of what seemed to be a good friendship. As she pounded on his door, Grace berated herself for forgetting the plant. She could have insisted that he take it back. Better yet, she could have thrown it at him. So maybe murder was creeping into her heart.

Nolan opened the door with a grin. "Hey! How-"

"Do you think that you are funny? Did you know that I had Cade read that *aloud* to me? What were you thinking?"

Before Nolan could answer, horrible tire screeches erupted from the corner and the two watched in disbelief as Craig drove up over the curb and into Nolan's yard. Before Grace could ask what was going on, Craig was at her side. Dispensing with a greeting, Craig growled for Grace to go back home.

Grace was incredulous. "Excu-"

"*Now* Grace! *Now!*"

Throwing both men a look of derision, Grace stalked home. Spotting Melanie watching the scene from the picture window, phone and card still in her hand, Grace changed the object of her fury. Bursting into tears she accused Melanie of being a 'spy and a traitor' before collapsing in her favorite chair.

~~~~*

Nolan didn't know what to think. Something was terribly wrong but he had no idea what the problem was. "Craig-"

"Look Burke. I trusted you. You assured me that you wanted to be a real friend to Grace, and against my better judgment I *trusted* you."

"What did I do? I don't understand."

"The card Burke. Did you really think we wouldn't be upset? That scripture is incredibly offensive"

"How can scripture ever be offensive, Craig? I don't get it."

Craig's face turned purple with fury. "That is not funny. I'm trying to keep my cool but you are insulting-"

"I am so sorry. I really thought that the scripture was a beautiful picture of Grace. I thought that she was the embodiment of everything it was..."

"You have some *nerve!*" Craig was exercising every ounce of control that he could muster.

"When 'the Preacher'..." Nolan was feverishly trying to explain but Craig cut him off.

"Since when does the preacher talk about *breasts* to an unmarried woman? Did you happen to notice the word *wife* in there Burke? Or were you so full of your own sick joke that you didn't bother to note that?"

Craig turned to leave. He knew if he remained any longer the temptation to flatten Nolan would be too great to fight.

As he stalked across the lawn to retrieve his car, he spat out his ultimatum. "Keep away from my sister Burke, or you'll wish you had."

Nolan barely heard him. Already in a cold sweat, he was frantically searching for his Bible. He finally located it in the front seat of his car where he had looked up the reference... the reference!

"Oh noooooooo what did I put on that card?"

He dialed the florist's number and asked to speak to the salesgirl who had written up his order. After asking what was on the card with the plant, he feverishly flipped from Ecclesiastes to Proverbs searching. "Five-nineteen... five... nineteen... here it is... As a lovely hind..."

Nolan sank into the nearest chair with his head between his hands. If the situation wasn't so serious, his quirky humor would have taken over. He had no idea how to fix the problem. He couldn't go explain; the Buschers wouldn't listen, not that he could blame them.

"I have to try. I'll call Craig first." Nolan remembered the pain in Grace's eyes and almost wept.

~~~~*

Melanie stared in shock as Grace sobbed. It had never occurred to her that Craig coming to her defense would upset Grace. Grace usually welcomed her brother's protectiveness. "Grace honey, I..."

Grace stood, tried to speak, and then rushed from the room. She knew that Melanie meant well but she was too hurt to think rationally. Craig flipped open his ringing phone as he stalked into Grace's living room. In a scene reminiscent of a Jane Austen novel, Melanie wept in one corner of the room, while his infant daughter whimpered in her car seat and Grace's sobs drifted down the hallway.

Hearing Nolan's voice on the other line, Craig snapped the phone shut and turned it off. Melanie's account of Grace's distress and years of experience told Craig to go home. He left a note telling her that he'd be by later and led his little family home.

~~~~*

Nolan pulled out his church directory and looked for the phone numbers of the elders. He didn't know them well, but had immediately been struck with the serious manner in which they took their office. Shepherding Christians in today's independent culture wasn't an easy job. Nolan was that it was the responsibility of every man to live his life as if being an elder in Christ's church was the only goal that he had in this life and these men seemed to have just that kind of attitude.

Thirty minutes later, Nolan sat with three of the five elders explaining the situation. He paced the floor as he told about the confrontation and his subsequent realization of why Craig and Grace were so upset. As soon as he gave the reference that was accidentally written on the card, the oldest man present snickered.

"I'm sorry? Did I say something funny?" Before the man could reply the full impact of the situation hit Nolan and he chuckled.

Several minutes later, the group of men were wiping tears of laughter from their eyes and trying to return to a more serious discussion level. "I know that I am supposed to go to them at first, and I did try to call but Matthew 18 tells us to go to them with others if they won't listen to you..."

Frank Welk, a big burly man with a full bushy beard, was shaking his head. "No, actually, we are to go to those who have done wrong to us, and if they won't repent then you take someone according to Matthew 18, but you did right coming to us. James chapter five says to 'confess your faults, one to another and pray for one another that you may be healed.' This is step one."

The men prayed and then discussed whether to call Craig or to have Grace come in alone. Nolan's plea for a moment to assure Grace of his chagrin without Craig staring holes into the back of his head was granted. Mrs. Welk was called to drive Grace to the church. When she arrived, one of the elders excused himself to call Craig and fill him in on the situation.

Nolan was a broken man as he stood before Grace. Several times, he opened his mouth to speak and choked up. Finally, one of the elders prayed and asked the Lord to give Grace an open heart to receive what Nolan had to say, and for Nolan to find the words to convey what was on his heart.

"Grace, can I read something to you?" Before Nolan could begin reading, Grace's expression softened.

"Furthermore, as to every man to whom God has given riches and wealth, He has also empowered him to eat from them and receive his reward and rejoice in his labor; this is the gift of God."

Grace shook her head. She didn't comprehend what Nolan seemed to be saying. "I don't understand..."

"I read that scripture yesterday morning and it made me think of you. I- I know how much you love the work you do, the service you offer to others and your creativity. It's all a huge part of how God has blessed you and you show that. Yesterday morning, well, I read from the end of Proverbs through the fifth chapter of Ecclesiastes. When I remembered that verse as I was writing out your card, well, I couldn't remember the reference. I wrote down Proverbs, but couldn't remember the numbers. Then, I went out to the car, found the verse, and went back inside to put down the reference. I didn't notice-"

"That you had the wrong book." Grace blushed. The verse was still embarrassing.

"Grace, I am so sorry- I would never- that is something so private, so intimate- I can't imagine..."

Grace shook her head. "No, please forgive me. I didn't ask you why or if you meant to write it, I was embarrassed and attacked- and Craig- I don't even want to know what Craig said."

Nolan reddened. "Um, he's pretty upset but I don't blame him. When I finally figured out what you guys were talking about-"

Frank Welk spoke up. "Grace, I actually think that this is going to get ugly with Craig. He has always been a little over protective of you. I'd like you to go see what you can do for tomorrow while we speak to Craig. I don't want you put in the middle, ok? We'll all come back together to pray once this is resolved."

Grace nodded and moved to the dining hall. As the door closed behind her, she heard Craig's car drive into the parking lot. It seemed to Grace that the whole situation had gotten out of hand and all because of her. If she had taken that card to Nolan and asked him to explain the use of that particular scripture, things would have been different. Now things were a mess.

Craig walked into the meeting room and slugged Nolan. Before anyone could react, he began a tirade that Grace could hear parts of in the kitchen. Attacking Nolan on every front, Craig let it be known his exact thoughts on the entire incident ending with his complete disgust at the meeting. The men listened in complete silence. Nolan held tissues to a bleeding nose and prayed harder than he'd ever prayed before.

The men's silence eventually took the wind out of Craig's sails and he finally seated himself in a folding chair that he moved slightly apart from the rest in one final show of anger. One of the elders began praying. Another elder took up the prayer and so they prayed around the room. Craig remained silent. As the final 'amen' was spoken, a mousy looking man, Seth Wolski, spoke.

"Craig, we are at a loss as to how to deal with you…"

"Deal with *me*! This man insulted my sister with suggestive and indecent comments. Whose side are you on?"

Seth sent a scathing look at Craig and demanded silence. "You have disgraced the name of Christ here tonight. I understand your anger but it is misdirected. You are wrong Craig. Nolan called us here to explain the situation and to request help in his quest to receive forgiveness. As your shepherds, we insist that you sit here, pray, open your heart, and then hear what this man has to say."

Nolan was shocked. Seth Williams looked like a mealy-mouthed wimp, but he'd been mistaken. Craig's face mirrored his. He looked toward Frank but Frank's eyes were stern. He nodded silently and Craig sighed. Praying when angry was never his strong point.

"Ok Burke. I'm listening. I don't want to but unfortunately, these men are men that I respect and I feel obligated to listen to their instructions. I can't promise that my heart is open."

Nolan began with an apology. Then he simply told his story. Point by point, line by line, he explained how the horrible mistake had occurred. Finally, Nolan paused. "Craig, I can not tell you how embarrassed and ashamed I am of myself. I was in a hurry and was careless. I'll never make that mistake again. But if you can forgive me..."

Frank held up his hand. "Wait. I am not certain that you have anything to ask forgiveness for. You didn't sin against him. Don't take upon yourself sin that you haven't committed."

Nolan shook his head. "I know that Craig takes his role as protector for his sister very seriously. I hurt my friend by hurting his sister and I want forgiveness for that."

Craig was in deep turmoil. He knew that Nolan was genuine. He knew that the man was telling the truth, but he didn't want to forgive. There was safety in Grace having a rift in the friendship. She couldn't be hurt when Nolan finally found the kind of woman that he was likely looking for. Craig wanted to nurse a grudge and just not take the chance.

"Craig, Grace has forgiven me. She knows that I didn't mean to hurt her. I have managed to salvage one friendship; I'd like to salvage another."

Melanie's quiet disapproval of his display of anger, Grace's obvious forgiveness, and Nolan's humility were enough to shame him. In complete repentance for his anger, Craig dropped his face into his hands and wept. The group of men prayed, talked, and despite the discomfort that men find in situations like this, sang a hymn. Grace heard them from the dining hall and smiled singing to herself with them, "...*Bind us together, Lord...*"

Chapter Thirteen

"Martha, can you call the Stern girls in and send out the Perkins'? Oh, and I think we could use some more help filling the plates. Is there someone washing dishes or something who can come in here?"

Grace rushed around the kitchen cutting, tasting, and supervising, all as she made batch after batch of gravy and mashed potatoes. The church was packed. It appeared that everyone had brought friends and family. As she mashed another large bowl of potatoes, Paige stepped into the kitchen looking like a model from Paris runway.

"Grace! I- can you come out here for a moment, I have to talk to you!" Paige was almost bubbling.

Mrs. Welk smiled at Grace and shooed her out. "Five minute break Grace. If you don't rest you'll drop and we need you too much to risk it."

Paige dragged Grace into the women's restroom and began talking animatedly. "Chuck Majors brought his brother Nathan tonight."

Grace waited. "And..."

"Oh Grace! When I first met him, you know what I thought he'd be like, but he is nothing like Chuck and..."

Paige's voice dropped to a conspiratorial whisper. "I think he's interested in me. He keeps looking at me and he-"

Grace smiled. "Of course he does! You look like a million dollars. I bet every man at that table is drooling."

"Well... Nolan looks kind of forlorn, but everyone else seems to be enjoying themselves. What did you do to him?"

"Long story. Trust me. I'll tell you later. So you're not interested in Nolan?"

"Nah, he's not for me. I think he'd be perfect for another friend of mine though..."

Grace washed her hands as a diversion and then headed back to the kitchen. She wandered through the dining hall to get a glimpse of Chuck's brother before getting back to work. She instantly regretted it. At every table, someone stopped her to speak to her. By the time she reached Nolan and Paige's table, she was feeling desperate. If this continued, it'd take her twenty minutes to reach her post in the kitchen. Nolan's eyes questioned her as Paige leaned over and whispered something to him.

Without hesitation, Nolan stood and escorted Grace to the kitchen. His presence seemed to deter everyone's attempts to stop her. People waved and praised the dinner but let her move freely through the room. Once in the kitchen, the obvious lack of helpers prompted him to tuck a kitchen towel into his waistband and ask where to start working first. Grace considered arguing and then 'called his bluff'. The result was hilarious.

Grace shooed him toward the sink and handed him a bottle of dishwashing soap and a dishcloth. "Here you go. I'll have someone tell Paige you've been detained. From what I hear, Chuck's brother won't be too upset."

"Nope. He's been eyeing her since Chuck introduced her as his 'on again, off again' girlfriend."

Grace stared. "He *didn't!*"

"Yup. Can you imagine? Nathan is obviously smitten."

"Smitten? That's a quaint word."

Nolan stopped a young girl serving and whispered something into her ear. The girl giggled and scurried out to the dining hall. "That'll make them both happy."

Three hours later, Grace discovered Nolan's plan. Nathan was asked to escort Paige home for him and was more than willing. Grace smiled as she saw her friend climb into an older model BMW and drive toward Paige's home.

She smiled into Nolan's equally satisfied face. "Thank you. I'd love nothing more than for Paige to find the right man."

"That, I know. I'm just glad that you aren't upset that I didn't want it to be me."

Grace laughed. "That's ok; I haven't given up hope, but I won't push. How do you feel about telling me what you're looking for in Mrs. Perfect?"

Nolan thought of his list. How would she react to something like that? It was intensely personal but he was curious. After a moment's deliberation, he decided to risk it and tell her. "Remember, you asked. It's a little embarrassing but I actually have a list- I call it my 'order form' that I've submitted to the Lord. I'm just waiting for Him to fill it."

"Order form? That's cute. I like it. So what do you want? Blonde, Red, Brunette? Tall, short?"

Slightly surprised, Nolan almost reconsidered telling her. He took a deep breath. "Not exactly. Those don't' matter much to me. I'm looking for a woman who is feminine. Completely committed to the Lord. Someone who has a sense of humor-loves being a woman but is strong too. She needs to love children and have a beautiful personality. That about covers it."

"You aren't asking for much. How do you intend to find this paragon?"

Nolan looked at her sideways. Should he risk hinting that he was increasingly finding her to be exactly what he was looking for? He took a chance and spoke. "I do want a lot. I also hope that somehow I can measure up to my ideal to provide what she's looking for in a husband."

"Well, good luck finding her." Grace's genuinely hopeful tone stripped the sarcastic tinge from the words.

"Well, I don't think she's as far from my acquaintance as I thought she'd be."

Chapter Fourteen

"So if you escorted Paige, who took Grace?" Traci was intrigued. She saw the change in Nolan and was fascinated.

"Craig and Melanie brought her there so I assume they took her home."

Mike's astonishment tickled Nolan. "You just assume!"

"After the past twenty-four hours, I'm being very cautious about how I step on toes over there."

Traci interrupted and changed the course of discussion. "So, tell me more about this guy Chuck and how did he get such a normal brother?"

Nolan launched into a comical impersonation of Chuck's arrogant thoughtlessness. The Finches assumed that he was exaggerating but he quickly denied it. "If anything, I'm convinced I'm downplaying this a bit. I cannot imagine why anyone would put up with him the way they do but I've never felt comfortable asking."

"Tell us about Grace."

Mike's words hovered in the air about them for several seconds. Nolan kneaded the back of his neck as he tried to remember everything he'd planned to say in the forty-minute drive to the Finch home. Mike and Traci's eyes sought each other, alarmed. What about Grace would make him hesitate to talk? He'd seemed so eager to share when he called but now that they were back on the subject, he seemed reticent.

"Grace isn't who I imagined and everything I dreamed. Oh, that doesn't make sense," he groaned.

"No it doesn't but it's a start. What does Grace do? Start there and maybe it'll be easier."

Traci's encouragement sent a wry smile over his lips. "Easy for you to say. What Grace does is part of what makes it so difficult to describe her. Grace is a homemaker."

"Well, that's what you've always hoped to find, isn't it? Someone who loves home and family? What kind of job does she have?" Traci clearly didn't understand his statement.

"Remember when Pastor Bjorn spoke about the real meaning of Titus two and how he said that the word translated 'keeper of the home' really means 'house despot' and derives from slave ownership? Well, Grace is definitely a house despot and she is her own slave."

"I don't get it." Mike and Traci stared at him as they spoke in unison.

"That's her job, her calling. It's her life."

"Huh?"

Traci bopped her husband. "You're so loquacious Mike!"

"I told you it wasn't easy."

"Does she have an income? Is she on welfare? What-" Mike seemed to have found his voice and fired questions at Nolan in rapid succession.

"Woah Nellie!" Nolan cried holding his hands up protectively. Then, not knowing what else to do, he told them Grace's life story, as far as he knew it, starting with her birth on her porch to the new hobby she'd taken up recently. "She's really good at it. I was doubtful so I went into that posh boutique that mom always shopped in for baby shower gifts? You know how she used to have me pick stuff up for her- Well, I went in and asked if I could see something smocked and I examined it. Grace's is ever bit as good, if not better. Hers seemed more polished somehow."

"She has a physics degree, could do almost anything she wanted and be quite well off, and she's Donna Reed?" The incredulous look on Traci's face was the first hint of what he'd have to deal with when his Rockland friends met Grace.

"When you meet her, you'll understand. I want you to come for church Sunday. Will you? Come Saturday night and stay all night if you like- I have room. Bring the kids and we'll roast marshmallows in the fireplace and pop popcorn. I'll throw a free date night into the mix... you drop off the kids and I'll watch 'em. There's a great restaurant-"

"Nolan!" Traci shouted, effectively stopping his momentum. "We'll come. You sound desperate!"

"He is. He's falling for this Grace. I can see it in his eyes and you heard the intensity in his voice. He wants an objective opinion!" Mike's voice was filled with glee.

They talked long into the night. By the time Nolan was ready to leave, Traci put her foot down. "Forget it Nolan, it's too late. You have a room, you know where it is, and you have clothes in there even. Go to bed. We'll see you in the morning."

"Send the kids in to wake me up. I need to be back in Brunswick before noon."

"Grace?"

"Having dinner at the Buschers and I'm Grace's ride so…"

"So this is getting very interesting. Very."

Nolan, with one foot on the stairs, paused. "I have a feeling that Mike is preparing for turnabout and fair play and stuff like that."

"What goes around comes around my friend. You reap what you sow. I-"

With out a second glance back, Nolan said, "You're such a cliché," as he took the steps two at a time.

The bed bounced. Giggles erupted and forced their way into his consciousness. Something tickled his nose, so Nolan grabbed it. A squeal pierced his eardrum giving severing all ties to sleep. "Uncle Nolan! I saw your Bible downstairs so I knew you were here."

"Hey tiger! How's my Mickey?" Nolan lifted his covers, looked under pillows, and peeked out the window behind his bed. "Ahh, now where did miss giggles go?"

London Finch squealed and dove for cover but not before she was enveloped in tickles. Mickey and London bounced and chattered until Nolan's body screamed for coffee. He tumbled from bed with a child on each leg hanging like barnacles on a ship.

"Where's Parker? Are your parents awake?"

"No, they're sleeping. We're supposed to take Parker in there if he wakes up. They sleep late on holidays. It's their day off." London's four-year-old voice amused him. He'd missed the children since he'd been in Brunswick.

"Well, you guys go see how Parker is doing and I'll get dressed. Maybe we can make breakfast for mom and dad as a surprise!"

The children raced to check on the baby as Nolan pulled on fresh clothes, washed his hands and face, and brushed his hair. Once the bed was made, he left his dress slacks, shirt, and jacket on the foot of the bed and put a twenty-dollar bill in the breast pocket of the jacket sticking out where Traci would see it. His pajamas, he folded and put back in their drawer leaving the room just as it'd been except for his clothes.

By ten, he'd made breakfast, helped the children serve it to their parents in bed, cleaned up the mess, and read a dozen stories to the children. Mike and Traci raced downstairs at ten-thirty apologizing profusely though thankful for time to wake up slowly and enjoy privacy. Fifteen minutes later, Nolan started his car and rolled down the passenger window talking to his shivering friends.

"We'll be there by four on Saturday," Traci assured him.

"Shall I make dinner reservations for you?"

Mike shook his head. "I'll call Marcello's in Fairbury. We'll do dinner and a movie over there and be back-"

"Then I'll meet you in Fairbury and I'll bring the kids back. I'll be there at four."

Before they could protest, he rolled up the window and drove away. Mike looked at his wife and grinned excitedly. "We could so milk this-"

Traci laughed and pulled him toward the house. "You're bad. You're very bad. I like it."

Chapter Fifteen

Amber was ecstatic. The smells coming from Grace's house were enough to make a stuffed lumberjack's mouth water. Thanksgiving with Grace was going to be so much fun. Marci was trapped in Chicago thanks to an untimely ice storm so Grace insisted that Amber spend the day with her at Craig and Melanie's.

Nolan's SUV crunched across the street and pulled into Grace's driveway. Amber met him at the door excitedly chattering about the day, the plans, and the food they'd be eating. "And I get to hold Graceanna when Mrs. Buscher needs me to!"

"Now that sounds wonderful. Are you going to share with me?"

Amber grinned. "When she gets heavy or stinky, you can take her."

Once Grace's Hungarian Coffee Cake was drizzled with icing, all three of them piled into his vehicle and left. Amber insisted on singing 'over the river' all the way there and the ways that they improvised to get the 'perfect' words made for a hilarious ride.

"I hope Aunt Fran won't be too hard on you today-"

"I've heard about her but I've not met her yet-"

Amber's little voice piped up morosely. "Lucky you. She always has something mean to say. Just ignore it like Miss Gracie says and it doesn't hurt your feelings too badly."

Grace shrugged and grinned at Nolan. "Children say it like it is, don't they?" She climbed from the car and grabbed the coffee cake. "Happy Thanksgiving; may the Lord bless you this day!" Grace called their traditional greeting as she marched up the walk.

A voice from inside the house nearly sent Nolan into a fit of laughter. "The Lord blesses those who leave His name out of it."

Nolan marveled at the way she seemed to forget recent tensions with her brother and ignore annoying aunts who try to grate on her nerves. As he reflected, he became concerned. It wasn't healthy to stuff down the frustration that Grace had exhibited toward her brother just days before. How long before that dam burst?

As Grace made room on a buffet table for all of the food she carried, Craig came over to Nolan's side. Before he could speak, Grace turned to him. "Oh Craig, good, can you put this in the fridge for me? I don't want the whipped cream to melt."

The next few moments were a bit chaotic and extremely funny. Grace pretended to trip over her feet and fell, pie first, into Craig's face. Nolan expected a roar of indignation to erupt from Craig's shocked face. His surprise was evident as Craig, Melanie and Grace dissolved into helpless laughter.

"I- I-" Craig struggled to speak through guffaws. "I didn't even see it coming. I figured you'd wait until you thought I was comfortable."

"I knew if I didn't do it right away, you'd be on your guard. Woohoo! That'll teach you.

"Melanie, think he's sweetened up enough?"

"Like a little whipped cream could cure him," Fran's voice interjected.

Nolan marveled at the way practical jokes could easily be enjoyed *and* forgiven in this family. His home had been loving, but slightly formal. They enjoyed humor but practical joking had been a rare occurrence; certainly nothing like the give and take that was sure to be a part of today's repartee.

Melanie eyed her husband warily. It appeared that Craig was inching toward an exceptionally flaky crusted pie. "Knock it off Craig or you'll wear the turkey too!"

While the rest of the group played games and sang songs from old Mitch Miller albums, Melanie and Grace worked on the finishing touches to dinner. Aunt Fran complained about the 'caterwauling' and then about screaming babies as Graceanna's wails drew Melanie from the kitchen when the baby became hungry. "Can you handle things Grace? Need me to call Craig in?"

"Nah, I've got it under control, let them play."

Grace continued stirring gravy and slicing canned cranberry sauce. She felt exhausted and attributed it to the events of the previous days. It had been a very rough week. A feeling of dizziness came over her but she continued with preparations. Gripping the counter next to the stove, she steadied herself.

Nolan watched in concern. After overhearing her conversation with Melanie, he'd decided to offer to help. It might be a chance to talk to her and see what she thought of him- as a man. "Grace? You ok?"

Grace turned around quickly. Too quickly. Dizziness overwhelmed her and she found herself lurching for the table. "Acck. The room is spinning!"

He seated the unsteady woman and continued stirring the pan she'd been working over. "What's wrong? Did you forget to eat?"

"No... I'm just exhausted. I don't think I slept well last night."

A cheer went up from everyone in the living room. The game of charades was apparently over. Amber dashed into the kitchen looking for nibbles and stopped short. She gave Nolan and Grace a funny look before turning and running back into the group. Nolan looked at Grace.

"Did I miss something?"

Grace shrugged. "She is a mystery sometimes. Her mother calls her 'intuitive'. I call her silly. I think she prefers silly."

Chuckling, they carried the bowls and plates into Craig's dining room and placed them on the large sideboard. "We'll eat buffet style. It'll be faster so the food won't get cold."

"Let me make a plate for your aunt. You go sit down and eat."

Fran accepted the plate smiling broadly at Nolan. Grace sat wondering if her aunt truly liked Nolan or if it was just the air of courtesy she put on at appropriate occasions. She was rude to most of her family, rude to service people and store clerks, rude to people who intruded into her living space uninvited, but the rest of the time, even if she didn't feel like it, she managed a cordial civility that always seemed out of character somehow.

Unaware of her niece's curiosity, Fran enjoyed her conversation with Nolan Burke. Over turkey, stuffing, and hot mashed potatoes that only Grace could have made, she quickly learned that Nolan Burke was one of *the* Rockland Burke' and that even if he and her family didn't know it; he'd be a part of it in the near future. His genuine interest in her and her life as a real estate developer in the early years of the Westbury boom gratified her and endeared himself to her.

An hour later the group lounged in the large family room, everyone too stuffed to make any unnecessary movements. "Why do we do this every year?" Melanie groaned and shifted the baby from her stomach.

"Because we're all hedonists if we're honest with ourselves," quipped Fran to an uninterested and non-listening room.

"Anyone feel like singing?" Craig's tone implied that his heart wasn't into the idea.

"Anyone feel like meditating day and night?" Nolan's quip earned him a few pained chuckles.

"Let's get up a good game of Twister! Come on Paige; show 'em what my girl can do!" Chuck's oblivious self-absorption appeared to be reaching new heights.

Nathan looked askance. "Um Chuck. Cool it. The girl is resting. It's what most people do when they finish an excellent Thanksgiving dinner."

Amber appeared to be the only one with any latent energy. Despite her obvious dislike for Chuck, she conned him into a pick up game in the back yard. "It'll be fun and they'll be ready to do something by the time we come in... come on Mr. Majors!"

As the back door shut behind the would-be soccer players, Nathan turned to Paige. "Does a nice, slow amble down to the park and back sound like too much of an assault on your stomach?"

Paige shook her head and the couple slipped silently out the front door. Nolan sighed. He'd considering making the same offer to Grace before the episode in the kitchen. Before he could formulate another plan to try to talk with Grace, Melanie stood to put Graceanna in her crib. Moments later Craig followed. "I'm going to lay down for a few. I feel like those decadent Romans who overfed themselves. I need a rest."

Fran stood and followed them to the guest room next to theirs. "If you need me, find someone else. I don't want to be disturbed."

"Looks like you're stuck with me." Grace's voice lacked any traces of mirth.

"Why do you say it like that? Are you still angry with me?" Nolan seemed confused.

"I don't know. Tiredness talking I guess. I'm not angry. I wasn't actually angry before- well, I was when Cade was reading this verse out loud and I didn't know how I was going to get out of it!"

Nolan's low chuckle was comforting. Their friendship had already resumed its comfortableness. "I appreciate your understanding. I'm still embarrassed. I mean, I don't even remember reading that verse before."

"I thing it's pretty personal between Mel and Craig." Grace blushed as she realized that she was passing on information that she shouldn't.

"Paige seems pretty happy with Nathan. Think they'll get a 'real' chance? I mean..."

Grace nodded. "Paige said that Nathan knows how to take care of it if he has to. I hope he's as wonderful a he seems- I'd hate to see her hurt again."

He hesitated. Would she resent him asking about personal things? "Paige implied that you'd been hurt yourself."

"Ahhh no." Grace's laugh was genuine. She looked at him with undisguised amusement in her face. "Paige persists on believing that my father's in home care assistant 'trifled with my affections' and then dumped me when he discovered how low the life insurance was."

"Can I ask an extremely personal question?" Ever since discovering that Grace was everything that he'd asked for in a wife, he had changed his perception of her.

She eyed him warily. "Well, I guess it depends upon the question."

"Have you ever considered marriage?" Nolan began to feel foolish for asking.

"Marriage in general, or to someone in particular?" Grace wasn't as oblivious to the change in Nolan's perception of her as he believed and she wasn't sure what she thought of it. It was one thing to desire a husband and children but her relationship with the Lord was so intimate- so special. She didn't know if she was willing to risk that changing- even for someone like Nolan.

"Well, how about both?" He was beginning to think that Grace was either incredibly dense, or she wasn't interested in sharing anything personal with him.

"Well, marriage in general? I've prepared for that my whole life."

Now this was going somewhere. "How? How have you prepared? What kind of wife do you see yourself as? What kind of husband or marriage have you been hoping for?"

"Well, it's a matter of what you think the design for men and women are, and what the purpose of marriage is. I believe that God has intended for most people to marry so I prepared for that- almost from birth. Craig too."

"What about when Paul says that he wishes that most people would remain single like him?"

"Look at the whole passage, Nolan. He says 'for this present distress'. He knew that a very difficult and dangerous time was coming, probably speaking of the fall of Jerusalem, and he still qualified it with, 'let each man have his own wife' etcetera because it's better to 'marry than burn'."

"Excellent point. So what did you do to prepare? What did Craig do?"

Grace spoke of years of the excellent example that her parents had exhibited for her and her brother. The lessons in homemaking and learning to serve others above herself were taught lovingly by her mother as she lived it. As Nolan listened, fond memories came over him. He remembered similar times of instruction that he'd spent with both parents.

"That's beautiful Grace. Tell me, why haven't you married yet?"

"Well, I'm not exactly old, but I've been called an 'old maid' by some of the little girls at the church; they like to read antique books. They assume if you're over twenty-two, your hopes are gone. But you didn't ask about that."

He hesitated and finally gave in. "So... how much older is Craig than you?"

Her laughter rang out gleefully. "That's a smooth one! I'm thirty-two. My birthday is July fourth.

"But you wanted to know why I'm not married. I'd say because no one has ever asked me but that implies that I'd just accept anyone."

"I can't imagine that happening. I don't think that Craig would go for it."

"Uh... no. That he wouldn't."

"Come on, tell me. If you could describe your husband if you could pick one out at a store, what would he be like?"

Grace grew thoughtful. Eventually she began describing a very special person. The warmth with which she spoke implied that she wasn't just making this up on the spur of the moment. As she spoke of the qualities she hoped to find, Nolan realized that she was describing a man much like, if not exactly like, her father.

"You miss him don't you?" The question didn't need to be asked.

"It's our second Thanksgiving without him. I miss him. Sometimes I feel so alone in that house without him. Everyone thinks that I am happy to be alone in my own little world that I've created. I've been told how lucky I am. I have a nice house that I can do whatever I want with. I don't have the hassle of in-laws or sharing the remote. Who wants to be alone like that for their whole life unless it's exactly what the Lord has planned for them?"

Grace paused a moment before continuing. "I don't want to presume to know the mind of God but I just don't think that God means for me to be single."

"You really want a home and family, don't you?"

"I don't want to sound pietistic, but while I truly do want a husband, children, and all that comes with them, I have a very close relationship with the Lord. I know that marriage will change that. It won't tear me away from the Lord but my relationship will change and I don't know if I want it to. Does that make sense?"

Nolan nodded slowly. "Do you mean something like a living example of 'the wife is concerned with the things of her husband but the single person, the things of the Lord'?"

"Oh what a relief for someone to understand," she sighed. "Most don't."

"What about Mr. Right? Do you know why he hasn't come along?"

Grace was thoughtful. She hated this part of the conversation. She was honest with herself but whenever she talked about it, she felt like someone trying to garner sympathy. "Well, the long and short of things is that I tend to be thought of as 'one of the guys'. I'm not exceptionally pretty, kinda overweight- ok, a lot overweight. I don't have a flashy career or any modern sophistication. I'm just an old-fashioned girl with a heart for hearth and home. Not a lot of men are looking for that."

"Does that bother you?" Nolan mentally refuted every point. Her beautiful personality and character shone in her eyes and illuminated a very gentle face. Who could notice her weight with a heart as big as she had, and there were too many sophisticated career women out there in his opinion.

"Not really. The right guy is either out there looking for me, or I am one of the exceptions; and as my dad said the day before he died..." Grace choked up a little as she tried to quote her departed father. "If you are one of those exceptions, Grace, that just means that God thinks you are exception-*all*."

"Well, you're already that. I-" Nolan was interrupted by a wail as Amber crashed into the room sobbing.

"Amber! What is wrong?" Grace's alarm brought a fresh round of wails from the child but before Amber could answer Chuck came striding into the room.

"What is wrong with her, one minute we're playing and talking and the next minute she's crying like a baby." Chuck's personality left much to be desired on most occasions but Nolan was particularly irritated with him at the moment.

Grace motioned for Nolan to take Chuck out of the room and held the weeping child. When the room was empty, and the girl's sobs quieted, Grace tried again. "Amber honey, what upset you?"

"I want mommy!"

Aunt Fran's voice hollered down the hallway, "Someone shut that child up! We're trying to sleep.'

Sighing, Grace tried again. "Did you get hurt?"

The child shook her head and sniffled. "I don't like him. I want mommy."

"Did Chuck say something that bothered you?" Grace began to fume.

"He asked when my mommy was going to get married again..."

"Is that all?" Grace knew it wasn't. It never was with Chuck Majors.

"No, he asked if I was going to be a good girl when mommy remarries so that the new daddy won't leave." Fresh sobs threatened to erupt.

Before Grace could answer, Craig and Melanie came hurrying in. "What's going on? Have we been asleep long? Amber honey, why are you crying?"

Amber ran to Melanie and began crying softly. Grace looked gravely at Melanie and made a face as she pointed out the window where Nolan and Chuck were in deep conversation. Motioning for Craig to follow, she headed out doors.

As they walked slowly down the steps, Grace filled Craig in and said, "Craig, it's time. He's gotten away with this kind of thing for too long. Do we need the elders or can you rebuke him first and contact the elders tomorrow if there's still a problem?"

Craig waived her to the side. "You are here as a witness as to what Amber said, *not* as a confronter. Keep quiet Grace."

Grace shut her mouth, with much difficulty, and watched the proceedings. Craig confronted Chuck with his words to Amber. The man's response was less than encouraging. "Yeah, so what?"

Grinding her teeth in fury, Grace fumed. *"Is this guy for real? Does he have no clue that he just hung himself? The **nerve**! At least the noose is good and tight now."*

Nolan was surprised to hear the grinding emanating from Grace's jaw line. His disgust and anger with Chuck evaporated in his concern for her. He realized, with amusement and a trace of amazement, that Grace's fists were clenching at her side in perfect synchronization with her jaw. Sheer willpower held a chuckle in check, as he noticed that her foot had a tendency to inch forward, then back again, as if ready to strike.

Craig's voice brought him back to the current situation. Slightly embarrassed by how easily distracted he was, Nolan tried to focus on the situation at hand. "Chuck, I don't think you are hearing what we are saying. I'd like you to listen, and listen carefully..."

Before he could summarize what Chuck needed to hear, a swift movement caught the corner of his eye, and Chuck yelped! "She kicked me! What's up with *that* Grace?"

Craig shot a look at Grace, but she spoke first. "I didn't *say* anything!" Craig's look would have quelled a meeker disposition. Grace, however, was made of sterner mettle. "You said not to speak. You didn't say I couldn't kick some sense into him."

Chuck seemed momentarily stunned. Nolan jumped at the chance to make his point. "Chuck. You essentially told a seven-year-old girl that it's her fault that her irresponsible father abandoned her. Tell me how this is acceptable behavior for a Christian."

Chuck, in his usual self-centered style, had ignored what was actually being said and responded only to what he *thought* they either were, or should be saying. Nolan's words seemed to sink in but a voice behind him managed to make a deeper impression. "Chuck, what have you said now?"

Nathan stood behind his brother with arms folded and steel in his eyes. Craig began pacing and ranting about Amber hurt and humiliated. Everyone jumped back in surprise as Nathan slugged his brother across the jaw. Everyone that is, except for Chuck. He almost seemed to expect it, and stood ready to accept the blow.

Chuck picked himself up from the ground where he'd stumbled, muttered a thanks for the dinner and drove away. Craig and Nolan stood by with shock, confusion, and a trace of envy running through their minds. Curiosity finally drove them to blurt out in unison, "What just happened here?"

"If there is one thing that I've learned about Chuck over the years, it's that he values brawn over brains. As you can imagine, it made for an interesting childhood."

The men groaned and chuckled while Grace and Paige looked at each other and shrugged. Remembering Amber and her distress, Grace went back indoors. The emotional drain was beginning to take its toll. As she seated herself, Melanie mouthed something to her but Grace's lip reading skills left much to be desired.

"Amber honey, can you get Grace something to drink?" Melanie went to the door and motioned for Nolan to join them. When Craig and the others followed, Mel waived them back.

Amber brought a glass of water and set it on the table before Grace. She gave an embarrassed glance at Nolan and hurried outside with the others. Melanie's face showed confusion. "Nolan, Amber is dealing with a lot of guilt right now. She saw Nathan punch his brother and blames it on her 'gossiping' about him."

An awkward silence fell over the room. Nolan looked at Grace, who looked at Melanie. Mel looked at Nolan as if waiting for an explanation. "Nolan, she thinks that it is gossip to tell us that a man said unkind things to her."

He waited for Melanie to continue. He was positively clueless as to what Mel was getting at. "Am I supposed to do something about this? You appear to be waiting for something from me."

"She said that you taught her that anytime you say anything about someone who isn't there to hear exactly what you said, that it is gossip and wrong."

Without a word, Nolan stood and went outside to talk with Amber. Grace and Melanie watched as he took her hand and led her down the street, talking earnestly as they went. Amber's uncertain face was evident from their vantage point. Craig, Nathan and Paige came indoors clamoring for an explanation.

After hearing the story, Craig sighed. "I'm glad to have him here. It's like having a close brother."

"Two days ago you were ready to murder him and now you're glad he's here. I don't understand you Craig Buscher."

"Well, I have to admit, I was a little unreasonable, but you just don't mess with my women."

Nolan and Amber returned a short while later to find everyone pouring over the special Christmas sales planned for the following day. "Come on guys; help us figure out where to go first."

Friendly arguments were swift to follow. With everyone having different store priorities, they finally split up into three groups. Craig eyed his sister and his new friend warily. Were they all playing with fire to throw the two together this often?

"Ok, so, with this plan we can all meet at Grimsby's for lunch. My treat." Nolan grinned excitedly. He hadn't been a part of a Christmas tradition in several years. Christmas was such a special part of his childhood memories and he was excited to join into the festivities again.

Grace squealed in delight. "I haven't been to Grimsby's in ages! Ok, gimme your lists. Melanie first."

The final plans were made over a pick-up dinner. Nolan looked at his watch before suggesting an end to the evening. "Ok, guys, what do you say? Shall we make it an early night? We have to be up at o' dark thirty."

Nolan's suggestion was readily accepted and everyone quickly gathered their dishes and piled into their cars. Grace hugged Amber and reassured her that everything was ok. "You're mom will be here in a few minutes so you can pick up your stuff at my house tomorrow, or I'll bring it Sunday."

"What about Ms. Fran?"

"Craig will take her home in a little while."

"She was nicer today. She played tic-tac-toe with me." Amber's voice dropped to a conspiratorial whisper. "I think she likes Mr. Burke."

"Well, he's a likeable kind of guy. I have to go now. Thanks for staying with me. I had fun!" Grace waved at Amber and Melanie as she drove away with Nolan

Nolan sounded sad as he drove toward their respective homes. "What's wrong Nolan? You seem a bit down."

"I just miss days like today. I am feeling very discontent. I want what Craig and Melanie have. I want a wife, a home that is my own, and a baby to snuggle with. I want a Christmas tree and stockings on the fireplace. And, I want someone to want it with me." He looked at his companion cautiously. "Pathetic?"

"I think after our conversation earlier today, you know that I don't think it's pathetic at all. At least I have Craig, Melanie, and the baby."

"Grace, would you like to go get a cup of coffee or something? Someone should be open don't you think? I'm not ready for this day to end."

Grace nodded. "Where could we go? Who is open today?"

"I'd offer to make you some at my house but Mr. Verily would have Craig on the phone before we got the door shut!"

Laughing with Nolan at the sight of her brother on the receiving end of a call from her back-up protector, Grace wondered where Nolan was taking her. "You know what Nolan…"

Nolan finished the thought. "This isn't a good idea."

He passed a tearoom parking lot and continued home. Grace sighed. "I've always wanted to see that place. The whole idea is fascinating. A boarding house with the gatekeeper's house as a tearoom. I'd love to own it." Grace giggled. "Hey, I'd settle for *seeing* it someday and Mrs. Stafford goes to our church!"

Chapter Sixteen

"Wait!"

Nolan slammed his foot onto the brake instinctively. *"What? Are you ok?"* He was prepared for another child to fly through the air, or at the least, a cat pinned under his tire. What he wasn't prepared for was her sheepish look.

"I forgot the lists. It's too early for me to think. I was in bed before ten and I feel like I didn't get *any* sleep."

Sighing, Nolan reached for her keys and got out of the vehicle. "I'll get them. Where are they?"

He stumbled through the unfamiliar house looking for the kitchen light switch. As he flipped the light on, he saw a scurrying that unsettled him. What would Grace do if she knew that there was another critter in her house? There were definitely disadvantages to living so close to the nearby fields. He'd killed a few of the varmints in his house just the week before and he wondered what they were doing bothering them in winter. Hibernation for mice should have been a requirement in Nolan's opinion.

After another quick glance toward the pantry, and with memories of a wild woman tearing apart her kitchen, he strode back out to the car. He had no idea how to tell Grace that she had unwanted visitors. Again. If he said anything now she wouldn't leave. With a slight twinge of guilt, he hurried into his vehicle and drove to the first store.

~~~~*

"Look! Isn't it sweet? Graceanna would be so adorable in this!" One look at the price tag and Grace hung the little jumpsuit back on the rack. "I'll have to make her one."

Nolan was having the time of his life. Grace was thoroughly enjoying herself and watching the process was one of the most delightful things he'd ever experienced. "You can make something that little?"

"Oh, this age is the best. You can make beautiful outfits with very little fabric. Very inexpensive."

A deep rumbling from Nolan's belly signaled the time to call Craig and Nathan about meeting for lunch. Everyone was seated around a table at Grimsby's a short while later. As they discussed the best entrées, everyone compared notes on their respective shopping trips. Most of the items on everyone's wish lists had been found, purchased, and were ready for the big wrapping party later.

As they strolled outside after the meal, Nolan handed Grace his keys. "Why don't you go ahead and start the car, I need to ask Craig something."

Grace took the keys and joined the other women and Nathan on the way to their respective vehicles. Before she was out of earshot, Nolan told Craig about the mouse. "What should we do? You know she'll flip if she sees another mouse in there. The last one was almost too much for me."

He heard the familiar 'beep beep' of his automatic car locking and alarm system followed by the starting of his vehicle's engine. Before he knew what was happening, Grace tore out of the parking lot and sped toward home. "Craig! She'll kill herself driving like that."

Craig was already jogging to his car. "Come on Burke, we'll go help. She'll be half done by the time that we get there but..."

"But what?" Nolan didn't like the look of alarm on Craig's face.

Before Craig could answer, Melanie came running up to them, panic-stricken. "Craig! Grace just *drove* out of here!"

Nolan looked from husband to wife, hoping that someone would enlighten him. "And your point is?"

Craig turned to Nolan with a grave face. "Grace doesn't drive Nolan."

"Well I knew she didn't have a car but-"

"There is a reason she doesn't have a car. She refuses to drive. I'll explain later but we have to go. If she gets pulled over they could arrest her. She has no license."

The scene at Graces house was beyond anyone's imagination or expectation. After hitting every red light in town, Craig pulled up to her house a full ten minutes behind her. The front door stood wide open without regard for the cold assaulting the house. All her hard work keeping out the elements was tossed out the door in the crazed search for a mouse.

Grace stood over the bathroom toilet sucking the water into a shop-vac. The kitchen was torn apart and Verily stood in the living room trying to calm her down and obviously relieved when the men arrived. Craig began explaining to Verily while Nolan went to Grace's assistance.

"Grace?" His voice was low and questioning. "What are you doing, Grace?" Nolan tried to keep his voice calm as he watched her flush the toilet and then suck the water up again in the vacuum.

"Drowning the little sucker. And don't sound so nice. You *hid* him from me!"

Nolan heard a tremor in her voice and calmly took the hose from her. He led her to the living room and indicated that she should sit before returning to the bathroom to deal with a very soggy rodent. As he carried the canister past Craig, he handed it out in jest and quipped, "Do you need this for evidence, or can I dispose of it?"

Nolan's nonchalance seemed to settle Verily's concerns and he shuffled toward home apologizing for being of so little help. Craig's fury was unleashed on Grace once their bemused friend walked away. Nolan listened to Craig's verbal assault on Grace's irrational fear of mice until he couldn't take it any longer.

"*Craig*! Stop. She's fine, she didn't hurt anyone, and she doesn't make a habit of stealing cars and assaulting mice with vacuums. Now settle down, go back to the restaurant, and get your wife. I'll sit with Grace and then we can all clean up the kitchen when you get back."

Craig seemed to calm down. He walked over to Grace and hugged her before suggesting that she go lie down for a little while. As he entered the living room and out the front door he turned to Nolan. "I am not going to pretend that I like this Burke. Something doesn't feel right."

"Is it because there is a genuine problem Craig, or is it because you feel threatened?" Nolan debated how far to take the conversation with Grace's excellent hearing just in the next room.

"She's my only sister Nolan. I'm all she has."

"And you like it that way." Nolan was treading difficult territory.

Craig sank onto the couch. "You're right. Since she was born I was taught that she was the most precious thing that God had ever given me and would ever be until God gave me a wife and I've taken that very seriously."

With a deep sigh and his voice heavy with emotion, he looked up at Nolan who sat in his chair looking uncertain as to how to handle the situation. "Too seriously huh. Lately anyway. Ever since you came into her life."

Nolan shrugged and let the man continue. He seemed compelled to talk and Nolan was more than willing to listen. "She's all grown up now and I forget that. It's a result of our upbringing. The men in our family take protecting our women very seriously. I think I went overboard after dad died trying to make up for the loss."

"It's possible. I bet she feels loved though. Every woman needs that."

Craig stood. "I have to go get Mel. Thanks for understanding."

Nolan began cleaning the kitchen in a slight state of shock. For the first time he and Craig had discussed Grace without Nolan feeling like a masher. Whistling as he scrubbed down shelves the spirit of the day took over and soon he was singing his own rendition of *Santa Claus is Coming to Town.*

"You better watch out
Or you're gonna die
You better watch out
I'm telling you why
Gracie's gonna see that you drown.
She's losing her cool
To stay you're a fool
Better get out
Before a cat drools
Gracie's gonna see that you drown.
She see's when you are sneaking
She don't think you're so great
She thinks that you are bad, not good
So get out for goodness sake

You better watch out
Or you're gonna die
You better watch out
I'm telling you why
Gracie's gonna see that you drooooownnnnn"

A muffled giggle brought Nolan out of his musical reverie. He stood in the middle of the kitchen with a broom for a mic and stand. To Grace, he sounded like a combination of Frank Sinatra and Vic Dana. In his opinion, he looked like a fool. Grace's applause rang through out the kitchen, and Nolan blushed.

"I'm calm now. I'd like to help clean up before everyone gets back here." Grace seemed subdued.

"Craig said he was taking them home."

"He forgot that we're wrapping here. I have all the paper!"

They worked in companionable silence. Nolan spent much of his energy trying hard not to laugh at the lengths that she went to avoid the vermin ever touching her food or dishes. She wrapped entire bundles of dishes at the back of her cupboards with Saran Wrap and zip lock bagged her trash bags. Before Nolan could poke fun at her, the rest of the group came hustling in from the cold.

"Come on Grace; it's after two. You ready to go get the trees? It's our first year with two trees!" Melanie's excitement was contagious.

Grace looked uncertainly at her kitchen. Was she ready to chance that she'd missed some area that the mouse had roamed? Or did she just not want to leave while she and Nolan were enjoying themselves? Nolan watched her struggle and couldn't take it anymore. Bending low, he whispered into her ear. "It's time to let this rest. You can deal with it tomorrow if you need to."

The move appeared quite intimate and personal to the onlookers but Grace and Nolan were oblivious to the scrutiny. Craig struggled against his fears while Melanie mentally began practicing the wedding march. Paige simply sighed. Nathan looked around at the group with an expression of comical inquiry. "Did I miss something? Aren't we going to find trees? You know those tall green things that you loop with lights and popcorn and load with ornaments and presents until the thing finally becomes a fire hazard and you cut it up and burn it?"

The group became 'guys against girls' as they piled into segregated cars and caravanned to the Christmas tree farm. The men planned their strategy while the women discussed how to thwart the men's tendency to grab the first tree and run. In the end, the result was stereotypical. The men agreed to every tree suggested, and the women found great delight in suggesting almost every tree.

Melanie found her tree first. The tree was wide enough to fill the picture window in her dining room. Craig pretended to grouse about having to move around the furniture and things, but it was readily apparent that he was as excited as she was. Grace deliberated between two trees until the decision made her head ache. Seeing her hesitation, Paige mentioned that she'd like the smaller of the two if Grace decided against it. Grace immediately chose the taller tree and motioned for the owner of the farm to come chop the trees down.

As the man began to saw the tree, Grace turned and fled. Her friends looked at each other in bewilderment. Shrugging his shoulders, Craig started to follow Grace but Nolan stopped him. "May I? Somehow I think I can get her to talk."

Grace was silently weeping in the back seat of Paige's sedan. Seeing Nolan enter on the other side, she quickly tried to hide the evidence of her distress. Nolan brushed away one last tear clinging to the corner of her eye with the back of his hand. "Want to talk about it?"

Blushing, Grace shook her head. Nolan tried a new approach. "Feel up to twenty questions? Nod or shake your head appropriately?"

With a sportive grin, Grace nodded. Laughing, Nolan began firing questions at her. "Are you too tired to mess with the tree?" Grace shook her head.

"Is it because it's the first time to have your own tree?" Another shake.

"Are trees too expensive this year?" Nolan knew the tree wasn't the issue but continued to discuss shopping and trees and decorations for a time.

"Does it have to do with driving my car this morning?" Nolan was risking a lot to bring the subject up, but he knew that this was likely the problem. If Grace didn't drive, and yet it was obvious that she knew how to drive, there was likely a reason that she didn't if Craig and Melanie had made such an issue of it.

"Oh Nolan, I could have destroyed your beautiful car. It wasn't even legal!" Grace's tears began to flow again.

"Grace… I wouldn't' care about that even if you had. We were concerned about you, not the stupid car. Craig said that you don't drive. Will you tell me about it?"

Grace took a deep breath. The tears wouldn't stop flowing. Without realizing what he was doing, Nolan gathered Grace into his arms and began silently praying as he wiped her tears away and made comforting sounds as if she was a child. "It'll be ok Grace. You're safe. I'm safe. Craig and his little family are safe. No one got hurt but a scurvy little mouse."

Nolan smiled at the sound of a weak giggle. Grace sat up, straightened her sweater, wiped her eyes, and looked into his troubled eyes. "Nolan. I haven't driven since I was sixteen years old. I can't believe I remembered how!"

"Why don't you drive? You couldn't have had your license for long,"

"I had it for half a year. We went down and I took the test the day after my birthday. I was so excited about it. Then, six months later, mom and I went to Rockland to do some Christmas shopping. Mom was tired when we got done so I begged to drive home. I wasn't used to freeways and things but mom let me drive anyway…"

"Oh Grace." Nolan took her hands. He knew what she was going to say before she could finish the story. He'd read similar stories in the Rockland Gazette for years. The Woodland Park Bridge had been covered with black ice. A car in front of her braked and Grace slammed hard on her brakes sending them into a skid from which she couldn't regain control.

"She didn't suffer. They told me she died instantly. I was in the hospital over Christmas that year. I'll never forget the look of shock and concern that came over her face as she woke up when I hit the brakes. She was more worried for me than the fact she was being thrown at a light pole at sixty miles per hour."

"She loved you Grace. It's what a mother does."

They sat in silence for a while. Nolan noticed that the group all stood near the car wanting very much to know that all was well but Nolan wouldn't budge. Grace had fears to deal with and stuffing them back into a little corner of herself wouldn't be healthy.

"Grace. When did you quit driving?" The question was a precarious one.

"Well. I did try to drive to school in January that year. I was fine until Paige asked for a ride home. They said that I just sat with my hands frozen to the wheel. I wouldn't budge. They had to call the paramedics to come and get me out. Dad always thought that once I had a break- was a little older and more mature, that I'd feel more comfortable driving but I just..."

Nodding, Nolan wiped the last traces of tears from her eyes. "You didn't trust yourself. You were fine driving *you* somewhere, but when it came to someone you loved..."

"You understand. Most people don't."

"I also understand that it isn't healthy for you to let this fear overcome you. It is very likely that if your mother had been driving, that you would have died instead. It was one of those things that only the Lord can understand right now."

Grace nodded slowly. She knew Nolan was right. Craig had pushed her for years to 'get over it' but somehow, Nolan's words seemed to hit home more truly. "Well. I do think you're probably right. I've prayed strength from time to time, but I know it wasn't truly genuine. I just wanted to 'do my duty so that I could say that I had been praying about it."

"Well, we all do that but it doesn't do us much good in the long run does it? Amazing to think of all the trouble that one little mouse has caused isn't it?"

"And that mouse isn't the only one in trouble. I can't believe you didn't tell me about it."

"Well, you are a little over the top when it comes to mice and we had a lovely morning planned..."

"I know I'm afraid of mice Nolan Burke. They're nasty little creatures that love to jump out when you least expect them but letting them roam about my kitchen just for a shopping trip..."

"I'm sorry. I didn't realize that it was just a shopping trip. I thought it was a time for you to do something with friends and your family. I thought it was about people and relationships. I guess I should have told you. You could have cleaned your spotless kitchen and I could have done your shopping for you."

Her expression grew cold and she leaned away from him reaching for the door. "Nice Nolan. Very nice. You have a talent for sarcasm. I'd love to spar with you on this but I have a tree that I really can't afford, to pay for and add to the rest of today's guilt pile. Excuse me."

Feeling guilty, Nolan urged, "Let me buy the tree for you Grace. I'd love to."

Grace shook her head emphatically. "I think not. If I want a tree, I can certainly afford to buy one. Spending this much money in one day always makes me a bit nervous but I'll be ok. I'm going to go take care of it, but thanks anyway."

Nolan knew he'd been forthright; however, her reaction was much stronger than he'd anticipated and immediately, he realized he'd pushed a wrong button somewhere. Hurrying back to where the group stood, he overheard her forced laughter and joking. She made a few self-deprecating remarks about her silliness and with apparent glee, marched off to pay for her tree while the men loaded it on to Craig and Mel's mini van. Nolan's mind worked silently as he wondered how to handle the situation.

Just as he'd decided to discuss the problem with Craig, Nolan spotted a little tree a few yards away. Barely over three feet tall, it looked perfect for the top of his coffee table. He hadn't planned to purchase a tree; he had no decorations, but the idea warmed him and he quickly decided to jump into the holiday spirit with both feet.

~~~~*

"Craig, I need to talk to Grace alone- sounds like a sermon by Luther doesn't it? Do you think you can keep everyone from bothering us for a few? I may need back up. Grace is being very stubborn about her money situation and I'm going to confront it now or it'll always hang over us."

Craig knew what Nolan was up against. He'd spoken to his sister time and again about laying down her pride, but to no avail. The idea of Nolan succeeding where he'd failed left a bad taste into his mouth but he knew it was only his own pride talking. The Buschers came from a long line of people who spent much of their lives fighting what his father called 'the chief of sins'.

Nolan asked Grace to help him set up his tree on the table in his living room while the others argued over the proper angle of the tree in its base. "They'll be there for hours, you willing to have mercy and help me?"

As they wrestled with the clumsy, too small, tree stand, they laughed and joked as if no uncomfortable words had passed between them. "Grace, I have to admit, I asked you to help me because I think we need to talk."

Grace looked up at him and tried to read his expression. "What about?"

"The conversation we had at the tree farm."

Grace stood, ready to walk back home. "I am not going to-"

"Stop being stubborn Grace. You are allowing your pride to override your common sense. Please listen to me for a few minutes."

Grace wanted to run. Instinctively, she knew that she was being unreasonable but with all of the opposition that she'd faced for her experiment, the last thing she wanted was proof for the nay-sayers. She sat down in Nolan's most comfortable chair and prepared to hear the worst. "Go ahead. I'm listening."

Not knowing where to sit, not wanting to seem to distance himself, Nolan finally sat at her feet Indian style. "Grace. As Christians, we are called to serve one another. You've read the scriptures; I don't need to give you book, chapter, and verse. You know that we are called to do this. Hypocrisy comes to mind Grace. You want the privilege of serving but deny others the ability to serve you, and it's wrong." Through great control, Nolan appeared to be outwardly calm; inside, his irritation was becoming difficult to control. He was not used to dealing with women, generally he avoided them, and at present, he was reminded of why.

Grace seemed to crumple for a moment. An expression of triumph lit his eyes and he quickly masked it, but not so quickly that it missed Grace's detection. Her chin drew up as she stood. "I'll consider what you've said. I think you'd be wise to remember that I am not your personal charity case."

Grace turned to leave the house but Nolan stepped in front of the doorway. Not amused, Grace stood facing him with arms folded across her chest. "Grace. This isn't about me wanting to be right. This is about me caring enough about a dear friend to speak the truth in love. 'Faithful are the wounds of a friend, but the kisses of an enemy are deceitful.' Proverbs something, something else."

As Grace considered the wounds her friend had inflicted, Nolan was briefly distracted at the idea of kisses. All kisses weren't considered of the enemy and his certainly wouldn't be deceitful. Grace's swift hug brought him back from his musings and she walked home alone.

"What was that about?" He chuckled as he realized how often he was talking to himself these days. His intriguing friend was rubbing off on him in many ways.

An hour later while Grace and Paige threaded popcorn and cranberries at a marathon pace, the men argued about the proper placement of lights. Nolan's frustration was slowly dissipating. Grace didn't act upset at him, and the family seemed oblivious to the previous tension. Just as he completely relaxed and fully entered into the festivities, Rolex entered the scene yapping and tearing among the boxes, playing tug of war with anything he could get into his miniscule snout.

"Grab him Grace! He's going to ruin something." Melanie's cry of distress woke the baby.

As Grace jumped about trying to grab Rolex, Nolan picked up an exquisite hand-blown glass star and carefully fastened it to the top of the tree. Seeing the lights dance about the base of the star gave him an idea. While the rest of the crew tried to save ornaments from imminent destruction, Nolan found a short string of all white lights and nestled them all into the base of the star. The effect was breathtaking. Light appeared to radiate from the tree-topper.

As Nolan stood back to admire the effect, a wail of frustration came from the kitchen. "Rolex got the angel! What will we do? I-"

The room grew quiet. The measured ticking of Grace's Grandfather clock mingled with the low tones of cheerful Christmas carols. All other sounds ceased as the group stared in disbelief at the top of Grace's tree. Nathan and Nolan looked at each other in bewilderment. The effect was breathtaking but it wasn't worthy of all of the attention.

Nathan finally broke the silence after a moment's pause. "Did I miss something?"

Grace picked up Rolex and left the room. Craig sat in the nearest chair and watched the play of lights on the star. Melanie looked around and took it upon herself to explain. "That star has been absent from the tree for a long time. Mr. and Mrs. Buscher bought it on their honeymoon. Grace bought an angel the year after Mom Buscher died because none of them could look at the tree without seeing her there placing it at the top and fiddling with the lights, just as you have done. From the way that Craig has described it, I think you've managed to make it look as good as she used to, and none of them have been able to accomplish that."

Concern shrouded Nolan's face. "Should I remove it? I had no idea…"

Craig shook his head. "No. It's time. It's a perfect year too with baby Gracie and all. I'm glad you did it. If you'd known, you wouldn't have and we would have continued to be held captive in the past. We only meant to not use it that first year, and then it was just too comfortable to avoid the pain."

Grace returned minus the critter and singing with the CD, began placing the cranberry-popcorn strings on the tree. With less jocularity than previously displayed, everyone enjoyed trimming the tree while singing 'Silent Night'. In grand Buscher tradition, the boxes were quickly stowed away and the lights dimmed in order for the tree to be admired properly.

The moment passed too quickly and with a little hop of anticipation, Grace shouted, "Presents!" and gleefully began rummaging through the hall closet for her box of gift-wrapping supplies.

New wrapping paper and bows were produced by a few of the shoppers and each person carefully separated their gifts that could be wrapped in the room, and which ones needed to be secreted into another room for wrapping. "There are different sized boxes in my coat closet. Just help yourself! I added some bags of beans, wood pieces, and a few rocks if you want to add weight to anything!"

Paper crackled and ribbon was curled as a wrapping frenzy began. Graceanna cooed and kicked from her infant seat at the sights around her. Paige noted the different way that everyone wrapped presents, especially Nolan and Nathan. Nathan took scissors and whacked off a piece of paper no matter what the size and if it wouldn't work one way, he'd find another. Nolan was methodical and precise with no ornamentation. His packages looked like they had been wrapped by a professional wrapper but the packages were sterile and void of all trimming.

Everyone dug through bags for their next item and wrapped amid songs and jokes. Occasionally someone would stand, grab wrapping paper, a roll of ribbon, and a spool of tape and dash into another room to wrap. The pile of gifts grew both under the tree and by their owners.

Paige was a whirlwind. Her business as a personal shopper ensured that she had more packages than everyone in the room combined. The deft way that she would wrap, tie, ribbon, bow, and label before going onto the next item amazed everyone including those who had previously watched her.

"Look at this. Do you think this guy's wife will like it? I was told to get the largest sapphire that I could find surrounded by a gaudy group of diamonds. Think this cuts it?" Paige looked disgustedly at the very large display of gemstones.

"Eeeeewwwwwww! Is that for real? Why would anyone want something that *huge* and for a ring? That'd be better as a pendant." Grace paused a moment and then whispered. "Well... the operative word there is *better*."

The group howled. Grace flipped through Paige's pile of gifts and found another jewelers box. "Is this one as bad?"

Paige's face lit up. "No! That one- oh my! I got a call from a man who had a huge business loss this year. He has a tradition of buying a new piece of jewelry for his wife every year at Christmas but this year he just couldn't go shopping. He said it was too painful to look when the things that he wanted the most, he couldn't afford. He gave me two hundred dollars and asked me to do my best. I found this for one seventy-five."

Paige opened the box and revealed an exquisite emerald flanked by two diamonds on a pendant. There was no chain but Paige explained that she was certain that the woman would have enough chains that could be used, and her husband could buy her another one later after they were financially back on their feet.

Grace fingered the trinket in its box. "Isn't it gorgeous? Look how the light catches that emerald and makes it look like the center is glowing. I never knew stones could be so pretty!"

Paige wrapped the jeweler's box inside a sweater box and laid plain white flannel around it to muffle any shifting sounds and to add weight. "She'll think she's not going to get one this year. I hope

Mr. Axell doesn't mind. He can rewrap if he does. I just thought it would be a nice surprise for both of them."

Grace brought out hot chocolate and chocolate dinner mints on a tray along with puffed rice treats and encouraged everyone to take a break. Nathan watched as Paige recorded each purchase and wrapping in her organizer and Nolan watched Grace. None of them were aware of the way that Craig and Melanie looked on the entire group with a parental eye. Little personality quirks were noted with elbow jabs and raised eyebrows.

At the end of the evening, bright and beautifully wrapped packages sat in the back seats of Nathan's car as he and Paige drove away, while Grace helped Nolan to carry the few packages that he had to bring home. "Ok Nolan. I see that there isn't a single package here to 'Grace'. Having trouble choosing, or do you have something hidden at home? Come on, you can tell me!"

She sounded almost giddy with excitement. Nolan looked at her in surprised amusement. "Too prideful to let me buy you a Christmas tree but you want to know where your Christmas present is?" he teased.

Grace's laughter rang down the street, into Verily's living room and warmed the elderly man's heart. "I am an enigma Nolan Burke! I love presents and surprises- the anticipation- and I am extremely obnoxious about trying to find out what you've gotten me. Ask Craig."

Nolan's expression gave him away. "You do have something for me! Come on. What is it?"

They bantered back and forth for a while until Nolan threw up his hands and said, "I give up! I'll never get a moments rest. I got you a mouse. Are you satisfied?"

Grace arranged the packages under Nolan's little tree and with a little wave dashed back across the street and into the warmth of her own home. Her giggle told him that she hadn't believed his assertion of a forth-coming rodent. Reaching one hand into his pocket, he pulled out a little charm from its wrapping. In his palm lay a silver charm of a comical little mouse running up a clock reminiscent of the children's nursery rhyme.

"I hope you like him Grace. I hope this little mousie is one you'll let live in your house," he murmured to himself as he watched Grace slip inside her house and sweep up her little niece in her arms.

From his vantage point, he could see her pointing out packages and imagined Grace telling the baby all about each one.

Chapter Seventeen

As Nolan pulled into his driveway, Grace hurried across the street. "Do you need help?"

"London, Mickey, this is my friend Grace." He smiled at her as he unbuckled Parker from his car seat. "And this is Parker! Guys, this is Miss..."

"Grace. I'm Miss Grace. We're making personal pizzas for dinner. Who wants to help me put toppings on?"

By the time Mike and Traci arrived to take their children 'home' to Nolan's, Grace had established a genuine friendship with all of them. London whined and wailed when her mother told her to put away the game they'd been playing and Traci's eyes widened in shock as Grace stopped the tantrum with a single shocked word, "London!"

"Sorry Miss Grace," the child apologized, chagrined.

"Don't apologize to me. Your mother deserves the apology."

To Nolan's surprise, Grace turned away from the child and helped gather jackets and shoes for Mike. London paused by Grace as her mother led her and Mickey out the door. "Are you mad at me Miss Grace?"

"I'm disappointed in you but you'll obey better next time."

"Grace, do you want to come have hot chocolate with us?" Nolan prayed she'd join them.

"I'd love to Nolan, but I'm exhausted. Why don't you all come over for breakfast? I have muffins made and I can scramble some eggs and cook some sausage."

Nolan scooped Parker up and carried him to the door. "Thanks for helping me."

"I enjoyed them. Thanks for sharing."

Traci watched the exchange with a fascinated eye. Grace was genuinely happy to have spent the evening with her children. Even she wasn't always happy for an evening with her own children. Instantly, she saw some of the attraction Nolan felt for the woman. "It was nice to meet you Grace. I'll see you in the morning and thanks for everything."

Once the children were snuggled in beds and Parker in his pack 'n' play, Traci curled up in Nolan's most comfortable chair, crossed her arms, and demanded, "Out with it."

"With what?" Mike and Nolan spoke in unison.

"She's a nice woman Nolan. She's not bad looking but she's definitely got a few pounds on her-"

Nolan's voice cooled considerably. "And your point is?"

"I'm curious to know why you chose the antithesis of every woman who has ever thrown herself at you. I'm worried that you've come here, found the opposite of what you could have had and decided it's better by the mere fact of its difference."

"That's ridiculous Traci! I've never heard you be so shallow-" Mike began.

"No, she has a point," Nolan countered. "I see why it might look like that. I wondered it myself."

"I think you're both brutal," Mike spat out disgusted at the turn of conversation.

"Look, I've been looking for a list," Nolan began as he walked to his computer and called up a file. He clicked the print button and waited for the paper to drop in the tray. "I started this list over two years ago- more like three and a half. Hadley Parkman proposed to me that night and I came home desperate for a wife that I could actually pursue first." He passed the paper to Traci. "Tell me which of those you think Grace doesn't fill?"

Traci waved the paper back at him. "I'd say all and then more that you should have put on there but Nolan, why did you happen to find the one woman who has these qualities and is so far removed-"

"That's enough." Nolan's voice was low and firm. He didn't like speaking to a woman, particularly another man's wife, with such an authoritative tone but he'd taken all the assaults on Grace that he could handle. "Where you see her size, I see her. Where you see her poverty, I see her generosity. I can't stand to hear you criticize someone you just don't understand."

A slow smile spread over Traci's face. "Now *that* is what I wanted to see or hear. I was afraid I'd turned you into a clinical monster when I pushed you to go where the most eligible females lived."

"I went straight for the most beautiful girl I think I've ever met. And she was all wrong for me. You'll know her immediately tomorrow."

"Not to change the subject or anything," Mike began, "but I'm afraid that if I don't ask now, I won't remember. How did Grace get that kind of response out of London?"

"That was amazing!"

"Grace doesn't tolerate it."

"Well neither do I but-"

Nolan's head shook as Traci spoke. "I know it sounds crazy but I'm telling you, Grace doesn't tolerate it so it doesn't happen. At first, I couldn't get any kind of reasonable response out of 'her kids'," Nolan made air quotes as he spoke, "when they were out of line but once I saw the difference, I got it. It was an option. I didn't think it was, but it was. I still expected them to act up so they did. When I quit expecting it and knew in my heart that I'd never tolerate it again, they quit."

"What happens if they try to see if you're serious," Mike demanded curiously. He'd been trying to gain control over his household since the day Michael Jr. was born.

"Well, they didn't try with me. I thought they would actually but Grace says she's noticed that kids don't try as much with men as they do with women. I guess they think women are pushovers."

Traci stood and refilled her cup. "So what would Grace do?"

"Depends on the situation. I asked once and she said it all boils down to making it not worth doing. Making whatever they do that is wrong more uncomfortable than just doing the right thing. The kids she babysits actually know that she'll call their mothers to come get them if they don't obey her, and some of them have mothers who travel out of state. They'll come right home, walk out of a business meeting, lose their job if necessary, because Grace says, 'come get your child.' The kids know it and they're not willing to go home to a mom that just had to do that so they obey." He paused. "But it's not just that. She likes them. She really likes who they are as little people and I think the children sense that and *want* to please her."

"I can't say I always like my kids," Traci whispered. "I love them but-"

"I know what you mean," Mike agreed. "You love them to pieces but sometimes you want to love them from a little bit afar."

"Bedtime bliss?" Nolan asked smiling. He'd heard them refer to the term often.

"Isn't that sad," Traci asked shamed. "Isn't it sad that I actually count the minutes until bedtime some days- sometimes from before lunch!"

"Think Grace could help?" Mike asked a little desperately.

"Can't hurt to ask."

~~~~*

After breakfast, Nolan took Traci across the street to show her where to find towels, soap, and sundries for the children's baths. Mike sat at her table watching Grace work and wondering how to broach the subject of his children. "I am still amazed at how you stopped London's melt down last night. Usually that would have been a twenty-minute nightmare."

"It was a simple attempt at a tantrum and she knew they aren't allowed at my house."

"How?"

Grace glanced across the kitchen. "How what?"

"How did she know they aren't allowed in your house?"

"She got upset when we started to play a different game and I told her so."

"You just said," Mike began incredulously, "'Sorry kid, no tantrums allowed,' and she stopped?"

"Close." Grace's smile disarmed him. "She wailed and I told her to hush. I said 'There is no whining allowed in my house. If you're going to misbehave, I'll have to tell Nolan to take you back to his house but it wont' do you much good. Tantrums aren't allowed there either.'"

"What'd she do?"

"She gave me a very endearing but challenging glare and told me in no uncertain terms that they *were* allowed in her house at home."

"You're kidding!"

With a slow shake of the head, Grace continued. "I think she needs someone to take the reigns of control back. She doesn't know how to keep the galloping emotions from running wild but you as the parent do."

"But we don't. We obviously don't. The melt-"

Grace shook her head. "These aren't meltdowns. These are tantrums. They are fully capable of controlling themselves they just choose not to."

Mike had the grace to blush. "Tantrum sounds so much worse-"

"Which is why you need to use it. If she were truly incapable of controlling herself, it'd be a good time to say so. She'd learn to differentiate between something out of her control and something she can control. Right now, she thinks that control is about how she uses her emotions to manipulate those around her. When it didn't work, she quit trying."

Shaking his head, Mike reminded her that she had tried again. "So what's the use if it only works for a little while?"

"But it didn't just work for a little while. You came back and she needed to see if the rules changed. I showed her that they didn't."

"How did you learn so much about children?" Mike asked amazed.

"I didn't. I learned about people. You have a business right?"

He nodded, curious as to where this was going. "Market analysis."

"So that means you have employees."

"Yes."

Grace grinned. "How often do they come in late?"

"They don't. Almost ever."

"Why not?"

Mike shrugged. "I don't allow it. If you work for me, you're on time or you're out. I pay my people well and expect integrity and hard work in return."

"It's the same thing with a child. They know what is expected and they give it. Consequences result when they fail."

"I can't fire my kids!"

"Well then," Grace challenged, "Perhaps your employees need a break. Maybe you need to make them eat lunch in their office if they're late or write a note of apology to everyone if they speak rudely."

"That's not much of a deterrent."

"My point exactly. Working for you is a privilege. It's an area of mutual respect but you are clearly the boss. You write the checks they do the work. If they don't do the work, you fire them and hire someone who will and they know it. Why treat children like you're just appeasing their desire to do a hostile takeover of the company, er, family? Why not admit that you're the CEO of the family, they're the 'employees' and there are rules they must follow or they'll face the consequences." She grinned. "No, I don't mean firing them but they are out of fellowship with their authority."

"I hate that word."

"Why? You are their authority. God placed you there. You can abdicate all you want but you're still responsible for your position as their authority."

"I guess I get tired," he confessed. "I hate constantly being in charge. Sometimes I just want someone to tell *me* what to do."

"Read your Bible lately?"

"Touche."

~~~~*

As Mike and Traci loaded their car, Traci pulled Nolan aside, hugged him, and looked seriously into his eyes. "She's a gem. She's wonderful. Don't hesitate, don't over think things. Pray about it, and then do it."

"Do you think I'm ready?"

"Take a day, go hiking, take a million pictures, come home, and ask yourself one question."

Nolan furrowed his brow wondering what that question could possibly be. "What?"

"How many times today did you wish she was there with you?"

The minivan turned the corner and drove out of sight but Nolan still stood in his driveway, Traci's words ringing through his ears. He knew the answer without leaving. "Too many to count."

Chapter Eighteen

December

"Grace? Come over here *now*. Please!" Paige's terrified voice burst over the telephone line.

"Paige! What is wrong?" Grace, alarmed by Paige's frantic and fearful tones, began looking for her purse and pulled on her jacket.

"That man- the one they've been trying to catch. You know- the ra-." Paige swallowed the word as though unable to speak it. "He came in and tried to attack me."

"Don't move. Call 9-1-1 and then hang up and don't move. Don't touch anything, don't go anywhere, and don't answer the door. Is it locked?"

"No. After he ran out I just grabbed the phone and called."

Grace insisted that Paige lock the door and then stand right next to it as she dialed for the police. "Don't walk around anymore than you have to. Maybe they can get a shoe print or a hair or something like they do in those TV shows. Who knows? I'll be *right there*. Does my key still work?"

Clicking off the phone, Grace dashed out of the house and ran to Verily's house. Moments later, they sped toward Paige's apartment. Grace mulled over the situation as her confused neighbor navigated the streets to get Grace to her desired destination. This was unusual. The attacker had previously attacked family neighborhoods. He seemed to stalk homemakers who were alone all day, not single women in apartments.

Halfway there it dawned on her that she didn't know if Paige had been hurt. Steeling herself for the worst, she spent the next few blocks begging the Lord for the right words to say and the wisdom not to speak when she shouldn't. "Grace, that's like asking Rolex to avoid the food in front of him if he's not really hungry."

"What Gracie honey?"

Verily's deep southern drawl soothed Grace's nerves. She explained that she was just concerned about Paige and promised to let Verily know why the woman had insisted that she come over later. Grace had decided not to share the information until Paige gave her permission to.

An officer pulled into the parking lot of Paige's apartment complex as Grace knocked on the door. "Paige, I'm coming in. Just wanted to warn you."

The door flung wide open and a disheveled and injured Paige threw herself into Grace's arms and sobbed. An officer raced up the stairs two at a time with his partner close behind him. "Is she alone? Is she safe? How long since the attacker left?"

Paige shook her head and told the officer what time the man had run off. She gave them a good description of the intruder and Grace sagged in relief when she heard that the man hadn't been able to do more than scratch her and bruise her shin. "I don't know what happened but I just kind of went nuts when he pushed in here. I kicked him and screamed and I don't know what all. I amazed myself! I am so mad at that guy I could tear his eyes out! He's such a small weasel of a man too! I can't figure out how he overpowered anyone!"

Later that evening, Grace recounted the story to Craig, Melanie, and Nolan. "They're 'processing' her now. They wouldn't let me stay since I'm not family so her mother is coming in from the city. I don't' know what happened but she kicked him in the face and a piece of his tooth was left on the coffee table with some blood so if they find the guy, they've got cosmetic evidence now and something about DNA. That's what they called it. I would have expected something more descriptive or scientific." Grace sounded disappointed.

"Maybe they just used that term so you'd understand what they meant." Nolan meant to tease but Grace nodded wisely.

"That's probably it. Anyway, she said, 'He looked a little familiar but I am not sure why.' Where do you think she saw him?"

No one could think of where she could have met the man. Paige didn't have much of a social life and none of them wanted to think that the culprit could be any of her clients or anyone from church. "Does anyone know where she lives? Her clients I mean, do they know?"

Craig looked with concern at his sister. Grace was creating columns on a notepad and organizing her thoughts. It was a habit begun in grade school by an exacting teacher, but it served her well at times like this. Years of reading her assignments from across the table and Craig had perfected the art of reading upside down. There was one column for church, one for business associates, one for the women who had been attacked, and one for commonalities.

Rolex tried to climb her leg and settle into her lap but Grace didn't seem to notice. Melanie took pity on the whimpering puppy and asked for Craig's opinion of the situation as she picked up the fur ball. "Where could this guy have gotten her address? Everyone in Paige's complex works all day. There isn't even an older neighbor home watching the comings and goings like Grace has here with Mr. Wirth."

"Or me. I have to admit that I've held more teleconferences since hearing that the lunatic was on the loose." Grace smiled at Nolan's admission. She knew that Nolan had been around more lately but had attributed it to the upcoming holiday season. She rightly assumed that January would bring a flurry of activity from her neighbor's house.

They all sat, talked and prayed as they waited for word from Paige that she had been released. It appeared to all that Grace was determined to discover where this guy picked his victims. Eventually Nolan went home to do some work and Craig and Melanie left soon afterward. As he pulled the front door shut, Craig looked into Grace's determined eyes. "Grace. Don't do anything stupid. You aren't a young Miss Marple. Call us when you hear anything and, we love you."

Grace went back to her columns. Church was a definite possibility and Paige did say that there was something familiar about him. "I wonder if he's some kind of repair man. That would make sense. Don't forget to ask Paige if she's had anything fixed lately."

She was still muttering ideas to herself and making notes when Paige arrived on her doorstep, duffle bag in hand and ready to spend the night. "I'm just not ready to sleep in that apartment. There is that dust stuff they used everywhere and it's still a wreck. My apartment manager's wife does housecleaning for a living. She's going to call me when it's clean again. I'm glad I got all of those packages sent off and delivered yesterday. Nathan had the morning off so he helped. I should have called him but-"

Allowing her to ramble from topic to topic, Grace hustled Paige into a guest room and helped her hang her clothes. She hung a warm pair of wool slacks with a marvelous cashmere sweater. "This is beautiful. Going somewhere special?"

"No, I just wanted something that made me feel nice, so mom stopped and bought it for me." Paige fingered the soft and warm outfit.

"I don't' want you to think you're not welcome but, is there any reason that you didn't go home with your mom?"

"You know mom. She's been a psychologist for so long that she'd have my head examined, labeled, and stuck on her trophy shelf inside forty-five minutes. I want to talk about it when I want to talk about it and only when I want to talk about it."

Grace howled. "And you came *here*? You know I'm dying to ask five thousand questions."

"But you won't make me answer if I don't want to, and you're interested in facts, not how I feel about the facts. That's the difference."

Grace noticed something in Paige that she'd never seen before. There was a confidence that her friend rarely showed. As Grace listened to Paige recount the ordeal at the police station, she shuddered. "Did you ever figure out what was different about his mustache?"

Paige shook her head. "Nope. But they think they did. The police sketch artist said that he thinks it was fake. They drew a few faces without it and they still look familiar but I still couldn't tell them where I'd seen him."

In a scholarly somber tone, Grace suggested. "Perhaps it is a physical manifestation of your reluctance to deal directly with the situation. When you properly investigate your true feelings about the situation, your resistance to remembrance will be swiftly overcome resulting in the ability to identify your perpetrator."

The women giggled. Grace had an uncanny knack for imitating Paige's overly serious mother. It always brought a smile to Paige's face when she was upset. "Hey, let's get you some dinner! I bet you're famished."

~~~~*

With a wave goodbye, and a thick notebook, Grace rushed from the house the next morning just as Paige emerged from her room. "I'll catch you in a bit Paige; I'm going to go check some things out."

At the library, Grace scrolled through page after page of newspaper articles on the recent attacks in the area. She filled in every detail that she could find on her chart and compared notes. The information wasn't very helpful. What she wanted to learn was if five out of eight victims had recently had the gas turned on to their furnaces or four out of eight received support from their churches after the attack. How many victims were not members of a church at all? However, the papers didn't give out that kind of helpful information.

Grace added new columns. Where did the women shop for groceries, department stores, did they attend lectures or plays? Frustration mounted. "Grace. Stop being frustrated and go look around Paige's complex. There's probably nothing there but it can't hurt to look."

With the tenacity that only comes from the vigilant pursuit of mice, Grace combed the parking lot, shrubs, and walk ways of the entire complex where Paige lived. "I don't know *what* you expect to find Gracie girl!" she sneered at herself.

Looking around at what appeared to be a sea of concrete and asphalt, Grace began walking up and down the sidewalks in the immediate vicinity. "Grace, you're even thinking like an officer now! Vicinity! That's-"

Grace got down on all fours to look closely at the object on the sidewalk. The absurdity of the situation struck her as hilarious. "How am I supposed to pick this thing up without damaging some kind of weird evidence that the police could get these days?"

Grace struggled back to her feet and brushed off her knees, noting the runs in her tights. "Expensive hobby Grace. Not smart."

Finally, in sheer frustration, Grace took out a felt tipped pen and created an outline of the fake mustache on the sidewalk, picked it up with a tissue, and carefully tucked it into her purse. She practically ran all the way to the police department. She was not prepared for the reaction that followed.

"Lady, do you know that your actions could be considered interfering with a police investigation? You have likely destroyed any evidence on this."

Grace looked at the unfriendly officer and sighed. She turned to leave but an officer at another desk stopped her. "Grace! Hey! Remember me?"

Grace's smile was warm and genuine. "Todd Mercer. It's good to see you again. It's been a while."

Grace explained to Todd why she was there and what the other officer had told her. "Well, Grace, that's not true. You weren't on a crime scene, you haven't interviewed any witnesses, and there is nothing wrong with bringing evidence down here. I'll talk to him. Joe's just mad that we haven't caught this guy. He's taking it out on all of us."

"I didn't want to move it. I tried to figure out how to call you guys but I didn't have a cell phone. I didn't touch it. I used a tissue..."

Todd walked her to her car talking casually about the case and how Grace was connected. He remembered their school days and how kind Grace had always been to him. While the other nice girls skirted around the Todd's mini gang of troublemakers, Grace had treated them all the same as everyone else. She smiled if eye contact was made and invited them to the church parties she attended faithfully.

"I never thanked you Grace. I should have." Todd's voice betrayed emotions he worked hard to hide these days. The rowdy boy who acted out to gain attention was gone. He was a respected member of the community now. He lived on 'the right side of the tracks' so to speak.

"Thank me for what?" Grace's genuine bewilderment showed him that some things don't change. Grace was still the modest person she'd always been.

"Just how you always treated me like everyone else. You were the only one outside the guys who did that."

Grace thought for a moment. "I don't want to cheapen your gratitude but honestly Todd, I didn't try..."

"That's my point Grace. Everyone else either pretended to be nice if they thought they needed to do their good deed for the day, or they completely ignored my existence, or worse." His voice still held traces of the boyish pain he'd felt as the more popular girls from the hill would tease him only to toss him aside before he got close enough to soil their air.

"Some of those girls from fourth period were rough on you weren't they Todd?"

He nodded and shuffled his feet before gathering himself together. "Let's talk about today. What's up with you? Can I buy you a coffee down the street? They've got a mean espresso if you like that kind of thing?"

Grace debated. She didn't know why Todd was asking. What would Craig say about coffee with Todd Mercer? His status on the police force nullified that argument but Grace wasn't sure. Finally, her blunt side won. "Why?"

"Huh?" Todd hadn't expected that. A yes, he would have been happy to hear but a little surprised as well. No would have been understandable, but why wasn't something he'd expected.

"Why do you want to buy me a coffee?" Grace felt foolish but she had to know.

"Well, because I'd like to have a few minutes to say thank you and ask to be your friend."

"Well a friend I can always use," she laughed and together, they strolled toward the coffee shop. Grace talked animatedly about her life and what she was doing, and then listened intently as Todd told of how he'd been encouraged by the track coach to enter the police academy. To the casual observer, Grace and the officer seemed unaware of their surroundings and they definitely seemed somewhat absorbed in each other when Nolan drove by on his way to a lunch meeting.

After talking for over an hour, Todd went back to work with new insight on the 'Housewife Rapist' and a new friend. He had told Grace about his online girlfriend and Grace sounded so excited for him that they arranged to have lunch later that week and discuss his friend Wendy. He hadn't expected to share so much but talking to Grace was like talking to an old friend with whom he'd lost touch. It felt good to be back. Although they'd never shared a friendship, somehow Todd knew that they would now be very good friends.

Chapter Nineteen

Nolan lost the account. His distraction over seeing Grace with a strange man had bothered him more than he cared to admit. His client, another woman sent by the disgruntled and rejected Michelle, had marched out of the restaurant with a disgusting stream of expletives. Picking up his proposal, Nolan absently paid the check and drove home in deep contemplation.

At home, Nolan sat in his most comfortable chair, his hands warming around a cup of his favorite coffee, gazed at his little tree lit up with multi-colored lights, and prayed. He wasn't sure why he kept dragging his feet regarding Grace. At first, he wondered if she wasn't interested in him and if that made him overly cautious. Then he surmised that she didn't know of his interest in her, but rejected that notion when he decided his actions lately should have been quite obvious.

Nolan stood and strode across the street to speak to Grace. It was time to quit dilly-dallying. It occurred to him as he knocked on the door, that he'd never truly expressed interest verbally in Grace or any woman. He was accustomed to running from women, and this time he didn't want to run away, he was ready to embark on a new adventure! He swallowed hard as he realized that his new adventure was a romantic relationship. Was he up to the challenge?

Grace opened the door while on the phone. She motioned him inside and shut the door quickly behind him. He listened to her chatting away with someone, probably Paige, about the internet. Grace was bundled in a warm sweater and thick leggings under her skirt. She eyed her wood stove with an air of someone who can't decide whether to add more wood or not. Nolan made gestures indicating his willingness to add more logs and received an appreciative nod as Grace hurried into the kitchen, still chattering about fabrics and trims, to make him some of her excellent hot chocolate.

He wasn't sure why Grace seemed so cold. Her house seemed almost stiflingly warm but he was willing to do anything to get him in her good graces before he brought up the subject that risked the condition of his heart. Nolan wondered if he could really gather the nerve to lay his intentions on the line and that is when it hit him. His reticence to speak clearly to Grace was because he knew it wasn't just a dinner invitation he wanted to secure. He wanted everything; Grace, her heart, and her quirky little ways that charmed him when he allowed himself the freedom to enjoy them.

Nolan was surprised at how little wood Grace had stacked on her porch. Long before she'd fired up her antique woodstove, Grace had piled a great quantity of wood on the porch where her wicker furniture sat during the warmer months. It was almost half-gone already. Gathering an armful, Nolan edged himself into the house and filled one of her wood 'barrels'.

An old oak barrel, cut in half, with carefully sanded edges, stood on each side of the stove. During the spring and summer months, huge houseplants filled each barrel while one sat on the stove. Today, one barrel stood empty, the other held only one log, and instead of a fern on the stove, a pot of chili simmered there. The room smelled heavenly. Grace's frugality never ceased to amaze him.

"Paige, I think I could do this but I don't know where I'd ever get the money for a computer and I hardly know how to use them anymore..."

Grace listened to obvious protest on the other end before continuing. "Paige, it's been seven years since I've really used a computer. They're probably different now... and I'm not familiar with the Internet anymore; I know nothing about html but I'll see what I can do. Maybe Craig has an old one he'd let me use or maybe I can borrow one from the office."

Grace nodded a few times and then promised to go to the Library soon and find eBay and see whatever it was that Paige was explaining. "Look Paige, Nolan is here and he's filling my wood box for me. I need to go and help him. I'm freezing in here. This is going to be a cold winter. Uh huh. Thanks again Paige, bye now."

Grace turned to Nolan and smiled. "Here, have some cocoa. Cold today isn't it?"

Nolan shrugged and made a comment about his activity keeping him warm enough as he searched for the right words to speak to Grace. "I- well, I've been thinking."

"I hear that's a pretty scary thing to do. I suggest that you find a different hobby. Something less stressful perhaps?" Grace chuckled at her own joke as she curled into her favorite chair and pulled a lap quilt over her.

"Grace, are you really that cold? Do you think you might have a fever or something? It's pretty warm in here."

Grace leaned forward and pulled her hair from her forehead. "Do I feel warm to you?"

Nolan reached toward her, only to jerk back suddenly. "I can't tell. I came here because we need to talk Grace."

"Well then speak o wise one." Grace hid a bemused smile behind her hand. He hadn't touched her, so how could he expect to tell?

"It just occurred to me today that I haven't made an effort to share how important our-" He paused searching for just the right word, "friendship is to me."

"Well I'm glad to know it. What do you know about Etsy?" Grace's mind still appeared to be on her conversation with Paige.

"Not much. Grace, what I'm trying to say is that you are really an admirable woman." Nolan prayed that Grace would focus on the discussion at hand.

"Do you think so? I don't know. I think that, really, I'm just different. I'm just a house-spinster."

"*What!*" Nolan's reaction to her joke was stronger than Grace had expected.

"Well, I'm not married so I can't call myself a housewife, and homemaker sounds so architectural to me. I'm a house-spinster. Cute huh?"

"I can't believe you'd call yourself that. A spinster is a skinny old woman with no warmth or friendliness and who makes misers look like spendthrifts! You're anything but a spinster, Grace and-"

Grace hastily interrupted. "Well, I may not be stereotypical. No one could accuse me of being skinny, that's for sure."

"Grace, that's not what I meant at all." Nolan's voice sounded strained as he began backpedaling.

"No, but it's the truth... prayerfully I'm warm and friendly, though right now I feel pretty chilled."

Nolan started to protest again but Grace's phone interrupted him. As Grace greeted someone by the name of Todd on the other end, Nolan stood, gestured that he was going to go, and dragged himself homeward. Had he seen Grace collapse into a fit of giggles, he would have been at a complete loss. As it was, Nolan immediately called Craig and made an appointment to talk. Talking to Grace had failed; maybe Craig would have some insights.

Meanwhile, Grace listened to the suggestion that Todd made. Several of the victims of the recent attacks wanted to gather for support and Todd thought Grace might be a good group leader for the women. "Grace, maybe, and you didn't hear this from me, but maybe one of these women will remember something in the group that they didn't before. You could ask permission to share everything with me just in case we didn't know about it..."

Grace realized that Todd was really stretching the bounds of his job by suggesting the thought but she pounced on the idea. "How about you tell them Thursday evenings at *The Assembly.* I'll make sure we have coffee, tea and something tasty. We can meet from 7:30-8:30 and you can come by around 9:00 or so and I'll tell you anything I hear that they'll let me share, and you can polish off any leftovers for me."

Craig listened intently to Nolan's ramblings. Grace had called him last night to warn him that Nolan might call and had collapsed into another fit of giggles upon hearing that Nolan had already set up a meeting. "He was trying to 'declare himself' or something Craig. It was so cute. I felt bad playing the dumb brunette, sort of. It was kind of funny..." Grace's voice replayed through Craig's mind, as Nolan tried to come to the point.

"Oh this is ridiculous. Craig, you were right. I don't know how you knew I'd fall for her, but I am. Falling that is. I tried to talk to her yesterday and see if she was comfortable with that but Grace- I don't know. Either she's completely clueless, or totally uninterested. She's your sister. What do I do?"

Craig unsuccessfully stifled a chuckle. Nolan's eyes were piercing- and not amused. "Nolan. Grace is a very intelligent woman. She'd have to be to survive the way she has this year. Do you know she's socked away almost five thousand dollars?"

Nolan failed to look suitably impressed. "And your point is?"

"My point is that Grace isn't clueless of your interest, and in my opinion, she's definitely interested."

Nolan shook his head. "I'm lost."

"Burke. What is Grace's defining characteristic? What is that one thing that sets her apart from most women that you've met?"

"She's strong without being brash?"

Craig's laugh resounded throughout the restaurant. "Ok, besides that. You've been around too many militant feminists my man."

"She's traditional, almost old fashioned but not caught in a time warp or anything."

Craig nodded. "And what would that mean in regards to relationships?"

"Relationships? Plural? Is there something going on between her and that officer I saw her with?"

"No, as far as I know, that man has an online friend he's been 'seeing'- however that works when you're online."

"Scary. Ok..."

Craig decided to help his friend understand. "Nolan, you've seen how Grace and my relationship works. You know how concerned I was about you. Why would you think she'd want to discuss anything between you two without knowing you'd spoken to me first?"

"I'm awfully dense aren't I?" Nolan sounded amused at himself.

"Nah. You've just never met anyone like Grace."

Nolan smiled. "You've got that right."

They drank their coffee in companionable silence. Nolan's head jerked up from his cup. "Craig! You didn't tell me to back off! Why?"

"Because I know you better now and because I only wanted to keep Grace's heart from being broken."

"And you don't think I'll do that now?" Nolan was encouraged.

"Mel pointed out to me that killing a friendship with you would break Grace's heart before you ever could. She's right. I treated you just like those women that you are so sick of."

Nolan's questioning look prodded Craig to continue. "I reacted to you solely based upon your physical attractiveness."

"You reacted before you saw me. You came charging over before you ever saw me."

"And as I left the house to come find out just what kind of man you were, I overheard my sister tell my wife that you are the most attractive man she's ever met."

Nolan grinned. "Is that so? Hmm… seems like I remember her making some comment to that effect once upon a time."

"Nolan, I have a suggestion for you though." Craig's tone was serious.

"What is that?"

"When you talk to her, start by telling her you've spoken to me, and then avoid the kind of conversation you have with the guys. I've learned in the last three years that women like to be talked to as much as they like to be listened to. If you think you've said enough, double that and you'll be set."

"Can I take her to dinner? Think she'll go for that?"

Craig nodded. "I think you might find someplace that gives you a bit of privacy though, but not too private. Just avoid anything that might appear inappropriate."

"And you're sure that she's not interested in this officer?"

Craig stood laughing. "Go call her. You've got it bad. Oh, and one last thing. Women are into feelings. Tell her what you're feeling. Trust me on that one."

"Feelings. Great. Do I have feelings? Better get some if I don't. Think the mall has a store with them?" Nolan began muttering something about how he didn't know how to become proficient at expressing his feelings at his age.

Craig walked away grinning. How much more funny could it be when your future brother in law begins to pick up your sister's quirky habits *before* he marries her?

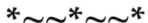

"Morning, Grace. I come bearing eggs, bacon, and orange juice. What do I have to do to beg you to cook 'em for us?"

The scent of blueberry muffins almost attacked his senses as Grace opened the door wider to allow him to pass. "Well, I've been craving an omelet..."

"I need to talk to you. You cook; I take orders and talk. Is it a deal?"

"No."

"Well-" Nolan paused, taken aback. He hadn't expected a negative response. "What?"

"I'll cook, you sit and talk. I don't handle helpers in the kitchen this early. Just sit down and let me function."

While Grace pulled out a non-stick frying pan and carefully laid the bacon strips in it, Nolan tried to re-gather his thoughts. He watched as she deftly whipped eggs and half-and-half together and chopped the tops of a green onion and tomato. "I went to see Craig yesterday."

"I thought you would.'"

"You knew all along?"

"Well, I think I figured it out the day before Thanksgiving," Grace replied as she poured the eggs into another hot skillet. "You said something like, 'she's not as far away from my acquaintance than you'd think.' Something like that. I'm not dense."

"You acted dense."

She whirled and glared at him. "I acted nothing. You didn't say anything so I didn't either."

His eyes held hers until she whirled to sprinkle the onions, tomatoes, cheese and torn bacon strips over the omelet. "But you knew what I wanted the other day and you played dumb."

Once the omelet was flipped in half, she turned and pointed her spatula at him. "You were beating around the bush. You knew how bothered Craig was by our friendship and yet you chose to talk to me without discussing it with him, and if that wasn't enough," her voice rose slightly as she scooped the omelet from the pan and slid it on a plate. "You were a little heavy handed."

His incredulous expression prompted her to do an exaggerated imitation of him. "'Grace, we need to talk.' You sounded like my father and I'd done something wrong. I expected to hear that I was on restriction."

Nolan started to protest but suddenly he saw himself with a serious expression and heard the words with fresh ears. He groaned. "Oh Grace-"

With a flourish, she handed him his omelet, a fresh muffin, and a glass of orange juice. He watched as she washed the pans and the baking bowls, and wiped down the stove. Once she cleaned the tiny kitchen, Grace settled into her chair with a hot cup of coffee, a quarter of the omelet, and her muffin.

He glanced at his watch. This had taken too long. He had appointments to keep and a project that needed finishing before he left. "I have to go. Can we continue this discussion over dinner? I'll take you anywhere you want to go."

"I don't know."

The answer hit him in the gut. Staring at her in disappointed disbelief, he scrambled to find a response. "Well-"

"Nolan, it's not you," Grace explained. "I want to say I'll go and I want to be excited about it. I want to think about what it could mean and enjoy it but the fact is, I don't know. I thought I knew yestrday but-" She struggled to explain without making him feel worse than he did. "Well, I just realized that I have to choose between two different relationships."

"Between what?"

Grace tried again. "I have to choose between my current relationship with the Lord and-"

"Grace! I don't want to come between you and the Lord, I want to share you with Him, not take you away from Him!"

Cocking her head, she waited for him to finish and then continued. "My relationship with Jesus as it is now, and how it will be later. It can't be the same. One isn't better than the other but I-" With a deep breath she shared part of her heart that no person had ever seen. "Over the years, I've made Jesus the equivalent of my husband. When I was seventeen, I was fascinated by the Catholic idea of nuns marrying Jesus as they took their vows and I realized that every Christian does that. It was a beautiful thing to me and, I confess, I felt a little sorry for Catholic girls who didn't realize that if they were a Christian, they were the Bride of Christ!"

Seeing that Nolan wasn't following her train of thought, she tried again. "A year or two later I realized that I could rely on Jesus just as a wife does on a husband. I could go to Him for the emotional support that wives seem to glean from their relationships. I could trust Him to be my protector and defender. Basically, I have a relationship with Jesus that means a change- not a bad one but a definite one- if I allow another man into my life and I have to really pray about whether or not I'm ready to do that now."

Stunned by the realization that Grace's reception of his affections wasn't the given he'd assumed, Nolan stood. "Well, will you call me if you decide that dinner is something we can do?"

"I'll call you either way. Thanks for understanding."

Nolan shook his head. "Don't. Don't thank me because I don't understand. You, Craig, Paige, Melanie- you've all talked about how you have spent your entire life preparing to be a wife, mother, and homemaker. You've been practicing this for years. You're the 'wife' of Jesus, the mother of every child you meet, and you're definitely a homemaker. You have everything you've ever wanted. You don't need a man. You don't need me. I just don't understand why-" He paused. "I'm sorry. Please forgive me. I'll wait for your call."

~~~~*

"Mike, she's not interested. I thought she would be but-" Nolan sat speechless in Mike's office.

"Are you sure about that? It sounds to me, from what you've described, like she's making sure she's ready for a new step in her life."

"What if she's not?"

Disgusted, Mike glared at him. "Then you wouldn't want her to go against her conscience or her heart just to pacify you I would hope!"

"Ouch. You're right. I was just so sure-"

"That's your problem Nolan. You've always been very sure of yourself but this time you have to lay it on the line and step back and wait."

A new realization dawned. "I am incredibly arrogant. I'm so used to being pursued by women that I don't know what to do when the one I want isn't sure she wants me. It's a blow to my pride at the least."

"You'll live. You would never believe the kick in the gut I had when Traci turned down my first proposal."

"Traci did what!"

"She told me that she might be damaged goods but she'd been repaired by the Master and He considered her priceless. If I wanted her, I had to quit acting like I was doing her a huge favor by asking."

"Ouch."

"Amen.

Chapter Twenty

"What do I wear Mel? I haven't been out to an elegant dinner since before Daddy died.

Melanie stood before Grace's closet in thought. With a mischievous glint in her eye, she reached for Grace's best dress. "We know he likes you in this one. Wear it."

Grace looked at the dress. "I remember him saying that. It took everything I had not to blush."

They talked, as Grace got ready for her dinner with Nolan. She brushed her hair and flipped it in the style that suited her best. Remembering the possibility of candlelight at the restaurant, she spent a few minutes carefully applying the cosmetics that she wore sporadically. Grace shivered.

"Are you cold Grace?" Melanie's voice held a trace of concern.

"I've been cold for the last three months. It gets worse all the time. I'm losing hair too. Look at this." Grace ran her fingers through her hair and brought out over a dozen strands.

As she rubbed lotion into her hands, Melanie remembered the dark circles under Grace's eyes lately. "You've been pretty tired lately too."

"That's the truth. I wake up in the morning and wonder if I got any sleep!" Clipping on her mother's earrings, Grace turned to Mel for final inspection.

"Oh Grace you look wonderful." Melanie watched as Grace reached for her glasses. She didn't need to wear them all of the time, but tended to wear them out of convenience.

A knock on the door threw the pair into a ridiculous fit of giggles. "You get the door Grace, I'll wash these. They're filthy. You must not have washed them after you baked last."

As Grace welcomed Nolan into the house, Melanie took the glasses into the bathroom. While washing them, she tried pushing one of the lenses to see if it would pop out but it held fast. With a sigh, Melanie dried the glasses and took them with her. Spying the glass case that Grace kept next to the television, Melanie inserted the glasses and made a show of putting them in Grace's purse.

"In case you need them. I need to go. The baby probably is getting hungry. You guys have fun."

An awkward silence pressed like a wedge as they drove toward an exclusive restaurant in Rockland. After several miles of watching cars pass on the freeway, Grace's sense of the ludicrous took over and she began laughing. Nolan eyed her with a trace of amusement. "Care to enlighten me, or is this a private joke?"

"It's us. You and me sitting here in total silence as if we were strangers or something."

Once again, Grace's forthrightness managed to break an awkward moment. Nolan thought a moment and then began talking. He told Grace about growing up with his parents in an exclusive area of Rockland. "You know Burke and Finch?"

"The financial offices down on Roosevelt?"

"My father and his best friend. Mike's last name is Finch. I told them when they were here about you. Actually, they came because I told them about you."

"They came to Brunswick because you talked about me?"

"I guess they took my seriousness seriously." Nolan continued his story. He spoke of being too focused and busy in school to make much time for girls and college years avoiding the typical college scene. When he spoke of the loss of his parents, Nolan's voice broke.

Grace watched him struggling to fight back tears and cautiously laid her hand on his arm. "I'm sorry. I know how it hurts. I'm so sorry."

Nolan smiled down at her through his tears. "I know you do. Unlike most people who say that, I know you know exactly what I mean."

He continued his story. He spoke of the lonely years as he built his business from the ground up. "I don't want to sound conceited Grace but I ran from women. I ran hard and I ran fast. Women literally threw themselves at me. At first, I didn't know if it was me, or the money I have accumulated or my parent's money and position in Rockland society. Combined with my inheritance, I am pretty well fixed and in Rockland, that fact wasn't easy to hide."

Grace laughed. "And your SUV, Stickley furniture, and original artwork didn't help!"

"Right. I guess. I've never thought of it like that. It was my dad's office furniture. I loved it, so I kept it. Anyway, I- I just left things as they were but I became lonely. Not the same loneliness I had dealt with before. I- I was lonely for things that I didn't have, or rather for someone that I didn't have.

"I started looking around but I wanted someone like mom and most of the women I knew were more like movie stars than real people or at least tried to be."

Grace nodded. She understood the idea but couldn't relate. "Must have been awkward."

"It was. That's when I started my 'order form'. I started with Christian. I slowly added things as they came to mind. I remember the day that I added loves children. I had just come out of this horrible business lunch. The woman was forward and awful. I made the unforgivable mistake of calling her Miss and that showed her true colors. She was almost venomous for a moment. As I walked away from her, there was this little girl blowing out birthday candles on a cake and I wanted nothing more than to be the man sitting next to her. He was obviously a very proud and happy father. I wanted that Grace."

Grace was a little surprised. They'd had deep and lasting conversations before now but this different. They'd discussed politics, the Bible, and favorite music, games, and movies. When it came to talking about himself, Nolan was a typical brief man. She knew that if they didn't cut to the chase, they'd have to continue their conversation in public.

"So exactly what are we discussing Nolan? I'm interested in your story, really, but you seem to be leading up to something. Can we talk about that before we get to the restaurant?"

"Oh Grace. That is what I like so much about you. You don't play games." Nolan didn't know what he was going to tell her and stalled for time. He wanted to say so much, but most of his thoughts seemed too premature.

Knowing she was waiting for some kind of comment from him, Nolan decided just to be frank. "Ok. If you can get to the point, so can I. You intrigue me. You appear to be everything I've looked for and prayed for in a wife. I want to know if you're interested in-well... "

"Please tell me that this isn't a proposal." Her tone implied that she knew it wasn't.

"Well. Not yet. I want to get to know you better. I want to spend time with you just talking, doing things, sharing things."

"You want a girlfriend?" Grace wasn't sure she liked where the conversation was going.

"Well... I want more than a girlfriend."

"Oh, you want a fiancée without a proposal, perhaps?"

"Grace!" Her chuckles made him smile. As ornery as she was being, her lighthearted bantering was definitely making this conversation easier. Taking a deep breath, he tried again.

"I want an understanding. I want to get to know you. I want to have the understanding that if you are who I think you are, and if I am who I hope I can be to you, that in a month or two, or four, or six, I can ask you to be my wife. And I'm going to warn you, I won't want a long engagement."

"I've never understood the reason for long engagements...they-." Grace's voice held a trace of amusement.

"You haven't answered the question."

Grace laughed outright. "I haven't been asked one. You've told me what you want, but I didn't hear any question in there."

"Grace. Are you interested in trying to build a relationship that could lead to marriage?"

Grace's silence unnerved him. When she'd called, he'd assumed that this meant she was ready to move into a different relationship. Now, he wasn't sure if she'd changed her mind and she wasn't interested, or if she didn't know, or if it was for some reason that he hadn't thought of. He was hesitant to push her. What if she said no? For the first time, the realization of how much that answer would hurt him came over him.

"I don't know. Why Nolan? Why me?"

Nolan was surprised. He'd steadied himself for the prospect that she might not know, but he'd assumed that it would be because she liked her life the way it is after all, or for some similar reason. He hadn't expected her to doubt his interest in her. "Grace, why not you. I brought a printout of my 'order form'. It's in my jacket pocket. Pull it out will you?"

Grace felt awkward as she reached into his pocket but did as he requested. "Ok.... Got it."

"Read it to me and tell me which request you don't fill." Nolan was sure that once she saw how perfectly she fit the bill, her doubts would dissolve.

"Christian, feminine- loves being a woman, strong, modest, a sense of humor, loves children, a best friend, an attractive personality..."

"Which one doesn't personify you? I added the last two after meeting you, I think when I was trying to get to know Paige, but I'm not sure. The rest I came up with before I moved here."

Grace nodded. "If I say that none of them fit me, I sound like I'm fishing for compliments. If I say they all do, I sound arrogant."

'Grace. What can I do? What can I say to make you believe me?"

Feeling like a heel, Grace asked one last question. "When your doubts are over, will you promise to tell me?"

"Doubts about what?" Nolan was genuinely clueless to her meaning.

"Whether I'm the right kind of woman for you. I can't help but wonder if I'm just the first woman that didn't run after you and you decided to settle for that."

His heart constricted. Strong Grace doubted herself. "Grace. My doubts are focused on my fear that you will not find me the man that you are looking for. I've pretty much made up my mind. I just want to know you better. It's selfish of me but I think if we can just spend more time together, maybe you'll decide..."

Grace laid her hand on his arm. "Nolan. Let's eat. I'm famished."

Chapter Twenty-One

Taking a deep breath, Grace knocked on Aunt Fran's door. The irritable "go away" was the closest anyone ever came to receiving a 'welcome' from the irascible old woman. She forced the door open with as cheerful of a "Hello Aunt Fran" as she could muster.

"Oh, it's you again. Honestly, if you'd just get a job, you wouldn't have so much time to waste annoying the aged."

"You're feeling chipper today," Grace commented dryly.

"What do you want?"

"Well, I have some interesting news and I wanted you to hear it from me."

Steel gray eyes met Grace's across the coffee table. "If you tell me you're pregnant-"

"Aunt Fran! That's just uncalled for. You know me better than that."

"Well, you know with your rolls, the chances of any man wanting-"

Grace stood. She knew this had been a bad idea but not coming would have been worse. "I'll go. It's obvious that you're more concerned with being crude, crass, and a curmudgeon than the normally loving and caring Aunt that we all know and love so I'll come back when you have had a nap."

She turned to leave but Fran's voice stopped her. "Sit down and cease with the alliteration."

Slowly, Grace turned and met her aunt's eyes. "Not until I know you're done insulting my character."

Shock filled Fran's face followed by laughter. "Deal. Why are you here?"

With a barely suppressed air of resignation, Grace returned to her seat and took another deep breath. "Nolan has expressed interest in forming a relationship."

"Girl, honestly. This is why you're pushing forty-"

"I'm thirty-two Aunt Fran."

Without a pause, Fran continued. "-and still haven't had a serious relationship. Do you hear yourself? 'Nolan has expressed interest in forming a relationship.' The guy wants you in every moral and carnal way imaginable." A hard look on Grace's face kept Fran talking before Grace could interrupt or leave. "-and furthermore, there's nothing wrong with that as long as he is willing to make an honest woman of you in the middle of it all."

"He's expressed a goal of marriage if that's what you're asking."

"Grace! Listen to yourself! Where is the interest? Where is your passion? Are you settling for the first man to come along? Granted," Fran continued with a gleam in her eye, "He's a wealthy good looking one from an impeccable family but still, if you are just not into him, don't do this."

A blush stole slowly up her neck and spread across her face. "At first I wasn't sure but when I was, I let him know and then we talked about it. Unless there is something major that we've missed, marriage is a given."

"You're a fool," Fran whispered.

Surprised by her aunt's change of tone, Grace glanced up at her curiously. "I don't understand."

"He'll break your heart. It might not be soon but someday- every man does. You can't trust them. I thought you had more sense but considering your rigorous brainwashing experience-"

"Aunt Fran..." Grace began warningly.

"I can't believe you don't see it. Even my brother hurt your mother."

"Anyway, I wanted you to know. I didn't want you to hear it from anyone else and you know how Brunswick is."

~~~~*

"Oh Verily, she was awful. Not that I didn't expect it. That's just Aunt Fran for you but-"

"Your Aunt Fran won't ever see good in anything until she's filled with the love of Jesus. She's just more honest than most people who are lost."

Confusion filled Grace's face. "What do you mean, 'more honest'? I mean, I know she's always been brutally honest..."

"Well, most people who are slaves to sin, have some kind of veneer or façade hiding their true condition. It's part of their sinfulness you know? They hide the rottenness within with the appearance of gentility."

"Slave to sin," she mused. "I can't believe I've never seen it before. I mean, of course I knew she needed Jesus but she's always been so ugly and I know so many non-Christians who are wonderful people that-"

Verily interrupted. "They are still made in the image of our Lord. It's a lie unless their actions come from a heart cleansed by the Lord but I've always appreciated knowing that with your aunt, what you see is who she is."

"Well, that's for sure. Whatever else she is, you never have to guess with her." Grace hugged the grandfather-like gentleman and smiled into his happy eyes. "Thanks. I needed to hear that."

"Well, *I* need to hear more about you and Mr. Burke. You shared with Fran but now it's my turn."

"We're exploring the possibility of a relationship."

"Romantical type?"

Grace blushed. "Well, that's the general idea but I'm not sure how romantic either of us really is."

"If you give him half a chance and a dash of encouragement, I'd say Nolan Burke is probably going to be an expert in the romance department. Men like him usually are."

Eyes sparkling, Grace laughed. "Speaking from experience Verily?"

Chapter Twenty-Two

"Grace, tell me... what did you talk about?" Paige was becoming exasperated.

"I told you. We talked about where we went to school, our different family lives, and our goals for our lives." Grace spoke the truth. However, she chose to leave out the more intimate subjects that she and Nolan had discussed. She didn't want to share everything. Grace was learning that she could be a very private person regarding certain topics.

'Did you hear what that gal from four streets over said about the attacker? That she thought he was a meter reader or something. That there was something familiar in the way that he walked?" Paige decided that if Grace wouldn't share, she'd talk about something else.

"Has anyone asked the different utility companies if they have any new employees or anything like that?" Grace planned a call to Todd.

"That's the weird thing. The meters for the whole building are on the opposite side of the complex from me. He couldn't have seen me, so he couldn't have known I was home." Paige was extremely eager to find the man who had attacked her.

"Ok. Who has been to your door outside of your friends in the last three months?"

Paige thought carefully. "Well, the handyman came in to turn on the heater but he only works for the three complexes owned by the company that owns mine."

"That rules him out I guess but we'll note it."

"The only one else is the mailman or the UPS guy."

Grace didn't appear to be listening. She was watching the television intently. Jumping up she ran to turn the volume up. "... this attack was more violent than previous attacks but the police indicate that they are confident that the new information from this attack will help them in their ongoing investigation."

"What did they say was different?" Grace seemed to be putting different things she'd read or been told together in one big puzzle.

Paige shook her head. "They didn't."

"It has to be a postal worker or a UPS driver. They're the only one that could have found you and someone else. You've seen this man many times."

Paige was thoughtful. "Most of the packages that come to my house come via UPS. I don't get a lot of postal packages. If it's the UPS guy, it's not the regular one because I would have recognized *her*."

"Her? Um... nooooo doubt it was *her*."

Grace grabbed her purse and asked Paige to take a drive. "Let's go talk to Todd."

~~~~*

Several hours Grace explained the story to Nolan over a cup of coffee at the local espresso café. "They're talking to all of the women to see if they've all received packages in the last three or four months."

Nolan was interested but concerned. "What happens if this guy finds out that you're looking for him and gets mad at you? What would you do if he came after you?"

Shaking her head, Grace reassured him that Todd didn't think that the attacker would stray from his pattern. "It's all about control or something. I don't understand it but I figure Todd knows his job. Besides, it's not like you or Verily would let a strange man get past my front yard and this guy always seems to go to the front door. How bold and brazen is that?"

Nolan reached across the table to cover her hand with his own. "Grace, just be careful. I don't think I could handle anything happening to you."

Grace grinned and changed the subject. "So, do you have a spare computer in your garage?"

"Computer? I've got a dinosaur in my garage somewhere, why?"

"I need a computer and I can't afford one."

Grace's tenacity always amused him. "Why do you need to get one?"

"Paige was showing me Etsy. It's a worldwide boutique for handcrafted items. Did you ever look on there? The stuff Paige showed me is amazing."

"Uh... no. I didn't know that. What does that have to do with you and a computer?"

Grace launched into her new idea. She told about how she'd set up an account; make some pretty little dresses for next spring and voila, a way to supplement her income. "Nolan, some of those dresses sell for hundreds... and a lot of them are down right ugly!"

Nolan stood and went out to retrieve his laptop from his vehicle. Hooking it up to the Internet connections provided at the café, Nolan called up the website and pushed it across to Grace. "Show me."

Grace found the links to the little girl's clothing slowly but surely. Eventually she called up pages and pages of 'boutique' clothing. After scrolling through auction after auction, Nolan noticed a trend. "Look at that! Daytona_Diva has sold dozens of things and several are to Munchkins_Mommy. Look at the totals to one buyer alone."

"See what I mean. I can do this. There is a seller... her name is something like UniqueBoutique or something, I liked her style. It was not as weird as the gal who calls herself Sassychic. I'm just old fashioned though. I like something a little more feminine and a lot less trendy."

"Where are you going to find a model? Do you have a digital camera? What about-"

Grace answered every one of his 'concerns' and continued to ramble about her ideas. Nolan didn't know half of what Grace was talking about but her enthusiasm was contagious. As they talked, Nolan began planning how to help Grace get started with her new project.

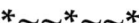

~~~~*

"Oh come on... what'd you get? I know you have something because you've got a new box under that dinky little tree of yours. It's only two weeks away, what did you get me?" Grace twirled the phone cord in her hand. She missed her cordless but as exhausted as she'd felt in the last few months, it felt good to be forced to sit to talk.

Nolan's low chuckle was the only response that Grace received. "Well fine. If you're not gonna tell me, then I'm not going to show you the cute outfit I made and I will *not* let you help Paige and I catch the creep that is attacking women out there."

"You're going to do what!"

Nolan's incredulous voice was loud enough that Grace winced. As Grace transferred the phone to her other ear, Nolan began shredding the mail. Seeing his unopened phone bill in tatters on his desk, he swept the mess into the trash and wrote 'phone bill' on the next day's to do list before moving toward the front door. He saw the package in question under his tree and had an idea. Scooping the box into his pocket, Nolan exited his house as he listened to Grace rambling about their plan on the other end of his cordless phone.

Grace, unaware that things were going to get more personal, continued her conversation. "You heard me. We figured out how Paige could 'see' him without him knowing it. We *were* going to have you here for masculine protection but..."

"Grace! You can't *do* that. Craig will murder both of us. You for doing something so dangerous and me because I will be near enough to take some of the fall out."

"You afraid of my brother?" Grace's amusement was not what Nolan had hoped to hear.

He harrumphed. "No. I just thought he made an excellent threat. Guess I was wrong."

"Sure and shootin' you are. I cry every time another woman is attacked."

A sudden pounding at the door startled Grace. Before she could get up to answer it, Nolan's voice over the phone said, "I'm coming in."

Suddenly her bravado began to crumble. She mustered all of her courage, hung up the phone, and smiled. "I see you're here! Good. So, are you going to tell me what's in that package?"

Nolan shook his head and pulling it from his pocket, tossed the package onto her lap. "We're not done discussing your flagrant lack of care for your safety. If you try to do this, I will call your cop friend."

"He knows. He can't encourage us but he hasn't exactly discouraged us either."

Nolan was becoming more frustrated by the moment. "Fine. I'll call the chief of police."

'He was my Sunday school teacher in the fourth grade. Just talk to him after church on Sunday." Grace's smug look was more than Nolan could take. Thoughts of padded cells in far away states began to invade his imagination.

"Nolan-" The man standing before her, silenced Grace.

"No Grace. You're not going to put yourself in harm's way. If you won't listen to reason, then do it for me, for Craig, for Graceanna, for Cade or whoever will prick your heart."

Tears pooled in Grace's eyes. "What about Paige. She's pierced my heart. She was hurt Nolan, and the guy who did it has hurt several women since. We know it has to be either a mailman or a delivery guy. Will you just listen to our idea before you come unglued?"

Grace sighed as Nolan shook his head. "It's too late for that Grace. I already did. My phone bill is in little pieces and I don't' even know how much it was- but I'll listen."

'It's really simple. I'll order something for Paige every day for a week. Everything will be delivered here. We'll track the packages as they come so that Paige will be sure to be here for them. She'll sit in her car in front of your house, and I'll answer the door, take the package, sign for it, and close the door."

"And where do I come in?" Nolan was obviously not impressed.

"You are here with me. You sit in the chair there… just so that he sees you and doesn't know I'm here alone all the time. Paige will watch him from her car. When she sees the right guy and he leaves, she will call the police and tell them." Grace's tone made it all sound so simple.

Nolan shook his head. "It's a good idea Grace, really. There are a few major flaws though. What happens if he sees Paige watching him? What happens if he copies her license plate? What if he recognizes me from deliveries to my house and knows that I don't live here?"

Grace grew thoughtful. In the manner of vintage cartoons, he would have sworn that a light bulb suddenly shone above her head.

"We cover her plates, you can call 9-1-1 if he even cough's wrong, and you can bring over your old computer and pretend to be working on it."

Nolan knew that the plan would work. He also knew that if the attacker really did show up, the chances of something going wrong were huge. Opting to change the subject, Nolan nodded at the package in Grace's hand. "Aren't you going to open it?"

Grace shook her head. "No way! If I open it, then I don't get to guess what's in it anymore!"

"Come on Grace... open it. I want an excuse to get something for you that I saw the other day."

Giggling, Grace tore at the package with exuberance. Finding the narrow jeweler's box under the wrapping Grace stopped short. "I have a watch. Why did you get me a watch?"

"Open it Grace. It's not a watch." Nolan's amusement was keen.

"I'm having fun guessing. Now leave me alone." Grace shook, she peeked, and weighed it against her watch, before finally taking off the lid.

"Tissue! You got me tissue! How did you know I was almost out?" Grace's giggles were infectious.

"Grace..."

Tossing a wicked grin in his direction, Grace folded the tissue back to reveal her gift. Lying in a bed of velvet was a lovely charm bracelet. White and yellow gold intertwined delicately in order for charms to hook onto the links easily. Grace lifted the bracelet, twisted it, and turned it to catch in the light.

"I can't believe that you bought me a *mouse*." Her voice failed to impart the disgust that she pretended to feel. After several moments of trying to connect the ends of the bracelet together, Grace handed the bracelet to Nolan and held out her wrist.

Taking the bracelet in hand, Nolan worked to open the clasp. "Need a little help with it?"

"I have a hard enough time trying to get a watch connected. I am not very coordinated with jewelry. I never have been."

Nolan carefully connected the ends of the bracelet around Grace's wrist. "I never noticed it before, but you don't wear much jewelry do you?"

"And where would I get the money to purchase it? I have more important things to do with my money. You know, eat, stay warm..."

Before Nolan could ask Grace's favorite stones, she was off on another tangent. "I have to show you the outfit. I think it's going to work well. I just have to set up that account and paint the pretty stand that Craig made me and I'll be ready to list it."

"I'll bring over my computer then. I figured out how to do it. I am going to bring my desktop computer and set it up here. I'll call and have you print anything I need and transfer files from the lap top every few days. How does that sound?"

Nolan had considered buying Grace her own computer system but knew that she'd object strongly to the idea. The next best solution was to set his system up at her house. The dinosaur that he'd talked about would drive her crazy with its lack of speed. He expected some resistance to this idea as well, and was prepared with all of the reasons that she should agree to his proposition.

"Great! When will you have time to transfer it?" Grace looked as eager as a child surveying the presents under a Christmas tree.

Nolan was momentarily stunned. All of the objections that he'd prepared himself for were left unsaid and Grace waited impatiently for his response. "Well, I think I can get it ready to move tomorrow..."

"That's great! I'm so excited. I want to list this dress; look!" Grace moved slowly, as if she was groggy, to the closet and pulled out a beautiful dress.

"Oh Grace! That is amazing. You did that? Already?" Nolan found it difficult to curb his astonishment. Knowing that Grace sewed was a far cry from seeing just how talented she really was.

They made plans for taking pictures and lessons in how to operate the software necessary for the upcoming clothing production. Nolan made a mental note to add a digital camera to his Christmas list for Grace. Taking pictures, developing film, scanning and uploading the scanned pictures would be a process that grew old quickly.

Grace yawned and shooed Nolan home with the excuse that she needed a nap before Cade arrived. "I'm so tired. I woke up feeling like a truck hit me. I can't seem to get any *rest* no matter how much I sleep."

Concern clouded Nolan's eyes. "Grace? Will you do something for me?"

"Sure, but after my nap, ok? What is it?"

Nolan hesitated. "Will you call a doctor and make an appointment. Tell them your symptoms and see if perhaps there is something wrong? You're always so tired and from what I understand, it's not like you."

Grace shook her head. "No can do. I have to pay for Christmas and then my house insurance is due in February and I have to make sure that I have a cushion in case it goes up. The bill isn't here yet."

"I'll pay for it. Please Grace." Nolan's voice was strained and slightly desperate.

Grace's chin came up in the familiar determined way she had about her. "Nolan-"

Placing one finger on her lips, Nolan shook his head. "Please, please don't let this happen again Grace. I know I brought it up. I know that you don't like to hear it. I know that you want to 'make it' on your own. I understand all of that, but please don't let your wants over ride your good judgment. Something is wrong, and over a dozen people are waiting in the wings just hoping for a chance to thank you in some tangible way after all you've done to help them. Please Grace; let us serve *you* just this once."

With those words, Nolan gave an astonished Grace a fierce hug and left. He knew he was taking a huge risk by speaking so boldly and not staying to discuss it further, but he also knew that when it came to Grace, he didn't always think rationally.

Grace sat in prayer as Nolan rose from the chair and left. Her heart knew that he was right. Her head knew that he was right as well. The problem was connecting heart to head and making the two do what she knew to be right. In the end, Grace knew that she'd be making a call to her doctor's office.

"Well, what do you have to tell him? You're tired- all the time-cold, skin is dry, losing hair..." Grace went through the mental list until she knew what to tell the doctor. Realizing that sooner would be better than later, she picked up the phone and made an appointment for two days later. She marveled at the amazing power that cancellations wielded as she hung up the phone.

With an impish gleam to her eyes, Grace headed for her door. In a few sluggish steps, she was across the street and knocking boldly on Nolan's front door. The man inside didn't know whether to answer the door, or put earphones on and drown out the knocks with music.

"This is either very good news Grace, or it's very, very bad news. Do I want to know which it is?"

Grace laughed at the man standing before her and tentatively opening the door. "Well, actually, that is up to you. I am here to strike a bargain."

'Uh huh." Nolan's face was wary.

'It's simple. I have made an appointment-"

"Great! I'm so relieved. Do you want me to go with you? I mean, I wouldn't go in the room- well, not with the doctor, but I could wait outside- in- Did you have a proposal for me?" Nolan couldn't seem to get his words organized properly. In trying to avoid the bargain aspect of the situation, he'd dug a very uncomfortable hole for himself.

"Proposal. Hmm. I thought that was something that men did. I'm kind of old fashioned for that but..."

"Ok, ok. Just give me the particulars." He delighted in Grace's quirky humor and her ability to interject it at any odd moment.

"It's simple. You agree to help us spot the Brunswick attacker, or I don't show for my appointment."

Nolan beckoned her inside as he moved into the kitchen and filled a glass with water. She watched fascinated as he swallowed a couple of aspirins and inhaled the water. "That must be a monster headache."

"Well, Grace, you should know. You gave it to me."

Grace's teasing dissolved immediately. She plumped couch pillows and pulled a throw blanket from the back of a nearby chair. "Here, lie down and close your eyes. I'll get you a cloth for that forehead. Where can I find one?"

"That's ok Grace. I'll be fine with the aspirin."

Grace pulled his legs up onto the couch and covered him with the blanket. "Come on, really, it will work quicker than the medication."

Minutes later Nolan was lying on the couch, tucked in with a comfortable blanket and a cool washcloth on his head. Grace sat on the floor next to the couch and occasionally flipped the washcloth over. "Feeling any better?"

Grace's tone was contrite. Nolan wanted to assure her that it would be ok, but Grace spoke first. "Nolan, you did know I was joking, didn't you? I really wouldn't skip the appointment. I don't operate that way. I just hoped that you'd see how important it is to us that Paige tries to see if she can recognize this guy."

Nolan, despite her objections, removed the cloth and threw it backhanded into the kitchen. To Grace's astonishment, it landed squarely in the sink. He pulled himself up onto the arm of the couch and rested his head in his hand in order to see her better. The tears in her eyes hurt him.

It had not taken Nolan long to learn that Grace did not cry frivolously. The one thing that would quickly move her to tears was the idea that she had caused pain or trouble for someone else. Watching her struggle to control her emotions removed a barrier that he'd erected during his conversation with Craig weeks before.

Sitting upright, he beckoned Grace to come sit beside him. "Grace, I want to pray. Come here."

With his arm around her shoulders, and her head nestled in his own, Nolan initiated the first of many special prayer times between them. He prayed for wisdom, for understanding of Grace's feelings, and for Grace to understand his concerns. He prayed for direction and that they would come to unified agreement on both the appointment and the identification scheme.

Amen was followed by Grace's sobs. Nolan was unprepared for the onslaught of emotions that his protective prayer brought upon Grace. Being just as surprised as Nolan, Grace had no idea how to control the swirling emotions that threatened to overwhelm her. They sat in bewildered silence as Grace worked to regain her dignity.

"I'm sorry, Grace. I didn't mean-" Nolan couldn't continue. His concern for her grew the longer she cried. Nolan smoothed her hair. He was surprised that he noticed how soft and silky it felt when his mind was so thoroughly occupied with Grace's tears.

After some time, they walked to the door with a tentative agreement. Nolan would talk to Todd Mercer and ask for help in avoiding any danger and if pitfalls could be avoided, he'd help Paige identify her attacker. Grace would be at the doctor's on Thursday. Nolan would drive her there, wait in the reception area, and then drive her back home. Grace noticed a mental shift that desired to honor Nolan's wishes and pondered it as he opened his door for her.

"Grace..." Nolan's words drifted into the frigid December air. He wrapped his arms around her and mumbled a few endearing words into her ear. A feeling of shyness overcame her as she listened to him share his concerns, fears, and love for her.

Grace had remained reserved to the idea that Nolan would grow to truly care for and love her but Nolan's hug, intimate words, and gentle, yet playful, kiss on her nose removed all doubts. Though not dressed for the impending snowy weather, Grace walked home warm and happy. She would have easily been persuaded to stay and talk further, but Nolan had seemed impatient to get back to work.

While Grace moved about her home praying and rejoicing, Nolan returned to his couch, pulled his blanket back over him and began praying in earnest. The more time he spent with Grace, the more freedom he felt to be honest about his feelings for her, the harder it was for him to behave in a brotherly manner. Reaching for his Bible, Nolan searched until he found the scripture that he was seeking. Turning to I Timothy chapter five, Nolan read.

"'*Do not rebuke an older man harshly, but exhort him as if he were your father. Treat younger men as brothers, older women as mothers, and younger women as sisters, with absolute purity.*'"

"Lord, I want to treat her as a sister, but if I only always treat her as I would a sister, she'll doubt my love for her. Show me the balance of courting her as Solomon did in his book of songs, and honoring her as a sister in the Lord. This is so hard Lord. Can't we just dash off to Las Vegas tomorrow?"

Twenty-Three

"Cade! That's not a word. I'm sure of it! I challenge you to a dual of dictionaries... Engarde!"

Grace quickly began flipping through her dictionary looking for the dubious word, farctate. "Aha...fa...far... farcta.. oh my, farctate is a *word*? What does it mean?"

Grace's laughter greeted Mrs. Crenshaw as she knocked and entered the house. "What's going on in here?"

"Lila, your son just bested me at Scrabble with the word- drum roll please farctate. The meaning of which happens to be: the state of being stuffed with food."

Lila Crenshaw gave her son a significant look before chuckling. "He's been scouring the dictionary for a word that he thought you wouldn't know and wouldn't believe existed. It sounds like he succeeded."

Cade gathered his books and started to put the game away but Grace stopped him. "No way, leave it there Cade. I'm going to show Nolan when he comes by."

After Cade dashed out the Crenshaw Suburban, Grace turned back to Lila. "Um, is there a way that he can stay with someone else next week? Paige, Nolan, and I have something we're going to be doing and there is a slight risk of it being unsafe. I doubt that it'd be a problem but I just don't want to take a chance."

Lila nodded. "Maybe Jon and I can switch around our schedules so that one of us is home with him over winter break. Unless I call, assume you're free until after New Year's"

Grace started to respond but Lila stopped her. "One thing Grace, this thing you're doing. How unsafe is it?"

Grace hesitated which caused Mrs. Crenshaw a little unease. "Lila, I'm going to be giving Paige the opportunity to identify her attacker. She won't be visible; she's going to park behind Nolan's house and then watch from his attic with binoculars. Nolan will be here setting up his computer. It'll be fine. Deliveries are made before 2:30 usually, but-"

Lila's voice was quiet and concerned. "Grace, be careful. I know it seems simple, but nothing ever is. I'll light a candle at mass for you."

Grace smiled, hugged her friend, and walked Lila to the door. She wasn't sure what lighting candles meant to a Catholic, but she assumed it was akin to 'I'll pray for you.'

"Nolan, I'm nervous. What if something is wrong? I thought ignorance is bliss and all of that. I think I want bliss." Grace was half joking with her companion as they sat in the waiting room. Grace filled out several forms and the more she wrote, the more nervous she became.

"Nolan, look at this. I have almost every symptom they list. Am I only supposed to tell them if it's debilitating or if I've ever had it or somewhere in between?"

Nolan covered Grace's cold hands and quickly prayed for peace. "Grace look. I've had half of these in the last six months at a time or two. I think it's a matter of whether you have them all together, or in conjunction with each other. Why don't you star the ones that are chronic or persistent or have been severe and tell him what you did? Dry skin on me wouldn't mean anything perhaps. But if you have dry skin, hair loss, and a rash, it might have something to do with each other."

Grace nodded and started making asterisks next to her symptom list. After pulling out her hand written timeline of symptoms and any thing that she could remember of possible triggers, Nolan submitted the paperwork to the nurse at the reception desk.

Grace fidgeted in her seat picking at her skirt and toying with her purse strap. When she began picking at her nails and cuticles,

Nolan took her hands in his and held them still. The effect was calming. Grace looked up at him sheepishly but in appreciation.

As they talked quietly in their corner of the office, Nolan played with the bracelet on Grace's wrist. "It looks nice on you. I didn't know if you preferred white or yellow gold so I got both."

"I love it. This mouse is adorable. As I can afford it, I'm going to get a charm of every fear that I have. It'll be a reminder to me that I should fear nothing but rather to rest in Christ and His protection."

Nolan nodded. Grace's words were true and full of Christian strength. They also struck a blow to his desire to be her protector. Grace noticed the change in his demeanor and tapped the back of his hand with her finger.

"What's wrong?" What did I say?"

Nolan looked into Grace's eyes as they filled with concern. "Selfishness. It'll get me every time."

"What are you feeling selfish about?"

Feeling somewhat chagrined, Nolan confessed his desire to be perceived as her protector. "Pathetic isn't it?"

Grace looked into Nolan's eyes and smiled. "I think it's amazing. I always hoped that someone would want that job someday."

"But you're right Grace; that is God's job." Nolan's voice held traces of regret.

"Nolan, no one said that God can't use you to do His protecting. Husbands are told to protect their wives, fathers are to protect their children, and brothers protect their sisters..."

"I'm not your father, brother, or husband."

Grace smiled at the disappointment in his voice. Occasionally she wondered if he would change his mind about pursuing a relationship with her but Grace was slowly learning that Nolan had made his mind up. He was waiting for her to know her own heart before committing himself permanently. Grace wasn't in any hurry; rather, she was determined to enjoy this time in her life.

"Why are you smiling like that?"

"You don't like bold and brash women, Nolan. You wouldn't want me to answer." Grace made simpering motions and batted her eyelashes as she fluttered a flyer for migraine medication like a fan.

Nolan's laughter rang out across the room. The receptionist looked up and smiled at him before reluctantly looking back down at the work before her. Nolan grew sober. "Come on Grace, tell me."

"Women really do throw themselves at you don't they? The receptionist seems quite taken."

"You saw it? It's not just in my head? Sometimes I wonder if I'm not just some conceited guy who thinks more highly of himself than he ought."

Grace shook her head. "I've smiled at people, and had them smile at me. I've seen women smile at men out of politeness, and in flirtation. She definitely was issuing an invitation of some kind."

"But you haven't answered my question. What bold and brazen thought made you smile to yourself like that?"

Before Grace could answer, the receptionist called her to the examination room. She stood, gathered her purse and notebook, and leaned down to whisper in Nolan's ear. "Yet. I was going to say yet. See you in a few."

Nolan sat and mentally retraced the steps that would lead Grace to answer with the single word 'yet'. What did that mean? Yet what? Why had she been so enigmatic?

Meanwhile, Grace sat in the examination room, half clothed on a cold padded table. Dr. Kline entered the room with a look of concern on his face. "How are you Grace? I'm not accustomed to seeing you when you're not looking like you're ready for the grave."

"Well, if you've read my chart…"

"I have. Now I can't make a definite determination but you have all of the classic signs of hypothyroidism- low thyroid function. I'll be ordering a blood test. Now let's see what we can see."

Dr. Kline examined Grace in his trademark tactful way. People often commented on the discreet manner in which he related to his patients and he often stated that patients shouldn't lose their dignity when they entered his office.

As Grace received instructions for blood work and nutritional advice, Nolan concentrated on ignoring the nurse and receptionist who took turns trying to catch his eye and tried to think of what Grace meant by 'yet'. The door opened and Grace, smiling and laughing with the doctor, brought him to meet Nolan. "Dr. Kline, this is my dear friend Nolan Burke, Nolan, this is Dr. Kline. He's the doctor who didn't get to deliver me after all."

Nolan and the doctor shook hands, and spoke for a moment as Grace made an appointment for the following week. Seeing the nurse try to catch Nolan's eye, Grace felt mischievous. "Nolan, honey, is there any way that you can bring me back next Friday?"

Nolan started. "Sure."

"No appointments that day? Do want me to call and make an appointment after you check your schedule?"

As Grace questioned him, Nolan gathered himself together. "If I've forgotten something, I'll reschedule. I want to be here with you."

While Grace confirmed the appointment, Nolan said goodbye to the doctor and stood beside her, his hand resting lightly around her shoulders. Enjoying herself, Grace smiled up at him as she paid for the visit. "Have a lovely day ladies."

As the couple walked to the car, they laughed. "That was so much fun!"

Nolan tweaked her hair. "I almost lost it when you called me honey."

Grace gave him a saucy grin. "You didn't like that? I'll have to remember to avoid 'honey' in the future."

Bending low to her ear, Nolan whispered, "Gracie, *honey*, you can call me any endearing name that you like."

"Uh uh, bub, Honey is my name- until I find a better one anyway. I had to think quickly."

The pair tossed out names of endearment as they settled themselves in Nolan's car and drove out of the parking lot. Grace gave a little shout of triumph. "I've got it! Nolie. I'll call you Nolie"

"I think not!" Nolan's tone was full of mock indignation.

Grace's giggles joined his chuckles. "Awww you don't like it? C'mon... what do you like? Hey, what does Nolan mean?"

A deep red flush crept up the back of Nolan's neck. "Noble."

"As in Noble Solutions?" Grace was trying to think of a new name based on the word Noble.

"It was my mother's name. She suggested it, I liked the way it sounded full of integrity, so I chose it." His tone was somewhat embarrassed.

"Well, English nobility consists of Lords, Dukes, Earls, Barons- I can't call you lord, you're not my husband. Duke belongs to John

Wayne and Earl sounds like the name of a dog. I think I'll call you 'sir'."

"Oh, that's endearing. I can just see those two women in there getting scared off by hearing you call me 'sir'."

Grace's laughter filled the car as Nolan pulled into a local restaurant. "Oh Nolan, I'm sure it's the way that you say it that makes it endearing."

Nolan was silent for a few moments. He wasn't prepared to be as open with her as he wanted to be. He was unsure of how quickly he could lay his full range of emotions on the table. "Grace, I don't think you have any idea of how much I'm holding myself back."

"Back? From what?" Grace felt the turn in the conversation shift from lighthearted to serious but didn't want to make too many presumptions.

Nolan looked confused. "Well, I don't know. I'd say from you, but that's not right. I don't ever want to hold back anything from you."

"So what is it?"

"Grace, I'll be honest. I'm waiting for you to make a determination about your feelings for me, and if you can respect me enough for a permanent commitment."

"Determination of feelings. Permanent commitment. You're such a man!" Grace giggled.

"I'm trying not to pressure you Grace. What I say and what I want are two very different things."

"So tell me Nolan, what is it that you want?" Grace's frustration was mounting.

"You."

"Me. You've got me. I'm right here. I'm not going anywhere."

Nolan shook his head, which irritated Grace. "Look Nolan. I'm not stupid but you're making me feel very dense. What am I missing? Is this one of those men vs. women-you'll never understand- Mars and Venus things? Am I being completely obtuse or are you being deliberately difficult?"

Nolan sighed. "The other day, I said some very intimate things to you."

"Yeah… you did. They were nice. I still turn them over in my mind. Then you sent me home so fast I couldn't figure out if you were just really busy or still upset with me."

"I just found you incredibly attractive and wanted to get you out of there."

Grace beamed. "Nolan. Thank you. That is one of the most beautiful things anyone has ever said to me."

"Huh" Nolan groaned inwardly. Could he have said anything *less* eloquent?

"You just told me that you find me very attractive. I've never been told that before."

A low chuckle rumbled from Nolan's throat. "Well, I can't say I'm sorry to hear that. I am surprised though. What is wrong with the men in this town?"

Grace's response brought him a twinge of pain. "Nolan, I've had a wonderful life. Everyone has always been kind to me, well, except maybe for Chuck, but he's never kind to anyone! But, well, I'm the girl that is 'one of the guys'. I'm the pal. I always have been and I encouraged that. Dad said it would protect my heart for the right man someday."

Nolan's curiosity got the better of him. "And did it? Did you keep your heart secure? Or did it just help?"

"It just helped." Grace looked at her hands and played with her fingernails.

"Who was he?" Nolan didn't know if he had the right to ask the question but his curiosity was aroused.

"Oh Nolan, don't you know? It's Jesus. I decided when I was fifteen that when I gave my heart to the Lord upon my salvation, that I gave it all to Him. Not just the dead, dirty, filthy, sin ridden part, but the part of my heart that wanted to be some man's special someone. I wouldn't give it away until the Lord told me I could. So, yes, it helped a little, but the Lord helped more."

Not knowing whether to hug her or give Grace a hard time, Nolan chose to thank the Lord for His hand on Grace's life. For the first time, Nolan realized that she truly was a provision from the Lord.

Twenty-Four

"Grace. It's now twelve days before Christmas. Let the fun begin."

Grace's laughter sang out over the telephone lines. "What are you talking about?"

"Open your front door." Nolan sat in his house watching through the window as Grace opened the door. Rolex scampered out of the house and barked furiously at the package that Nolan had left on the mat just minutes before. Before Grace could pick up the box, the dog dashed across the yard and over to Nolan's house.

"I've got him Grace. Open your gift."

"Are you nuts! Out here? It's *cold*!"

Grace's incredulity amused Nolan. "Ok, go inside, but open it in front of the window. I want to watch this."

"Do I open the card first or last?" Grace shook her head at the silence on the other end of the line.

"Umm, I guess so. Yes. Open it first." Nolan's voice grew certain as he decided the best order of opening.

The sounds of an envelope opening sparked a boyish eagerness in Nolan. He'd always loved giving gifts. Christmas and birthdays were his favorite days of the year as a young boy. The planning, purchasing, and even the wrapping of the gifts brought much excitement and pleasure to him. However, nothing was as wonderful, as the carefully executed presentation of a gift.

Nolan smiled at the metallic tinkle of a musical card playing *The Twelve Days of Christmas.* "Do you like that song?"

"I do now. I love it now! Can I open the box? Hey... Twelve days of Christmas... does that mean that I get twelve presents?"

Her eagerness encouraged Nolan. He'd had some concerns about whether or not Grace would enter the spirit of the game. "That's right. This is day one."

"But the twelve days of Christmas are *after* Christmas!"

"And I wanted to do it before. Sue me," Nolan laughed.

Grace tore open the box eagerly. Nestled in the bottom and surrounded by shredded Christmas paper sat a box with "Partridge Farms" stenciled on the top. Grace opened it to find the most delicious smelling pears she'd ever seen. The fragrance permeated the room.

"Oh Nolan... they're wonderful! How did you find a place called Partridge Farms?"

"Well... Melanie said she knows how to stencil so I..."

"Well come on over, bring back my escape artist, and get some. These are good!"

~~~~*

Grace smiled as she watched Nolan's long strides across the street. He held a gaily-wrapped box and wore a goofy smile. The gifts weren't nearly as fun as watching Nolan's delight in giving them. It was slowly becoming apparent to Grace, that some of Nolan's frustration with her inability to accept help stemmed from his love of giving. They were very similar in that manner.

Grace met Nolan in the front yard. Arm in arm the pair walked up Grace's steps and entered. "Paige should be here any moment. She phoned from behind your house. She's really getting into this whole spy thing."

"Really? She's coming here first?"

Grace nodded. "She went by Craig's office to thank him. Did I tell you?"

"No, how did you convince Craig. He won't tell me."

A trace of guilt crossed Grace's features. "Well, I started by giving him a fake ultimatum, kind of like I did you, but he knew I was bluffing."

"What kind of crazy threat did you have for him?"

Shaking her head, Grace pled the Fifth Amendment. "If you want to know, ask him.

"Anyway, I finally asked him if he thought that Christ was strong enough to protect me. Then I asked if he thought you were an adequate protector. Then I suggested that he come be in the house as well. I finally got through to him. I think he'll be glad when Paige can identify the guy and get him off the streets. The police are close, but identifying him *outside* a lineup would help I think."

Nolan handed Grace her package and gestured for her to open it. Inside a beautiful candy dish was laden with Chocolate turtles and Dove chocolates. Grace set the dish on her dining table after sampling the chocolates. "These are wonderful. Turtle-doves- cute"

Before Nolan could reply, Paige crept in through the back door. "No one saw me! Nathan is over at your house Nolan. I'm going to sneak across in a bit and then he'll openly come out and help you with the computer stuff."

Lunch came and went and no packages were delivered. Nolan fiddled with wires and set up programs as slowly as possible. The extra linen closet next to her coat closet made a perfect mini-office. Everyone was getting antsy. Finally, the familiar brown truck pulled up in front of Grace's house. As Grace signed the receipt, she glanced at the man's face. It wouldn't be him. He was too tall, too heavy set and he was dark haired.

As the man drove away, Paige and Nathan walked across the street in deep conversation. Grace and Nolan felt the disappointment keenly but weren't surprised. They couldn't expect to catch the man on the first try.

The couples played games and chatted through dinner. Grace had planned to make a meatloaf, but Nolan and Nathan begged for pizza. As Paige and Nathan left to make a soda run, Nolan and Grace sat on opposite ends of her couch in deep conversation.

Nathan had spoken of wanting an even number of children and, subsequently, had sparked a discussion of desired numbers. Nathan and Paige had bantered numbers back and forth while Grace sat silent on the couch. When the other couple left for the store, Nolan asked Grace what was on her mind. "You've been so quiet. What is bothering you?"

"I don't know. I've never thought about 'how many'. I just didn't give it a second thought. Have you?"

"Well, no. I did pray once for a half a dozen little Graceannas though."

A small smile tugged at the corner of Grace's mouth. "Would that happen to have been after a dinner with Melanie when she tricked you into holding Gracie?"

"Yes... she was so dear and tiny. I wanted to take her home with me." The wistful sound in Nolan's voice was very endearing to Grace's heart.

"Well, how do you decide how many children to have? You can say, 'I want two, or four, or five or twenty', but how do you know how many you should really have?"

Nolan shook his head. He'd never considered the idea. "I don't know Grace. I don't remember the Word talking about choosing the number of children but they probably didn't have birth control then either."

"True. So with birth control available, how do you use it to God's glory? What does God consider to be right? One child? Two? How do I know what His will is?"

The couple continued their discussion until the pizza and drinks arrived. Grace tried to rally above her troubled thoughts as she suggested a game of Hearts. Long after her guests left for the night, Grace was in prayer and study over the evening's topic of discussion.

The phone rang next to her and she answered it absentmindedly. The distant tone to her voice when she said 'hello' told Nolan that Grace was still troubled with her thoughts. "Can't sleep?"

"I'm studying. I can't find anything. I only read positive things about children and families. When people like Rachel and Hannah couldn't have children, they found it very disturbing. They became distraught. Rachel wanted more than one, but was that because her sister had more or because she truly wanted children. And Jacob. He's a dussie."

"How's that?" Grace's earnestness pulled Nolan from an exhausted stupor.

"Well, Rachel pleads with him to 'give her children'. You know what he said?"

"I think I remember that story, he said it wasn't in his hands or something."

Grace nodded at the phone. "That's right. He said- here, let me find it."

The pages of her Bible rustled as Grace tried to find her place again. "Here Genesis chapter thirty. It says,

"'When Rachel saw that she was not bearing Jacob any children, she became jealous of her sister. So she said to Jacob, "Give me children, or I'll die!" Jacob became angry with her and said, "Am I in the place of God, who has kept you from having children?"'

"Hey, I just noticed something."

Nolan finished Grace's sentence in the familiar manner that close friends do. "Rachel said children. Plural. She didn't just want a child, she wanted at least two."

"I wonder why. I mean, most people today, if they were infertile anyway, would be thrilled for just one child. Why wasn't Rachel asking for *a* child? Didn't Hannah ask for a single child?"

Nolan didn't know how to answer her. "Maybe Rachel's feelings about children weren't rational. Her sister goaded her constantly. Maybe that had something to do with it."

"That's true. What did Mary do?"

"Grace." Nolan was growing concerned. "Why is this so important to you?"

Grace's voice broke as she spoke. "I don't know. It's just bugging me."

"Can you trust the Lord with it? Can you turn it over to him?"

Grace nodded. She didn't realize how often she spoke with gestures rather than words. "I guess I'll have to."

"I'll be praying for a peaceful rest for you, and Grace?"

"Yes?" Grace was already beginning her prayer for peace and understanding.

"I love you." The phone clicked before Grace could respond.

Chapter Twenty-Five

"Three French Hens. Wonder what he'll have this morning Grace? We can't have poultry on this side of the street. Cross that highway and he'd be ok so it won't be that. Maybe he'll give me Cornish Game Hens to make dinner for him. He sure is having fun..."

Grace continued to ramble through her morning preparations. Today she planned to list her first boutique outfit on Etsy. Would it work or not? Not allowing herself to 'take heed for tomorrow', Grace prayed for wisdom in how much time to spend on each listing and for help in getting her pictures just right. She'd spend her morning learning how to use the web page software that Nolan had installed on his computer.

The phone rang and Grace pounced on it. "Morning!"

"Well morning sunshine! You're chipper this morning!" Nolan smiled as he teased Grace. Holding the digital camera he'd purchased the day before, Nolan debated deliberately scratching it so she wouldn't notice it was new.

"When is Paige coming today?" Grace seemed anxious to get the plan on the road.

"Nathan said they'd be over by noon. Are you going to work with that program this morning?" Nolan looked at the camera in his hand.

Upon hearing Grace affirm her intention to learn how to use the computer programs in order to begin her Etsy 'career', Nolan decided to jump in and see how she handled his purchase. "I've got something for you. I'll be right there."

Grace waited in anxious expectation as Nolan came across the street with two boxes in hand. One box was wrapped in gold paper and tied in a silver ribbon bow looking elegant and tempting, while the other appeared to be some kind of appliance. Waving at Verily who was sweeping his sidewalks across the street, Grace welcomed Nolan with a brief hug. Nolan almost forgot the gift he'd brought in his surprise at the warm greeting.

"Hey, if I go home and come back, do I get another hug?" Nolan's eyes twinkled with mischief as Grace gave him a playful punch in the arm.

"Nolan, you can have a hug anytime you want one. You just have to ask."

"Ah but Grace, I liked the spontaneous hug that you offered."

"Not too brazen for you?" Grace eyed the package in Nolan's hand.

"Grace, you couldn't be brazen if you tried. You wouldn't know how. Want your third day gift?"

"*Yes!*" Grace playfully jumped as if Nolan was holding it over her head and caught the package up in her hands. "It's so light! It could be a gift certificate for a poultry farm but I kind of doubt it."

Nolan's voice was low and wheedling. "Open it Grace. I'm dying to know if you like it."

Grace unwrapped the simple little box and found she was partially right. "It is a gift certificate! And if I order some kind of poultry it'll make me completely right. When are we going?"

The couple discussed the best time to make reservations at the elegant French restaurant while Nolan showed Grace how to operate the camera. They took pictures of the dress from every angle and Grace worked hard to manipulate the pictures to look as nice as the other listings. Paige and Nathan arrived bearing a large submarine sandwich, chips and sparkling cider. "We're celebrating the soon-to-be capture of our elusive attacker!"

"Paige you're crazy but you're fun!" Grace immediately began cutting the sandwich and setting the slices on plates laden with chips and fruit.

Nathan left for work as Paige settled herself in Nolan's house. Nolan and Grace went to work trying to create auction pages that looked as professional as the ones doing well on eBay. The UPS driver came and Nolan signed for the box while Grace continued to get the lighting just right.

Five minutes later, Nolan noticed that Paige hadn't come over or called. "Grace. I think something's wrong. Paige hasn't called and she's still at my house. I'm going over there. I'll call you if there's a problem."

Grace followed him to the door praying. She hadn't really expected today to be 'the day'. It was only day two. She was certain that it would take the whole week, if not longer, before they saw the man they hoped to identify.

The phone rang. Instead of answering it, Grace ran across the street and flung open Nolan's front door. "Where are you guys?"

Grace followed the sound of Nolan's voice down his hallway to a front bedroom. Paige sat on the floor of the doorway, paralyzed and clutching her cell phone in her hand. "What happened?"

"I don't know. She's just sitting there. She won't answer me, and I can't get the phone from her."

Grace sprang into action. Sitting next to Paige, she wrapped her arms around her friend and began rubbing her arms. "I need a blanket and you need to call Todd Mercer now. Did the guy at the door have red hair?"

"No, it was brown, why?"

"Get Todd over here and get me a blanket. I think you should call 9-1-1 too. She's very cold and not responding. I think she's in shock.

Todd and an ambulance were on the way, and Nolan carried Paige into his living room and laid her on the couch. "Do you think it just shocked her or did he see her? Why is she like this?"

Grace shook her head. "I don't know. I really don't understand it but she was unusually strong after the attack. Maybe she just collapsed in relief."

The sound of the ambulance siren grew louder as it approached the house. Paramedics rushed in followed quickly by Todd and his partner Rick Marlowe. In moments, the paramedics had Paige loaded and on her way to the hospital. Todd turned to Grace and smiled.

"She's going to be fine. She identified him I'm sure. She's not talking yet but I am sure that's what it is. Which of you saw him?"

Nolan held up a hand. He wasn't happy to see the officer standing in his living room. Despite his better knowledge, he couldn't forget the picture of Grace walking down the street talking earnestly to the ruggedly handsome officer. "I did."

"Did he have red hair and a mustache?" Todd noticed the coolness in Nolan's response but attributed it to his role as an officer. People often became defensive with him just walking into the room.

"No. Brown hair, no mustache. What can that mean?"

Grace looked up from her seat on the couch where she'd been praying. "Maybe he uses one of those 24 hour hair dyes?"

Todd nodded. "Probably. We've got a call into the local UPS yard. They're going to tell me who delivered the package that Nolan signed for. I need the tracking number from that package."

Before Todd could continue, Rick spoke up. "What you people did today was brave, but very stupid. You may have injured your friend's health, you could have put him in danger and you could have interfered in a police investigation which is a felony."

Grace nodded. "I realize all of that, but Paige wanted to and she has the legal right to watch and see if someone delivering packages looks like the man who attacked her. She's stronger than she looks. She'll be ok."

As the two officers left, following taking down their report, Todd winked at Grace and waved as they drove away. Nolan watched the exchange with a frown. Grace, noticing the look of irritation on Nolan's face, misunderstood and grew angry. "Nolan, if you weren't convinced, you shouldn't have agreed. I'm not really in the mood to discuss this right now. I'm going to go home."

Nolan stood watching Grace move swiftly toward home. His mother's voice echoed in his head as he watched Grace enter her house. "Son, don't let a friend walk away from you angry. Confront the problem before it grows too big to handle."

He jogged across the street, knocked on her door, and entered without waiting for an invitation. Rolex bounced and danced around his legs as Grace sang of Scotch lassies coming over the ocean to be with their true love. "Grace?"

She jumped, dropped a plate, and whirled around to face him. "You startled me!"

"I'm sorry Grace. That's a beautiful song. Would you leave your homeland and move across the ocean to be with the love of your life?"

"Well, living in America, that means I get to go to Scotland. Land of the crags and the sheep and thatched cottages... Oh yeah I'd go. I've always wanted to see Scotland."

"Why are you angry with me Grace? What did I say?" Nolan's tone showed Grace that she had been wrong.

"I'm not. I thought you were sorry we'd helped Paige today. The look on your face when Rick and Todd left-"

Embarrassed, Nolan decided to come clean. "Grace. That wasn't anger you saw. You saw pure, unadulterated, jealousy. I noticed Todd's interaction with you and when I remembered the last time I saw you two together-"

"What last time?" Grace found Nolan's jealousy charming but didn't know what to think about the comment about 'last time'.

"Well, several weeks ago, I think it was the day after Paige was attacked, I saw you and Todd outside of that little coffee shop on Warner Street."

"That was the day I found the mustache and took it into the police station. Todd and I had coffee and caught up on each other's lives."

"I know, and I know he has some kind of online friend, but-"

Grace interrupted eagerly. "Actually, I introduced him to Marci and I think they are hitting it off."

Nolan nodded. "Are we ok Grace?"

Grace nodded as she rushed to answer the ringing phone. A few short sentences later, she hung up and turned to Nolan. "Do you want to drive me over? Paige is there and coming around. I'm glad I listened and didn't insist on going with them. It sounds like the officers are there now."

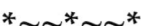

Wednesday brought the surprise of a new cordless phone that rang four times to awaken Grace in the morning. She laughed to discover that Craig had installed it as she slept the night before. Craig teased that Nolan had begged to be allowed to help so he could determine if she snored, but Grace dismissed him with a laugh.

The morning news announced that the man arrested the night before for the attacks on eleven Brunswick women, had confessed to all charges against him. The announcement brought relief to more than the friends of Paige Matthews.

Paige was kept in the hospital for observation overnight and released. Nathan's possessive attentions as he took her home were charming to observe and Grace and Nolan enjoyed speculating how serious the relationship was growing as they watched the solicitous care Nathan showed as he settled Paige into his car and drove toward her apartment.

Thursday, Nolan knocked on Grace's door, as she was finishing her time of prayer and Bible study. He pulled a blindfold over her eyes and led her to his car. Once out of town, he passed her a basket with hot tea, Danishes, and fruit

"Where are you taking me?" Grace was enjoying herself immensely. She loved surprises.

"Ok, take your blindfold off. We're going to a favorite childhood place of mine."

"Does this have something to do with 'five golden rings'?"

Nolan's grin answered for him. Grace smiled at the thought but wondered what golden rings had to do with the man's childhood. "Sure, leave me hanging."

"It's supposed to be a surprise. If I tell you, it's not a surprise!"

The car ride was a long one. They laughed, told funny childhood stories, and their understanding of each other developed to a deeper level. Two and a half hours later, they took a side road that led to a small replica of a European Village.

"You're taking me to Little Vienna! I haven't been here since I was in Jr. High School."

Nolan smiled. "They brought us here in seventh grade but my parents came every year. It's where they went on their honeymoon and we all came every year for their anniversary. I liked it because I always got a room at that little inn on the square all to myself."

"They let you stay in it alone?" Grace couldn't imagine such an idea.

"Well, we had those connecting doors. They were always open when I went to sleep and closed when I woke up. I thought it was magic."

Grace laughed at the picture of an awed child Nolan waking up to a door that was shut when it'd been open. "You had a delightful childhood didn't you?"

"My parents were masters of creating special experiences to enrich my life." Nolan's voice was laced with longing as he remembered the parents he missed so fiercely.

Nolan pulled into an almost empty town square. Thursdays were usually fairly free of tourists, even though it was just days before Christmas. Leading Grace through the park on the square, they found an old-fashioned carousel in the center of the park. A few mothers sat watching their children ride the horses and several more sat on the horses next to, or behind their children on horses.

"The brass ring! You're going to try for the brass ring aren't you?"

Nolan nodded and held up his hand, all five fingers extended. "This one happens to have five brass rings and a bunch of iron ones. I thought it might be a fun diversion from chocolate and pears."

"Five? You're going to try to get five rings? Are we going to ride this thing all day? I tried for a brass ring when I was in Jr. High! It's not as easy as it looks!"

Nolan's smile disarmed her. Grace looked carefully into Nolan's eyes and groaned in mock disgust. "You've done this before haven't you?"

Catching her hand, Nolan ran for the entrance to the carousel and they each chose their animals. Grace sat sidesaddle on a lion beribboned to show his regal bearing. "If I'd known we were doing this, I would have worn something else!"

"Nolan smiled and shook his head. "You're perfect the way you are. You look like English Nobility parading through the jungles of India."

Smiling Grace bopped Nolan with her purse as they came close to the first ring. Leaning carefully, the man snagged it with and presented it to Grace with a flourish.

On their second pass, he leaned behind Grace to grab a ring near her side. Grace's laughter rang out as she held two rings in her hands. The children around them stared in awe. Swiftly he stood on his feet and leaned across the other way to snatch one that came in quick succession.

Grace quickly realized that Nolan had a talent for ring grabbing. Laughing through the final two rings, Grace felt the carousel slow down to stop. She whispered something into Nolan's ear before dismounting from her lion and handing the rings out to the children nearest to her. "If you give this to the man when he comes around, he'll let you ride again."

They stood and went to sit on the booth like benches and smiled at the children's delight in riding again. As they exited the carousel, Grace noticed Nolan slipping a bill to the operator as he passed. "Did you pay him for the rides?"

"Well, the brass ring tradition wasn't meant for big adults like me. It wouldn't be right to take advantage of them."

"You are a fine man Nolan Burke. A very fine man."

They strolled hand in hand through the village as Nolan shared his childhood memories. From the fountain he fell into after making a wish, to the little shop where his father purchased Nolan's first knife, he had a story for almost every brick and cobblestone.

Grace found it fascinating to discover the rich heritage that a man, completely alone in the world, could have hidden away in another side that others didn't see. "Thank you for sharing this with me."

They ate lunch in an authentic Austrian restaurant sampling Weiner Schnitzel and Apfelstrudel. The proprietress tried to encourage the couple to try a sachertorte but, overfull from their lunch, they refused as graciously as possible before strolling toward the river that ran past the town and through an authentic watermill.

"This river runs into Lake Danube near Fairbury, I remember thinking that they should have built this village down there," she mused as they neared the water.

Skipping rocks across the surface of the side creeks and throwing an occasional snowball at each other, Grace and Nolan spent a glorious afternoon just enjoying each other's company. As the day drew to a close, Grace found herself not wanting it to end. The thought of sending Nolan home alone was frustrating.

Friday dawned bright and clear. Fresh snowfall was evident by the hushed sounds of children hurrying off to the bus. Grace dressed quickly and brushed her hair as she threw open her living room drapes. The sight before her sparked an uncontrollable fit of giggles.

On her lawn, in all their tacky glory, sat six of the most ridiculous Easter geese she'd ever seen. Dressed in prissy bonnets, the 'geese' had laid plastic Easter eggs all over the snow-covered lawn. The incongruous mixture of pastel and lace bonnets with

Christmas wreathes draped about the necks of the geese was a remarkable sight. Children giggled and pointed as they passed her lawn with its gaggle, carefully positioned for maximum comical effect.

She picked up her new cordless phone and dialed Nolan's cell number. His drapes were closed and the driveway showed tire tracks so she was certain that he'd gone to the city for a lunch meeting or to de-bug some program that he'd written. Nolan answered on the fifth ring.

"Sorry Grace. I had to pull over. The traffic is murder out here. What can I do for you?"

Momentarily forgetting the purpose of her call, Grace looked at her phone before speaking. "How'd you know it was me? Why didn't you just ignore the call?"

"I have the phone velcroed to my dash and the phone flashes your name and number if I enter it into my 'address book' that is in the phone."

Nolan smiled at the mental picture he had of Grace. He could just see her nodding into the phone and trying to keep a straight face as she commented on the spectacle, he'd made of her lawn. Leaving that morning, without seeing Grace's reaction to his artwork had been hard. Nolan observed that work could be a serious detriment to one's social life.

"Grace? Did I lose you?"

Grace shook her head and answered. "Nolan, I have to tell you, this is a spectacular sight on my lawn. I'm likely to be in tomorrow's paper you know. Meanwhile, I'm becoming quite nervous about the next few days."

Nolan's hearty laughter warmed her heart. "I assure you, there will be no more fowl play at your house."

Grace dissolved in a fresh burst of giggles and said goodbye. Seeing her little dog come crawling out from his bed on the back porch, Grace picked him up. "Rolex, would you just look at what that man did out here?"

Grace sent her little dog out into the yard. The pooch yipped and yapped at each goose, pulling on some of the wreaths, and knocking a couple over. With a triumphant bark, the fur ball grabbed green egg in his little snout and dashed back into the house.

Grace spent her day with Melanie and Gracie-anna finishing the plans and the shopping for Christmas Day. On their way through the mall to Melanie's favorite home store, Grace saw an exquisite sweater in a store window. In an instant, she threw aside her desire to be fiscally responsible.

"Melanie. I want that sweater. I could wear that with my royal velveteen skirt to that party at Nolan's friend's house next week. I've got to have it."

Without a moment's hesitation, Grace went into the store, found her size, tried it on, paid for it, and left the store swinging her shopping bag and feeling wonderful. Melanie dropped Grace off at her doctor's appointment where Nolan planned to meet her, drove straight to Craig's office. When Craig heard the story of Grace's purchase, the man smiled a special smile that Melanie knew was reserved only for his sister. "She's in love Mel. My baby sister is in love."

Grace sat in the doctor's private office waiting for the verdict. Dr. Kline took her suggestion and let her sit in the office and rest from her shopping trip while he took the next patient. Nolan hadn't arrived yet and she hoped he'd make it before she received her 'verdict'. Moments after she finally relaxed, an attentive nurse ushered Nolan into the office.

Nolan sat next to Grace and took her hand in his. He was startled by how cold her hand was. "Grace, I'm so sorry I'm late. Your hands are like ice. Are you nervous or just cold?"

Smiling into the handsome man next to her, Grace shrugged. "I'm always cold. You know that."

A voice behind them spoke out. "Not for long. My suspicions were confirmed Grace, you have low thyroid function. I'm going to start you on a synthetic replacement for the thyroid hormone."

For the next several minutes, the doctor told Grace what to watch for in order to determine if she became over medicated. Nolan had many questions for the doctor and Grace took notes. Surprisingly, the answer seemed to be simple. The doctor instructed Grace to take a tiny little pill, and the pill was instructed to make Grace well.

At home, Marci brought Amber to Grace for a few hours while she went to dinner and a movie with Todd Mercer. When Nolan noticed his little friend bouncing her way into Grace's house, he gathered a computer videogame console, a new soccer game, and made a beeline for Grace's house. He'd noticed that the girl needed male attention and had made a point of spending as much time with her as he could whenever she was with Grace.

After a meal, hot chocolate and a frenzied game of Yahtzee, Grace begged for a nap. Nolan encouraged her to rest while he and Amber battled it out on the electronic soccer field. Twenty minutes later, the score stood tied. Amber tried not to squeal as she scored another goal.

"Are you going to marry Miss Grace?" Amber's voice was hushed over the sounds of the game in which both of them were engrossed.

"Well, Amber, I hope to. What do you think? Should I ask her to marry me?" Nolan was somewhat taken aback but intrigued by the girl's question.

Amber nodded emphatically as she swerved to kick an electronic soccer ball that rolled across the screen. "What will you say?"

"Say?"

Amber sighed and tossed her joystick aside allowing Nolan to score the winning point. "How will you ask her? Will it be romantic?"

Nolan shrugged as he packed up the game gear. "I'm not sure. I'd like it to be but that's kind of personal."

"You've got to make it romantic. She's going to remember it for the rest of her life! You can't just go in there and say, 'Oh by the way, I thought it might be cool to get married. What do you say?'." Amber sounded quite affronted that the perfect situation hadn't been arranged before now.

Nolan chuckled and tweaked her hair. Amber's giggles resounded through the room. "Shhh! We don't want to wake up Grace. She needs her rest. So, where did you get your notions of romantic proposals?"

Amber grinned. "My mom likes to watch old movies. They're really mushy sometimes. The guys always say something really romantic to the girl and how can she say no when he says something so great? You gotta say it right."

Nodding absentmindedly, Nolan began mentally rehearsing how to ask Grace to promise to become his wife. Looking over at Amber, he sighed. "I'll never come up with anything that sounds as good as a movie. I'd be smart to just drop a ring in her lap, get on my hands and knees, beg, and pray for the best."

"No way. You need to do it right. Miss Grace deserves the best and you've got to give it to her." Amber's voice showed traces of disgust. Hey... I have an idea. I'll be Grace, you practice on me." Amber's delight with her idea was evident.

"Oh but Amber, it's so personal. I don't think Grace would like to know that someone else heard her proposal before she did.

Amber clapped her hands and bounced on the couch in delight. "If you can't tell me then it's perfect. And then the preacher will say you may kiss the bride!"

Nolan lifted Amber's little hand and kissed it in the manner of days gone by. "Thank you Milady Amber. I can't wait to ask her."

"Do you have a ring? You've got to have a ring. Grace is old fashioned. She won't want to have to pick it out herself. It'll make her feel weird. You really should have one."

"I don't know what she likes." Suddenly, Nolan realized that marriage might be easier than the process of getting there.

"Well, Melanie told mom that Grace likes apples and pearls, but Miss Grace told me that she likes Black Fools Gold." Pride shone in Amber's voice as she relayed this very important information while Nolan did his best to keep from laughing.

"What's this about fools gold and pearls?" Grace's voice startled the co-conspirators.

Nolan scrambled to find the right words to cover his tracks. "Well, we were just rehearsing."
Amber interjected her contribution before Nolan could continue. "For kind of a play thing. Nolan was being the handsome prince. He makes a good one huh. I was Milady Amber."

"Sounds like a nice play. I want to see it when it opens ok?" Grace heated tea as she listened to the pair joke about Nolan wearing tights and a medieval tunic.

Before Nolan could open his jaw, Amber quipped, "Don't worry, you will."

Chapter Twenty-Six

Saturday dawned early. Day seven arrived. Grace wondered just what to expect as she tried to imagine what would happen with swans. "Lord, yesterday's foray into the wonderful world of front page small town news was quite intriguing, but can you help him find something less public for his swimming swans?"

Two hours later, Amber arrived at her door shivering and dressed in a Swan Lake costume complete with tutu. Standing in Grace's living room with her mother taping every minute for posterity, Amber read a short poem written for the occasion. Her sweet little singsong voice was filled with excitement.

"Seven swans a-swimming will soon be swans a-dancing
You can just call it my peculiar form of romancing
And I would like, to ask from you, if I may be so bold
For just one hand, through out the night, for this poor gent to hold."

The little 'ballerina' hugged Grace and handed her a creamy envelope of tickets to January's performance of the classic ballet in Rockland. Grace's eyes began to fill with tears. Nolan was going 'all-out' with this little game of his. Ballet tickets were limited to Grace's dreams and far away from her budget.

Marci nodded and pushed the camcorder into Grace's hands. "Take this and go talk to him. He loves you, you know."

"I know." Grace hurried across the street, camcorder in hand.

Nolan stood shivering in his doorway. With less reserve than Grace usually carried herself, Grace jogged up to him as if to hug him but stopped short. "Thank you."

A fleeting look of disappointment masked his eyes before he smiled down at her. "You're welcome. Do you like ballet?"

"I watch it every time it's on the TV but that's not very often these days... What's wrong?"

Nolan waved off the question. "I'm glad. These are good seats. My father was a donor to the Rockland Arts Association so I grew up on a wide variety of cultural things."

"Nolan, you're avoiding my question. I saw something in your eyes. What's wrong?"

Marci watched the scenario with excitement. An engagement was looming. Nolan listened earnestly to something Grace said before bending low to whisper into her ear. Marci's romantic side drank in the scene. Grace wrapped her arms around his neck before handing him the camcorder. Marci drove off with a wave and a sigh. It couldn't happen to a nicer couple.

Grace waved to Nolan and Marci as she hurried back into her house. She had a busy day ahead of her and she needed to get to work. Nolan and Grace were having dinner at Craig's house that evening so Grace wanted to be well rested before they left.

~~~~*

The conversation around Craig and Melanie's table was full of Christmas plans and special secrets. Nolan seemed jittery and nervous which bothered Grace seated across the table from him. Before she could gently kick his shins to catch his eye, Nolan stood.

"I have a, well, toast isn't correct. Hmm- I guess I have a request to make of you Craig."

Grace's eyes opened in surprise. This was not what she'd expected from Nolan. Before she could react, Craig spoke. "Anything for you Nolan. You're almost like family now."

Nolan swallowed hard at the word 'family'. How would he ever say this right without looking like a fool? "Craig, I would formally like to request your blessing on my pursuit of Grace's hand..."

A deep hush fell over the table as Craig worked his jaw trying to contain his emotions. Grace, strained to the emotional breaking point, finally spoke. "That's odd."

Nolan was taken aback. "What's odd?"

"You only want a hand? No feet, legs, head, arms?

Nolan's rumbling chuckle was interrupted with one last barb. "Oh and by the way, if Craig won't give his blessing, I will."

~~~~*

Grace found Nolan's "Lily Maid" goat's milk soap assortment a hysterical alternative to a lawn full of cows and milkmaids. "Where did you *find* this?"

Nolan's laughter seemed to wash away the edginess that surrounded him. "My mother."

Grace quirked a single eyebrow. Quickly, Nolan explained that his mother had purchased the lot of soap from a schoolgirl selling soaps and lotions to go to camp. "It was either give you mom's soaps or buy you some cheese with a feminine sounding name. I opted for the soaps. I called the company, they say that it's perfectly safe to use the soap and they still smell nice."

Grace cut him off with a smile. "You don't have to apologize. You gave me a piece of your mother. That's a pretty special gift."

"Piece of mom?" Nolan shook his head in confusion.

"The story Nolan. Your mother bought something from a little girl, something she probably didn't want. She made a little girl's dream possible. That's a side of her I expected, but you hadn't shared yet. Thanks!"

The couple had been talking on their way to church and as they pulled into the parking lot, Grace smiled over at Nolan. "This has been the most fun week I've ever had. Have I thanked you?"

"Of course Grace, if you hadn't voiced your appreciation, which you have of course, your eyes, your smiles and even your occasional tentative affectionate expressions, have told me that you were pleased."

"Tentative huh? Maybe I need lessons in showing proper affection."

As they walked up the steps, Nolan whispered one last thought into Grace's ear. "I'd be happy to volunteer as your teacher."

~~~~*

Monday morning found him at a jewelry store explaining his mission to the woman behind the counter. "I want a diamond in it.

Something small. She likes pearls and opals but the last jeweler I spoke to said that they're too soft for everyday wear. I'm hoping she'll never want to take this off. I also want plenty of gold in the lower part so it can easily be sized in pregnancy. I don't want her to have to go without if her fingers swell."

The sales clerk was growing caught up in the excitement in finding the perfect ring. When Nolan requested Black Hills Gold, she'd assumed that the man was working on a budget. She kept showing him inexpensive alternatives until eventually Nolan realized what she was doing. After assuring the woman that he'd pay thousands for just the right ring, the search was on in earnest.

Nolan checked his watch again. What was keeping Paige? She'd agreed to meet him at the last jewelers an hour before. Snapping open his cell phone, Nolan dialed her number. As Paige answered with her trademark, "Good Morning," Nolan felt a tap on his back. Turning, the man laughed, snapped his phone shut and gave Paige a fierce hug.

"I'm so glad you got here. I was getting worried."

The sales clerk watched and sighed. It was so romantic to watch them talking and laughing. "Well, are we ready to look again? Mark is going to bring out another tray that we had in the vault."

Turning to the woman at the counter, Nolan introduced Paige. "Beth, this is my…"

"Fiancée. Nice to meet you Grace. You are a very lucky woman. Nolan is a great guy. What a catch!"

Paige shook her head violently. "Nope. Nolan's not mine. Would you like to see a picture of Grace? She is my best friend and Nolan here is pretty lucky to have *her*."

Beth gave polite attention to the photo and turned back to her job of selling jewelry. Paige waved everything aside. "No. This isn't right at all. I saw one on my way in. It's perfect. That's what took me so long. They're holding it for us right now."

Torn between wanting to rush to purchase the ring, and feeling a desire to purchase something from his helpful sales clerk, Nolan turned to Beth and asked for one more item. "I need a charm. For a charm bracelet of course. Something that has to do with money. A piggy bank, dollar sign- anything that makes you think of money."

Paige looked at him questioningly but Nolan was too absorbed in a display of charms to notice. "What about that one? The penny.

That's original. I like it. I'll take it. Can you wrap it up and when I get back, I'll put it on my card? I'll be back in a few minutes."

Tossing his business card on the counter for Beth to use in writing up his receipt, Nolan hurried off with Paige to purchase the ring Paige had picked out for him. As he examined the ring his shopping companion had chosen, Nolan smiled. It was perfect.

A full-blown tri-colored gold rose was nestled in a swirl of gold. A single tiny diamond created the center of the rose and shone beautifully. It had all of the originality of Grace and yet the traditional diamond that just seems to belong with engagement rings.

The date he planned to propose was engraved into the band for Nolan's benefit. He knew that he'd not be tempted to postpone his proposal if there was something written in gold telling his original intentions. They picked up the gift-wrapped charm and strolled out of the mall. Paige teased him all the way to her car. After setting the packages in her trunk, Nolan gave her a brief hug, thanked her and walked back to his car. In thirty-six hours, he'd know if Grace meant it when she gave her blessing to him proposing.

In Brunswick, Nolan stopped at the dance studio and called Grace. He'd made arrangements to have a single private class with the instructor before paying for nine weeks of ballroom dancing. He stepped outside, crossed the street, and entered the same coffee shop that he'd seen Grace and that officer talking near.

Grace walked in looking rosy and happy. "Verily was going shopping so he dropped me off at Grant's Groceries."

Grace had awakened full of curiosity. Her first thought of the day was, "What will he do for nine dancing ladies? Wonder if that Irish Step Dancing troupe is back in town? Lord, this is just too much fun. You're too good to me."

Sipping coffee with Nolan, Grace knew that he was about to reveal his latest 'gift' and was almost bursting with anticipation. Nolan watched the emotions glowing in Grace's eyes and worked hard not to laugh. Craig had assured him that Grace wouldn't object to the dancing lessons but Nolan wanted to be certain.

"Grace. This is day nine. Nine ladies dancing. What do you think about dancing anyway?"

Grace gave him a wry smile. "What kind of dancing and who's doing it?"

'Well, Craig assured me that it would be ok but, Well, I've always pictured myself having a very special dance at our- with my-" Nolan swallowed hard.

"What is your gift Nolan? If you and Craig are in favor of it, I dare say I will be too."

~~~~*

For the first time in his life, Nolan understood the common phrase, 'she took my breath away'. Grace was ready for the party at Mike and Traci's. The emerald green sweater looked marvelous with her royal blue velveteen skirt. She wore her charm bracelet on one hand, its lone charm dangling from the center.

Thankful for the lack of an audience, Nolan swallowed the lump in his throat. "Grace, you look..."

A slow smile crept across Grace's face. "Really? I look all right? Am I over dressed? Under dressed? Both?"

With one hand, Nolan tucked a stray hair behind Grace's ear and whispered. "You look perfect. I have something for you."

Grace accepted the pretty little box. Not sure what to expect from Nolan, she opened the box gingerly. Nestled in the bottom of the tiny box lay a golden 'penny'; a charm for her bracelet. "Nolan, thank you so much but what does the penny signify?"

"Your fears. You said that you wanted to make a bracelet of all of your fears. You're not truly afraid of money, but you do allow your pride to make you fearful of spending it. So I thought it might be appropriate." Nolan's eyes were hopeful. He hoped she'd understand. Grace was so strong in so many ways, he hadn't been able to come up with any other fears other than the fear of driving and Melanie had already shown him the little VW Beetle charm that they'd purchased for her stocking.

On the way to Rockland, Grace toyed with her charm. The motion and movement made Nolan wild with frustration. Every movement seemed to grate on his nerves. Finally, Nolan picked up Grace's hand and asked permission to hold it. "Do you mind?"

Grace found his request endearing. Wrapping their hands in her other hand, she nodded. Looking down into the valley that Rockland encompassed, the lights of the city were breathtaking. Unconsciously, Grace began singing her favorite holiday song, *Silver*

Bells. Nolan's rich baritone joined her and the car resounded with harmony such as they sped toward their destination.

"Grace, that was marvelous. I've heard you sing but it's always been in mock exaggeration with those funny old songs you love so much. I had no idea your voice was so lovely."

Grace beamed at Nolan's compliment. Slowly she was learning to appreciate and bask in the wonderful opinion that Nolan seemed to have of her. Rather than doubt his words, she smiled. "Nolan, I've wanted to sing with you ever since I heard you singing behind me that first Sunday at *The Assembly*."

"Oh… May I ask Mike if we can sing? His wife plays the piano and always tries to get people to do an 'impromptu' talent show. They usually get me to do *Battle Hymn of the Republic* since it was my father's favorite. I've sung it at these parties since I was four, but I'd love to sing with you instead."

Grace nodded. Looking at the clock, she gave a murmur of dismay. "Oh Nolan, aren't we going to be early? Should we stop and get a cup of coffee or something? It's only six o'clock now and you said the party starts at seven."

Nolan sagged in relief. He'd been praying that Grace would notice and save him from making the observation. He didn't want to be too obvious. "Oh my, you're right. We didn't hit much traffic did we? Well, I know where we can get the world's best hot chocolate and a beautiful view of ice skaters. Some are budding professionals."

"That outdoor skating rink down by the park? I'd love to see it. My father took me when I was ten but I was lousy on ice skates." Grace sat up in eager anticipation. Nolan's relief was lost on her as she watched for the right exit and chattered about the falls and tumbles she'd taken on her one and only jaunt on the ice.

In minutes, Nolan and Grace were wrapped in blankets on the benches near the ice sipping cocoa and watching the skaters. One little girl, hardly over five or six years, was spun and jumped like a professional. "I've watched her go from barely moving across the ice to her first jump that she landed, to spinning like that. She's incredible."

Grace looked at Nolan in surprise. "What's her name?"

He shrugged. "I don't know. I've wanted to ask her mother- that's her, over by that tree, but I always thought she'd think I was a creep out to harm her child so I never did."

"What are we going to sing?" Grace was cold. Talking would keep her teeth from chattering so she worked hard to keep the conversation flowing.

Singing was the last thing on Nolan's mind. His throat was thick and his mouth was dry. He ordered a second cup from the mobile vendor as the man passed by again and seared his tongue drinking too quickly.

"How about one of your oldie songs? Are there any that I know? It might be a nice change."

Grace rattled off the names of dozens of songs, most of which Nolan didn't know. Out of desperation, she began rattling off the names of songs in every musical she'd ever seen. From Anchors Aweigh to Sound of Music, Grace tried to find the right song. By the time she got to My Fair Lady, Grace was certain that the idea was doomed to failure. *"On the Street Where You Live?"*

Nolan's voice rang out clear and true before Grace could suggest any other song. Taken aback, it wasn't until the line about being several stories high that Grace picked up the harmony. People stopped skating to listen as the song carried across the frozen rink. Muffled applause resounded around them as people clapped through their mittens as the singers finished.

Gathering his nerve, Nolan turned to Grace. "Grace, I-"

Words escaped his memory. All the practice that he'd done in the few days previous was for naught. Looking into Grace's eyes, all Nolan could think of was the pain of possible rejection. Finally, in a moment of determination he spoke.

"Grace, I love you."

"I think I am beginning to realize that you really do." Grace looked intently into Nolan's eyes. Smiling softly and with the hint of tears in her eyes, she voiced her feelings for the first time. "I love you too, very much."

Her confession of love for him demolished any remnants of the beautiful proposal he'd formulated. Somewhat panicked, Nolan gathered Grace into his arms. Holding her closely, he tried again. "Will you marry me Grace? I-" Nolan's mouth went dry again.

Before he could swallow and try again Grace began weeping silently. Not knowing whether or not to continue his proposal, Nolan tightened his arms about her and pulled her closer to him.

Whispering into her hair Nolan tried again. "Oh Grace, I-"

A burst of sobs cut him short. He pulled Grace closer to him and tried to soothe her. "I'm sorry Grace. I botched this terribly. I really wanted to make it special for you but all I did was hurt you. Please Grace, just don't tell me that you've decided against me. Maybe we need more time. I'll wait for you to be ready…"

"No, Nolan. That's-"

"No? "

Grace smiled up at him through the tears that still streamed from her eyes. "I meant yes. Nolan I'll marry you tomorrow if you want me to. I was just overcome… I'm either in love or ridiculously hormonal or maybe it's this stupid medication."

Deep chuckles erupted as Grace burst into a fresh round of sobs. Moments later Nolan and Grace dissolved into chuckles and giggles as the absurdity of their behavior hit them. "It's the most wonderful thing to ever happen to me and I'm crying like I'll never see you again."

Nolan smiled tenderly at her as he pulled the ring box from his jacket pocket. A crowd had gathered several yards away to watch the proceedings but they were too engrossed in each other to notice. As Grace opened the box and saw the ring lying there, she looked back into Nolan's eyes. "Are you sure Nolan? Once this is on my finger, you'll have a terrible time getting it off me so I have to know. Are you sure?"

"About you?" Nolan was eager to see the ring on Grace's finger. He had no idea how to answer Grace's questions.

"You had very specific ideas about what you were looking for in a wife. Do I really meet those criteria? I don't ever want to wonder if you 'settled' for me. Can you understand that? I mean am I really what you've been praying for?"

"Grace. I don't want that list. I just want you. If you didn't fill everything on the list to perfection, I wouldn't care. I'm just doubly blessed that you do."

A moment of uncertainty passed as Grace digested his words. Another awkward moment almost passed as Grace handed the ring to Nolan. Surprise and pain crept into his eyes until she said, "Nolan, would you put this on me? I have enough school girl romance in me to think it'd be special to have you put it on for me."

As Nolan slipped the ring on Grace's finger, a cheer went up from the crowd. Surprised, and more than slightly embarrassed,

Nolan and Grace hurried back to the car and drove toward Mike and Traci's. They rode in a sweet silence until Grace finally spoke. "What will your friends say? Will they approve of me?"

Nodding, Nolan traced the outline of her hand with his fingers. "Mike knows that I planned to propose. Now I know why he told me to bring you in the back way. He thought you might want a moment to 'freshen up' as he put it."

"I guess Traci cried when he proposed."

"I guess so. I think I remember my mom saying she laughed and stalked out of the restaurant." Nolan parked the car in Mike's driveway.

"You're kidding! What did your dad do?"

"Followed her, stopped her, pulled her into a nearby doorway, and kissed her. Apparently that kiss changed her mind."

Grace gave him a sidewise glance. "Maybe I should have said no."

~~~~*

"I'd like to make a little announcement. Well, maybe it's not so little but Nolan asked Grace to marry him tonight, and she has accepted. Let's congratulate them and wish them many years of happiness."

Mike's announcement was received with cheers and warm wishes. The women surrounded Grace hugging her and commenting on the unique ring, Nolan had purchased. The men laughed and clapped Nolan on the shoulder. Nolan reached Grace's side quickly. With his arm around her shoulder, it was obvious to the entire room the pride he felt as Grace's fiancée.

Hours later, as Nolan bid goodbye to his friends, Grace and Traci cleaned up in Traci's kitchen. "Grace, I can't tell you how happy we are that Nolan found you. He's been so alone in the world since Mom and Pop Burke died. The women at church, you met them, they're wonderful women but Nolan was always looking for someone like Mom Burke and our ladies are too sophisticated for that. You're real."

"I can't believe he chose me. The women here- they're beautiful and intelligent and-"

"And completely uninterested in creating a home. Mom Burke and Mother Finch spoiled our men with excellent home lives. These men of ours love home and family more than anything. I wasn't trained for home making like you were but I'm learning. Fortunately, Mike loves me anyway."

Traci and Grace chatted unaware that their words were overheard. Two women from Nolan's former church looked at each other in surprise. They could see why Grace had captured Nolan's heart. She was genuine, loving, and friendly. While not the most beautiful woman at the party, her face shone with an inner beauty that these ladies rarely saw. The women were all that Grace had said they were and more. They were just not, what a man like Nolan Burke was looking for.

The next day dragged by as if being played through slow motion. Grace waited anxiously all day for ten lords to leap into her life. She racked her brains trying to figure out what Nolan would do. She imagined Russian Cossacks dancing in a foreign film and rabbits jumping across her lawn with names like Sir Bunnyhad or Lord Bouncewood.

Grace found herself twisting the ring on her finger and reliving the prior evening. "Engaged. Grace Lynn Buscher, you are engaged!"

A letter arrived in the afternoon mail. Grace opened the missive to discover instructions for Grace to be ready to depart to the city at three-thirty. Grace read the note carefully. *"Grace... this is somewhat of a dressy occasion.* **Bond Street** *is holding a dress for you, should you choose to accept it. They're ready to deliver at a moment's notice. Please feel free to have the dress sent, but don't feel obligated. I'm sure you own many pretty dresses but thought it might be fun to have something new as well."*

Grace hesitated before picking up the phone. As she started to dial, she switched the last four numbers and waited for Melanie to answer. "Mel? I have a dilemma."

Encouraged by Melanie to ring for the dress, Grace showered and readied herself for the evening. Seeing the dress that Nolan sent, Grace sighed. Purple. She should have known it would be purple.

Fingering the fabric, Grace marveled to realize the dress was created from faux suede in royal purple. The little mandarin collar was cut from black velveteen and matching French cuffs made for an unusual yet simply elegant dress.

Nolan risked a low wolf whistle as Grace invited Nolan inside. Her blush told him that she wasn't offended by his attempt to compliment her while trying to interject a small amount of levity to the situation. He hadn't seen her since walking her to the door the night before. Craig and Melanie had been waiting at Grace's home to congratulate them. Nolan had mentally kicked himself as he walked to his home. What was he thinking when he decided to call them?

From the moment Nolan and Grace became engaged, until the moment that Grace opened her door, dressed in the beautiful dress he'd provided, Grace and Nolan had hardly spent a moment alone unless navigating the freeways between Brunswick and Rockland counted. As he looked at his fiancée Nolan realized that many plans needed to be made and quickly. Excusing himself to the restroom, Nolan made a call to his credit card company requesting a card in the name of Grace Lynn Buscher be over-nighted to his house. A wedding would be in the works in the matter of days.

~~~~*

Grace laid her head on Nolan's shoulder as the Sugar Plum Fairy danced across the stage. Whispering, Grace tried to express her delight in the evening that she'd had. "It's so beautiful Nolan. Thank you."

As the audience filed out of the theater, Nolan suggested dessert and coffee at a local restaurant. "We have plans to make you know."

An hour later, they poured over Nolan's pocket calendar and trying to determine a wedding date. Grace worked through March, April, and May, desperately trying to find a date that would work around Nolan's most important business needs. Near tears, Grace looked up at Nolan. "I don't want to wait until June. What will we do?"

Nolan flipped back to February. Grace started to make a sound of protest but when she saw that there were three open weeks in February with little to be done she sighed. It'd be a lot of work but she couldn't afford an expensive elaborate wedding anyway. "Let's do it. Think about it. Our rehearsal dinner can be at the church and it'll still be decorated from the Valentine Party on Wednesday. With our anniversary one day after Valentines day, surely you won't forget one of them!"

The date was set. On February fifteenth, Grace Buscher, would become Mrs. Nolan Burke. Looking up at Nolan as he walked her to her door, Grace smiled. "It truly is a wonderful life, isn't it?"

~~~~*

"A DVD Player? What does that have to do with piping- and Nolan, I've been calculating expenses, and this is an extremely expensive twelve days you've given me."

Nolan laid aside the electronic cables he had been arranging and drew Grace to the couch. "We have to talk Grace. You've been living very frugally, and quite well I might add, for many years. Some of it is your upbringing, but I think naturally you are a frugal person and that is a wonderful thing. I am not concerned in the least that you'll leave me a pauper inside of a year but Grace-"

The look on Grace's face alarmed him. She seemed ready to bolt. "What have I done wrong Nolan?"

"Grace, I can afford to spend what I've spent this week without missing much of it. My business is good, and I've rarely touched a dime of my inheritance. It's invested well and earning healthy profits even in lean quarters. I need you to learn to trust my judgment on what I can afford to spend."

Grace nodded. Just as Nolan felt like he was getting through, her face changed again. "But-"

Sighing, Nolan waited for Grace to continue. "Go on."

"Why buy a DVD player? In about seven weeks, we'll be married. I can use yours!"

Nolan went back to work in silence. Grace wondered if he was angry, frustrated, or perhaps he realized that he could have prevented double buying and didn't appreciate being reminded of it. His voice startled her minutes later. "Grace, I don't own a DVD player. I bought this for us to enjoy. If you really don't want it, I'll take it back."

"Nolan! I didn't say that. I was just trying to help-"

Nolan's frustration boiled over. "Grace. It hurts to try to do something for someone only to have the decision questioned as a waste."

An unusual bite came to Grace's voice. "I'm sorry! I didn't mean to question your impeccable judgment, I just asked!"

Nolan looked at Grace's angry face and sighed. He started to pick up his tools to go home but Grace stopped him. Grabbing her coat, she opened the door. "Don't bother Nolan. Finish your project. I'll go."

Nolan began praying fervently as the door slammed shut behind her. "Lord, of all the stubborn self-reliant women, I had to pick her! I don't understand. She's being completely unreasonable. If she doesn't trust that I can make a decision about a silly piece of electronics, will she trust me when it's something major? Did I let my love for Grace...?"

Grace. Nolan knew he loved her. The past two years had been difficult and extremely tight financially for Grace. He'd taken her questions personally instead of looking at what was behind them. She loved him and wanted only the best for him.

Nolan grabbed his jacket and rushed out the door. Looking up and down the street, Nolan couldn't figure which way Grace had gone. Did she go to Verily Wirth's? Seeing her footprints in the snow, Nolan tracked them as faithfully as a bloodhound. He followed them around the corner to the bench that a kind neighbor had set behind his fence for the schoolchildren to use. Alone on the bench, weeping, sat Grace.

Nolan slowed his jog down to a walk so as not to startle her. Several feet away, he called her name. Grace didn't seem to hear. Reaching her side, he pulled her up into his arms. "I didn't think we'd have our first 'real' argument and have to make up in public like this but perhaps it is best."

Grace continued to sob as Nolan whispered apologies. "I didn't think Grace. I took it as you rejecting my surprise for you. I should have known better."

Shaking her head violently, Grace pulled her head up. "No, you were right. I needed to trust you. You tried to do something special for me and I didn't accept it graciously. I'm discovering that I might find submission more difficult than I thought. It might have been a mistake to live alone this past year. It encourages a very independent spirit. I thought it would foster a deeper reliance on the Lord, and in some ways, it did. I wouldn't have chosen to see the special relationship that I have with the Lord change for just anyone..."

Nolan nodded as he listened to Grace talk through her thoughts. He led her home trying to understand the differences between their worlds. He'd grown up with any need, and many wants satisfied almost before they became needs or wants. As he returned to his electronic mess, Nolan smiled at Grace as she fussed about trying to help him. "It's ok Grace, right? We're ok. We talked about something and we'll need to talk about it again I'm sure. But, we handled a problem and we can handle the next one."

With the DVD player set up and ready to use, Craig and Melanie arrived with Gracie-anna. Rolex went wild at the smell of the baby and promptly snuggled down at the base of her car seat. "He got us a DVD player. Isn't it neat- hey, Nolan? What does a DVD player have to do with eleven pipers?"

Nolan pulled a disk from his jacket pocket and inserted it into the player. Grace watched carefully as he pushed buttons and started the machine. The swelling of bagpipes filled the room and Grace sighed. "How'd you know that I love the bag pipes? I'm sure I've never told you."

"Lucky guess Grace. Lucky guess." Grace missed the wink he threw at Melanie as everyone settled down to watch the rugged loveliness of the Scotch countryside and the beautiful steps of Scottish dancers.

~~~~*

Christmas Eve dawned with a fresh powdering of snowfall. Nolan watched anxiously for the FED EX truck to bring him the credit card he'd ordered for Grace. After yesterday's discussion, he knew that she'd resist using it but Grace deserved the wedding of her dreams and he was determined to provide that for her.

Grabbing the CD he'd purchased the night before, Nolan walked across the street to deliver his final gift for the twelve days of Christmas. When he realized that his gift giving had become overwhelming, he'd cancelled his plans for twelve live drummers drumming, in favor of a CD with a military band playing 'Little Drummer Boy'.

Craig and Melanie arrived simultaneously with Nolan and everyone crowded into Grace's house eagerly. Nolan was amazed. Overnight, Grace had transformed the house from the average decorated home to a Christmas Wonderland. Stockings hung from the mantle looking shelf that ran along one wall. Candy and cookies were everywhere and the smell of baking ham already permeated the entire house.

The festivities began in earnest. Nolan played the song for Grace as she scooped her little niece up in her arms. Craig pulled out an old turntable as well as his parents Mitch Miller albums, and the foursome sang and laughed until lunchtime.

Craig excused himself for a short while as the rest of the party ate a light lunch. When he returned, Craig called the room to attention. Sitting next to Grace on the couch, he handed her an envelope. "I didn't want this gift to get lost in the shuffle tomorrow so I'll give it to you now. I have a little story to tell.

"When Dad got sick, he knew he wasn't likely to be here for your wedding. He asked me to do two things for him. First, he wanted me to protect you from men who would only break your heart. I hope I've done that. I'm sure Nolan wouldn't and I don't think anyone else has."

Grace silently wept at the picture of her father handing the reigns of protection over to her brother. How she missed the man who had shaped her notion of what a Godly man should be. Craig continued his voice husky with emotion.

"The second thing he did was to give me this. It's an account Grace. I changed it to your name today and there is a Debit card in there. Dad wanted to be sure you had a nice wedding. There's also a letter from him that I was supposed to give you the other night, but I had it in the bank vault."

Grace accepted the envelope as she hugged her brother. Her wedding was something she hadn't been willing to think of yet. She knew that there was little money in her accounts to cover basic expenses, and while Melanie and Craig would love the opportunity to provide her with a nice wedding, Grace didn't like to think of the money being spent on her when Graci-anna would need so much over the coming years.

Nolan watched the scene, understandably moved. He thought of the card in his wallet that bore Grace's name. Once again, he'd jumped the gun. He moved to sit near her feet and looked up into Grace's eyes. "I think it's wonderful of your father to provide for you like that. I only hope I am as thoughtful with our-"

Grace interrupted him quickly. "You will be. No one could think otherwise."

~~~~*

"Presents! Nolan... wake up! It's time to come have presents!" Grace banged on Nolan's door impatiently.

Nolan opened the door slowly. He looked like a little boy standing there in his flannel pajamas with sleep still clouding his eyes. "Is it morning already?"

Grace found herself involuntarily tracing his jaw line with her fingers. "I've never seen you with stubble!"

Nolan wrapped Grace's hand in his and kissed the back of her fingers. "How about I go get dressed? I'll be over in a few minutes. I obviously need to shave."

Grace nodded and started to leave. Turning to him with a whimsical smile, she stopped the door before he had it completely closed. "Nolan? I think you look fine the way you are. Don't bother shaving. Takes too much time anyway. We've got *presents* a-waiting, food that's a-cooking, lots of songs a-singing, *fun* aaallllllll dayyyyyyyy."

As Nolan hurried into his clothes, he heard her singing her way back across the street. A quick glance at the mirror proved that a shave was definitely in order. Picking up the shaving cream, Nolan hesitated. Had Grace just been eager to begin opening presents or was she implying that she liked him unshaven now and then?

Reluctantly he set the razor down. Rubbing one hand over his chin, he made a funny face at himself in the mirror before hurrying to the living room. His presents were piled into a reproduction of a vintage wagon for Graci-anna. He grabbed the wagon handle, pulled his load across the street, and entered Grace's home with a cheerful 'Ho Ho Ho!'

The morning passed in a flurry of wrapping paper. Paige, Nathan, and a tag-a-long Chuck stopped by to exchange gifts. Grace managed not to laugh at the roll of paper towels and can of peanuts tied together with ribbon that Chuck bought each of the women.

Nolan unwrapped his present with trepidation. He wasn't sure if Grace would use this day for a practical joke, but he didn't put the idea past her either. He unwrapped a very 'fuzzy' pillow. Flannel squares stitched together in order to create a very unique effect. Grace took the pillow from him and reached inside a pocket that Nolan had missed. Almost instantly, she pulled a blanket from inside the pocket. Grace flipped the pillow piece inside out and presto... a blanket. "You can put your feet in that pocket if they get cold.'

Nolan felt that any gift would be inadequate after the last week and a half but he'd really tried. Mike had given him an enlarged picture of them singing at his party. Nolan inserted that picture into the first page of a leather photo album and on the next page, Nolan taped a business card for a local photographer for their engagement pictures, courtesy of Melanie's forethought.

A mini version of the album was included. In the little album, every picture that Nolan could find of he and Grace was included. From a snapshot of him playing soccer with Amber, to them teasing one another on Thanksgiving, to a cut out newspaper picture of the geese on Grace's lawn, no picture was overlooked.

Chuck interrupted in his usual, inelegant style. "You'd think she'll be seeing you enough without pictures too."

Nathan and Paige took his words as their cue to leave. Goodbyes were said and everyone waved as the trio drove toward Paige's parents' home. "What will Mrs. Matthews say about *Chuck*?" Grace questioned dryly.

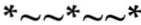

Dinner was over; the gifts were carefully put away or packed into Craig and Melanie's car. Melanie sat in Grace's most comfortable chair nursing Graci-anna while Grace divided the leftovers. In time, the group sat around the room reminiscing about past Christmases.

Taking a sip of his hot apple cider, Nolan gathered his courage. "I have a request to make of you. It would mean a lot to me if some part of my family's heritage could be a part of this wedding. Just using Dad's money to pay for rings or a honeymoon isn't very meaningful.

Nolan took a deep breath. He looked at Grace, then at Craig. Mentally pleading with Grace and Melanie to understand, he made his request. "I know its tradition for the father of the bride to pay for the wedding, the dress, the veil etc. I'm supposed to pay for a rehearsal dinner, the rings, and the honeymoon and I promise you, I will be content with that. But if you would consider allowing me to provide Grace's dress and continue what has become a Burke family tradition..."

Gracie-anna's coos and giggles were the only sounds in the room. Melanie watched as Craig's eyebrows drew downward into a scowl, and as Grace tried to formulate her thoughts. Nolan's shoulders began to droop and Melanie could see he thought he'd offended the family.

Before anyone spoke and said something that would wound, Melanie decided to ask a question. "You said something about a Burke family tradition. What is that tradition; can you tell us about it?"

She laid her hand on Craig's arm and whispered to him. Grace overheard but Nolan was too far across the room. "Craig, let's listen to him; we love him and we know he loves Grace. I don't think this is about money, Craig. Just listen."

Nolan cleared his throat, took a sip of his hot apple cider, and spoke. "May I explain? I have a story of my own to tell, a little in the same vein as Craig's story yesterday. I've been hesitant to mention it because I don't want to step on toes or cross family traditions that you might have.

"My great, great grandfather married an orphan loaned out to a local farm. The family who took care of her in exchange for the work she did- they weren't wealthy but they were good to her. When Great Grand Father Bart asked Melinda Potts to marry him she came with nothing. No real family, no 'hope chest,' nothing. Grandfather didn't mind; all he wanted was Melinda's heart."

As Nolan told the story, Grace could almost hear his mother's voice telling the tale to him repeatedly as a child. The phrases that Nolan used indicated years of storytelling behind them. Grace reached for Nolan's hand as he continued the story.

"The Warners, the family that took in Great Grandmother Melinda, had a daughter, Emily-Jane, who was a very good friend to Melinda. Grandfather Bart conspired with Emily-Jane to pick out the dress that Melinda would have if she could afford any dress she wanted. Then Grandfather Bart prayed. He wasn't a wealthy man but he'd saved as much as possible, almost from the day he met Melinda, in hopes that they could start life with a healthy nest-egg.

"Melinda and Emily-Jane found the wedding dress late one afternoon. The town only had one old fashioned mercantile. The dress had been sitting in the window for quite some time and had become dusty, but Melinda loved it. It was made out of a cheap cotton material but she didn't care. Emily-Jane showed Bart the dress and he immediately went to discover how much it would cost. The storeowner was so happy to find someone interested in the dress, that he gave Grandfather Bart a significant discount. The dress was wrapped up and sent by the owner's son to Melinda's house.

"It washed up beautifully. When Melinda finished with it, the white was spotless and every wrinkle ironed out. A few stitches in the sides helped to make the dress fit better and the following weekend, they were married.

"Almost thirty years later, Melinda pulled her wedding dress out to show her daughter in law to be. As she told the story, the young girl held the dress up to her in front of a mirror and twirled a bit. Ellen Jackson, my grandmother begged to wear the dress. Grandmother Melinda was delighted to hear that it would be worn again. With four sons, and no daughters, she had just assumed that the dress would stay in its wrappings until it turned to dust. Those two women worked hard to remove the yellowing of age and repair the places where the stitching had grown weak. When my grandfather saw his bride coming down the aisle, she was wearing his mother's wedding dress."

Grace sighed as she thought about the pretty muslin dress. She was certain that the dress was a common muslin, but how pretty it sounded! She imagined that Nolan was about to tell them that his mother had also worn the dress. Would he want her to wear it as well? She wasn't sure if she liked the idea or not. There was something sweet and sentimental in the idea, but what if it looked terrible on her? Nolan's voice broke through her thoughts.

"… Mom was too big for the dress, and it had disintegrated to the touch in some spots. Mom's father wanted to buy her a dress, but with the medical bills that his wife's health incurred, he just couldn't afford it. Mom decided to wear her navy blue suit, like most of her friends did during those war years, and she determined to be happy with wearing her mother's veil. Dad remembered the stories that he'd grown up hearing and was sorry that his wife couldn't wear the dress that both his father and grandfather had seen their brides in. Taking a risk, Dad went to dinner one evening at Mom's family's house and he told the story. Then he talked about how he wanted to carry on the tradition but the dress just wasn't a possibility."

Nolan took a deep breath. He knew that he was entering delicate territory. "Dad requested permission to pay for Mom's dress as his wedding gift to the bride. Grandmom Winston was irate. She cried, she shrieked, she wailed. She was kind of an overly emotional woman according to Dad. Well, Dad started to back-peddle but when he heard something about surprises and maidenly modesty, he realized that his future mother-in-law thought he wanted to pick out the dress- to see it before the wedding. Once he assured them that all he wanted was the privilege of assuring his bride of the dress of her dreams, things calmed. After some consultation among the family, it was announced. The tradition could be continued. Mom would choose her dress, Dad would pay the bill. My father loved giving gifts but I think he considered the greatest gift he ever received was seeing mom walking down the aisle of that little chapel wearing 'his' dress. Their wedding was really small. Most were those days. He shipped out to the South Pacific two weeks later but he carried their wedding picture with him through battle for 'good luck'.

"It was 'over there' you know, that Christ claimed my father's heart. Mom was home, getting letters sporadically. After a time, she noticed that he was sharing insights to things than he ever had. He mentioned praying for her and his letters took on deeper meanings. Somehow, even through the cuts by the censors, mom could see that Dad was a new man. By the time he got home, Mom was ripe for the gospel. I was born a good eighteen years later."

Nolan finished his story and the room fell silent again. Craig seethed in his corner, not quite believing that this wasn't about money. Grace looked from Nolan, to Craig, and finally at Melanie in complete confusion.

"Nolan, would you excuse us, I think we'd like to discuss this alone if you don't mind. Maybe you can take a prayer-walk or something. Give us about thirty minutes or so?"

Nolan nodded, kissed the top of Grace's head, and whispered. "No matter what you decide, I'll support you. What I want most is for you to be happy with your wedding day."

As the door shut, everyone began talking at once. Melanie, despite her proper Southern upbringing, grew frustrated and whistled an ear-piercing whistle. Everyone quickly looked at the baby who ceased her coos. The baby wiggled and blew raspberries as if to beg for more.

"Whew. Thought I'd scared her. Now listen, you two. I have something to say."

Melanie waited until Grace and Craig both were paying full attention to her words before continuing. "You know that this proposition goes against every thing I have been brought up to expect, to appreciate, and to believe to be right. Men just don't buy their wives wedding dresses. If Craig had asked, it would have hurt me to do it, but I would have refused. I would have worn a twenty-dollar clearance dress from a department store before I would have allowed Craig to buy my dress. Then again, I'm just a traditional Southern girl with a father who loved providing me with the wedding that I had with all its own traditions and things. Craig almost went crazy a few times over things he thought were no big deal."

Craig's face began to clear. The thundercloud that had covered it when Nolan had made his request slowly dissipated. He should have known his wife would speak rationally.

"Grace you should know," Melanie continued, "Craig planned to purchase your dress himself. He wanted to give you the gift of whatever dress you'd like to have. Like Nolan, he didn't want to pick it out for you or even see it. He just wanted that honor and I knew you'd understand it and at least you'd have a dress that you loved."

Melanie took a deep breath. With eyes begging patience from her husband, she turned back to Grace and concluded her thoughts. "But Grace, this is your dress- your wedding. This is your special day, and if you want to bless Nolan by allowing him to give you this gift, I think even Craig will stand beside you and support you. And Grace, it is a beautiful thought. Really, I understand his desire to give this to you, I truly do. I think even Craig, if he thought about it, would admit that he would have done the same for me and if a similar tradition was in the Buscher family, Craig would have wanted to continue it as well."

Craig sat silently. He was livid. To him, the idea of Nolan paying for any piece of Grace's wedding was preposterous. He knew Nolan's net worth. He'd paid for a background check and done a little research about Nolan when Grace's neighbor-turned-fiancée first arrived. This was not a man who would miss any amount spent on a lavish wedding. He actually felt insulted that Nolan would mention it.

Before he could speak, Grace spoke absentmindedly. "Well, I know it's not about money. He knows I have the money. So, we can't take offense about the money. I've already hurt him by being bothered about him spending so much money on me. I'm not going to do that again."

Craig sighed. Grace nailed him with her comments. "Grace, as much as it kills me to say it, Melanie is right. This is your decision. I won't try to influence you so if you don't want to be influenced, don't ask my opinion. You'll have to let us know what you decide. Talk to Mel if you like. I think she's capable of being a little more objective." Craig stood, picked up his infant daughter, and left the room.

"Mel, does Craig really want to buy the dress, or did he just think it would be a nice gift and one that would help stretch the wedding dollars. I looked at the bank statements; there is just over three thousand dollars in there. That's a lot of money but we both know, it'll only pay for a very, very simple wedding."

Melanie smiled. "Craig is a man. He would think it fine if you showed up in your denim skirt and favorite flannel shirt. It only matters to Nolan because it's a tradition."

"He won't have family there, only his father's partner and his friends. I've always thought that the groom's family got short-changed in a wedding but I don't know. I know that Nolan would handle me telling him 'no' better than Craig would. Maybe it means more to Craig then?"

Melanie shook her head. "No, the Buscher pride is just stronger than Nolan's desire to continue a tradition."

"I know you wouldn't do it Mel, but I don't know if I can break a tradition like that." Grace seemed more bothered by the idea than Melanie expected.

"Grace, I don't think Nolan is bothered by breaking tradition. I don't think that matters to him at all. I think that he's more interested in the joy he'd receive in continuing it. Does that make sense? It's like when you want to buy a friend a birthday present for their party and then hear that they've requested no presents. You're not sorry the present buying tradition has been broken, you just miss honoring the friend with a gift."

With a hug for Melanie, Grace went in search for her brother. "Craig? You know I've considered you my 'protector' since daddy died. You know that I've tried to give you the respect and honor that a role like that deserves. I'm not going to give Nolan any answer until I either have a 'no, I do not approve at all, or a 'you have my blessing to do this'."

While Grace and Melanie had been talking, Craig had stood before the Lord in prayer. He knew that it wasn't a sin for Nolan to buy the dress. He knew that he could care less if they just got the whole thing over with the next weekend. He knew he was choosing to have his pride hurt by the offer and he knew, without a doubt, his reaction was sin. "Grace, you have my blessing to make any decision about this dress that you like with two provisions."

"What are they?" Grace wasn't sure she liked the idea of provisions.

"First, you pray about this before you even consider it. I think we're all making a mountain out of a molehill here but maybe it's for a reason.

"Second, that you do what you really want and what you really think the Lord would have you do, not what you think will make everyone happy."

Grace found Nolan in his kitchen, drinking a cup of his favorite coffee. "Care to take a walk?"

Nolan dumped his coffee out and followed Grace from his house. "Well, we've decided that we don't know. Craig said something that is making me wonder but I'll let you know in a day or two ok?"

Nolan stopped in the middle of the sidewalk. Neither of them noticed that they were standing in front of Mr. Wirth's picture window. The elderly man sat in his recliner and watched as the couple talked, remembering days gone by.

"Grace, if I thought you would feel at all obligated, I wouldn't have asked. I thought it would be nice to carry on traditions, but traditions are here to serve us, not for us to serve. If you decide to allow this, just have the bill sent to my house. I'll know then. Otherwise, let's not speak of it again ok? I'll understand either way but I don't want you to feel obligated to come to me and tell me yes or no."

"You are too good to me Nolan. You really are. I'm so happy that I could just-"

Nolan found Grace's abrupt silence amusing. Pulling a sprig of mistletoe from his pocket, he held it over Grace's head. "Kiss me? You could kiss me perhaps?"

Verily silently cheered as Nolan held the mistletoe above Grace's head. He seemed to hesitate until Grace nodded. Unaware that they had a witness to their first 'real' kiss, Grace and Nolan seemed reluctant to part.

Nolan's voice was deep with emotion as he whispered. "Merry Christmas Grace."

Twenty-Seven

December

As he entered *Brunswick Haven*, Nolan asked a passing attendant where to find Fran Buscher and was directed to her room. Fran opened the door holding a tissue to her nose and scowling. "What are you doing here?"

'I'm very happy to see you too. We were sorry you didn't feel well enough to spend Christmas with us."

'I wasn't. All that yammering about Jesus and stars. It's ridiculous. Grace brought me my gifts this morning. She always makes me food and this year she gave me a scarf."

"I brought you a gift as well." Nolan pulled a box from his jacket. "Merry Christmas."

Fran glared at him suspiciously. "You're here about Grace. I thought she looked too happy. I should have checked her hands."

Smiling, Nolan nodded. "Yes, you should have. The left one is sporting a new ring."

The disgust on Fran Buscher's face surprised him. "You could have any woman in Rockland- almost. Why not someone more sophisticated?"

"Because then she wouldn't be Grace. I want Grace."

'Can you put up with her Jesus talk?"

Nolan sighed and sank into her extra chair uninvited. "Ms. Buscher, I wouldn't want her if she wasn't a child of the Lord."

'Oh not you too! How did I get stuck with a family of raving fanatics? I have managed just fine without Jesus all of these years-"

"I beg to differ."

"What?" Fran protested indignantly.

"Jesus has been with you every moment you've been near Grace or Craig- even their father and mother. Jesus was with them and therefore you haven't gotten along without Him."

"Well He hasn't done anything so grand for me so He can just stay away."

Nolan stood and smiled sympathetically. "Ms. Buscher, if it wasn't for Jesus, you'd be all alone. Without Jesus, your family would have given up on you years ago and you know it. They love you but love can't cover pain unless something deeper heals the wounds."

~~~~*

Paige, Melanie, and Grace sat at Melanie's kitchen table making lists of things to do. Grace wrote down the money she had to spend on the wedding and everyone looked at it with determination. This wedding would stay on budget, and would be the nicest wedding anyone could come up with in seven weeks time.

Paige was in her element. "Ok, Grace. The dress is the first thing. We can spend weeks searching stores, websites, catalogs, etc, or we can decide what you want it to look like and just take it to a seamstress."

"I just assumed Grace would make it." Melanie looked at Grace with huge question marks in her eyes.

"I did too. I even sketched a few of them last night. I'm wearing mom's veil though. I know that much."

Paige put on her professional mantle and spoke seriously to the two women. "We have seven weeks to come up with tuxedos, dresses, flowers, the cake, the photographer, the decorations, the food- Grace won't have time to make her dress."

Grace nodded. "And I've never been good at making myself highly tailored clothes. It's easier on someone else. You're right. So who do we get to do the dress?"

Several calls were made to Nolan as the trio tried to determine a color scheme. Finally, Nolan gave up in despair. "Grace, choose whatever color you want and don't tell me what it is. It'll be a surprise for me."

London and Mickey were nominated flower girl and ring bearer. Nolan named Mike as his best man and Craig and Nathan

Groomsmen. Grace asked Paige to be her maid of honor, and Melanie and Traci as attendants. The entire wedding party would be odd. It was quite unavoidable with Craig walking Grace down the aisle and then standing with Nolan during the ceremony but this was how Grace wanted her wedding and everyone stood behind her.

Melanie secured the church and called her friends until she found someone who knew how to get wholesale flowers. Paige found dresses for all of the attendants and Amber in the exact same shade of plum. She ordered tuxedos with matching ties and to Grace's relief, the attire for all attendants was found, purchased and on it's way the first week.

Grace planned a menu of hors d'oeuvres that could be prepared before hand and frozen. A call to several bakeries made her angry. "I had no idea that cakes were so expensive! If I'm not careful, I could spend several hundred dollars just on flour, sugar and eggs. What do I get for my money? Cake for everyone and someone gets carpel tunnel syndrome from squeezing the silly bag of frosting. I'm going to tell Nolan I want to elope. That solves the dress issue, saves a ton of money and everyone can just congratulate us at church."

"No you won't missy, I've already reserved a room at Grimsbey's for your shower. It's in three weeks by the way so I need a gift list by Friday. I'll register you to save time."

"You make me sound like a purebred dog. Ick." Grace laughed as she joked with her friends.

This would be a wonderful wedding. Even if it killed her. And if she continued to feel as badly as she did now, it would kill her. Grace couldn't wait for Dr. Kline's medication to start working.

As the women continued making plans, Nolan stopped in. "Don't want to bother you ladies; this shouldn't take long.

"Grace, I need to know if you have a passport."

Grace shook her head. "Will I need one?"

Nolan flipped open a folder containing passport applications, and a list of instructions. "When you get this filled out, I'll need copies of your birth certificate, your driver's license and we'll need two passport sized photos."

Giving Grace a quick kiss, Nolan hurried out to his Expedition and drove away. The three women stared at each other in shock. Finally, Paige spoke. "Where are you guys *going*?"

"I don't know. Out of the country, I guess. I'll have to pull down the suitcases won't I?"

Grace's comment showed the other ladies that she was clearly stunned. Paige made a note on her list to find out if Grace should pack for warm or cold weather and Melanie placed a call to Nolan to get the particulars. Patience had never been Melanie's strong point.

Hearing Melanie's squeal, the two women looked up. Grace could hear Nolan laughing. "Ok, Nolan, I'll call Dr. Kline to check on shots. I doubt she'll need them but it doesn't hurt to ask. Thanks and- she's going to love it- No, I would never tell- It's too much fun keeping her in suspense.

~~~~*

"I like this one. The fabric is just what I want. Can we get this locally or in Rockland? I don't want to take a chance on ordering..." Grace stood in what seemed to be the millionth dress tried on in one morning.

Allie Thompson was carefully taking measurements of both Grace and the dresses she tried on. The woman had turned her garage into a sewing studio and she specialized in wedding dresses. Melanie walked around the room looking at different dresses and trying to imagine this many wedding dresses in one place when none were for sale.

"How did you ever afford to purchase so many dresses?"

Allie laughed as she made notations on her pad. "I actually buy them at garage sales, thrift stores, second-hand stores, and occasionally on eBay. If I can get a dress for under fifty dollars, it's worth the investment if I don't have the size and style already. It gives my brides something to work with."

Finally, Grace picked her dress. "I want this style. The princess seams really seem to give me a 'leaner' look which is always a blessing! The neck is wrong; I want to turn this basic style into as much of an Edwardian styled dress as possible. No high necklines... let's do an illusion of a high collar. I love their simply elegant sleeves... Now how can we imitate their skirts with that beautiful insertion lace and still have the long lines of the dress?"

Allie showed the three women swatches of fabrics that the stores in a one hundred mile radius kept in stock as well as her personal selection of laces. It was two-thirty before Grace got home from the session and she was exhausted. When she realized that school was out for the week, and Cade wouldn't be coming, Grace pulled her favorite quilt over her on the couch fell into a deep sleep.

Nolan found her resting late that evening. Grace hadn't called to welcome him home, and her house was dark. Concerned, he'd crossed the street and found her door unlocked. As he saw her sleeping, a rush of protectiveness washed over him. He reminded himself that Grace was still a weak woman. Until her medication took over and really did her some good, she wouldn't be able to handle as much work as she would try to do.

He turned on her lights and tried to reload her stove as quickly as possible. As he stirred the coals, Grace stirred on the couch. "Is something wrong Nolan?"

"It's just getting chilly in here. Thought you might like some heat."

"I picked out my dress today. I think it's going to be lovely. Paige knew a seamstress that is amazing. She thinks my dress will be finished in three weeks. She always stops taking orders in the middle of November and doesn't start up again until March. Paige worked her shopping magic and she's starting now so I have a dress!"

Chapter Twenty-Eight

January

Three weeks later, Nolan found Grace working hard in her kitchen. Her forehead dripped with perspiration and her hands shook from exhaustion. Taking one look at her, Nolan determined to try to get her to call the doctor.

"You look done in Grace; couldn't you pay for someone to do this?"

"I'm just tired. I stayed up until midnight last night addressing the invitations and writing thank-you notes."

"Did it have to be done then?"

Grace nodded wearily as she stifled a yawn. "The invitations have to be mailed this week."

"But the thank-you's- couldn't you have written them later? The shower was just three days ago."

"I know but there is so much to do. I'm so glad that my dress is almost finished. In one week, I'll have one thing completely done. Mom's veil is airing out now and will be ready to wear in time. I've found a pair of shoes that match and I think I know what I'm doing with my hair."

"You'll look lovely Grace. Of course, I'd think so if we went right now and stood before the Justice of the Peace as we are."

Grace began searching for a new package of egg roll wraps. Peering into the fridge, she groaned. "I knew I'd need more wraps. Would you mind getting me some more? I could check my email while you were gone and then be ready to roll again. I'm so tired."

"Why didn't you just buy them, Grace? This looks like an enormous amount of work. The Mandarin House would have been able to handle an order for a couple hundred egg rolls but you can't handle it all by yourself!"

Grace pulled money from her purse and handed it impatiently to Nolan. "Because I'm almost broke and I can't afford it. Please, go get the wraps. I'm stuck until it's done and I've got to get these frozen."

Before Nolan could answer, the phone rang. "Can you answer that for me? I need to use the bathroom."

Nolan answered the phone. He asked to take a message and snatching up a pen, wrote it on the pad that Grace kept near the phone. "Thank you- yeah, ok. I've got it."

Grace dragged herself into the room moments later to find Nolan trying to wrap an egg roll. "This is hard work. Everything squishes out of the sides or it splits down the middle."

"I know what you mean. I wasted a whole package before I figured out how to do it right. Who was on the phone?"

"Paige. She said that she's looked at all of the warehouses and there aren't any cheaper flowers than carnations unless you wanted to go with just baby's breath."

Grace sighed. Turning back to her re-organizing the preparations, she began talking to herself. "I wonder how pretty you can make baby's breath. It might be pretty original- some sheer ribbon, and maybe a silk flower or two..."

"Grace?" Nolan's voice was tight and somewhat stern. "What's going on Grace? I think we need to talk. Living room perhaps?"

Grace absentmindedly followed Nolan to her favorite chair and wearily sat down. "Can we make this fast? I've got to get those egg rolls in the freezer."

"Ok Grace. Spill it. What's going on? You're killing yourself making egg rolls, you've got Paige searching for the cheapest flowers available and then you're willing to do without all together? What else are you skimping on? Who have you hired for our photographer?"

Grace sat up a little straighter and tried to clear her face of exhaustion. "I love cooking, I don't want to waste good money on flowers that will just be dead in twenty- four hours, and I have Todd Mercer lined up to do the photography. He's the in house photographer at the police station when the regular is off duty."

"Grace! You're out of your mind! I do not want Todd Mercer doing my wedding pictures." Nolan's voice edged up a notch with each irritated word.

Grace smiled slightly. "You really are jealous of him aren't you?"

Nolan stood and began pacing. "Grace. This has nothing to do with jealousy. It does, however, have everything to do with me not wanting to explain to our children why our wedding pictures look like *mug shots*!"

"Don't be silly Nolan. Todd doesn't even do mug shots. He takes pictures of crime scenes-"

Nolan lost all control. Grace, however, didn't know it. She'd yet to discover that when Nolan shifted from visibly angry to absolute silence, that his anger level had reached the breaking point. In a matter of seconds, Nolan was in danger of saying something that they'd both regret.

"Grace Lynn Buscher-almost-Burke. That is worse. I refuse to have someone who is skilled at taking pictures of shot up corpses, taking pictures of the day that is supposed to be the best day of our lives."

Grace stood to face him. "Well you don't have to talk to me like a child who has done something unforgivable! Calling me by my full name- almost anyway. What is so bad about saving a few dollars and having someone who knows something about a camera take the pictures?"

Nolan's voice dropped to dangerous sounding levels. Grace realized after the second word that she'd misjudged his reaction. Nolan wasn't calming down, he was beyond livid. "Grace. This is the day brings us together as husband and wife- the day in which the Lord takes two independent people and melds them into one. Do you really think so little of it?"

Seeing Grace's features start to crumble, Nolan pulled her to the couch and sat beside her. Mustering all of the inner strength that he could, Nolan tried again. "There's something under all of this but I don't understand it so help me. What is the problem? Why are you doing this? Your brother gave you money for the wedding..."

"That's just it Nolan! I've done everything I can think of to stretch that money. Egg rolls aren't marvelous but they were the easiest things that I could do myself! If I had someone else do it, it would have been triple what I spent. I still have the fruit, vegetables, sparkling grape juice- and that's just the food! The cake is five hundred dollars!"

Nolan spoke before he thought. "I'm surprised that you didn't make that too!"

Not catching the sarcasm in Nolan's tone, Grace answered defensively. "Well, I would have! I just don't know how to decorate cakes! I had to cut corners somewhere! Three thousand, two hundred and twenty three dollars doesn't *go* very far these days. Not with wedding stuff. It's all so expensive! I shouldn't have paid for the girl's dresses- I didn't have to-"

Nolan's jaw visibly dropped at the announcement of her wedding budget. From what Mike's wife had told him, her father had spent over five thousand on her dress alone. It dawned on him that Grace would work until the wedding was a perfect tribute to the fact that you can have an exquisite wedding on very little money. Then, she'd sleep through their honeymoon and into the following month just to recuperate from the work.

All of Nolan's angst fell away as the vision of what Grace would put herself through to make this day happen appeared in his mind's eye. "Grace. I need to thank you. Really. What you're doing is amazing. I don't want to throw in any 'buts' but I am. Grace, you are working yourself to death here. You look ready to collapse."

"I think those pills aren't working Nolan. I don't feel any better since I've been taking them." Grace looked at Nolan in frustration and sighed.

"Grace. I want to take care of the reception. I'll find some one who can cater it. You know, one of those places that does it all. You can give me the name of your cake decorator so they know what to expect."

Grace started to protest, but Nolan stopped her short. "By the time the reception arrives, we will be married. Why shouldn't I pay for my wife's first meal after we're married?"

'Craig…"

Drawing Grace to him, Nolan began praying. Grace found the gesture irritating. How do you argue with a man who is standing before the throne of Almighty God in prayerful petition? She considered his move a dirty trick and was determined to let him know it.

As he finished his prayer, Grace seethed. Unaware of the brewing storm beside him, Nolan stood, gathered his coat and gloves before kissing Grace's nose and opening the front door. "I'm going to go to Craig's office and discuss this with him. I'll call you from the city. I have a late meeting tonight and an early one tomorrow so I'm staying over at Mike and Traci's. She's threatening to let the kids play dress up in her gown unless I watch them for an hour tomorrow around noon."

Grace stood watching him leave, fury mounting with each step. "Does he think he's God incarnate? Does he have any idea what a low down rotten-"

Trying to take her mind off the situation, Grace grabbed her jacket and purse and hurried to meet the two o-clock bus. She wasn't about to waste ten pounds of egg roll stuffing and if Nolan insisted on hiring a caterer, then fine. He could just eat every last one of the egg rolls himself- even if it meant she served them on their fourth anniversary, freezer burn and all. Grace made a mental note to wrap the rest of them poorly and then put them at the bottom of the freezer so they'd get nice and ugly by the time Nolan could eat them.

Late that afternoon, Cade and Grace rolled the last of the three hundred egg rolls. The kitchen resembled the carnage of a disaster movie and Grace was exhausted. Nolan called to see how she was doing but Grace's short responses seemed to discourage Nolan's desire for conversation. The call was brief and Cade noticed.

"You didn't talk very long to Mr. Burke. Don't you like him anymore? Are you still getting married?"

Grace, still exhausted from the day's work, forgot that she was speaking to a child and spoke her mind freely. "Just because Nolan is being an overbearing, manipulative, irritating, controlling fiancée doesn't mean that we don't love each other or that we can't work it out. After I throttle him all will be well..."

Grace continued to clean her mess as Cade watched in fascination. He'd seen Grace angry occasionally, but it was usually directed at small furry rodents. When his mother got angry with his father, the silence in the house was so loud, it hurt his ears. Grace was talking and even joking and she was mad. He finally decided that adults were simply weird.

Mrs. Crenshaw arrived to pick up Cade. Grace could hear the young boy chattering all the way out the front door about how Grace was mad at Nolan. Shaking her head at the bluntness of children, Grace went back to repack her freezer, trying to squeeze just a few more packages.

Craig arrived shortly after six-thirty. Grace wondered what Nolan had said to send her brother before he went home to his family. Sitting together in the living room where each had taken their first steps, the brother and sister just looked at each other with understanding.

Craig spoke first. "Melanie reminded us to remember that Nolan loves you and only wants the best for you."

"Well, I love him too. The dirty rotten low down scoundrel. And those are his good points I'll have you know."

Craig's low laugh brought back memories. Before Grace could travel too far down memory lane, Craig's voice brought her back to the present. "Care to tell me about it? Are you really set on doing everything yourself?"

"It's not that Craig, really. Honestly, I'm furious with him right now, but it's only because he snuck out of a perfectly good argument by praying. What a cheese."

"He did what?" Craig knew Grace made sense to herself but he was clueless as to what she was trying to convey.

Sighing, Grace relayed the events of the afternoon in precise detail. Relating what each party had said, almost verbatim, she worked her way past the egg rolls to the flowers and finally to the catering comment that sparked the impromptu prayer. As Craig listened, he was both amused and intrigued.

"Sounds like a smooth way to get out of an uncomfortable situation. Maybe I should try that with Mel."

A murmur of indignation erupted before Grace realized that her brother was teasing her. She stuck her tongue out at him in a very juvenile fashion. "I'm gonna warn her brother mine."

Moving back to the subject at hand, Craig started over. "Grace. Tell me. Why do you only have thirty two hundred dollars? I know that's all that was in dad's account but I know for a fact, you've saved five thousand dollars in the past couple of years. What about that money?"

"I thought I should have that to give Nolan. I mean, he's taking on a lot of responsibility-"

Craig's laughter filled the living room and annoyed Grace. "Listen little sis, if you put that five thousand into one of his bank accounts, it'd be the equivalent of someone adding five bucks to mine. It's a drop." He saw her dismay and rushed to clarify. "Don't get me wrong, it's an amazing thing you've done. I know he was impressed when I mentioned it to him but saving your dollars to fill his coffers when you need it to save your health and sanity isn't a very wise use of your money."

Thoughtfully, Grace relaxed in her favorite chair and thought about Craig's words. He was right. Nolan would have a hard time appreciating the gift of five thousand dollars if their wedding was an embarrassment to him. He was accustomed to a much more lavish lifestyle- his friends were accustomed to a different kind of affair than the potluck receptions so popular at *The Assembly.*

"I think you're right Craig. I honestly never considered that money an option. It was saved for the future- whenever that is, and now certainly wasn't it."

"If you had ten thousand dollars to use to cater the reception, what would you serve? Would you hire the work out, or would you do it all yourself?"

No answered followed. The fire crackled in Grace's woodstove as she tried to think reasonably. "Well, I'll be honest. If I wasn't as tired as I am, I'd probably still try to do it, but it seems like every day I get colder, more tired, and more irritable.

"If I had six months, I'd still try to do it I think, sick and all. But honestly, if I had ten thousand dollars, right now, I'd pay to have it done in a heartbeat. This is very hard work and I'm just tired Craig. I'm not used to feeling so tired."

"Have you called your doctor recently? I think he needs to know this. I want you to call him tomorrow."

"I will. You think he can do something? I feel worse than I did before." Grace's voice was as tired as her face looked.

"I think he just needs to give you a stronger dose or something. Meanwhile, we have to settle this food thing. What do you have done?"

"Egg rolls. That's it. I have to work on some kind of punch, and the day of the reception, I'll have to cut veggies and things. I wonder what kind of difference five thousand would make in catering options. If I had ten thousand, I wouldn't care. I'd just spend it and let someone else do the work while I agonized over majorly important details like silver or gold for attendant gifts."

Craig pulled a check from his breast pocket and laid it on the coffee table. When Grace saw the name on the account, she looked quickly up at her brother. "You? When I saw you pull that check out I-"

"I know. Nolan offered me one but I turned him down. Silly tradition or not, I want to help pay for my sister's wedding somehow and since I haven't received a bill for your wedding dress, I decided that I would step in here- but only if you want me to Grace. This is still your wedding."

"But can you afford it? I mean, I can't imagine spending that much on food... I wouldn't spend it all, really, I'd give you the remainder of course, but it's too much, Craig. You have a family to thing of-"

Craig interrupted her ramblings. "Grace, I'm beginning to understand Nolan's frustration. He's trying to provide for you- ok a bit prematurely perhaps, but you've gotten to where everything is a matter of dollars and cents."

Grace sat up and smiled. "You're right. I'll find a caterer tomorrow and have them send you the bill. I'll keep it affordable but nice. And tell Mel that she's a pretty lucky woman. She's got herself a man that is almost as wonderful as mine.

"I've got more important things to think of and to do than stress over egg roll skins and out of season fruit prices. This is my wedding and I'm not going to get bogged down in details that don't bring me happiness. Thank you Craig. You've always been the best of brothers."

Feeling somewhat dismissed, Craig grabbed the stacks of egg rolls she'd asked him to store in their freezer and left for home. Knowing Grace as he did, she was still fighting her flesh. She knew that he was right, but wasn't quite ready to own it. In a day or two, the 'old Grace' would be in place and no one would remember the day that Grace Buscher threatened to make her husband-to-be eat egg rolls until he learned to despise them.

Chapter Twenty-Nine

Nolan entered Grace's home with some amount of trepidation. He'd known Grace was angry with him, and when he saw Craig's reaction to the story, Nolan realized that she was likely more angry than he'd anticipated. He had no idea what kind of reception he'd receive.

He found Grace sitting at her kitchen table surrounded by price lists and a bowl of beef stew that looked like it'd been sitting there a little too long. All the lists worked on a 'per head' value. You could have very simple finger foods set up buffet style, or a four course elegant meal. It all depended on how much you wanted to spend per person.

Grace heard Nolan's entrance but didn't respond. She was still fighting her frustration and didn't want to say something she'd regret. Feeling his hands resting on her shoulders, Grace sighed. "I called the doctor. He tripled my dosage and called in a new prescription."

"That's good. And how are *we*? You feel like talking or would tomorrow be better?"

Grace stood, scraped her bowl of stew into the trash, and moved into the living room. Since knowing Nolan, she'd sat on her living room couch more than in all the years they'd owned it. Though she generally preferred the recliner, sitting on the couch gave the neighbors no doubt that their behavior was properly circumspect.

"I was furious at you yesterday Nolan."

Sighing, Nolan took her hand. "I didn't really understand it, but after talking to Craig, Mike, and Traci..."

"Did you tell all of them how you ducked out of a discussion by praying? That was a cheap shot Nolan."

"I honestly wasn't thinking about avoiding the discussion. I just wanted to kind of diffuse tension. When I saw it fail, I left. Cowardly of me, I know."

"Well... I can't argue there." Grace softened her words with a slow smile.

Many things were settled that evening. Grace learned a new appreciation for Nolan's desire to protect Grace from anything, even herself, that would cause her pain. Nolan learned that women need to talk, even when it seems irrational to try to communicate. Grace also learned that she'd made assumptions about Nolan's interest in the wedding. She'd plowed forward, making decisions without consulting her fiancée on his ideas and preferences.

As Nolan left, Grace was excited to learn that their travel arrangements were made for the honeymoon. "You don't mind me making our destination a surprise?"

"It's not like I won't find out soon enough. Just tell me what to pack and I'll be happy to wait until they announce departure times for our flight. I'm having a blast trying to figure it out. It's kind of like a Christmas present but you don't have a box to help you determine what it could be.

"Paige says we'll be headed to some tropical island."

Shaking his head, Nolan opened the door. "Feel that? Pack for that or a little cooler. I'm not sure of exact temperatures but I do know it'll be pretty cold."

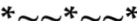

~~~~*

Three days later Grace awoke feeling refreshed for the first time in months. With all of the preparation for the food being handled by the local catering company, Grace spent leisurely days searching for just the right gifts, shopping for a few new outfits to take on her honeymoon and choosing flower arrangements. Nolan hired a chamber group to play at the reception and before Grace realized what had happened, she had a marvelous group playing for her wedding. All that remained was for Grace to pack for her trip and to get the house ready to close up for two weeks.

As Grace folded a new sweater into her suitcase, she heard tentative knock. Grace eagerly welcomed Verily into the house chattering all the while about her preparations. Noting that he seemed to be on a 'mission', Grace sat next to him on her couch and listened as he explained his visit.

"Miss Grace, honey, I had to come see you before your weddin'. I've watched you grow into a fine woman and nothing pleases me more to see you married to a good man like Mr. Burke. My Marlee never had much that was really special but after we were married for about twenty years, I decided to save up enough to buy her something nice for our fiftieth anniversary. She got the cancer about five years too early so I took what I'd saved and went and bought her the prettiest thing I could find with it. Marlee wore it until the day she died. I wanted you to have it."

Grace's eyes filled with tears as Verily handed her a hand carved jeweler's box. When she lifted the lid, she gasped at the lovely bracelet of hand knotted pearls that lay on a bed of velvet. "They're exquisite Verily! Thank you!"

Her beloved neighbor beamed. As he showed her how to operate the unusual clasp on the little string of pearls, Grace remembered the many lessons she'd learned at his side. Verily had been the only one able to convince her to try to ride a bicycle and the first person to come to Grace's rescue when a large mastiff 'attacked' Grace at age five and attempted death by slobber.

"Verily, have I ever told you how much you've meant to me all of these years? You taught me the names of all the trees and flowers when I was eight, you listened to me cry when Paige and I had that awful argument in junior high, and you were at the hospital with me while Dad and Craig buried mom. You've been the grandfather that I didn't really have and I want to thank you."

Overcome with emotion, her lifelong friend simply took her hands in his as he struggled to speak. Finally, Verily Wirth chose to pray. "Lord, please keep your hand on little missy's life as you have since the morning she was born. Guide her into being the fine wife that I'm sure you intend for her to be. Teach her to look to you first in her marriage, just as she has all of her life.

"Show her husband how to serve you and honor her. Give them the wisdom to raise the children that I am asking that you give to them. Grace will be a wonderful mother, Lord. Hear my words oh Lord, and please make them conform to your will. For Jesus, I thank you, Amen."

Grace sat in a contemplative silence as Verily walked to Nolan's house to offer similar words of encouragement and support. "Lord, you've blessed me in so many ways. I'll never be able to express my gratitude enough. I can't believe he picked me."

~~~~*

"And then I'll ask you if you'll love, honor, and the rest- you'll be encouraged to kiss and then…"

Before the minister could continue, Nolan kissed Grace lightly on the nose. "Will that do?"

A titter of laughter rippled through the room as they skipped down the aisle like children at a Maypole. The wedding party left to attend the rehearsal dinner while Grace and Nolan took one last look at the church before the minister locked the doors. "One more day Grace. I was beginning to fear it would never come."

Chapter Thirty

February

"Will you, Nolan, promise to honor, cherish, and love Grace as Christ loved the church? Will you be faithful to her in word, deed, and thought for as long as you both shall live?" Nolan's reply resounded proudly throughout the church.

Turning to Grace, the minister smiled and spoke. "Will you Grace promise to love, honor, respect, and submit to Nolan, as our Lord bids us to in His Word? Will you be faithful to him in word, deed, and thought for as long as you both shall live?"

Grace's 'I will' was strong and confident. They exchanged their rings, kissed, and the minister spoke the words that the congregation waited eagerly to hear.

"It is my privilege to be the first to introduce to you, Mr. and Mrs. Nolan Winston Burke.

Grace startled as the skirl of a lone bagpiper, in the corner of the room, began to draw the plaintive tones of *Amazing Grace* from his instrument. Nolan's grin combined with Grace's rosy cheeks sent a low chuckle throughout the crowd. As the music swelled, tears formed in Grace's eyes and only willpower held them back. Bagpipes always tugged at Grace's heart in a way she never quite understood.

The couple meandered their way down the aisle, stopping to hug and accept congratulations from those who sat along the aisle. It was a custom at The Assembly to greet as many people on the way down the aisle to reduce the time and wait in the receiving line. Those already greeted were ushered directly to their seats and encouraged to enjoy a few appetizers while Grace and Nolan greeted everyone else.

After the final posed photographs, Grace and Nolan hurried into the reception hall to begin the festivities. A cheer rose as the couple entered and Nolan smiled to see Grace's blush. He'd never realized how much Grace disliked being the center of attention but her discomfort was obvious to him even if not to the rest of the room. He gave her hand a gentle squeeze as they sat at the head table surrounded by the wedding party.

Aunt Fran stood. "Before everyone starts their pietistic speeches, I want to say something."

Grace's heart thudded as she waited trepidatiously for what horrible thing her aunt would say. Nolan's jaw tensed but Grace reached for his hand and squeezed it. "It'll be worse if we protest, just smile," she warned.

"I didn't think Grace would ever find someone Craig or my obnoxious brother approved of. I expected to have to leave her my money just to keep her off welfare but apparently I don't have to die precipitously." Fran winked at her niece. "However, I have to say, of all the men she could have picked, I think Nolan is probably the most tolerable. I know he has to love her, why I can't say, because a man like him could have had someone beautiful, wealthy, sophisticated,"

Her aunt's unique blessing on their marriage struck a humorous chord in Grace. She pulled Nolan's ear closer and whispered, "You know, all the things her plain, fat, socially-backward niece isn't." Grace's obvious amusement kept Nolan's irritation at bay.

"- so I just want to tell that man that now that he's married her, he'd better make her happy." Fran swallowed and a hint of unexpected emotion deepened her voice. "Or I'll make sure he wishes he had."

A round of hesitant applause followed Fran's unexpected speech. Grace stood, wove her way around the table, and hugged her aunt. "Thank you Aunt Fran. I love you too," she whispered. Louder for the rest of the room to hear, she quipped. "I'll pay you once I get my hands on his checkbook ok Aunt Fran?"

Despite careful plans to ensure that they didn't spend their reception on their feet, the plan failed. After twenty or thirty minutes, Nolan led his bride to the dance floor. "I've waited so many years to finally dance with my bride at our wedding. Many were more than a little impatient. If I had known the prize at the end of the journey-" Nolan paused and pulled his wife a little closer. "I'd have been even more impatient!"

The room erupted in laughter. Paige sighed in delight as Grace and Nolan waltzed around the room as though they'd been dancing for years. "Isn't that beautiful? I've waited for so many years to see her that happy."

Nathan started to reply but Chuck interjected before he could speak. "I'm surprised she didn't try a diet or something but for Grace, she looks kind of nice."

Paige and Nathan's eyes met and they stifled a laugh. Nathan leaned over and whispered, "You know, if Grace's Aunt Fran were just a few decades younger..."

While the reception festivities drew to a close, Nolan and Grace made preparations to leave. Grace's reaction to the sleek white limo that sat in front of the church was priceless. She was as excited as a teenager at her first prom, while fighting her tendency to balk at the extravagance of something as expensive as a limousine. "Oh Nolan, it's beautiful!"

Nolan helped her into the waiting automobile and smiled into the last of the photographer's incessant camera shots before firmly closing the door and signaling the chauffer to drive away. "I have never been so thrilled to get away from dear friends in my life!"

Grace whispered a hearty 'yes' as she leaned back into the comfortable cushions. The couple looked at each other with strange expressions on their faces. "Do you feel it Grace?"

"Yeah. Weird. Really weird."

Nolan nodded. "I want to roll the windows down to show we're not doing anything 'unseemly'."

"Well, it's too cold so let's don't and pretend we did, ok?"

"Are you feeling alright Grace? Tired today?"

"Nope. A little worn out from the last few days and today's little tensions but mainly I'm just hungry," she confessed. Grace hadn't found time to enjoy any of the food at the reception.

"I thought you would be. I have dinner reservations at *Gatekeeper's Tea Room*. Would you like to go now, or would you like to take a drive in the car first?"

"Who knows when I'll get to ride in such luxury again? Let's drive and let what is left of my nerves completely settle so I can enjoy the meal."

Their drive was quiet and lovely. Instead of popping corks of champagne, they stopped at a mini mart to purchase bottled water and candy bars making their driver scratch his head. What an unusual couple! They drove to Lake Danube and watched the water lap onto the ice rimmed shores from the warmth and comfort of the vehicle.

After their drive, the car delivered them to the front door of *The Stafford House*. They sat in the Tea Room at dinnertime feeling very self-conscious of their clothing and the obvious attention they attracted. As much as she hated the attention, Grace loved her gown and was determined to wear it as long as possible.

"I feel like I'm in a glass house."

"You are. Don't move right!"

Grace jerked toward him in their little corner settee involuntarily. "What?"

"Gotcha." Nolan's playful smile prompted Grace to bop him with her napkin.

"I'll get you for that!"

The other diners enjoyed observing the bride and groom as they bantered and teased. Grace indulged in a little discreet flirting with her husband while Nolan simply enjoyed Grace. The dinner was delicious and afterward, Nolan led his bride slowly up the long driveway to the Stafford House Inn.

Several hours later, Grace gently folded her gown. As she laid it in the suitcase, Nolan came across the room to finger the sleeve. "That fabric is beautiful, so soft, and silky. That seamstress has my gratitude."

"What for? A huge bill and a dress I could have made if I hadn't been so lazy?"

Nolan tipped Grace's chin and winked at her. "Nope. For saving my bride's sanity!"

Thoughtfully, Nolan observed as Grace zipped the suitcase shut and set it aside. "Grace, I hope our daughter wears that dress- or maybe our son's wife will want to- like Grandmother Jackson did. It'll take an incredible woman to fill your shoes though."

Before Grace could absorb the compliment, she quipped mischievously, "It'll take an incredibly *big* woman to fill this dress!"

What Nolan whispered to Grace that evening, no one but he and Grace knows, but when they arrived home from two weeks in bonny Scotland, a new Grace walked beside her husband. She held her head just a little higher, and spoke with a tad more gentleness and confidence. Everyone in their lives agreed; Grace Burke wore marriage very well.

Hungarian Coffee Cake

In glass bowl mix 1 pkg of yeast with 1/4 cup very warm water and a pinch of sugar.

½ stick of butter
¼ cup of sugar
1 egg
¾ cup of milk
3-6 cups of flour

Set aside for later:

2 cups sugar
¼ - ½ cup of cinnamon
1-2 sticks of butter

Heat milk, sugar, and butter in a saucepan until butter is completely melted. Beat egg and add to mixture. Let cool to very warm rather than 'hot' and add yeast mixture (assuming it has bubbled) to this. Beat egg and add to mixture. Stir in 3-4 cups of flour. Add flour until the dough is just barely not sticky. Knead well. Place in greased bowl and cover with a towel. Let rise.

Take an angel food cake pan with a *removable center* and grease well. Melt butter, mix cinnamon and sugar to taste... generally is best if slightly too cinnamony.

Use a biscuit cutter or a lid to large cinnamon container for cutting circles. Flour the surface of your baking area and when the dough has doubled, punch down, and roll out to about 1/4" thick or so. Try to handle the dough as little as possible once you've rolled it. Cut circles by dipping in flour when necessary.

Dip each circle in the butter, and then into the cinnamon/sugar mixture and start layering from the outside in. Alternate brick-style. Do not pack the layers but rather lay the circles against the previous layer. When you get to the middle, tuck extras to fill the circle without packing it. Layer leftover circles standing up in a mini loaf pan and bake with the rest of the coffee cake removing as soon as the tops are golden brown.

Pre-heat oven to 400 degrees. When layered pan has risen to "plump", place on cookie sheet and in hot oven; bake for 25-45 minutes (seems to depend upon the oven.)

It is done when the tops of the 'cake' is golden brown from baking, not from cinnamon. Let cool for 5 minutes, and then remove the center of the pan and place on a plate.

Icing

2 cups confectioner's sugar

1 ½ TBS soft butter

½ tsp vanilla flavoring

3-4 TBS milk

Mix well and adjust milk for your preference in drizzling.

Drizzle with icing over the top, down the sides, and for holidays, add maraschino cherry halves for a festive look.

We prefer ours hot from the oven or, if served later, wrapped well in aluminum foil while hot to 'sweat' a bit.